INDIANS, ROGUES
— AND —
GIANTS

Leif HerrGesell

INDIANS, ROGUES
AND
GIANTS

The Tale of Lt. St. Crispin Mull

TATE PUBLISHING
AND ENTERPRISES, LLC

Indians, Rogues and Giants
Copyright © 2013 by Leif HerrGesell. All rights reserved.

No part of this publication may be reproduced, stored in a retrieval system or transmitted in any way by any means, electronic, mechanical, photocopy, recording or otherwise without the prior permission of the author except as provided by USA copyright law.

The opinions expressed by the author are not necessarily those of Tate Publishing, LLC.

Published by Tate Publishing & Enterprises, LLC
127 E. Trade Center Terrace | Mustang, Oklahoma 73064 USA
1.888.361.9473 | www.tatepublishing.com

Tate Publishing is committed to excellence in the publishing industry. The company reflects the philosophy established by the founders, based on Psalm 68:11,
"The Lord gave the word and great was the company of those who published it."

Book design copyright © 2013 by Tate Publishing, LLC. All rights reserved.
Cover design by Jan Sunday Quilaquil
Interior design by Jake Muelle

Published in the United States of America

ISBN: 978-1-62510-929-3
Fiction / Historical
12.12.14

To:

Katie, Emily, Andrew and Nathan

and

the men and women of
NMCB's 18 & 40 Afghanistan 2010

FOREWORD

I have settled on writing this story down for posterity some twenty-five years after I first acquired the information. It was during the last war that we fought with the British (1812) that I first heard of St. Crispin Mull. I was serving as a volunteer in the militia of Sackets Harbor, New York, where I owned a small farm at the time. I was just thirty years old in 1813 when the British Army came over from Canada, along with a pack of Indians to burn our ships and stores and reduce our forts in the town.

After a very sharp fight, which we nearly lost, the English and their allies pulled off in whale boats and divers bateaux and escaped via their ships on the lake back to their own towns and fortresses. There was much litter left about after the heroic fight, and I happened to retrieve an officer's haversack in which we soldiers carried our eatables and sundry utensils. I peeked inside the worn canvas pack and noted a large bundle of papers, which appeared to be correspondence. Thinking that it might be of vital military importance, I sat down under an oak tree and began to peruse it. I was only a corporal at the time, but I was seeing that the officers were all busy with reorganizing the companies and regiments, as well as putting out the many fires that had been lit to deny the enemy our stores. I took it upon myself to analyze the information and determine if it was of any value.

I had over six years of formal education, including Latin and mathematics before my parents had moved to Upper New York from Connecticut in 1795. Armed with this knowledge, I felt equal to the task I set before myself.

The sheaf of loosely stitched papers was not military in nature at all. What I held was an original manuscript written by a British officer, Evelyn Norris, about the exploits of an officer with whom his father had served during the French and

Indian War. Along with the author's manuscript were original notes in his father's hand and dated around about the time of our American Revolution. Clearly, Evelyn Norris had added his own researches to complete those of his father as there were additional notes in the same hand as the manuscript and dated in the last few years, which you will remember at that time was eighteen and thirteen.

I did not divulge to anyone the fact that I had acquired the papers, but instead, I went to the grave-digging detail and inquired about the British dead to see if the author had fallen in battle. If he was still alive, perhaps, I could return his work to him after the hostilities had ended. Clearly, the work was one that he considered important due to the fact that he brought it with him on such a dangerous campaign. Clearly, he did not want to be separated from it. As I looked amongst the dead and asked the burial detail if they had a list, I began, for some odd reason, call it prescience, to believe the worst. Sadly, I was right. There, finally, in stiff and silent repose, were the mortal remains of the Author-Captain Evelyn R. Norris son of Captain Thomas Norris of the Fifty-Sixth Regiment of foot.

Delving into the notes, I learned that Norris's father, Thomas, had been an ensign in the British Fifty-Sixth Regiment during the Seven Years' War (also called the French and Indian War) and had left the regiment as a captain in 1769 when his son, Evelyn, was born.

Young Norris joined the army in 1786. I suppose they must have shared stories, and his father, doubtless, regaled him with tales of his days in the Fifty-Sixth of Foot, and this is, I suppose, how the son came to hear the long sad, sordid, and fascinating story of Lieutenant St. Crispin Mull. What prompted him to write the tale told to him by his father is open to conjecture. At the time of our battle in Sackets Harbor, Norris the Younger was fighting in a Canadian Regiment and was himself passing his middle years. I had every intention of returning the haversack and papers to his widow who lived on the other side of Lake Ontario.

They say the road to Hades is paved with good intentions, and if that is so, then I can claim—sadly—to have added a brick to that corrupted path. After I had finished reading the intriguing but unfinished manuscript and notes, I put them carefully away in my own desk so that I could return them to the bereaved widow. The war passed, and the notes became forgotten until recently when I began to set down for my heirs an accounting of my part in the battle of Sacketts Harbor. Remembering the notes, I reread them and decided to finish and edit the manuscript, which Captain Norris had begun all those years ago in part to expiate the guilt I have felt at not returning the haversack and papers and partly because the story is so fascinating that Captain Norris's research and literary efforts need to be appreciated by others. Oddly and mysteriously, the Fifty-Sixth Regiment has been removed from the establishment, and all memory of the Old 56th has been erased from the annals of British arms. Even as the printer's ink dries on this tale, I have begun my researches into the mysterious "Cheviot Guards" and hope to soon tell the reader what bedevilment or adventure may have become of them.

Here then is the tale of Lt. St. Crispin Mull.

—Arthur Tancred Pocock, Esq.
Leviticus, New York
April 15, 1837

"I, St. Crispin Mull, being a man fallen from grace and about to meet his maker, give this testimony of my own free will. God grant that the crown may be merciful to her wayward son. I have been many things in my day, but now stand with the lowest. I am accused a murderer and a common thief. The only crime I am guilty of is avarice. May my maker forgive me. I have fallen in with rogues, supped with rabble, and slept with whores, but I have never killed an innocent nor robbed a living man. My last wish is to redeem myself before God and King as a soldier doing battle against our popish enemy."

THE BLACK DRAGOON

It is rare when a man so handsome and so keen and as well made as St. Crispin Mull finds himself locked in the Albany Gaol, but such is his tale.

Born to Ezra Mull and Abigail McHughes in Glasgow in the year of our Lord 1734, wee Crispy Mull was the treasure of his mother's heart. Perhaps the cord wrapped around his neck should have been an omen of things to come. Perhaps the way we enter the world foretells the way we will exit it. The midwife slipped her finger beneath the cord and lifted it off the bairn's throat until Abigail had finished pushing. While the blood was still wet on her thighs and the sweat was curling off her temples, the purple-gray infant began to cry. St. Crispin Mull had made his first narrow escape. He was named in honor of one of the twin Patron Saints of Cobblers and tanners. His father had thought the name sounded grander than Thomas or David, and calling him St. George after the patron saint of England would have gotten him a beating even in lowland Scotland. Most referred to him as Crispy or, when need demanded formality, Crispin.

In the weeks, months, and years to come, the lad would experience the rough and tumble of all wee boys, but Crispin Mull was different. Of course, he fell and skinned his knees and, on another occasion, nearly drowned in the River Clyde. Other boys took a beating from their da for lesser offences, but Crispin never got caught. Most likely, that is how it all began. Crispin knew he was "lucky." He stole a meat pie right from under the nose of a street vendor and ate it under the cart and, for good measure, took another for the walk home. He punched a chubby, gap-toothed bully boy twice his size right in the nose, and the lad ran, crying even though he was ten and Crispin was eight. His torturous birth had left his mother barren, so she poured all her affection and love into her only child, always forgiving any youthful transgression the boy committed.

Ezra Mull had a thriving business supplying the scientific community in Glasgow and Edinburgh with everything they wanted in the way of specimens for dissection, examination, and rigorous description. From live salmon to rare plants, mummified toads from china, dead alley cats, two-headed lambs, the odd, purloined corpse or skeleton, and even a small whale calf, which beached in the Firth of Forth one July for no apparent reason other than faulty navigation. An associate of Ezra's, an ancient, gouty Jew named Jakob Schultes, realizing its scientific market value, hauled it by cart to Glasgow where Ezra paid two guineas for the now rather ripe example of cetaceous progeny. He turned a tidy profit of five pounds on the stinking carcass when the bastard son of the late 16th Earl of Sutherland, Rabbie Gordon, bought it for dissection in his apartments in Edinburgh. The earl's stuttering son was preparing a boring and erroneous treatise on mammals of the sea and was only too eager to piddle away his inheritance on rotting whale meat and pickled seal pups as long as it extended the knowledge of mankind. Ezra gave the money to Abigail, who salted it away in an iron-banded copper coffer under the stone floor of the bedroom. Of course, she gave young Crispy, now twelve, a few pennies to fritter away on sweets.

Ezra and Abigail lived fairly in the years before Crispin, but it was their long-term goal to lift the Mulls above their current social station. Ezra proposed that if they scrimped and were careful with their purchases, they might set aside enough so that by the time Crispy was seventeen, they could buy him an ensign's commission in an English Regiment of Foot and, thereby, make a silk purse of a lucky sow's ear.

Colonel Sir Beverly Blanchard of the Fifty-Sixth Regiment had issued orders for the reordering of the companies and the formation of new flank companies. Sergeant Major Spurling was given the onerous task of shepherding the newly commissioned ensigns as well as overseeing the drilling and instruction of the troops. Generally speaking, a new ensign is not a terribly useful item in the life of a regiment. With little knowledge of military life and without the trust of the commander, they have little to do other than the work that the lieutenants and captains will not do unless placed in a situation in which there is no junior sergeant or ensign. The work in question most often was keeping the company records and overseeing the digging of offal pits for the disposal of things, which, if left to the air, produced residual odors less than savory, never gentlemanly, and definitely not conducive to ingesting stewed oysters. If a detail was to be ordered to town to pick up a pot of fresh eels for the officers' mess or cabbages and turnips for the regimental kitchen, then more often than not, an ensign was chosen to lead the three privates necessary to manage the successful transfer. Senior sergeants were far too important to be wasted on such trivial matters. Outranking only the privates and corporals, ensigns invariably but quietly turned to the seasoned sergeants for direction. Of course, as an officer, it was unseemly for even a junior ensign to be seen requesting or receiving instruction from a man of the ranks. St. Crispin Mull was now to discover the life of the regiment.

"Here's the cold coin, Ensign Mull," said Sergeant Major Spurling, placing the purse in Crispin's hand. "Watch them men going with you—they're not gentlemen like yerself." In a more conspiratorial tone, he leaned close to Crisp. "Ye might ha' time fer a nip at the Crown an Scepter, laddie, but don't be late getting them eels to cook. The colonel likes his supper prompt. There'll be the very divil ta pay an all the papist saints in Rome won't save ye if it's late."

"My thanks for the warning, Sergeant Major, and I'll remember what ye said about the men." Crispin grinned, eager to begin his mission, the first duty he had been given since settling in with the regiment a fortnight before.

Reaching the village of Hart was no difficult task; Private Lane of Dublin and London volunteered that they had nearly worn a rut down the middle of the road running errands for Old Barley Blanchard. The colonel had received his unofficial moniker from the troops for the amberish color of his hair, which resembled a tankard of ale. Of course, no one ever called him Old Barley if he was within a hundred feet for fear of the Gunner's Daughter or worse. Acts of insubordination generally involved a sweating sergeant standing in his small clothes beating the blood out of some poor sod who couldn't hold his tongue or who had imbibed too much and wagged on like a fishwife. The Gunner's Daughter was one of Old Barley's favorites. When the offender was taken down off the cannon's wheel, he was usually dragged face downward through a bit of muck or along the length of the picket line so that he got a good mush full of horse dung. Then the whips were scraped to clean off the blood and then oiled and hung up till next time.

Said Private Lane of Dublin to the likable new ensign as they strolled briskly toward Hart, "Ensign, sir, you seem like a fine man and a credit to yer people, and as this is yer first official duty, the lads an' I would like to buy yer a nip at the Scepter to welcome you to the regiment on behalf of the ranks. What're ya say?"

"I say lead on, Private Lane!" Crispin Mull trusted his luck and his apparent growing popularity with the men.

The truth was that Crisp had grown up with men just like Lane, and if his father hadn't saved the price of the commission, he would himself be a private in the ranks. It wasn't Crispin's nature to look down on an Irishman just because he was Irish. After all, he himself was lowland Scots, looked down on by the Highlanders as some form of traitor and looked down on by the English as a second-rate citizen. Crispin knew what it was like to be looked down on because of some accident of birth. What

Crisp could not know was what it was like to be unlucky. Good looks and his uncanny luck had often made up for the lack of title and fortune.

Private Lane, on the other hand, was serving in the Fifty-Sixth after being recruited out of Newgate Prison. Lane had had a lucrative trade, supplying women to lonely members of the House of Commons from outlying districts. All this was well and good and could have gone on indefinitely except that one of the members refused to pay his bill, which had grown rather hefty after six months of frequent use. Lane finally lost his temper one night when he was in his cups and sent a note to a patch-eyed strangler whose demesne were the closes and alleys of London. Trepan arrived at Lane's rundown pleasure house and came in by the back door. The two had been acquainted for years. Lane used Trepan for jobs that were unclean, and Trepan sated his desires with women he could never afford otherwise. Lane explained that a certain member of the Commons needed to choke on an oyster or trip and fall on his own knife or be struck by an errant chamber pot. Trepan agreed that something would most likely happen to the unfortunate gentleman as everyone's end is preordained. In the meantime, he would like to sample the wares upstairs.

The upshot was that just as Trepan emerged from the shadows and struck the honorable member in the head with a chamber pot, his foot became stuck fast in a gap between cobbles. Literally brought to heel. Trepan sang from the docket like a spring thrush, and Patrick Peter Lane, whoremonger, went straight to prison without hope until a few years later when he was offered the opportunity to enlist in the Fifty-Sixth of Foot, rarely named as the Cheviot Guards. Trepan escaped as he was being dragged to the gallows by biting off the eyebrow of one of his guards and showing nothing but his heels. The honorable member of the House of Commons, Sir Douglas Barden, outlived his attacker by many years though he had a permanent droop to the left side of his mouth and a dent in the right side of his head from the chamber pot. The dent remained until he died some forty-six years later.

He patched up things with his wife and never again frequented houses of pleasure and was reelected seven times to his seat in the Commons. Other than the occasional tremor or seizure, he lived hale and hearty, dying quietly in the night at the age of ninety-nine. Though he lived soberly, he passed with a crooked smile and obscene amounts of cash made in illegal contracts for inferior rope sold to the Royal Navy. Had the right honorable member died when Trepan struck his porcelain blow, Crispin Mull would have been denied the companionship of P. Peter Lane as Lane would surely have swung.

The interior of the Crown and Scepter was dark and pleasantly smoky with the strong underlying aroma of oak casks, roast beef, and the sweet warm baking of singing hinnies. The leaded windows let in little light, and it took more than a minute for the eyes to adjust to the dimness. Private Lane and his companions sat at a table near the fire and stretched out their feet before them while Ensign Crisp stood with his long straight spine turned towards the flames. God was in his house and all was right with the world were the message leaking from Crispin's expression. Mother would be right pleased to see that her wee laddie was in charge of three grown men, the youngest of them was a year older than Crisp, and all of them were calling him sir!

The smash-faced barman, one Joab Kinney, an Irish, brought out a battered tray of tankards, bobbed his bald, spotted head at Crispin and caught the coin that Lane flipped at him. His acrobat-like agility was remarkable for a man of his immense girth. He wiped the coin on his apron, which was pinned above is celestial sized belly and eyed it suspiciously in the poor light.

"Good ta see yer payin yer tab, Lane," the publican tossed over his shoulder.

"Pay 'im no mind, Ensign. P. Peter Lane always pays back everything eventually. Neither a borrower nor a lender be, but if yer gonna ask fer an advance, never fergit a goodness is my motto." He shared this with everyone who ever borrowed from him. "Since we are on the subject of finances, mayhap you would like to listen to a little business venture that I've in mind to include you in?"

"I have little to no knowledge of business, Private, and it takes all my pay just to maintain myself in food, lodgings, and uniforms, but if you can find a way to increase my fortunes, I am game," replied Crispin, feeling a pleasantly warm glow from the ale spreading towards his toes.

Lane signaled the barman for another round of ale and then began a beguiling and lengthy tale of his "cousin" in the rum trade who was looking to expand his business but needed help because he had no friends in government. The nameless cousin had begged P. Peter Lane to intervene with some influential officer who might be able to help him get his cloven hoof in the door with army contracts.

"Now, I understand yer no general, but you seem like a man destined fer greatness, Ensign. I've no doubt, but I'll be callin' you major before you shall be callin' me corporal. Do you think you might help my cousin out, sir?"

"My da always told me to look out for ma own interests, Private Lane. What I should like is to become a major or at least a captain. Do ya think ye could make tha' happen? If the answer is yeah, then I'd say we ha' a deal. If nay, then I think we should finish our round and fetch the eels." Crisp picked his tricorne off the table and cleared his throat.

"Not so fast, Ensign. Where's the rush?" returned P. Peter Lane. "I think we still ha some time fer both talk an eels." He motioned Crispin to slow down. "I think we might be able to reach a mutually acceptable arrangement, sir. I think I see how ye might git a promotion, and I think ye might be able to return the favor." Lane placed a special emphasis on favor.

The one-time crafty whoremonger outlined a devilishly simple plan to make Crispin the hero of the hour. Old Barley's wife and clubfooted daughter lived in apartments over the only other inn in the village. The Black Dragoon was a small step uptown from the Crown and Scepter. In a town with only two inns, that wasn't saying a great deal. Old Barley had rented out the entire upstairs and had installed Madame Blanchard and his comely but clumsy daughter in the four good rooms.

The Black Dragoon looked out over the village from a small eminence at the north end of the main (and only) thoroughfare. The fishmonger's shed was a half mile beyond and down a track near the river. Nearly twice a week, Beverly Blanchard sent a detail down to the fishmonger to purchase oysters, eels, or some other morsel of the deep. Blanchard, not wanting his family too near, preferred to stay in camp with his men until the weekend when he would be forced to ride the two and a half miles to the village. It was agonizing enough to spend the weekend listening to his wife complain about the lodgings, being away from her friends, and the lack of society for young Sally Anne.

The major problem for Old Barley was that he couldn't send his wife and daughter back home to live at Blanchard Hall until he devised a plan to get his mistress out of the house. Beverly Blanchard was many things, and well planned wasn't one of them. He had asked his wife and daughter to come stay with him because his mistress had demanded that if she didn't get to visit him at Blanchard Hall, then she would publicly expose him. Beverly was unlike his peers—he lacked the resolve to take care of the situation once and for all. Peggy Fairchild was a fine, saucy auburn-haired girl who had started life as the oldest child of a dressmaker. Her shapely figure and sparkling blue eyes soon caught the attention of many a young rake, and before long, she had taken up the life of a kept woman. Beverly Blanchard was smitten and entrapped in her romantic snare. It never occurred to

Old Barley that he only had to say the word, place, and the right amount of coin in the right hands and Peggy Fairchild would just be gone from his life. Word amongst the other colonels and the few others who knew of Peggy was that Beverly did all his thinking with a certain extremity, which it is not necessary to name.

While P. Peter Lane did not know about Peggy, he knew exactly where Madame and Sally Anne Blanchard lived. He rightly surmised that if they were saved from a group of toughs bent on rapine and robbery, then the rescuer would be in very good standing with Old Barley. That officer not only would receive a promotion but would likely have the colonel's ear regarding the business of the regiment, the kind of business that involved the purchasing of watered rum at premium prices with "gifts" for the officer or officers granting the contract. Lacking any other plan, it seemed brilliant on the surface.

On the appointed day, some of P. Peter Lane's old associates gathered in the predawn gloom under cover of a beech grove down near the fishmonger's shed. At the same time, in the camp of His Majesty's Fifty-Sixth of Foot, Ensign Crispin Mull was pulling on his worsted stockings and slipping his feet into brass buckled shoes. After a light breakfast at the ensigns' mess, Crisp would gather his three privates and start the forty-minute walk into Hart in order to get the oysters from the fishmonger for the colonel and the major and also to pick up two bushels of turnips for the ranks. Because the pickup was larger than a pot of eels, they had brought along a large pushcart which Private Spooner was propelling. Crispin walked in front with his sword and pistol buckled on, and Lane and the third private, Lear by name, walked alongside either wheel. The sky was just brightening, and it was a few minutes before six in the morning. The overcast kept it from becoming light quickly. As Crisp and his detail trundled up the main road, lights began to come on in cottages, and smoke puffed lazily out of chimney pots.

The five toughs hiding under the sylvan boughs passed a rum flask between them.

"Remember, take whatever yer want, but don't hurt no one bad. The innkeeps got a blunderbuss under the bar, so don't let 'im get it. The ladies is off limits, right?" said the biggest and ugliest of the ruffians.

"Say, Shep," piped up another. "Der ye suppose we could torch it?"

"Listen, Burnie," said Shep. "Leave off settin' her a fire, and we go in an we git out as soon as the reglers hit the front door. We duck out the back with what we can carry. We meet back at the river an' row downstream just like Lane said." The five toughs picked up a small log they had brought for the express purpose of battering down the back door of the inn.

The Black Dragoon was still a hundred yards distant when Crispin heard the first screams. A woman flew out the front door and fell down the steps. "Robbers! Help! They're killing my man!" She ran towards Crispin's detail.

Lieutenant Crispin Mull drew his sword and pistol, and the privates each drew their bayonets. They never brought their muskets with them on a victualing detail. Crisp had agreed with Lane not to harm any of the hired toughs and only to make a show of it and drive them off. A dull roar echoed from inside of the inn as a firelock was discharged, and voices could be heard yelling and screaming. A shabbily dressed, unshaven tough in baggy sailor's slops barreled out of the front door with both of his hands clamped to his smoldering head. Wisps of smoke curled up from his burnt, greasy hair, and rivulets of blood ran down his stubble-covered cheeks, making his face a mask of ghastliness studded with rotting teeth bared in pain. Crispin and his men reached the front door just as the scalawag disappeared around the back corner of the building running for all he was worth towards the river.

As Crispin stepped into the dim interior of the inn, he saw a great heap of a man in a dirty frock coat and workman's cap making for the back door. Crisp hauled up on his tower pistol. Thinking only to make a good show of it, he touched off the round. Shep's pulpy-eyed head slammed forward, and he tumbled out the open door into the daylight, collapsing in a lifeless pile of dirty, wrinkled clothes, shaggy, unwashed beard, and rapidly clotting blood. Yells and curses could be heard throughout the inn mixed with the voices of terrified women. The remaining three toughs still in the inn put up a mock fight with the soldiers who were all in on the deception. Fortunately, none of them knew about Shep or their comrade with the immolated scalp. Windows flew open, and then, all three made timely exits, unlike their ill fated companions. Carrying off silver plate, a clock, a whole still flapping salmon, and for no good reason, a cracked chamber pot, the three headed for the rendezvous on the river. Crispin dashed up the stairs and made a show of calming the hysterical Madame Blanchard and her comely but clumsy daughter.

"Ladies, rest assured the villains have been dealt with an' tha inn is secure. One of the divils lies cold on the stoop. I warrant he won't be terrorizing anyone. I shall send one of ma men for reinforcements, and we'll smoke out these rogues. I'll order a coach to take you to the colonel immediately."

Crispin posted Lear and Lane on the front and back doors respectively and sent Spooner, who was now mounted upon a borrowed shire horse, back to camp for the colonel and reinforcements. The innkeep who had blasted the one villain in the head with his blunderbuss lent his pony and cart to the cause and, reloading his weapon, escorted Madame and Sally Anne Blanchard up the road in the cart behind Spooner. Meanwhile, Crispin began to organize the gathering mob into a pursuit party. Naturally, not wanting to catch the thieves, he sent all the men home to pack a lunch and to gather weapons. Rallying back at the Black Dragoon half an hour later, Ensign Mull led a cautious pursuit towards the fishmonger's shed, leaving Lear to report to the officer in charge of the reinforcements. As the angry but fearful townsmen approached the fishmonger's shed, Crispin hailed the building.

The fishmonger came out, wiping his hands on his bloody, scaly apron. "What's all the blasted commotion about?"

"Have ya seen anyone about this mornin', Mr. Suply?" queried Crisp.

"Nay, I've not, Ensign. What was all the racket comin' from the Black Dragoon? It sounded of nastiness and bloodied knuckles."

"Indeed it was nasty, Mr. Suply. Have ye seen four rogues coming this way, one of them holding his head with his hair on fire?"

"Nay, but there were voices down near the river this mornin'," replied Suply. "I figgered it fer some of the local laddies goin' fishin." Suply stuck his fish-gutting knife into a stump next to the shed door.

"Our thanks to ye, Mr. Suply," said Crisp. "Thieves attacked the Black Dragoon this morning. They were seen coming down this way. We'll have to search yer shed by yer leave." Crispin knew the stall would give the surviving house breakers a lead in their flight.

A half-dozen men armed with old swords and pikes surrounded the fish shed while Crispin and the remaining two men in the party cautiously entered. The interior was lit with several fat lamps that guttered and cast long shadows in the early morning overcast. Wicker baskets sat on the floor in confusion. Some were filled with writhing eels; others were heaped with oysters and cuttlefish, and still, others held innumerable fish. There was nowhere for a tough to hide, so Crisp and the others backed out into the morning.

"Mr. Lane, pick the finest oysters and take them back to the camp. Don't forget to pick up the turnips. I'll take these men and search the riverbank for a mile or so. If you should chance to see the reinforcements, tell them what we're about," ordered Crispin.

P. Peter Lane was beginning to think he had created a monster. The lad took charge as though he'd been born to the manor. He seemed to show no remorse at having shot down poor Shep Wells, and he seemed to have a natural instinct for getting at what needed to be done. Lane feared for the remaining toughs if Mull caught up with them. Without Lane to remind the lad about their agreement and with Lear and Spooner dispatched to other duties, the only thing to save Lane's friends was a swift current carrying them out to sea.

Lane surmised correctly. Crispin was becoming emboldened. *What*, he thought, *is to stop him from apprehending and executing the toughs?* Society would be shed of cutthroats; no one would be the wiser to his dealings with Lane, and he would seem to be the bold and dashing officer capable of leading a company or even a battalion. Crisp's luck was showing itself again.

The men fanned out along the riverbank and beat the bushes with their swords, but the only thing they flushed were a pair of ducks, a swan, and a three-legged tabby cat out mousing. As they neared the end of their mile, they came upon a muddy spot on the bank, covered with footprints and the crease created by a small boats keel. Clearly, the toughs had debarked, and likely, they had an hour's lead. The only way to catch them now was with a small boat or with fast horses in pursuit along the bank.

Crispin paced and thought for several minutes. At last he spoke. "All right you men. I think we've done all we can on foot. Perhaps I will take two men and continue the pursuit while the rest of you return to the village. Send back a fast horse, and commandeer Mr. Suply's boat. If we don't catch them, we'll surely drive them from the district."

Crispin took the only two men who owned firelocks and set off at a brisk pace, hoping he might catch up with the toughs before the reinforcements came up. It dawned on him while he had time to think that if any of the thieves were captured, they could inform on him and Lane. They would either need to get away clean or have to be cut down like the brigands they were. The greatly diminished pursuit party had gone no more than another half mile when horses could be heard thundering up behind them. Crisp halted his companions. Three officers' flapping red-coat tails came pounding up, and their horses were well lathered and blowing steam in the early morning light. The regimental major, flushed with the excitement of the chase, was accompanied by two captains mounted on the colonel's horse and remounted. Shiny pistol butts showed in their belts, and each carried an officer's fusil.

"Ensign! Mull, isn't it? Where are the blackguards now?" asked the major who had rarely deigned to speak to Crispin before this.

"Well, sir," returned Crispin, "I believe they are about an hour ahead of us on the river. I have dispatched—"

"I know about all that, Mull. You did a good job of keeping us well informed with messengers. Right good fun, this. Like chasing old foxy Reynard himself. Listen, you continue along with your two men here, and I'll take captains Lyon and Nash and fetch up these ruffians and hang them by their cullions! Sound the chase, Nash! Come along as quickly as you may, Mull!"

Captain Nash brought a shiny hunt horn to his lips and gave a blast, and away the three went with great gusto. Major Patterson slapped his hat against his mount's foamy flank. The horses seemed as eager and excited as their riders, carrying their heads high, manes flashing with a great thunder of hooves, and farting they roared down the greensward that ran along the river.

Blast and damn, thought Crisp. *If they don't kill them, I'll land in Newgate for sure.* Crispin wasn't aware that he would more likely be executed for his role than to be locked up. Nothing to do but trust to luck. Crispin put his head down and plodded along with his townsmen, stalwartly keeping apace.

The entire district around Hart was abuzz with the news of the attack at the Black Dragoon. When all was said and done, the damages to the Black Dragoon amounted to about six pounds in smashed crockery, broken chairs, and stolen fish and chamber pots. While the loss of first-rate borders was not to be laughed at, the throngs coming in to see the place where Shep Wells had met his rogue's end more than made up for the losses. Ale and meat pies were sold briskly. Stewed oysters and claret less so, however, there were a number of officers from the regiment who had to remain in camp during the riot and manhunt who later just had to come in to see what that new young ensign had done. They were more of the oyster and claret crowd and provided a dash of color and civility against the rustic, dull backdrop of the locals. Most visitors quaffed ale and whispered while pointing at the swan shot holes in the ceiling beams. That was where most of the charge had gone that had removed the one tough's cap and scorched his scalp. Examining the rapidly fading bloodstained stoop and praising the marksmanship of the new young ensign, the patrons removed themselves to the quieter and cheaper surroundings of the Crown and Scepter.

After several days, the furor died down, and life began to return to normal in Hart. Farmers argued wool prices, housewives gossiped, three-quartered tabby cats moused peacefully by the river, and another ensign was seen leading a detachment into town to fetch a pot of eels and a half-dozen bushels of cabbages. Crispin Mull cooled his heels for a week, hearing nothing more on the subject than the praise of his captain and the adoration of the other ensigns. Everywhere he went, lieutenants glowered jealously, and the ranks nearly bowed and genuflected. Senior sergeants now included him in their conversations, even asked his opinion of military matters, and privates asked him to settle their disputes, but there was no talk of a promotion or reward.

One problem still remained. While Madame and Sally Anne had been happy to leave the Black Dragoon, they were not terribly happy with the life of the regiment and demanded to be sent home immediately. Beverly Blanchard was coming to the end of his rope, and he was quite sure that when he reached it, he would find that Madame had fashioned a clever knot around his cullions! Unless Peg Fairchild could be persuaded to leave Blanchard Hall and keep her mouth shut tight, Old Barley was in for a hot time when Madame "Old Barley" Blanchard caught him out. Backed into a tight place with nowhere to retreat, Beverly showed uncommon guile.

The candles guttered in the draft as the door of Colonel Blanchard's headquarters swung open. Old Barley had occupied the office of the tannery for several months while his men slept in drafty little tents. Winter cantonments were being constructed from the various barns and warehouses that made up the abandoned tannery. Ensign Mull leaned into the door and heaved it shut against the clammy gale. The milky rotten smell of soaking hides still pervaded even here.

"Ah! Mull, good of you to stop by," said Blanchard as though Crispin actually had an option and would turn down an order from the commander. "That was excellent work you did last week, and you cannot know how much I appreciate your efforts on behalf of my wife and daughter."

"Thank you, sir," replied Crispin. "And may I say, it was ma pleasure to serve yer family."

"Well spoken for a Scot! Let me say that after reviewing the reports from yourself and Major Patterson and after interviewing Private Lane, I must congratulate you and offer you this reward." Old Barley picked up a small leather purse from the padfooted gaming table that served as his desk. "Five guineas. I know it seems a large sum to one so young. I hope you will use it to improve your appearance or further your career in some way. The army needs daring young men like you. Carry On." Blanchard began shuffling through the papers in front of him.

Crisp pivoted smartly about and started for the door, silently fuming. How dare Blanchard. For all he knew, the attempt on his wife and daughter had been genuine, and all he could offer was five guineas for their safety. Killing a known reprobate was only worth five guineas! Damn that Lane. Crisp had risked all and barely had enough to buy a new sword and knot.

"Oh, Mull! I almost forgot."

Crisp was just shutting the door and ducking his head into the wind and rain.

"I have another mission for you. Perhaps more rewarding than your latest action with an enemy."

Crispin approached the desk and stood at attention.

"Relax, boy. You have shown that you have metal and can control yourself in a taxing situation. I would have promoted you for gallantry for your deeds at the Dragoon, but it would have been a bit much with four of the rascals escaping. What?" Old Barley began to pace with his hands behind his back. "And if Major Patterson and Captains Lyon and Nash had succeeded where you failed, then I should have been forced to reward them as well."

Crisp could not see how the escape of the other four had been his fault. Blanchard was leading up to something.

"The mission I have in mind for you is secret but should confer military preferment if you are successful. A promotion, in case you need that spelled out. I know you Scots are a more blunt and simple folk." Beverly reached down and picked up a piece of paper from his desk. He continued, "I have here a letter commissioning to the rank of lieutenant for Ensign Mull. The price of the commission will be paid anonymously, and no one the wiser since this is a secret mission." Blanchard's eyes narrowed, and he bored into Crispin's eyes, trying to see his mind. "I am also going to assign Privates Spooner, Lear, and Lane to this mission, and the man whom you tell me is most deserving will receive a promotion from my own hand to the rank of corporal, and the others will get a guinea each for their efforts. If you fail, Ensign, you will bring ruin upon the regiment and yourself." Beverly failed to mention that he was the one who would be most ruined.

Old Barley began to explain that there was a woman at his home who was a spy and a threat to the Crown, that she sang a siren song, and anyone who listened to her lies was likely to end up dashed on the rocks of a broken future. He told Crispin that she had been lured to his ancestral home under false pretenses and that she must now be dealt with. She went by the name of Peggy Fairchild, which was undoubtedly a fiction. She was most likely a French courtesan, carrying out a mission of intrigue, intended to bring embarrassment on certain persons highly placed in His Majesty's government. He further told Crisp that it would be up to him and his detail of men to nullify her with all which that implied. When one's father dealt in snatched bodies, the truth, or rather the lack of it, was nearly as transparent as the skin of a corpse dug fresh from the grave. In other words, Crisp was not buying the French courtesan tale and suspected that Old Barley had been dipping his quill in an inkpot other than Madame's.

A DASH TO THE SEA

Blanchard Hall was well removed from Hart, being nearly twenty-five miles distant to the Northeast. Crispin rode Old Barley's remount, a slick little chestnut gelding while Lane, Lear, and Spooner walked. The trip took three days, and the detail stopped every night at a hedge inn. Private Lear went mildly lame from bad shoe leather and had to limp the last six miles or so leaning on a stick.

Blanchard Hall lay like a wart on an otherwise smooth face. The low, squat stone manor house appeared to be about three hundred years old and lacked any redeeming architectural appointments. The landscape was nonexistent unless one counted the sole large oak in front and the three or four high, suckered stumps that stuck up like rancid teeth. The barns, orchards, and gardens were to the rear and looked mundane and utilitarian.

Old Barley had suggested a straightforward course of action—take the infernal woman well away from the house, allowing no one to see you and silence her. None of this was according with Crispin's new ideal of an officer and a gentleman. Old Barley was full of suggestions and short on efforts, or so Crisp had begun to suspect. Crisp approached the front door of the many-roomed manse. Lear sneaked around back as much as one can sneak on sore feet and when there is absolutely no shrubbery and it is broad daylight.

Lane was in the barn, talking with the coachman about harnessing up the team. Spooner stayed with Crispin and checked his flint and priming. Old Barley Blanchard had insisted that the detail be fully armed and ready to attack or defend. Crispin laid his hand on his small sword hilt and lifted the bronze doorknocker.

The door swung open, and a young woman in a rather expensive-looking green satin gown trimmed in lemon velvet stood before Crispin. She smelled like a lavender pomander, and her red-brown hair was piled in a fetching manner. Crispin Mull's experience with women was rather limited. Never having known a member of the fairer sex conjugally, Crispin was a bit overawed. His sole experience in matters of amour had been limited to an abbreviated grope of the bosom of the sister of a country friend from near Paisley. The young lady, only fifteen at the time (two years Crisp's senior), had been more than willing and seemed to show rather a bit more experience than was common. Unfortunately for Crisp, her father seemed to regard the virginity of his daughter as one of her more compelling selling points for potential suitors. He loudly and bluntly told Crispin that if he should lay hands upon her again, her bosom would be the last thing Crisp would see in this mortal world before he found himself face to face with a fiery demon. Crisp was quite sure that the girl's father was a far greater threat than burning demons sticking red hot pokers in his eyes. Presbyterians, it seemed to Crispin, relied a good deal on brimstone, pokers, pitchforks, and whippings to drive home a point. Crispin had steered wide of women for the last four years, but every Samson has his Delilah.

"Mistress Fairchild, I presume?" asked Crisp in as official a voice as he could muster. Major Patterson had been a suitable role model for the pomposity, arrogance, and hence, the proper bearing of an officer.

"I am that person, Ensign, and how may I help you? One also presumes you are here on official business of the colonel's regiment," said the twentyish beauty.

"Indeed. Colonel Blanchard requires you to accompany me immediately. You are to pack your things forthwith and mount the coach. We will take you to Whitehaven, and your passage will be booked for France." Crispin was all for keeping up the pretense that she was a French spy. Sadly, no one had bothered to let pretty Peggy in on the whole spy ruse, and thus, she was quite puzzled by the offer. Crispin straightened up and attempted to appear as old as possible, which is quite difficult when one only has to shave every other day.

She leaned forward and whispered in a conspiratorial tone. "Is the colonel going to join me in France? I presume this is a secret mission, Ensign," she continued in a more petulant tone. "Hasn't Beverly had enough of that harpy wife? Couldn't he just join me here himself?"

Crispin stepped forward, forcing the young woman back into the entry hall. A maidservant peeked around a corner, trying not very hard to remain unseen. Clearly, Old Barley had communicated with the staff as he said he would and ordered them to assist the ensign and stay out of the way. Once inside, Spooner closed the door and stood with his firelock diagonally across his chest blocking the path back out.

"Mistress Fairchild, my private here will escort you to your chamber and see to carrying your things once they are packed. I'm sorry we don't have time for any more questions," said Crispin, cutting short her query and leaving her gape-mouthed. Spooner strode forward and took her by the elbow, herding her toward the stairway at the far end of the parquet-floored entry hall. Crisp tried hard not to be overly impressed by the wealth in evidence throughout the house. He did not want to appear the country bumpkin.

Peg Fairchild was naive upon occasion and mostly unlettered. She had never read Cicero—most women had not—nor even some of the more popular new novels. Yet she was no gibbering idiot either. Peggy realized quite quickly that she was not going to see her beloved and exploitable Sir Beverly Blanchard. The private's grip on her elbow was firm almost to the point of painful, and the simple message it sent was, "If you resist, I'll break your arm." Peggy briefly thought about seducing the private and soliciting his assistance in making her escape. Was escape even necessary? Surely, Beverly was only banishing her until such time as he could safely bring her back without Madame Blanchard's knowledge. Beverly would never hurt her. Of that, she was sure. Old Barley had professed his love to her every time they had made physical union, and here was where Peg's naiveté showed itself. She truly believed that Beverly's profession of love was genuine and that someday he would cast off Madame Blanchard and take Peg for more than a romp. She naively dreamed of becoming Lady Margaret Blanchard.

Crisp handed Peg up into the carriage and climbed in behind her. Lear rode the back like a footman while Spooner rode at the coachman's side, and Lane rode rearguard on the colonel's horse. With three days behind them, they had but five ahead to make Peggy disappear and to send the coach on to the camp of the Fifty-Sixth.

The coachman, young Bob Tofts, was informed that he was to say nothing of the event and was to tell Madame Blanchard that the delay was caused by a necessary repair to the coach's front axle, which had broken on the way to fetch herself and Sally Anne. The repair had taken three days, and then the remainder of the trip had taken several more. In reality, Bob had been given five shillings and told not to spare the horses. With the four soldiers guarding it, the coach was impervious to attack by the rapidly fading threat of highwaymen, and the team was in fine shape. Bob drove them with an expert hand. Over deeply rutted roads and narrow arched bridges, the coach flew down to Penrith and onward to Cockermouth and then the coast road, slewing sideways in the turns and sometimes even rocking up onto the outside wheels. Run to a lather and then walked out and lightly watered at stations, they made the run from Blanchard Hall to Whitehaven in a little over two days giving him a night and part of a day to rest the team before they dashed the final stretch for Hart and the regiment. The team had suffered coming through the Cumbrian Lake District west of Cockermouth, but young Bob had eased up in time and spared them from foundering.

Crispin's instructions were explicit. Get rid of the infernal woman. It was not in young Crispin's character to willingly execute innocent women. That was more the purview of Trepan, Patrick Peter Lane, and the like. The lad hadn't felt even a moment's remorse at the death of Shep Wells. As undeserving an individual as Crispin had ever seen, this was largely because Crispin had never seen the denizens of the dark and festering world of London's waterfront and back alleys. Crisp began to believe that he had taken deliberate aim. Ensign Mull was beginning to associate himself with that superior class of human beings—nobility, gentry, and officers.

Of course, Crispin's ignorance could never have allowed him to see that poor Shep had been the sole source of income for a family with six members under the crown's lock and key. Shep had come from a long and ancient line of thieves and hightobys. His father, three of his brothers, an uncle, and a cousin had been rounded up. The Wellses had attempted the theftdom of a brewery. While the gang had successfully broken and robbed the strong box, they had attempted to make good their escape in a rickety ale wagon laden with full casks. They absurdly reasoned that they would have ale enough for everyone for a matter of weeks and that mayhap they might even be able to sell it in the black market. Tragically, the spavined beer wagon was too cumbersome and slow, and the Wellses were too far gone in their cups to make good the retreat when the constabulary caught up with them. Shep alone had the good sense to remain mostly sober. As the torch and rider bearing horses had borne down on the wagon, Shep had leapt overboard into a wickedly thorny briar patch. After their capture and a brief trial, they began their long and damning sentence. Shep had visited often and became their only provider. Crispin's act of manslaughter had ensured that the Wellses would live out their rather pitiful lives on gruel and water with one blanket each, never again seeing the light of day or toasting a cup of ale. In Crisp's mind, Shep had signed his own death warrant the day he decided to act with Lane and rob the Black Dragoon, even though it was partly to Crispin's benefit.

Peggy Fairchild, however, was another story. The harmless and attractive lass was not the public menace that Crispin had suspected Shep was. In actuality, Shep had hardly risen above a public nuisance. Peg's nearness throughout the race to Whitehaven had been a sore reminder to Crispin of his own maleness. It seemed that at every turn, Peggy would allow the coach to throw her into his arms even when they were careening in the opposite direction. Peggy had poured out her heart to Crisp, telling him a complete fiction. She explained how she was the orphaned, bastard daughter of a member of the House of Lords and that she had been shunned by her wealthy but heartless father and was raised by a prelate from Somerset and so on ad infinitum. Crispin, of course, chose to believe the pleasant fiction over Old Barley's story of the French courtesan cum spy. In truth, Crispin knew that both were lies, but he preferred to accept the young lady's story for now as long as it meant she would continue to throw herself into his waiting arms.

It was near the end of the trip with only perhaps fifteen miles to go that one of Peg's perfect bosoms popped out of its nesting spot just as they careened around a turn. It was a rather neat trick, and to the unsuspecting Crisp, it merely appeared to be a timely and pleasant coincidence. Peggy's warm breath flavored with the scent of herbs sent Crisp over the edge, and he grasped her about the waist and kissed her with the appetite of a starving man. With a hoisting of her sail-like petticoats, a popping and rending of buttons, and a fair amount of sweating, lad and lassie came together in the way that God intended for newlyweds. When the squealing, grunting, and heaving of bosoms was over, Crispin sat spent upon the seat until a slewing motion sent him sprawling onto the floor. Crispin had now known a woman in the conjugal sense, and he was sure he wanted to know her better and as often as possible. Women, Crispin Mull was certain, were a wondrous, great thing and altogether wasted in the cooking of meals, bearing of children, and the emptying of chamber pots. Like a hungry satyr, he could see the fairer sex only as *le femme coquet* awaiting his pleasure. Peggy helped him up and suggestively rebelted him, smiling like a worshipful slave before her all-powerful pharaoh. Crispin was about to discover that *le femme coquet* made Shep Wells look like a winged angel and a messenger of peace and harmony.

The plan was that when they arrived in Whitehaven, Crisp was to locate a certain smuggler and arrange to have Peggy taken to Liverpool where she would be put aboard a brig bound for the West Indies. The coach arrived in the town at just after sunset, and Bob found a tavern and livery where he could water the horses and wet his whistle. Lear stayed with him while Lane and Spooner went off in search of the smuggler whose hideout was known only to Lane. P. Peter Lane had a wide assortment of contacts, and even though he came from London, it seemed that wherever he went, he was not without contacts and business partners from the past. He didn't elaborate on how it was that he came to know a smuggler from Whitehaven, but Crispin suspected from past conversations that it had to do with the Indian women that Lane had made available to his clientele. It was becoming entirely clear what line of business P. Peter Lane had been in, but he was starting to suspect that the private had more about him than the ordinary street rat and procurer.

P. Peter Lane had told Crispin about the smuggler who, in turn, had portrayed the smuggler to Colonel Blanchard as one of his own contacts. Crisp had managed to dissuade Old Barley from homicide, and truth be known, Blanchard did not want to see Peg killed but merely felt it necessary to maintain appearances. It was good if soldiers thought their commander was ruthless and even slightly bloodthirsty. Crisp had suggested to the colonel that Lane might be of special use in this delicate affair. Lane it was who came up with the plan to send the girl to the Indies. Whitehaven had been chosen because of Lane's contacts and the fact that it was a large enough port that a young lady might draw little attention to herself. Crispin and his men had removed their identifying regimental coats and had donned nondescript oilskin greatcoats. Crisp remained in the coach, gently petting Peg's sleeping brow while Lear fetched a pitcher of ale, a loaf, and a cold joint of mutton from the inn.

Old Barley had been right; Peg could sing a siren song, and Crispin's personal ship was straying dreadfully close to the rocks. He toyed with the idea of stealing away into the night with her and leaving the regiment behind. Then, he heard Lane's voice from the night before. "That saucy piece would roger a horse if she could ride him a mile rather than walk!"

Little did Crisp know that Peg was not truly asleep. Sensing danger, perhaps because he had stopped stroking her hair, she decided it was time to snare the young ensign once and for all. Peg began to murmur in her false slumber, "Oh, Crispin! You're so strong" and other similar endearments intended to bend him to her ways. Crispin, like every young man who has fallen in love with a slightly older woman, gave his heart to her in an instant. He gently kissed her brow and quietly climbed out of the coach to stretch.

He hadn't had his shoes off in several days, and his clothes had been slept in for the last six. Crispin was not aware that he could have ordered one of the men to polish his shoes and press out his uniform. Ensign Mull made up for a lack of martial experience with braggadocio and bluster, but like nearly every young man, he lacked the confidence to order and demand obedience from his elder subordinates.

While Crispin commanded, it was Lane who laid the plans and arranged the details. Details had long been one of Lane's specialties. He picked the dresses his strumpets wore, and he made sure that every gentleman's choice of belly wash was close at hand. While his actual establishment was a rundown, shabby, former vicarage, he made sure the bed linens were always clean and the doors letting out onto the streets were carefully guarded to ensure privacy for his customers. In all, P. Peter Lane had employed some sixteen people either on their backs at a washtub or in the kitchen. Like most successful rogues, petty and great (Lane fell somewhere in the middle ground.), he sat at the center of his self-made realm like a gangly, unwashed spider. Lane knew every twitch of a thread, and he knew where every ha'penny was spent and every guinea made. If the cook tried to water the soup and steal the stock, he knew. If one of the girls took a tip and tried to keep it from him, he knew. If one of the guards fell asleep on the job, he knew. Based on experience, when all was said and done, P. Peter Lane had more ability to command than Major Patterson of the brave Fifty-Sixth. Had he learned to speak more like a gentleman and had he turned his efforts to more wholesome pursuits than procuring, he might have made an honest merchant or even a regimental sergeant major.

Lane had taken pains to make sure that everything went right on this delicate mission. If the ensign succeeded, then Lane would become a corporal, which meant more pay and a degree of trust. Mull would become a lieutenant and would be indebted to him along with the colonel. If all went right, his watered rum trade might set him up for his old age. The army had gotten him out of gaol, given him coin for ale, and allowed him to prepare his finances for a life afterwards, as long as some damnable war didn't come along and blast and dash his plans. P. Peter Lane was enjoying himself nearly as much as when he was a part of London's shadow world.

While Crispin slaked his thirst with good ale and soothed his rumbling belly with bread and mutton, Lane was making the final arrangements with Captain Keyes. The good captain had been in the smuggling trade for over thirty years. His gaff-rigged top'sl cutter, the *Emily Jane*, was a sleek fast little vessel with a crew of eight besides the captain. The title of captain was stretching his importance but not his skill at outmaneuvering the Revenue Cutters. Keyes had never met his match for seamanship and charged accordingly. Whether he was bringing, illegal spirits from France or Indian wenches fresh from the Carib, he demanded a high price for delivering on time and without fanfare or damage. The captain's den was nothing more than a tumble down fisherman's cot with moss covered walls and leaky thatch that attracted no attention and where no exchequer would ever think to look.

Spooner waited outside in the bushes above the stony track that lead to the hovel. If anyone followed, he was ordered to dispatch them with the bayonet, firing his musket only as a final resort. No one knew of their mission, and it was unlikely they would be followed, but as Lane was fond of saying, "Ignore the little things and the hangman gets his due."

"Listen Tim," said Lane. "The colonel's tasty habit is in a coach up at the tavern. We'll bring her down when you give the word. I've the coin here. Yer ta take her to Liverpool an' see her off ta the Indies. Right?" Lane had quoted a price to Captain Keyes lower than what Old Barley had been willing to pay, so he had already skimmed the top for himself.

Keyes leaned across the inlaid mahogany table he had salvaged from a wreck in his younger days. "Pete, you've naught ta fear. I told ya what with the price yer payin and what I can make on her in Liverpool, she's a right good investment." The captain planned on selling her to a sugar cane planter he knew. The fellow was in the market for an English-bred house servant and bed warmer. The planter who was visiting relatives in Huddersfield was leaving for Bermuda in four days. The planter and Keyes had served aboard the same letter of marque privateer chasing Spaniards in the War of Jenkins' Ear.

Captain Keyes pulled an enamel and gold watch out of a threadbare brown velvet waistcoat pocket. "Bring her down in an hour, an' if she's half the wench you said, I'll cut ma price for old time's sake."

Things kept looking up for Lane. Now, he had only to separate Old Barley's itch from the boy hero. He had been afraid the lad would get stiff in his breeches if left all alone in the coach with the wench for too long. P. Peter Lane had dealt with situations like this many times before when members of Parliament had fallen in love with his merchandise. Patrick Peter Lane had never himself been in love with a woman. He considered them a millstone around his neck. Women were for riding, renting, and removing. His own mother had been slatternly, and her sluttish ways had driven her husband, no account Gil O'Brien, to the highway. P. Peter Lane had taken his name from a gravestone in Killarney rather than be known as his mother and father's son.

Lane could understand the predicament that Old Barley found himself in, but he could not precisely sympathize. Men like Blanchard and the ensign were fools, and Lane had always been ready to separate their like from their money. Fool is as fool does.

Lane and Spooner came up to the coach and peeked in. Peggy Fairchild was nibbling at a cut of meat, and Crisp was pouring her a tot of wine like she was the virgin princess and he was some gallant of old. "Sure, it's time, sir," said Lane. "The captain'll be waitin' fer us, and we've no time to lose."

"Don't ye suppose we could talk about this, Lane? I'm sure we could work something out where Mistress Fairchild could go to London or Edinburgh, or perhaps I could send her to ma parents in Glasgow."

Lane took a deep breath and sighed as though he were explaining something to a rather slow-witted child. "Sir, the colonel's counting on you to preserve his good name. If his name is blackened, then so is the regiment's. For the Fifty-Sixth, sir, do the right thing. Her lips may taste of honey and her skin be milky smooth, sir, but she has the heart of an adder," reasoned Lane.

Peggy shot him a murderous glare, and her nostrils flared, but she knew if she opened her pouty mouth to protest or if she gave Lane too hard a time in any way, he would hurt her and think nothing more of it than if he had kicked a starving mongrel pup. On the trip from Blanchard Hall, she had a chance to plumb each of the men. Lear and Spooner were simple. They would do what Lane told them. Lane would do whatever served his purpose. Peggy was not struck by the irony of this at all. Crispin Mull was her only chance, and now, she could see the boy lacked the strength to have his way over the older and more worldly Lane. She had played her best hand and lost.

Lane led Peg down the path to Captain Keyes's trim little cutter. Crisp had remained behind, pounding his fist against the coach and alternately railing at Lear who had remained behind with him. Altogether, Crispin's first foray onto the field of romance had been an abysmal failure. He had tilted with his lance and been unseated by fair lady. He longed for another encounter even though his first was only four hours past. Lear remained silent as usual.

Tom Lear came from the midlands. His father, a farmer, had two boys, the younger of whom was a not terribly independent thinker. Tom had always done what his brother or his father had told him to do. His father was cleaning the horse's feet one day when a fly with apocalyptic timing bit the animal right in the tenderest part of the rump. The poor beast flinched and kicked out, meaning no harm. Unfortunately, the head of Lear's father was immediately behind the tray-sized iron-trimmed hoof. Tom had found him an hour later staggering about the farmyard, moaning, and bleeding quite profusely from the upper part of his face. Tom called his brother, Harry, in from the fields, and they dressed the wound with a cold cloth and laid their father in the shadows near the cool hearth. Tom went to fetch the doctor who lived over seven miles away. Happily, Lear's father passed away before the physician could bring him any more pain and suffering, and Harry became the master of the house forthwith. Harry had long had an eye on a local girl whom he now planned on marrying. The will of Lear's father had left poor Tom with a good shovel, a new pair of sturdy walking boots, and a treasured blackthorn staff. It was clear that his father's living and dying wish had been that Tom take the road and seek his fortune, or so said Harry.

The recruiters of the Fifty-Sixth found him a few weeks later in a tavern counting his last few pennies from a ditch-digging job. Adventure, they said, awaited a brave lad around every turn when he joined the army. The chance for advancement, they said, was there for every strong, courageous youth that dreamed of commanding a regiment one day. Why, women threw themselves at the feet of men in red coats. The Fifty-Sixth, they said, had the finest reputation and accepted only perfect physical specimens. Come have an ale, and drink to adventure, they said. The colonel, they said, is the bravest of brave, second only to the great Marlborough himself. Colonel Blanchard was Julius Caesar come back to life, they said. Have another ale, they said. Tom downed the tankard with the thirst of Akbar the Saracen, and when he got to the bottom, there was a shilling. Tom plucked the shilling out of the pewter mug and held it up to the light coming in from the many-paned front window. Here, they said, the lad has taken the king's shilling. Does everyone see?

Tom signed his name where the sergeant showed him and then sold his shovel to a chap who looked like he could use a new shovel. Tom was actually too young to join on his own, but with no one to speak up for him, the recruiter was asking no questions. Two weeks later, Tom found himself in a pinchingly tight-fitting red coat with forty pounds of equipment in a sheepskin pack on his broad back, following a corporal to the home of the Fifty-Sixth Regiment of Foot, who some used to style the Cheviot Guards. That was all two years ago, and Tom was now content with the life of a soldier.

Adventure had never found him, but as long as he stuck by Lane, he had a full cup of ale. Peter Lane knew fine spear carriers when he saw them, and he recognized in Tom Lear two of the requisite traits: the ability to remain silent when told to and the ability to follow orders unflinchingly. While King George never consulted Lane on matters of the law, the one thing that they could agree upon was what made an outstanding henchman. Tom also had thought Peg a strapping lass in need of the services of "Private John Thomas," but Lane had warned both him and Spooner not to lay a hand or anything else on her. Tom sympathized with the poor ensign. *A love struck lad is a pitiable sight*, he thought

Peg stumbled and tried to stay upright on the steep path leading down to the water. Spooner had tied her hands behind her, so she had no method by which to check her momentum or keep her balance. Lane led the way, and Spooner, with his brown bess musket at the charge bayonet and a wary eye, took the rear.

William Spooner was a quiet man. Not the shy and pleasant kind of quiet but more the eye of the storm kind of quiet. Bill had that presence that made others uncomfortable. He never said two words, and no one, not even Peter Lane, could say what he had been or done before the army, and he seemed to have no interest in telling anyone. It was as though he had just appeared out of nowhere. The truth was that Bill Spooner could kill with his bare hands but did not enjoy the work particularly, which ironically is why he joined the army—to get away from killing.

Spooner had worked at divers slaughter pens and knackers yards. Most of the meat and black puddings on London's tables had been brought there, at least, partly compliments of William Archimedes Spooner. A slaughter yard is an unattractive place on the very best day, which happens to be holidays when no animal is being summarily transported to the great beyond. On those days, a great herd of animals spends their last hours quietly munching feed in the yards, unaware of their own role in the grand scheme. As soon as the holiday is over, they spend their hours munching away to the accompaniment of the thump and whack of the knacker's hammer. The coppery smell of blood permeates the air as the swine and cattle are bled out and then swung high. Fresh hides pile up each morning to be carted off by the tanner, and the knacker leans on his hammer at day's end, the sweat dripping from his brow. And if all his customers were present, a mountain of meat would be lying still at his feet. Bill Spooner saw death as a chore not a passion. All his years swinging the hammer had left him with little appetite for chops or roasts or sausages. Multitudes had supped each night on Bill Spooner's handiwork, but Bill himself went home and ate a bit of bread and a bowl of boiled turnips or potato and leek. On holidays, he added a small pudding to the menu, and even now in the army, he traded away his portion of beef or pork, which his messmates thought queer but didn't dare to mention. Each man always gave half his potato or a bit of turnip to Bill in exchange for the salty overcooked flesh.

Captain Keyes and his tiny crew waited on the shingle, standing ready to put out in an instant.

Lane tossed the purse of coin to Captain Keyes. "Count it out. Treat her well or however ye have a mind to." P. Peter Lane shoved Peg forward and threw her small trunk after her.

Two of the sailors grabbed her up by her bound elbows and waded her out to the shallop and heaved her up and over the freeboard so that she landed rather unceremoniously in the tiny boat.

"Patrick," said Keyes, "ye know I'd not damage goods of value. It's been fair doin' business with ye. She's a rum doxy as my dad always said." Captain Keyes flipped a gold Louis d'or back at Lane and then waded out behind his remaining two crewmembers. Good to his word, the captain had given Lane his due.

Spooner and Lane watched without passion or sympathy until the dainty but fanged cutter-weighed anchor and hoisted sail, slipping off into the gathering fog. The job was done, and P. Peter Lane was a stealthy step closer to securing the rum contracts for the Fifty-Sixth of Foot.

The only way that Lane could think of to improve upon his overall good fortune of late was to loan some of his newly earned wealth to an officer. Many of the officers of the Fifty-Sixth, like a great many gentlemen, were inveterate gamblers, and no few lacked the willpower to leave the gaming tables when the cards and the gods of fortune were against them. With mounting debt, they borrowed from anyone in order to pay for their uniforms, bed, and board. Lane could demand extravagant interest and add another officer to his collection of favors owed.

Lane and Spooner mounted the path back to the town, sure that, at last, Peggy Fairchild was no longer Old Barley's problem.

Timothy Keyes was not unlike most salt-rimed men of the sea. Short on words, long on sense, he brooked no riot, argument, or misbehavior aboard any vessel he commanded. In fact, Tim Keyes had only commanded two ships. The *Emily Jane*, which classified as hardly more than a decked over pinnace with a modest hold and a tiny cabin, was his current hull. Like many a seaman, he had begun his career as a gunner and worked his way up over eight years. Hacking down his enemies and choking on the noxious fumes from hundreds of kegs of burnt powder, but slipping in the blood of his shipmates had taken a toll.

Privateering was not for the faint of heart but could, under good circumstances, reap huge rewards as the crew shared in the spoil of any vessel captured. The more rank a sailor had, the greater his share of the bloodied prize, and Tim had risen in his career to be first mate on the letter of marque vessel, *Shrike*. Letter of marque ships were often the finest and best-equipped ships that investors could buy.

It was his goodly share as mate of the privateer that had allowed him to borrow the additional cash to purchase the *Andrew Morgan*. The *Andrew Morgan* had preceded the little cutter *Emily Jane* by more than a decade and had carried a crew of seventeen, carrying aloft a good bit more canvas on an extra mast and boasting four deck guns and a bow and stern gun at each end respectively The *Andrew Morgan* had made Captain Tim Keyes a second fortune, running passengers and provisions back and forth between Scotland and France during the late Highland rebellion. After successfully outrunning a frustrated English ship of the line, she foundered on the rocks in 1747 after having heroically delivered a group of exiled Jacobite Chieftains to Calais. Tim had sworn by his cutlass that he would never again support a political cause, and true to his oath, he never took another cargo aboard that was running from the hangman. Stalwart and wise, Captain Keyes heaped on all sail and sped away from danger now rather than seek it out.

The *Emily Jane*, being a daintier vessel than the *Andrew Morgan*, sported only two swivel guns and a two-pounder bronze stern gun, which was intended to deter chase in the final extremis.

Keyes arrived in Liverpool with barely a day to spare and thought himself in fine shape to sell the wench and return to Whitehaven with no one the wiser. What he had not counted on was the customer leaving early. Word had reached his old friend, the planter, of a hurricane hitting the Lesser Antilles and nearly wiping out his plantation. Keyes's old shipmate had taken the first boat to the Indies in hopes of salvaging his rather substantial fortune. English-bred serving women were hardly first in his mind, and he had even forgotten to send a note to his old friend Tim in Whitehaven. Keyes had inquired at the ship he thought his friend was taking and had found out all.

Now with a fancy strumpet and no customer, Keyes had regretted giving P. Peter Lane a reduction. "Who, in the name of all that was holy, would want the kidnapped mistress of a regimental commander?" he asked himself. No good answer was forthcoming. Captain Tim knew he was not safe, keeping her lying about for long. If she were unbound, she would run. If she were seen bound, Tim might find himself answering to the admiralty. Peg had not yet made an effort to arouse attention, but Keyes was certain she was only awaiting the right opportunity.

During the three-day run, she had stayed in the captain's tiny cabin where she had slept on the deck—that is to say the floor under her blue woolen cloak. Tim had given no more than a moment's thought to ravaging her and perhaps even keeping her for himself but decided she was too great a trouble. Keyes had never been one to go in for rapine and whoring, and unlike most of his fellow seaman, had never felt the burn of the surgeon's hot copper wire. Diseases of the loins were not worth a moment's stolen pleasure with some gap-toothed, wrinkled, rum-soaked harridan. He had heard tales of the beauties of the South Seas, but never having sailed in those waters, he had only seen the used-up sailors' whores of Marseilles, London, Amsterdam, and Copenhagen. As far as Tim was concerned, Peg was no more than a gentleman's fille de joie. Courtesans and mistresses were costly, overrated copulation that demanded pretty things and constant attention, and that kept a man from getting about his business.

The woman could not stay in England. She could bring ruin upon everyone, so Tim was racing about the docks, seeking a way to rid himself of this winsome anchor and recoup what he had lost to Lane. He toyed for an hour or so with the idea of sending her on to the Caribbean and billing his old shipmate later. The only problem with that plan was that he would have to pay for her passage now, and he might never be repaid. No, he would not lose money on this deal, and if he could help it, he would still see more profit.

At last, Tim found himself standing lost in thought when he looked up to see a group of dock workers, carrying chests of tea up onto a fair-sized brig with a savage maiden, naked as a worm, for a figure head. The *Indian Rose* was the name painted across her stern, and after a couple of well-placed questions, Tim was able to learn that she was bound for Rhode Island with a load of tea and pigs of iron for the colonial market. Tim hunted up the captain, one Isaiah Harding of Providence, Rhode Island. Yes, he said he would be glad to take aboard a passenger for the right price.

Tim explained that he had his wife's sister begging at his table and that he could no longer afford to keep her about and would the good captain take her for the price of her indenture less ten pounds? "Good god!" exclaimed Harding.

"Was Keyes trying to sell his own sister-in-law?"

"Why, no," stammered Keyes, trying not to queer the whole deal, but didn't he have a right at least to recoup her board? After all, she could sew and clean. Her indenture would more than cover her passage and still leave Captain Harding a tidy profit. For a delicate thing, she had a prodigious appetite and had nearly eaten him out of home, he continued to lie. She would likely be seasick and eat next to nothing on the crossing, however.

"What price did you have in mind?" asked Harding.

Why, ten pounds was not out of line, thought Tim.

"Two," said Harding.

"Eight," countered Tim.

"Four and not a farthing more," insisted Harding. Captain Tim knew when he faced a hard bargainer.

"Done," said Tim. He would deliver the girl tomorrow morning before the *Indian Rose* weighed anchor. He breathed a deep and silent sigh of relief.

Tim explained all this to Peg on his return to the *Emily Jane*. He hoped she would play along and not give him a hard time. Quite the contrary, she screamed, extended her claws, and took a tigress swipe at Captain Tim's face, landing a not ill-aimed hook. Three red stripes welled up with blood just as Tim's rope-callused fist slammed into the side of Peggy's auburn-maned head. The fair wanton hit the deck without so much as a thump or a wiggle. Corpses have danced livelier jigs than that girl as she lay motionless. Tim was an experienced man with his fists and knew just how to strike a blow that would stun but neither kill nor maim nor mar the face of a wench. Captain Tim and one of his crewmen dragged Peggy a quarter of mile through the murk to the *Indian Rose*.

"She went lunatic an' hit her head," said Captain Tim to Captain Harding. "I thought it best if we brought her over like this. She's not as like to hurt herself or anyone else this way you see." The Yankee skipper ignored the bloody welts on Keyes's grizzled cheek.

Isaiah Harding was no country rustic, and he needed no more explanation. He motioned for them to bring the senseless Messalina aboard, and then two of his crewmen took her to a spartan cabin below decks. He paid Keyes the devil's four guineas they had agreed upon.

So it was that Peggy Fairchild passed out of England and was bound for a land teeming with garishly painted red savages and wild animals where civilization rarely penetrated more than one hundred miles inland—where no one had heard of Sir Beverly Blanchard and no one gave a fig for the former mistress of a colonel of Foot. Little did Peggy know that all her social graces and romantic machinations would avail her naught in her new home. She awoke from her stunned faint just as the coastline of England was slipping away over the horizon. With a fair wind and favorable seas, Peg would step ashore in Providence Town in six weeks. The crew would look less pagan in their freshly washed shirts and neckerchiefs, compliments of Peg Fairchild, washerwoman. Captain Harding would have a quick in his step that his wife had not seen since their wedding night, and this would bring Peg to even more despair and woe, but that is all for later.

✧

Crispin Mull sat dejectedly in the coach as Bob Tofts gave the horses their head and galloped for Hart, the wheels of the coach hardly touching the track as it bumped and jostled over the road with sparks flying from its iron-rimmed wheels. P. Peter Lane rode on behind, and Spooner and Lear took up their positions at the front and rear of the hurtling coach.

ABOARD THE MATADOR

The entire regiment was drawn up at attention; their hair was freshly floured and clubbed. Buckles gleamed and boiled leather neck stocks kept everyone's head held up high. Booted and wigged, Colonel Sir Beverly Blanchard strode out in front of the regiment, followed by his staff. Major Patterson cleared his throat and read aloud the commendation and promotion, etcetera, and so on and so forth ad nauseum.

Ensign Mull stepped out smartly from the ranks and approached the greatly relieved colonel with as precise a military bearing as he could muster. He touched his hat respectfully, stood at attention, accepted the promotion with the left hand so that the right hand is free to touch the hat again, returned to the ranks, made a right-about turn, and he was done. In less than three months, Ensign Crispin Mull had achieved the promotion that took others years. His meteoric rise had not been politely ignored by the other ensigns or lieutenants, and Crisp was in for a bit of a hard time. With diligence, hard work and some luck, which as it may happen he enjoyed in great quantity, Crisp might hope to make captain in a few years.

Lane stood before the colonel next and was promoted to the rank of corporal and given a guinea for valorous and honorable service to the king and country.

The word went out through the regiment that Corporal Lane and Lieutenant Mull had been chosen for a secret mission following their courageous action at the Black Dragoon.

Whoremaster, swagman, kidnapper and conspirator to murder, P. Peter Lane's chequered past was serving him well as only he might expect. It is said that rogues prosper while honest men toil from sun to sun.

Spooner and Lear received their guinea each from Crispin's young hand along with a kind and grateful word passed on from Old Barley.

※

Two years passed, and 1755 dawned frosty and cold on the first of the New Year. By now, Corporal P. Peter Lane had acquired the substantial rum contracts for the Fifty-Sixth of Foot by extorting the cowardly officer in charge of supplies.

Continuous loans to cover poorly made wagers had left the luckless captain indebted to the felonious corporal. The men of the regiment noticed that their rum was less efficacious and its merrymaking qualities were greatly lacking; however, several bottles of Tokay bestowed upon the right officers had silenced the grumbling. No one had even the slightest idea that Lane was the actual supplier of spirits. A wagon from Carlisle arrived each month and unloaded the correct number of barrels along with a case of wine and spirits for the officers, courtesy of Messer's Patten and Collett.

Patten and Collett were merely the current names of two professional pretenders with whom Lane had been acquainted for years. The two, for a nominal fee, diluted the rum, purchased the cheapest wine and spirits they could, and then turned them over to the carters, who then trundled them to the camp of the Fifty-Sixth. Corporal Lane never touched a bill or receipt, and no one was the wiser as his accounts grew from wee little stacks into great heaps.

By forgiving another officer his imbecilic debt, Lane had managed to get himself promoted yet again when the sergeant of his company died of blood poisoning. The poor sergeant had been "accidentally" shot by one of his own privates when the "clumsy" soldier's musket had discharged prematurely during a loading and firing demonstration staged for the locals on market day. The sergeant's ugly, ragged hip wound had gone putrid, and the poor man had died screaming through his nose whilst choking on gobbets of blood and sputum. Sergeant Dick Cameron parted the veil and left vacant an honored place in the ranks.

The preceding year of 1754 had been one of great moment in the world as the two great powers, Britain and France, squared off yet again like two spoilt and effeminate pugilists. Both monarchs were bedazzled by their own brilliance, which was reflected in the weighty, jewel encrusted crowns that sat upon their rather soft fat heads. Had King Louis of France and George the Second of Britain been allowed to scratch at each other like two hairy maidens, the young men of England, Scotland, Wales, Ireland, France, Canada, and the British Colonies in North America not to mention the peasants of divers other nations on the continent, would have been spared a great bloodletting.

Centuries of enmity would be resolved on the battlefields of Europe and America in the coming years. In England and on the continent, the conflict would be called the Seven Years War; and in America., it would bear the confusing appellation of the French and Indian War. Falsely leading one to believe that it was a fracas between the Gaulish Canadiens and their erstwhile allies of the forest. In truth, the American side of the war was perhaps the most unpredictable and murderous, and the stakes, the most lucrative.

The Seven Years War was only an extension of King William's War, Queen Anne's War, and several other major and minor skirmishes in which the French and Anglo peoples found themselves for over four hundred years. Throughout the first half of the eighteenth century, the two combatants continued to master the art of war and spent vast fortunes periodically arming and training professional armies. It was into this gladiatorial arena that Lieutenant Crispin Mull had placed his figuratively sandaled foot.

About the early spring of 1755, the Fifty-Sixth Regiment of Foot had been ordered to America via the Caribbean. Stopping off briefly at the island of St. Kitts to deposit two companies at the fortress there, the balance of the regiment was to continue on to America to assist in the reduction of French fortresses and the chastisement of the natives supporting Froggish claims to regions close by British settlements. The royal governor of the Island of St. Kitts politely feted the officers and introduced them to the few young ladies who were of available age and appropriate station and whose skin was fair and free of slave or Indian taint.

Drunk on rich food and too much wine, several of the officers slipped down to the waterfront where they sampled more exotic and duskier entertainments. Crisp danced with the winsome planter's daughters and sipped fine wine from elegant stemware. With his eye on making captain in the next year or two, Crispin had only to land a brightly gowned, flapping angelfish that had a fat dowry and graceful social connections. The young lieutenant had learned over the last two years to play the parlor and drawing room games of the rich and deliciously powerful.

Meanwhile, P. Peter Lane and the rest of the soldiery remained aboard the transports, drinking watered rum and dicing with tricked dice supplied covertly by Sergeant Lane. Lane naturally had Lear and Spooner running the games, and none of the other soldiers were the wiser. Should someone challenge Lear or Spooner, then Lane would step in and "confiscate" the bones. Lear and Spooner got to keep half of their stealings, so the games were worth the risk. Lear played on the gun deck while Spooner's game was on a hatch cover on the main deck.

P. Peter Lane wandered back and forth between the two holystoned decks, making idle town talk with the soldiers and sailors, contentedly puffing away at his stubby white clay pipe and taking mental notes on the rising piles of coin in front of his two henchmen.

Lane hoped that the regiment would soon arrive in the colonies. There was nowhere to go aboard ship or on this tiny island. Once in America, if it appeared as though the regiment might actually be sent into the fever-filled wilderness, Peter planned on making good his desertion by using the ill-gotten gains from his dice scheme to pay for his passage back to England. The three leaky transports carrying the regiment and the cannon-studded ship of the line escort still had to sail their way up the coast of the colonies before the troops could be deposited at New York. Lane calculated that the soldiers and sailors would be broke before they made landfall in the colonies. He safely surmised it best if he allowed them to keep some of their paltry pay lest they become overly suspicious. They would require loans in New York to augment their losses anyhow. He plotted on using the profits from the enormous interest he would charge the honest corporals, privates, and his fellow sergeants as the foundation for additional loans to the officers at even greater interest. Some of the small loans to officers would be forgiven in order to obtain special favors and ensure protection for his varied business ventures. With cat-like agility, Patrick Peter Lane always landed on his feet and, like an assassin's shadow, left no trail.

 Lieutenant Crispin Mull had steered clear of Lane for the last couple of years, realizing that once the grasping sergeant got his talons into a body, it was painful to break free. Crispin was now an accepted member of the officer cadre of the Fifty-Sixth of Foot and was paving his own path to success through the no less dirty channels of "gentlemanly" society. While some of his fellow officers were less conspicuous in their consumptions, it was only for lack of ready cash, not any moral prerogative, that they galloped with the lasses less or gambled more infrequently. Only a few of the older married officers kept their swords sheathed and played with their children instead of Jacks and Knaves. Lieutenant Mull had his eye on being one of the youngest colonels in the army, and he recognized that a good marriage and a solvent purse were the keys to his campaign. In England, Crispin could never hope to marry well enough to enter into the middle or upper echelon of military life. In the islands or in the colonies, there was likely many a rich merchant's daughter who would gladly give her dainty, alabaster hand to a captain of regulars who had real hopes of one day gaining a colonelcy.

Colonel Washington of the Virginia Militia lit the torch that fueled the flame, which the winds of war fanned into conflagration. The blueblooded young colonel was certainly no wise and experienced centurion. The squire marched into territory claimed by the French but desired by Virginia Colony and attacked a party of French Regulars led by the intrepid Ensign Jumonville. Poor Jumonville, along with nine of his men, was cut down in the sneak attack. Like a bold cockerel, Washington remained in the region and closeted himself and his tiny army in an ill-placed, drafty, mud-ridden excuse for a fort. A sizeable force of natives and Frenchmen of Fort Duquesne then laid siege from two neighboring hillocks and enfiladed Washington's deteriorating and demoralized troops. By the by, Colonel Washington signed a capitulation which allowed him to skip off to Virginia with his drums-a-beating. Alas, the young would be Tiberius had inadvertently put his name to a document, which admitted to the assassination of Jumonville. Washington would learn to read the fine print more closely in the future before agreeing to apply his signature.

This faux pas would give the French precisely the prod with which to goad their cross channel enemy—England. All across the long and tree-canopied frontier, savages and whites began to slit each other's throats. Most of the happy and successful slashing and scalping was initially perpetrated by the Indians. The unlettered and incohesive tribes had slowly been losing ground to the cunning and guile of British land speculators and the colonial governors who pushed the rustic colonial mob westward. The French gleefully hoped to contain the English along the coast while keeping the lucrative fur trade of the interior for themselves. Britannia girded her ample loins for war. Regiments like the "Cheviot Guards," the Black Watch, and the numerous other companies along with battalions of colonial recruits followed the smoke of burning cabins and blockhouses that foretold the war-painted terror that poured from the forest.

The small convoy of transports and escorts bearing the Fifty-Sixth of Foot slowly advanced northward toward the coast of the Carolinas.

※

Captain Miguel Antonio DeVaca had called the capes and islands of the Carolinas home off and on for the past two years. His schooner, El Matador, with a crew of forty-one-plus, the captain had been preying on unarmed merchantmen with singular success until the past two weeks. Miguel, known as Red Mike by his crew, had been born in Spanish-held Florida.

Miguel's sire had been an officer at Spanish St. Augustine and his dam, an Irish missionary nun bound for Brazil, who was rescued from a storm-wrecked ship. Quite obviously, she had not remained a nun. Miguel's father had fallen in love with the fair Colleen and married her as soon as he learned that she was swelling with his child. Tragically, Miguel's father was struck and killed by lightning while making water against a tree. Some in St. Augustine whispered behind their hands that it was because he had despoiled a bride of Christ. The new babe's mother removed herself to Maryland, an English colony with a large Catholic population. Miguel was raised without a bit of Spanish on his tongue, and other than his olive skin and raven hair, he would have passed for an Irish country lad. Miguel's mother had remarried, this time to an Irishman who crabbed and hunted on the Chesapeake Bay. Miguel kept his last name, but everyone knew him as Mike. Young Mike learned to handle small boats and fowling pieces, helping his stepfather, Gavin Burke, hunt Canada geese, ducks, and shore birds.

By the age of fourteen, bright Mike had signed to crew aboard a privateer with letters of marque to cruise against Spain in the

War of Jenkins' Ear, which came to be known as War of Austrian Succession. Young Miguel fetched the powder by the pail full for the guns aboard the *Dread Angel*.

By the ripe old age of twenty, Mike had earned the "Red" that preceded his name. *Dread Angel*, the infamous brig commanded by Joshua Russell, took a French vessel by stealth and coupe de main. With the captured crew tied up in the main hold, Russell had offered a double share of the prize to any member of the crew who could sever two heads with a single stroke. Several of the *Dread Angel*'s crew tried and failed, leaving for each effort only one decapitated corpse and one gasping, horribly mangled French sailor. Finally, Mike's turn came, and he stood his victims back to back and kindly blindfolded them together with a single black silk scarf. Mike had honed his cutlass to a razor edge, and now he swung it with all the cruel force his tanned, sinewy arm could muster. Two blinking heads wobbled, ghastly on the gory deck of the *Dread Angel*, and Red Mike had committed his first cold-blooded murder.

Other sailors and passengers had felt the nick of Mike's cutlass or had received a wound in honest manly combat, but never had he killed two defenseless men for a double share of loot.

The war had ended, and Russell had no intention of returning to more humble means of employment. For a half-dozen years, he preyed on Frenchmen, Dutch merchantman, and Spaniards as he desired even though peace had been resumed and his letters of marque revoked. He had gone pirate. With the coming of Seven Years War, he once again sought legal letters and tried to wheedle his way out of a noose. The commander of His Majesty's squadron in the West Indies, however, could not tolerate a pirate even if the fellow was preying upon papists and Dutchmen.

Captain Joshua Russell was six feet tall with a shock of straw-blond hair, and in a black velvet and brown brocade coat with a silver hilted small sword, he cut a rather memorable figure. Foolishly, he thought to spend a night ashore in Nassau Town. Sadly for piracy and privateering, Captain Russell was recognized over a glass of madeira by one of the rare survivors of his depredations, and he was promptly arrested. The *Dread Angel* sneaked back out to sea that very night without further incident, and Captain Joshua Russell danced the hangman's jig and then hung in chains above the navy dock for all to witness. Red Mike was elected captain simply because he was handsome, lethal, and all hands hoped, lucky.

Captain DeVaca did what Russell couldn't and, a few months later, obtained legally issued letters authorizing him to prey upon the merchant fleet of France. He took prize after prize, and the crew agreed to anything he proposed. Unwisely, he chose next to cruise the coast of the Carolinas, thinking if they were successful enough there, he might retire and let someone else take command of the brutal schooner. An earlier generation of royal governors had had their fill of "privateersman," and the current crop would have none of the outlawry and buccaneering their predecessors had profited from. Red Mike's avarice was outstripping his judgment. Now he sought to do business with anyone who had a mind to condemn his prize and pay him off.

DeVaca had not seen his mother or stepfather in nearly seven years and strangely was saddened by the fact that he might have shamed them, and he wished to explain himself and ease their lives with some of his violently accumulated wealth.

The dashing captain brought the *Dread Angel* into Easton, Maryland, one wind-whipped night. Before dawn, the crew had careened her and were inspecting the bottom of the hull for rot, scraping off the inevitable encrustations. Teredo worms had holed her like a sieve. The *Dread Angel* was a lost cause. Her hull was weeks or days from failing, and without significant and costly repairs, she would be unseaworthy. The crew split up and agreed to rendezvous in three weeks to see if they could locate another likely vessel.

During the interlude, Mike would visit his parents and beg their forgiveness for his sins. It was in the second week of his separation from the crew that Mike's first mate came to him secretly with the news of a schooner moored near Queenstown in one of the many inlets of the Chesapeake. The crew regrouped, plus four, bringing the total to forty-two including Red Mike. Several of the innocents that had been lead into brigandry by those happy sons of Satan were boys no older than Mike when he had signed aboard with Russell. Red Mike set a plan in motion that would let them take the ship without a shot being fired or an alarm raised before they were long gone upon the waves of the Atlantic.

Just as Mike had planned, the vessel fell without a shot; the lone watch stander was strangled in the dark just before dawn, his feet drumming against the deck as his face turned blue. The name of the ship, now long forgotten, was painted over and the name *El Matador*, a bow to Red Mike's Spanish heritage was emblazoned across her stern in blood red letters.

<hr>

As the transports climbed the coast off the Carolinas, riding the Gulf Stream, Crisp was given the duty of walking the men about the main deck for exercise.

In the cramped quarters of the transport, each soldier had to await his turn with the others, as the main deck was too small for all to go out at the same time. The slop buckets, full of stale urine and waste, would be taken up and dumped and the men allowed to stroll the deck and fill their lungs with fresh salt air. Below decks the smell of the slop bucket mingled with the ripe odor of unwashed bodies, pipe smoke, and cooking fumes wafting from the galley. The walk about was one of the few opportunities to break up the sameness of the days. Lieutenant Mull's task was to organize and oversee the walk about.

Three senior sergeants were stationed about the deck—one at the bow, one amidships, and one at the stern. The sergeants were allowed to smoke and relax but were to keep their eyes open in case any of the men started trouble.

Soldiers at sea were a riot waiting to happen. Like the oft-mentioned fish out of water, they too were out of their element, and they were often seasick and were unused to the constant close quarters confinement. These conditions could easily lead to friction between the men. Fistfights were not uncommon, and upon occasion, a blade would appear, and it was then time for the sergeants to move in with truncheons.

Other junior officers were in charge of arranging some light duties and entertainments for the distraction of the troops. The lads were allowed to bring along a mascot such as a cat or bird and musical instruments as long as they fit in their packs and took up no valuable space aboard ship. Displays of pugilism with the attendant betting were not unheard of, and of course, church services were made available but not as popular as two ham-fisted straw heads pounding each other to jam. The ship's captain would lead the service with selected readings, and an assortment of Cromwellian psalms would cap off the ecclesiastically uninspired worship. While all the men were required to attend worship, very few could be called religious except for their drinking, cursing, and gambling, which they attended to with greater regularity than their immortal souls.

It was while Crispin was enjoying a pinch of snuff and inspecting his nails for dirt that disaster hit the transport. The sergeant at the stern shouted the warning. A thundershower several miles off the starboard quarter had suddenly spawned two waterspouts, which were heading toward the small convoy with great speed. Crisp's transport trailed the column, and the southernmost spout was bearing down on them before the helm could respond.

The gape-mouthed soldiers all stopped in their tracks, their conversations cut off in midsentence as they saw catastrophe bearing down on them. Suddenly, they were in the midst of a maelstrom of flying water. The ship heeled over hard to port and, with unbelievable rapidity, began to spin counter clockwise on its beam ends. Men were swept off the deck and sucked up into the funnel with sails and snapped yardarms and splintered masts.

A heartbeat of calm ensued, and those men that had been able to grab a mast or a flapping ratline were dropped to the deck in a sodden, winded heap. Then the eye of the elemental storm passed over. The whole ship shuddered as it was lifted off the water and rolled over, just inches from the waves. With a whip-cracking sound that was lost in the roar, it was dropped back into the ocean with its keel snapped and lay on its back like some mortally wounded leviathan. The spout continued on its way as the remainder of the storm stirred up the water and pelted the other untouched vessels with driving rain.

The remaining four vessels of the convoy all turned their glasses on the broken and sinking wreck. Signaling back and forth, no one had spotted even one lone survivor as the capsized victim slipped beneath the gray-green water and headed for Davie Jone's Locker. The sixth-rate ship of the line escort came about smartly after the storm passed and cruised through the area seeking any sign of life and finding none. The job was so complete that there wasn't even a keg or a shoe or any piece of flotsam to show where two hundred and fifty-three men had met a watery end.

The two hundred and fifty-fourth man had remained lucky as usual as had a dozen others. The thirteen soldiers and sailors who miraculously survived had been amongst those caught in the column of water and dropped several miles west of their original location. Most of their fellow air travelers were lifeless corpses when they entered the water. The few that still breathed were scattered over several hundred yards of storm tossed water, mostly unaware of each other.

Crispin found himself gripping a spar and spitting out water when a dead rat plummeted out of the sky, knocking him unconscious. When he came around again, he was facedown in the water, and his spar was nowhere to be seen.

One minute, he had been thinking of nothing more than a conversation he had had the night before, and then almost the next, he was ripped off the ship's deck and nearly drowned in the wild ride of the waterspout. The fall of eighty feet into the water had all but killed him, but when he came to and reached the surface, he found the spar inches from his nose.

Crisp hadn't even had the chance to assess his situation. He was still in shock from the suddenness of the whole ordeal when the drowned rodent hit him smack on the head. The rat had been carried thousands of feet up into the funnel and had taken a minute longer to fall than Crisp. Crisp never knew what had hit him in the head nor was he ever aware of the brief and fruitless search of the escort. He only knew he was likely to die in the next few hours.

The water was cold enough that he was already starting to shiver, and the choppy whitecaps limited his view in any direction. He had never been to sea and had no idea where he was or what to do. He rolled over onto his back, floating in the buoyant brine, thinking he would take a pleasant rest and let the waves take him when they were ready.

Little did he know that the convoy had been cruising a mere eleven miles off shore and that the waterspout had taken him to within eight miles of land. The winds from the storm had lessened his distance from shore another mile, and so Crispin was within sight of land had his view been from the deck of a ship.

Seven miles is still seven miles too far for most any man, and Crispin would likely have drowned within sight of shore if not for the happy occurrence that followed an hour behind the convoy, lurking off their larboard quarter.

Red Mike had shadowed the convoy, hoping to exploit some weakness and unaware of the vast overwhelming power of the squadron until he was much closer.

The past two weeks had been rather slow for the *Matador*. Mike had succeeded only in taking a small sloop with a cargo of household goods bound from Charlestowne to Port Royal Sound. While Mike enjoyed the comfort of a wing back chair in his cabin and had also taken possession of a cracked but convenient chamber pot, the remaining goods had fetched a poor price in Spanish Florida, and the crew was eager for more lucrative plunder.

The only sails they had sighted since returning from St. Augustine had been those of the convoy. Ordinarily, Mike would have sighted a dozen sail and been able to choose his next victim carefully. As luck would have it, he was just never in the right place, and traffic along the coast was particularly slow for several days for no good or apparent reason.

So when the convoy was spotted, Red Mike shadowed it just to give his men something to do. The *Matador* was quick to respond to the helm, and when her captain saw the waterspout, he put about and headed closer in shore, leaving the storm off his stern and a steady land breeze on his larboard bow. Once he was sure the storm had abated, he stood further out and picked up the convoy's trail, unaware that the transport had been sunk.

"Summin' in the water two pints of the starboard bow, Cap'n!" bellowed the lookout.

The sailors crowded about the rail, and a dozen climbed into the rigging to see what had attracted the lookout's attention. As the nimble schooner came near the soaker, they dropped the ship's boat and sent three men out to pull the lunger out of the drink.

Crispin's eyes fluttered as he felt the boat hook tug at his clothes. Strong hands reached out and grabbed hold of his collar and pulled him aboard the ship's boat. In less than an hour and a half of being cast adrift, Lieutenant Crispin Mull had been pulled from the reaper's grip again.

Of the thirteen hardy men who survived the sinking, only six would see land again.

"Stand him up, dammit!" shouted Red Mike. "Let me see what kind of fish we've caught here." Mike looked Crispin up and down. "Give the poor bastard a draught of rum and a blanket."

"Thank you, Captain," replied Crisp. "And to whom do I owe my gratitude?" Crispin shrugged into the blanket, tugging it close around him and trying not to let his teeth chatter.

"Well, fish, I'll tell you who I am when I find out who you are and whether or not I keep you aboard or put you back. And then, of course, we have the matter of your passage, if I say you stay." He put special emphasis on *if*.

Crispin looked shocked by this statement. "Why on God's green earth would you save a man only to put him back in the ocean? Are you some kind of heartless pirate then?"

Crisp looked more closely at his rescuers and realized that all of them had the marlinespikes and knives that every sailor carried for mending ropes, but many also showed a boarding axe or dagger in their belt as well. Little did Crispin know at the moment that most of the weapons were stashed away until called for.

"You're not on God's green earth yet, mate," growled Mike. "This is my sea, and neither the devil nor the lord holds sway in these dominions. As to my heartlessness, you'd do better to ask my crew." Red Mike pointed up to where the *Matador*'s red ensign signifying no quarter, snapped in the breeze.

"I'm Miguel Antonio DeVaca. I hold letters of marque from His Majesty King George's Governor of New York. We are charged with disrupting the trade of King Louis's dominions in New France," finished Mike with a well-practiced Spanish accent he had learned in Florida along with a few quaint phrases. He failed to mention that he had taken more vessels flagged by his own nation than any other and that he broke out French colors whenever he set about taking a ship.

Crisp shifted his feet in the puddle collecting under him and watched the grim silent crew. "I see. My apologies, Captain DeVaca. You are, of course, entitled to earn your bread in whatever way you see fit, and it was unwise of me to call your generosity to account." Crisp had just noticed, and was rather relieved, that his coat had been torn away in the storm, and there was little about him that marked him as an officer, or so he thought.

"I don't know how you came to be in the water, fish, but I'd hazard that you were a high-handed officer and your men threw you overboard," guessed Red Mike. "Only an officer could insult me by calling me a pirate in one minute and then try to talk his way out of it the next." DeVaca turned to his first mate, Socrates McFadden, and ordered a cutlass be brought to him. Mike always wore his own sword as he didn't have to scamper up the rigging like the crew, and he also wore it as a badge of rank. The mate returned with a battered old saber taken from a long-dead Dutchman.

Crispin took the Dutchman's sword and locked eyes with DeVaca. "You don't offer a gentleman much option, do you, Captain? Perhaps you could return me for a reward? By the by, I was not thrown overboard. My ship was sunk by a waterspout, and as far as I know, I am the sole survivor."

He assumed a fencer's stance and shrugged off the blanket. Crispin was quite sure he stood no better than a fifty-fifty chance of besting DeVaca. Little did he know that the odds in his favor were no greater than zero. Everyone knew that privateersman were little better than pirates who were quite adept with edged weapons, and this captain seemed no frail exception. Crisp, on the other hand, had only had two lessons in saber fencing from a friend in the dragoons and had never heard many pirate stories.

Red Mike sprang at Crispin and, in a fluid set of moves like a gypsy dancer, knocked Crispin's saber to the side, grazed his cheek enough to draw blood, and then slapped Crisp solidly in the side of the head, stunning him yet again.

Crispin began to think himself unlucky as he lay temporarily paralyzed on the deck. He had been sunk, cast adrift, and rescued by men who could only be described as pirates, only to be insulted and assaulted. He did not know, of course, about the rat that would have been the sugar on the pudding.

Red Mike stood over the top of the unmoving castaway. "Clap iron on him, and put him in my cabin. Pour some more rum in him and on him. He might have a point. Mayhap we could curry some favor by returning him to the bosom of the governor." The crew snickered at his sarcasm and knew the privateersman was scheming already.

Sergeant Patrick Peter Lane had found a section of splintered iron-collared main mast and clung to it like a drenched but game rat. The second day after the sinking, Lane had finally sighted land through a dehydrated haze and managed to slowly paddle his way to shore with the help of the waves and the tide.

Lane still wore his regimental coat and belt with triangular bayonet. After several hours of drying in the warm April sunshine, he came around enough to realize that he needed both drink and food, and that he had no idea of where to find either of these things.

The shoreline was covered with sandy dunes, and it appeared that beyond them was a forest of towering trees. Surely if he had made it ashore, others had as well, hopefully along with some of the ship's stores. Delicious things to eat began marching through his head until he remembered that there was nothing delicious about army food.

As his mind began to clear, Lane remembered that the crewmembers had mentioned that they were cruising the coast near Cape Fear. It seemed an appropriately named place to be wrecked and marooned. Lane started inland, following a small creek. He hoped and prayed, something he had never done, that farther inland he would find sweet water instead of the salty swill that exited the channel in a brackish rut at ebb tide.

His stomach rumbled again, and he was sorry for the first time that he had not even a bit of wormy army bread. Army victuals were usually supplied by men who were as conscientious as the rum contractor for the Fifty-Sixth of Foot. This generally meant that the flour had been stretched with sawdust and that the meat had the brine drained off in order to lighten the load, and had therefore turned, or worse, gone maggoty.

As the tree line neared, he began to have grave doubts about stooping beneath the boughs. Lane knew as much about the forest as a woodcutter knows of London after sunset and that is to say damn and blasted little. Hunger overcame fear in the final consideration, and Lane hoped to locate someone who could feed him and point him toward civilization.

He reached beneath his waistcoat to reassure himself of the presence of his money belt. Even though the coin had nearly pulled him under Neptune's waiting cloak, he had refused to let go of his hard won wealth. In the end, he had found the shivered mast and saved himself and the mintage.

Lane had no idea if there were Red Indians in the Carolinas or where the towns and villages of the colonists were located. To Patrick Peter Lane, the map of the colonies was mostly a large blank. He knew the three principle cities along the coast were Philadelphia, Boston, and New York, and that said cities were in the north of the continent. He recalled hearing one of the besotted members of the House of Lords talk of a city in the south called Charleston and once one of the clients had talked of the damn fools in the burgesses in Virginia, whatever that was.

Penniless Irish boys whose parents spend their nights in drink and whoring and their days passed out from the evening's carnality, rarely see maps or the like. P. Peter Lane had once seen a map in a naval captain's possession, but it had shown the land about the man's farm in Essex and contributed nothing to Lane's understanding of the world, had he even understood what he was seeing, which in, point of fact, he didn't.

Sergeant Lane could write his name and could read haltingly, thanks to one of his better-taught wenches. He racked his brain trying to remember anything he might have ever heard about the Carolinas and especially anything that may have been mentioned aboard ship. Blank. His memory was an absolutely clean sheet of paper.

No, that wasn't exactly right. One of the sailors had mentioned that Hatteras was to the north and that they would stand farther out to sea as they approached that cape as it was quite hazardous. He had said they would need more sea room to avoid the treacherous reefs, rocks, and islands. None of this seemed likely to help Lane out of his present predicament.

Lane guessed he had several hours before darkness fell and then the devil knew what lurked in these forests of perdition. He had kept his flint and steel in a tin box in a pocket in his waistcoat where he could get at it easily to light his pipe. Blast his pipe was in his mouth when the storm hit. No pipe and nip tonight.

⁂

A soft brown face, at once both noble and savage, leaned in close to Crispin.

"You damn people awaken Davy. You about the luckiest man I ever see," said the face. Crispin had no idea that the phrase to "awaken Davy" meant to cause a storm.

He just terribly wanted to rub the salt and caked blood out of his eyes, but his hands were pinioned behind him, and he seemed to be manacled to a post. A tankard of watered rum was poured over his head, and then he was roughly toweled with a linen. He knew it was rum by the delicious odor it gave off.

When he opened his eyes again, a huge brown man in black linen breeches and a dirty white brocade waistcoat sans shirt was standing in front of him.

"My name is Socrates McFadden, an' I be the first mate of the *Matador*. You do what I tell ya, you live. You give me any lip, I gut ya like a little bird. Captain's gonna come see ya, an' you best speak more better than you was jabberin' before." Socrates jammed the cup between Crisp's cracked lips and poured the final dribble into his throat, nearly gagging him.

"Trepan!" called Socrates over his shoulder. "Damn that crooked little bastard!" Socrates turned and stumped out of the cabin.

Crisp looked about at his surroundings. The cabin was tiny, no more than eight feet square. Built between oaken frames in the stern, it admitted a little light through the gallery windows in the fantail. A small rug from Cathay lay on the floor with a curtained bunk in one corner and a small writing table in the other. A wing-backed armchair stood before the table and a chamber pot with a crack in it perched on the floor next to the bed. A brace of sixty-nine caliber holster pistols, a sextant, and a French shelf clock made up the only other items within Crispin's view.

Directly behind him, and therefore out of his sight, was a blunderbuss hanging beneath a small cupboard that held a few books, including Defoe's *Robinson Crusoe*, a copy of the British Navy's *Fighting Instructions*, and *Famous Pirates of Spanish Main* by E. Thomas Lodge, physician to the royal governor of Virginia in 1738.

Beneath the cupboard was a sea chest containing clothes and a small quantity of gold and silver specie of various mintages. Captain DeVaca, like all men who lived occasionally outside of the law, did not keep his horde near where any crewmember could see it and become homicidally larcenous. Red Mike had hidden his lucre well, and only he knew the location.

Crisp sat silently trying to focus enough to imagine the options before him. These privateers clearly were interested only in profit, and therefore, unless he could show himself profitable, he was likely—to make an understatement—in a bad way. He considered offering to write his own ransom note. He began to draft it in his head.

"Dear General," he began.

No, that wasn't endearing himself enough.

"To my esteemed commander, I have been rescued by a ship's captain to whom I owe my life. The bearer of this note will gladly make disposition for my return. The good gentleman is desirous of a just reward. Colonel Blanchard is acquainted with my career to date and can, therefore, help to place a value upon my safe return to my regiment.

He wasn't exactly a prisoner in the sense of a prisoner of war. Crisp realized he had been plucked out of the water out of curiosity, like one of the specimens his father used to sell. Perhaps stupidly he had offered the notion of reward, and at that point, he ceased to be a curiosity and became a potential investment like a load of lumber and cheeses.

He continued, "I am afraid, General, if payment is not made, these fellows will not hesitate to do me some grave harm. I place myself at your mercy and pray that God will not desert me nor courage fail me in this, my hour of darkness. With deepest respect, your humble servant, etcetera.

The last line before the request for mercy had driven home the dire straight in which Lieutenant Crispin Mull now found himself. He began to repeat the draft in his head so that when quill and ink were supplied he could calmly set words to paper.

Socrates McFadden and a filthy one-eyed sailor came back into the cabin. The "Patch" who Socrates referred to as Trepan had a bowl of porridge in one hand and a tankard in the other. Brown Socrates stepped behind Crisp and loosened the iron bracelets.

"Touch nothing," said Socrates. "Eat and when yer done, the captain wants to see you on deck."

Socrates McFadden had been born a slave on the fetid coast of the Spanish Main. His mother was said to be the most beautiful coffee colored African wench to ever grace the sheets of Don Roberto Jose Rivera Lopez plantation. The Don was not short on names or manly desire.

Socrates's sire had been born a free Indian high in the mountains. His father and mother had married at the Lopez plantation and raised three of their own children in slavery, the third of whom was to become Socrates McFadden.

When he was still tiny, Socrates, his parents, and his two sisters were taken and sold to Portuguese slavers. Don Berto had fallen on hard times and sold everything he had to sell, including his slaves. He broke up families and sold them like goats or sheep—two here and a half dozen there. It pained him horribly to part with the African beauty; she had been a supple if unwilling bed partner. A beating applied to her husband now and then had reminded her of her duty.

Socrates, only four at the time, had watched as his parents were dragged off in a cart to a neighboring plantation. The Abbot of the mission of San Sebastian had purchased his sisters' freedom but had run out of money, and so the handsome little brown boy had stood with tears in his eyes and waved good-bye even as the gavel came down on his own pitiful sale.

Ian McFadden had been in port on a horse, buying expedition when he had heard of the auction. McFadden owned two sugar cane plantations in the Leeward Islands and was always in need of slaves for the brutal field labor. The little boy would work at the side of one of the older wenches until he knew the job and, after a few years, had the strength to pull his own weight in stone. If the lad survived childhood and adolescence, then he might be paired off with one of the younger field wenches and allowed to breed other little brown slave babies. If he showed a stubborn or violent streak, he would be sold off if at all possible. If not, well then, Ian McFadden would shoot him himself. Bad bucks were like wolves among sheep—let them live and bloody ruin would come of it.

The boy was named by the master for his deep thoughtful eyes. On the plantation, he would never be allowed to learn to read or, for that matter, to go near a book so that he could revel in his namesake.

At fourteen, Socrates had been caught by the overseer lying with a girl near his own age. This would have gotten him a stern yelling at and perhaps a stripe or two across his back if the girl hadn't been the overseer's own lily-white daughter. The man set on the boy with a thick walking stick, screaming at his fleeing daughter with spittle flying from his curled lip. He would have broken the lad's back and left him to lie in the field collecting flies if Socrates hadn't fought back. As the cane came down for the third time, the boy ducked and grabbed up a rock of a size a little bigger than his fist and slammed it into the man's temple. The overseer stopped dead in his tracks and then slowly sank to his knees, falling face forward with a trickle of blood running out of his ear.

Socrates knew he had committed red-handed murder, and he felt free for the first time in his young and until now innocent life. The girl had fled for home at first sight of her enraged father, so she wouldn't give the alarm until he was found dead, which likely wouldn't occur for some hours. Socrates took the man's boots and waistcoat—which seemed a good fit—along with the straw hat; he cut the figure of a black artisan. He picked up the offending stick and began the walk into town where he would try to blend in for a few hours until he could find a ship that would take him aboard. Failing that, he would rejoice in a few hours of freedom and then find a good place to go and hang himself.

He had heard tales of other escaped slaves doing the same thing when they knew the net was closing around them and that their end would be deliberately and especially painful. Escaped slaves were beaten within an inch of their lives and often set upon by dogs used for boar hunting. Horrible wounds and maiming were considered the normal results of evenhanded discipline. Slaves who killed or defied authority violently were made example of for all to see, and often, their naked tortures were witnessed by the simple expedient of dragging the victim in a wagon from plantation to plantation for all the slaves to see.

Socrates had no intention of being whipped unto death and then hoisted like a trophy of the hunt for all to see. Being left as an example at the docks or crossroads was the worst way to meet your end, thought the boy.

He stopped at a creek and dipped his neckerchief in a small mountain stream that tumbled down from the hills and meandered across the fields. A palm tree standing near the road offered shade, and a respite from the sun for a few minutes was what he needed before he continued his fateful journey.

Socrates stared out across the fresh cut cane from his seat beneath the tree and gazed upon the turquoise of the sea, imagining all the lands beyond his island. The lad could barely remember the trip with Ian McFadden, but a vague recollection was just enough to fuel his youthful imagination.

The memory faded and turned to darkness with torches burning around the manor and Master Ian standing on the steps before the assembled hands. "If any of you think to insight servile insurrection on this island, look upon Mr. Millard's buck who thought to strike his own master." A canvass covering the back of a cart had been pulled away, and there was the flayed carcass of a man tied to crosstrees. "This, my dark and ignorant children, is what will happen to any who takes up a weapon or raises their hand against a white."

McFadden had stomped back into the house, and the slaves had silently drifted back to their huts, each quietly alone with his or her own fearful and angry thoughts.

Socrates had thought the notion of striking at a white the most foolish thing he had ever heard of until today. Never again would any man, white or black, lay a hand or a cane on him.

Socrates McFadden had found a place on the crew of the *Dread Angel* that very day, and no one cared the color of his skin. The mere fact that he was strong and able were enough. He proved himself fearless in combat and once juggled the heads of three Frenchies like grotesque melons to the raucous applause of his shipmates. On another occasion, cornered on the deck of a feisty Dutch merchantman, he had held three Hollanders at bay with his gully knife and a belaying pin. In the end, the fight finished with two of the Dutchers with their throats slit and the third paddling frantically away from the gathering school of sand sharks.

As an intrepid gun commander, McFadden had proved himself both accurate and indefatigable. His gun had taken a direct hit in a duel with an offended French vessel, and Socrates, by himself, had righted the iron long nine using the rammer as a fulcrum and jamming a load of case shot under the carriage to level it. The blood-spattered berserker reloaded it alone, shredding the opposite ship's main'sl with a load of chain shot. Minutes later, Captain Russell took a boarding party over and conquered the stalled ship as she fought to get under way and clear her decks of torn canvas and rope.

※

Crispin stood on the deck, ignored by the busy crew. Those sailors who didn't have a watch or duties were asleep below decks until their turn came. Captain DeVaca was engaged in conversation with a used-up old salt whose bleary eyes were covered with cataracts and who seemed nearer to his end than his beginning.

DeVaca finished his dialogue and came at Crispin like a man who meant business.

"Well, fish, what's your story?" queried Red Mike.

"Captain DeVaca, I am Lt. St. Crispin Mull of His Majesty's Fifty-Sixth of Foot, bound for New York to fight the French. As I mentioned, I was wrecked when a waterspout sank our transport. I can assure you that the army will reward you for my safe return," said Crispin calmly and very politely, not forgetting the recent object lesson in manners applied by Red Mike's absurdly quick cutlass.

"Well, Lieutenant, it seems you are valuable enough to keep aboard, but do not expect to be returned quickly. We are two hundred miles from the nearest English port and headed in the wrong direction. My plans will take us away from Charlestown, and I have no notion to sail up the James River and present myself to the Governor of Virginia so that he may hang me from the gibbet for exceeding my letters. Governors, Mr. Mull, are a mercurial lot. When they've need of ships of war, they gladly welcome men like me as privateers, and when they have shaken hands and supped with their enemy, they say cease and desist, Master Privateer, and go back to making shoes or catching fish," lectured Red Mike.

"I understand perfectly, Captain, but surely, there is some other way to contact the authorities," suggested Crisp.

"If I were so inclined, then that would be a perfect plan, Mr. Mull. I am not so inclined. This is a ship of war. We prefer to earn our keep more honestly than by kidnapping. We will be intercepting a merchantman any day now, and my men prefer a certain amount of bloodthirsty commotion and canon smoke. It is good for the bowels. Surely, as a soldier, you understand this. We are not peaceable men, Mr. Mull. My lads will transport you to a suitable port and accept emolument when they have satisfied their more warlike habits. Si?" All this was said with a colonial

English accent, with the notable exception of the final word, which was spoken with a practiced Spanish accent.

"In the meantime, Captain, what am I to do?" asked Crispin.

"In the meantime, Mr. Mull, you may enjoy the pleasure of our company. You may do as you are told, and you may enjoy seeing men of action in action," tossed back Red Mike.

And so the next several days passed. Crispin slept with the crew below. He ate nothing more elaborate than their daily fare of salt beef, peas, and hardtack. During the day, he stayed out of the way. Red Mike had given him paper and quill and allowed him to draft the letter that would be required if and when they decided to contact a neutral vessel.

Finished with that, Crisp closely observed for the first time the multitude of actions it took to maneuver a ship. The hands would all stand idle, waiting for the ship to tack or for Mr. McFadden or the captain to give an order, and then all hands would heave to the lines and sheets. Other sailors would be busy below deck, splicing lines and mending sails with needle and thread. Crispin was astonished at the amount of industry these cutthroats showed. He had imagined that privateersmen were a lazy lot who only worked when absolutely necessary and who spent their days in drunkenness and riot. The *Matador* was a tighter ship than the transport he had been on.

Crispin knew that his only chance at escape lay when the ship put in to dock or moored near shore. He simply didn't have enough knowledge of small boats to be sure of himself were he to succeed in stealing the ship's boat which trailed behind on a painter. If he made it ashore, he had only to report himself to the authorities or put enough distance between himself and the privateers in order to convince them that pursuit was not in their best interests.

It was on the fifth day aboard the *Matador* that things heated up. A sail was sighted, hull down early in the morning off the starboard stern quarter, beating its way south. Crisp watched as the dot on the horizon grew larger, and Captain DeVaca gave orders to come about. The captain of the other vessel was attentive and saw the *Matador* reverse its course, so he became suspicious. As the *Matador* began to close the many miles between ships, the captain of the prey piled on all sail just to see what the *Matador*'s intentions were. Captain DeVaca backed sail and let the other ship regain a little room in order to assure them his ships intentions were not hostile.

"It does little good to show your hand too early," Captain DeVaca told Crispin. DeVaca had called Crispin to his side, obviously enjoying the opportunity of having an audience. When the other ship seemed less wary, Red Mike would slowly slip closer and try approaching within hailing distance, he explained. Then he would haul down the British ensign, and up would go his personal banner with the hellish skeleton of Red Mike DeVaca. Privateers wear on their backstay whatever colors suit their need and the line between lawful and outlaw is often a matter of zeal and avarice. If the other vessel showed guns or guts, then he would promptly order a broadside from the *Matador* be thrust into the flanks and belly of the prey. If the other ship were wise and surrendered, then Red Mike would lead a boarding party over to take the helm and subdue the crew and assist in lashing the ships together until the transfer of any booty was completed.

The final disposition of a ship depended entirely upon who the capturing captain was and who and what were aboard the prey. If the prey was large and the privateer ship small, it was more likely to burn simply because the conquerors could not afford to crew both vessels. If the ship were of good lines and in fine repair, the captors could either take it for themselves or sell it. In these declining days of freebooting, when the Royal Navy reigned supreme a quick escape and few survivors to tattle was more the method. Red Mike had no intention of trading the *Matador*, so the fate of the ship depended entirely upon the actions of her crew over the next several hours or so.

Six hours had passed, and DeVaca was close enough that he could read the writing on the stern through his glass. *Silas Canterbury*, it said. She was a small brigantine with fully eight good feet more of deck and three more feet of beam than the *Matador*, but she showed no gun ports, and he could see only three guns to a side located on the weather and poop decks. *Matador* had five guns ranging down each side of her flush deck plus two in the stern and one in the bow. Altogether, one broadside launched forty-five pounds of screaming, smashing iron when one took into account the three wee one-pound swivels. Equally as important, the sailors of the fiery *Matador* could deliver a broadside every two minutes and a half. While she was no threat to a man of war or even a well-skippered brig in open battle, there were few others of equal size who would dare to stand against the *Matador*. The men on deck would throw grappling hooks and try to pin down the prey's crew with musket fire while they pulled her in like some giant harpooned sea monster.

As the *Silas Canterbury* came within hailing range, Red Mike called out to her that he wished to bespeak the captain. An older gentleman came to the poop deck of the prey. He called out and inquired of Red Mike which vessel was he and from what town. The distance narrowed. Mike called out that he was from Old Bristol in England, and that he was the Merry Elizabeth. The other captain turned away and began speaking to a crewmember. Several men from the cautious *Canterbury* disappeared into the cabin. Mike put down his glass and ordered the British colors lowered and the red skeleton hoisted. It seemed to matter not in the least that the *Canterbury* was most certainly a British colonial vessel and in no way French or even Canadian.

"Prepare to fire!" he yelled. "Boarding party, prepare your hooks. See to your firelocks! Buena guerra!"

The *Silas Canterbury* had already realized her terrible peril and put the helm over hard in order to turn away from the broadside. Several men scampered up the rigging and began firing muskets down at the *Matador*'s decks, but the range at seventy-five yards was still too great for accurate musketry. The *Matador*'s gun muzzles thrust out of the gun ports like the many heads of Cerberus, the hound that guards the gates of Hades. With four men to a gun and fifteen in the boarding party, that would leave only seven to man the yards, the helm, and the swivels.

Once they had grappled and lashed the prey vessel, the gun crews would leap on her deck and join the boarding party while Socrates McFadden would take command of the *Matador* in Red Mike's absence. Muskets and swivels would support the boarders from the deck of the Devaca's ship if called upon.

The *Silas Canterbury* answered her helm and heeled to larboard as she tried to shy away from the broadside like a startled doe. Red Mike bellowed for all hands to hear. "Fire! Bring us along her larboard side, Mr. Dodens. Boarding party, prepare to cast your hooks."

As the *Canterbury* heeled, she was hit with a slightly raking broadside. Two of the shot landed at her waterline, which became exposed as she leaned into the turn like a fleet and trim racehorse. Three of the balls burst along the hull just a foot over her waterline and punched on into the holds, wreaking havoc as splinters flew everywhere like savage arrows. The distance between the two vessels was a mere fifty yards.

The quick thinking of the captain of the *Canterbury* had forced Red Mike to act sooner than he pleased, and he kept the *Matador* from getting the other vessels weather gage. By the time the two ships had completed their course changes, the *Matador* lay almost directly astern the prey and could only bring her swivels and bow chaser to bear. Mr. Dodens had not been dexterous enough to echo the *Canterbury*'s helm. The swivel was quickly moved to the forward starboard rail where it could fire at a sharp angle, enfilading the *Canterbury*'s helm by firing obliquely across the *Matador*'s own bowsprit.

The bow chaser barked loud and deep, rolling back on its wooden trucks. The bar shot screeched through the fantail lights of the *Canterbury*. Continuing along its path of destruction, the shot smashed through the stern cabin and slammed squarely into the leg of a deck hand, leaving a bloody gore where once his limb had been and gouged a red trough out of the deck, before it tumbled over the rail and plummeted into the sea. The swivel coughed sharply and a load of scrap metal flew like oversized swanshot into the helm. The steersman crumpled at the base of the wheel, struggling to get his blood-pocked legs back under himself, finally collapsing in a tangled knot of his own entrails.

A handful of sea jackals had climbed into the yards and began firing down on the deck of the *Canterbury*. While their fire was inaccurate, combined with the cannon fire, it drove the crew of the *Canterbury* below decks and kept them from the sails and sheets. The ship continued on its course, and with no one at the helm, it was only a matter of time before the wolvish privateersmen brought her down.

The brave captain of the *Canterbury* took up a musket and pistol and fired at the cutthroats in the tops, hoping to lead by example, but it was in vain. The privateersmen all directed their fire at him, and one lucky ball found its mark, striking the courageous captain in the upper thigh, making him fall.

HONOR AMONGST THIEVES

P. Peter Lane had been walking through forest and swamp infested with mosquitos and snakes for two days. His pocksy face was now covered with bites, the backs of his hands were scratched from thorns, and if not for his knee high canvas gaiters, his worsted stockings would have been hanging in tatters.

What little feverish water he had found had not been sufficient to slake his thirst, and he had eaten nothing. *Surely some of the plants are edible*, thought Lane, but he had no idea which ones, and he thought for sure that he would die of starvation. The stagnant water had come alive once with the writhing of a tangle of water moccasin vipers, but Lane could not bring himself close enough to strike one with a stick nor to impale one on his bayonet, which was a good thing as P. Peter Lane's sole experience with snakes had been watching a tightly caged king cobra eating wharf rats down Thames side. It never occurred to the sergeant that if he fitted his bayonet to a long pole he would have a weapon for defense and hunting.

Lane was alone in the wilderness and began to have thoughts about his own immortal soul and its state of readiness for eternity. The account, P. Peter Lane knew, was a bit overdrawn, and he feared that unless he squared things with the Almighty, he might just become the devil's footman.

Using the sun for his guide as much as possible, Lane continued to stumble west and then north, but at each swampy pothole, he was forced to skirt the edge of the water, leaving him confused and often off his mark as to direction. When the branches closed in such that he could not frequently access the sun's location, he became despondent and walked without a care for direction and, in this way, slowly wandered beneath the trackless canopy. As darkness came on, Lane became sure that the LORD was giving him a taste of his eternal damnation.

He gathered wood and kindling and slowly struck flint and steel, catching the spark in his char cloth and blowing it to a glow until it ignited the bird's nest, twigs, and larger tinder. He was near the end of his tether, and lying next to the flames hardly sufficed to keep off the growing chill of hunger and exhaustion.

What Lane didn't know was that he was near salvation and companionship and that he had only to survive until morning to enjoy the fruits of civilized conversation. Near midnight, his heart began to slow and shivers ran the length of his boney frame as the flames died and the embers winked out one by one.

☆

Crispin stepped aboard the *Silas Canterbury* and gawked, unsure what to do or how to behave. The crew busied themselves with securing the two ships and with rooting about in every hold, cabin, locker, and nook and cranny. Sea chests, baggage, and bedrolls were piled at the foot of the main mast while Socrates McFadden led a detail of privateersmen in taking inventory of the holds.

The crew seemed quietly jubilant, and Red Mike DeVaca stood feet apart and chin thrust up, surveying his handiwork and seeing to it that no fighting or mischief broke out between his men. His arrogant smirk and cocksure pose left one reminded of Drake and the defeat of the Spanish Armada or of a Carthaginian captain who had just rammed and sunk a Roman Trireme.

The crew of the *Silas Canterbury* had emerged with their rope callused but unblooodied hands above their heads and stood near the bow with three bristling guards watching over them with loaded firelocks and gleaming gully knives. Crisp felt sorry for them but was impressed with the orderly, military management that Red Mike exercised over his band of rogues and cutthroats.

As he advanced toward the stern, Crispin came upon the moaning form of the fallen captain. He had tied his neck scarf about his leg and slipped the rammer from his pistol into the knot, twisting until the tourniquet stanched the flow of blood.

"Is there anything I can get for ye, sir? A drink of water perhaps? I'm afraid they have no surgeon aboard," said Crispin.

"Thank you, young man. I'm too damned weak to stand and help meself. I would care for a drop of rum, if ye have any about ye. I take it yer no one of these brothers of the coast?" asked the captain quietly, gesturing towards the privateers.

"No, sir, I am but a guest like yerself." Crisp excused himself and went looking about for some rum to give to the poor wounded mariner.

He knew things were not about to get better for the crew of the *Silas Canterbury*. Crisp found a partly empty jug of spirit lying amongst the loot at the mast, and no one seemed to mind his helping himself to so trivial an item. He showed it to the lad guarding the pile just to be sure, and after the youth had drained off a noggin or two for himself, he let Crispin go on.

The rum reminded Crispin of Lane, and he half prayed that the sergeant had been killed in the wreck. If Lane had passed away, then that would leave only Crispin knowing all the truth about the circumstances of his promotion.

Rum had been a prominent part of many major events in his life, and Crisp noted how nearly every important event involved the imbibing of spirituous drink. His father had once said that spirits were the jugulum of every business transaction. Ezra Mull used large words and tried to sound as important as the nitwits, ne'er-do-wells, and pompous fools that were his clients. He nearly succeeded. Mull, the senior, had also enjoyed a dram every night at the Cock and Bull, a local inn, and it was there that Crispin too learned to drink. It was also where his father often heard tell of strange cargoes, neighbors recently consigned to eternity, and five-legged kid goats—all of which were highly marketable in the right circles. Crispin's father was well connected to those circles. One of his clients had once required the head of a felon for experimentation on the nature of the criminal mind and how one could identify criminal behavior in the face. Ezra Mull had thought of asking the eminent scientist why he didn't go to the jail and look at the faces of felons, but thought better of it and instead had a body stolen from the gibbet, which was then decapitated in a butcher's shop for a shilling or two. The remaining parts were pickled in brine and stored against later requests. Surely, some wealthy buffoon would require an abdomen for dissection and examination of the stomach juices.

The captain of the *Canterbury* had pushed himself to a sitting position, and Crispin suspected his future was no brighter than the stolen corpse of a felon. Mull left him with the jug before beginning his own exploration of the ship. No one, it seemed, cared if he showed himself about, and all the crew were busying themselves with booty and nautical tasks.

The crew had ransacked every locker and sea chest, and Crisp found that nothing of consequence had been overlooked. As he poked his head into the main hold, he saw lanterns bobbing about in the darkness, which would undoubtedly be Socrates and mates. The hold seemed to be filled with tools, furniture, and crates of pewter and china dishes—all things that had to be imported in the sugar islands. The ship's carpenter from the *Canterbury* could be heard banging away stopping the influx of water where the ship had been holed by the *Matador's* guns.

When the crew of the *Matador* had completed the transfer of booty and had stripped the ship of everything useful, needful, or of momentary fascination, they would set her ablaze since she was unlawful fare. Like all sailors, they celebrated with drink, music, and revelry. Red Mike would allow them to bask in the glow of victory, which, in this case, came from the flames of a burning brig until they were nearly incapacitated, and he would then fire a shot or two in order to get their attention. Once they had ceased their bacchanalia, he would order the watch posted and all hands to sleep in order to sober up.

Captains have found themselves astride a barrel in deep waters without a friend in sight for this kind of autocratic behavior, but Red Mike had the respect and devotion of his men as long as he kept the spoilation coming.

The crew of the *Canterbury* were given the chance to sign aboard for shares or to choose a darker, more deadly path. One young lad alone chose to sign with Red Mike while the others would stalwartly stand by their fallen captain.

Red Mike ordered the ship's boat from the *Canterbury* put over the side, and the men of the doomed hulk were put off into the water. Only six at a time could fit in the ship's boat, which left more than half paddling about in the water. Socrates threw a small cask of fresh water and a sack full of ship's biscuit into the boat and then thoughtfully added a length of rope and a compass. In this way, the men in the water could cling to the boat by means of the rope, and the wounded captain could navigate.

It was doubtful whether all the men would make it to shore, which lay approximately thirty miles to the west, but still, their odds were better than some watery outlaws would have preferred. Out and out pirates like Teach, Morgan, or Captain Bartholomew Roberts would have put them in the water without a boat or provisions and consigned them to Poseidon's keeping. Red Mike DeVaca would kill for money or in self-defense but had not yet a heart black enough to kill out of sport or hurry. He still told himself he was a privateersman, a convenient half-truth.

Crispin looked at the valiant captain and silently said a prayer for the man as the boat pulled away from the *Matador*. Courage and spleen had seemed lacking in no few of the officers of the Fifty-Sixth, but here was a staunch man who, through moral and financial obligation, had played his best card to preserve his crew, his vessel, its cargo, and his honor, and would likely lose at least his leg if not his life.

Captain Miguel Antonio DeVaca had left nothing of value behind. The *Silas Canterbury* was stripped to the last rope, block, and pail of oakum. The ship's stores along with the cargo would be sold off in St. Augustine. The Spaniards were always hungry for trade and asked no questions of the captain and crew of the *Matador*. The governor knew that Red Mike was more a pirate than a privateersman, but as long as his bloody depredations were against the English and French, who was he to complain? The goods could be bought for half price, and the English were punished for their protestant arrogance if even only in the slightest way. So it was that Crispin found himself even farther from his destination than when he first was cast down into the sea.

Sergeant P. Peter Lane lay shivering and moaning in the dark and did not hear the quiet snap of a bayberry twig and the nearly imperceptible rustle of last year's leaves. The few remaining sparks had winked out at one o'clock in the cold morning as a solitary figure lurked about in the shadows, trying to identify Lane's supine form near the barely smoldering ashes.

Bill Spooner had been attracted to the fire but had been suspicious and cautious enough to approach slowly, moving from tree to tree. Spooner already had seen two Indians as he had watched a junction of footpaths. The savages had seemed harmless enough, but their polished bows and pointy arrows had been enough to convince Spooner to remain well out of sight in the palmetto groves.

The second night in the woods, Bill had thought he had smelt wood smoke and followed his burnt and peeling nose, but it was a few hundred yards through the scratchy tangled undergrowth until he had come upon the fire near the edge of a swampy pool. Lying near the smothered flames had been the form of a man. In the near pitch-black of the cypress grove, it had been difficult to tell who the sleeper was.

Corporal Spooner crept closer, coming at the recumbent body from the back so that he would have a moment's advantage should the man awaken. When he got within a few feet, he could see the contrast between cuff facings and coat, and he knew it was one of his comrades. Reaching out with the toe of his shoe, he nudged the man, not wanting to be too close when he awoke. The soldier barely moved but groaned quietly and shrugged his shoulder away from Spooner as though to say, "Be off with ye." Even in the dark, Spooner could see the other man was near the end of his rope.

William Archimedes Spooner was not a man given to thinking a great deal, but here was a poser. Should he take a man who was clearly sick under his wing, or should he guarantee his own safety by leaving the poor sod? The man was from his regiment and deserved a certain amount of loyalty for that alone, yet a dying man would only slow him down. *What would Lane do?* thought Spooner. Lane had always done the deep thinking for Spooner and Lear. He certainly wouldn't have hampered his own survival by carrying a useless man. That solved it. He would sneak back off into the forest, leaving this poor cat's paw, whoever he may be, to his own end.

Spooner stooped over the sleeper once more time and decided to remove the triangular bayonet. His fingers noticed something hard and flat beneath the waistcoat and wrapped around the waistband of the breeches. The corporal slipped his hand under the weskit and grasped the money belt. Lane moaned fearfully again, and Spooner paused in his groping for the buckle. A second later with a quick flip, he snugged the buckle up and then backed it off so that it would slip free. LORD but it was full! There must be at least fifty guineas in it (There were fifty-six plus small coin to be precise.) He threw the money belt over his left shoulder and tucked the bayonet into his belt. He could always use another weapon besides his folding knife and his own bayonet. Corporal Spooner slowly and carefully crept back into the trees another several hundred yards before he sat down to rest and await sunrise.

※

Rather than die, which would have been the easy thing to do, P. Peter Lane groaned and peeked out from behind his bite swollen eyelids seeing the misty gray dawn of the Carolina fens.

It took more than a few minutes for him to become cognizant of his surroundings and to be able to force himself to a sitting position. The fire was out, and a bull alligator roared somewhere in the deep recess of the mossy swamp, but even that fearsome noise elicited little response from the semiconscious, formerly whoremongering sergeant. Even had he been fully conscious, it is doubtful he would have known the source of the sound as the closest Lane had ever been to an alligator was a stuffed caiman that sat in the shadows of a tavern owned by an ex-jockey from Ipswich.

Lane sat back on his hands with his legs stretched out in front of him and his chin sagged to his chest. It was in this orientation that he discovered the fact that someone had stolen his money belt. It took several seconds for the truth to settle into his muddled brain, but finally, his wits quickened, and he leapt to his feet with an indignant yelp. Lane's eyes darted around the pathetic campsite. He was hoping that the belt had fallen off during his search for firewood. Alas, it was nowhere to be seen. Perhaps he had lost it somewhere else in the soggy forest. But no, he remembered checking it the last time he had made piss just after he lit the fire the night before. Blast and damn, someone had taken his bayonet! That cinched it. Whoever had taken the money belt had also taken the bayonet, and now he was without means of defense or money to buy his way to safety, presuming, of course, that he could find someone who could be bought. Lane was unsure whether Indians used money or not.

⁕

Bill Spooner had decided that his best hope lie in moving north as much as possible. He recalled speaking to one of the sailors who came from Pennsylvania, and the tar had mentioned the colony was north of their present position just off Cape Fear. The man had talked so highly of the land and city "Phillydophia" that Spooner thought it must be a good place to go. Bill Spooner knew that if he kept the sun to his right and rear and left, in that order, he must surely reach it, eventually. As the sun had risen, Private Spooner had struck out to find civilization and succor.

Sergeant Lane, on the other hand, was now furious and more determined than ever that he should live and return to England to live off his ill-gotten wealth, but first, he must find the man who had robbed him and make him pay. Lane had no clue where he was or how he would find this man or how he would get home to London. He needed a plan, but first, he needed food and water. Finding some berries near at hand and some less than poisonous water, Lane sat down to ponder upon a plan.

Unfortunately for P. Peter Lane, the berries were more poisonous than the water and the handful that he had eaten would have felled an ox, which would have known enough not to have eaten them. At first, he thought only that his stomach was upset with the fare because it was the first thing he had eaten in several days. The vomiting, however, was unremitting, and suddenly, he became dizzy and disoriented. Lane realized, as his belly began to cramp painfully, that he had survived the night and the rigors of the swamp only to be felled by a handful of berries. P. Peter Lane knew that his life was about to end. What rankled most was that he would never get even for the theft of his guineas. Doubled over on his knees with his forehead touching the ground, Sergeant P. Peter Lane of the Fifty-Sixth of Foot choked quietly, and then a long shudder ran down his spine, and his greedy heart ceased to beat. It had all happened quickly, and even Lane had been surprised by the rapidity of it.

His corpse would stay in the same position for several days until the bloating gases caused the carcass to tip over on its side. A family of opossums would be the first to sup on P. Peter Lane, followed by a gray fox, and finally several days after the body cavity was exposed, the maggots would start to devour the souring meat. In the end P. Peter Lane's grave would be five acres of swampy forest through which the animals dragged his parts. The buttons and buckles of his uniform were found two years later by a savage boy on a hunting expedition with his father. The gnawed and jawless skull, dropped by a scavenger, would tumble into the black water of the swamp. Slowly sinking into the silt, there it would become the primary resting place for the remains of a sergeant of the Fifty-Sixth of Foot.

✣

Miguel Antonio DeVaca had sold off the cargo of the *Silas Canterbury* and distributed the spoliative shares and again was cruising the coast of the Carolinas and Virginia, making his way toward Canada and the popish sailors of New France.

Crisp slowly became accustomed to life aboard the *Matador*. When the larcenous crew found their next victim two weeks after they left St. Augustine, Crisp was becoming restless. He had amused himself in the Spanish town as much as was possible with no coin and with a sailor always at his side. Red Mike had permitted Crisp to go ashore on his oath that he would not try to escape. The crew had felt sorry for him in his penury and so they had bought him strong drink at the tavern.

Nearly five tedious weeks had passed since Crispin's transport had been sunk, and he was beginning to become nervous out of boredom and lack of activity. For the past several days, he had been employed in mending sails as instructed by Mr. Dodens who often took the helm.

Dodens, a squat, grizzled Dutchman by birth, had been at sea for most of his sixty years. Pirating had claimed his soul in the year of Our Grace 1711, and he hadn't sailed an honest day since. Cataracts were clouding his once blue eyes, but his instincts and touch on the wheel were so magnificently skillful that sight was nearly a hindrance. When he wasn't at the wheel, Humphrey Dodens took it upon himself to teach Crisp the ins and outs of seamanship as it were, and so the lieutenant's nautical education began.

Crispin had little interest in the handling of sheets and halyards, but the activity made the hours pass more quickly. Splicing line with the whalebone marlinspike kept the hands busy while Daddy Dodens told tales of the sea—some believable and some no more than bold tarradiddle.

Hump talked of watching as a pirate comrade gambled his own hand away. Two of the loser's mates had jumped upon him, pinioning him to the ground, and then chopped off the tattooed wager in two shakes of a lamb's tail. While the screaming, amputee ran about with blood spewing from his stump, and the other two had shaken hands with the severed fist and played with it as a gory backscratcher. Of course, the foolish blackguard had died of a fever several days later, yet his hand lived on in pirate customs. Whosoever owned the hand could play it against a final roll for whatever amount was required to cover any bet. As the years mounted, the hand withered and became a talon-like brown relic traveling from one port to another, changing ownership every few months at the most. As the legend spread, both honest seamen and buccaneers together would add to the mythical stories of the "Dull Gunner's Claw." Perhaps the last time this curious and grotesque relic was mentioned in recent times is when it was listed in the estate of the late destitute Captain John Paul Jones. It is unlikely that Humphrey Dodens ever witnessed the severing as the first mention of a "Dead Man's Hand," "Gunner's Claw," or "Powder Monkey's Paw" as a lucky talisman is in the journal of Machias Corbett. The journal entitled *A Missionary to Madagascar* was published in 1695, nine months after the kind Christian Prelate was hung by Henry Avery, captain of the pirate ship *Fancy*. Reverend Corbett retreated to heaven after failing to save their unrepentant hearts. Preaching the gospel to pirate ears is a dreadful dangersome task. According to tradition set down by Corbett, the hand can be recognized by the tattoo of a setting sun encircled by seven evening stars, setting it apart from sundry pretend monkeys' paws and fraudulent specimens claiming the title of the "Dull Gunner's Claw."

In the weeks to come, two other prizes fell to the *Matador*. By the by, a third ship was boarded, and Crisp had now become entrusted enough that he was given a much abused, dulled cutlass, and posted as one of the guards over the handful of prisoners gathered as usual in the bow.

She was a Holland brig, fair and well founded, with new standing and running rigging and a load of cheap goods for the fur trade. Old England controlled the vast and lucrative shipping in and out of her colonies, but the prices were not always the best for those forced to purchase English hard goods. No few daring men smuggled in goods from other parts, most usually in a vessel falsely flying British colors. It was not uncommon for a bold captain from another nation to undertake a voyage to New England's coast to deliver barrels of beads, countless hand mirrors, colorful shirts, bolts of bright fabric, war hatchets, and of course, fancy goods for the civilized market.

Red Mike had spotted the brig rounding Boon Island on a larboard tack, making for Cape Neddick just before sunset. The Matador caught the vessel when it was still miles out, and as they crossed her bow, each of the iron guns marked its place on the Dutch ship. The name on her stern had been hastily painted over, and she flew the British Jack of Union, but DeVaca knew that no vessel would venture so close to shore at day's end on a calm sea unless she were smuggling. Clearly the *Guilderhoose*—he would learn her name later—was making a rendezvous bent on avoiding giving the king his due.

Red Mike had hoisted his French pennant and his intentions were clear as he bore down on the interloper. Crisp stood at Hump Doden's shoulder with quiet excitement, wanting for the first time to leap across the rapidly closing gap between the two ships. After crossing the other ship's bow, the *Matador* had raced ahead trying to put the helm a lee and luff up so that they might come about and bring themselves alongside for another go at her, if necessary. The smuggler let fly his mainsheets, and Crisp could see that her bowsprit was a knot of broken wood and snarled rigging where several shots had struck home. The captain of the prey had no intention of fighting it out and brought his ship to as the *Matador* came alongside. Each of her guns trained on the *Guilderhoose*'s deck.

Mike demanded the captain and his crew to come aboard while the half-drunken, raucous crew jeered at the Dutchmen wildly shaking their muskets and gleaming knives. Half the battle for DeVaca's crew was in scaring the fight right out of their less bloodthirsty opponents. The men of the smuggler rowed over to the *Matador* post haste.

DeVaca had moved into the northern waters off the Massachusetts Bay Colony after two captures in Virginia's waves. He knew the Royal Navy would not take kindly to his poaching, so he had wisely relocated, hoping to direct his attention at French shipping, thereby hopefully gaining some goodwill with the English while he filled his own purse at French expense. The *Guilderhoose* was in British colonial waters and had merely been too ripe not to pluck. The Dutchmen were a little more welcome by the authorities than the *Matador* and were only slightly less likely to be hunted.

Half of the crew, including Crisp, had gone aboard the *Guilderhoose* when the dogs of war sounded the cry. The French raider *La Revanche* of ninety men and sixteen guns was bearing down on the two tightly lashed ships with a bone in her teeth. She had been cruising off the Jeffrey's Bank, taking Yankee fishing boats and hoping to net some fat English merchantman headed for Boston. Captain DeVaca did not see her name but knew by her lines and colors that she meant fire and destruction.

Closing his telescope, he issued a stream of orders; the vessel was still miles off, but Red Mike also knew he had only minutes to loot the *Guilderhoose* and cut her free if he were to make good his escape. Crispin and another fellow by the name of Mungo Ulmen jumped into the hold with two rogues who had been taking inventory and began throwing bales of cloth and small kegs of beads up through the hatch. Within seconds, the crew had formed a line and was rapidly passing the stowage over onto the *Matador*. Two sailors stood by with well-sharpened hatchets ready to cut the ship free while a handful prepared the *Matador* to get underway.

It was during the ensuing confusion that a frightened half-wit amongst the *Guilderhoose*'s crew wrested a pistol away from one of the *Matador*'s and made a pell-mell dash for Red Mike. Crisp had just returned topside to begin helping to secure the Dutch cargo now aboard the *Matador*. If the French vessel decided to give chase, the *Matador* could little afford to have her holds in disarray. Crispin looked forward towards the commotion in the bow of the smuggler and saw the pistol wielding Dutchman pounding across the deck towards Red Mike. The other Dutchmen were hollering, trying to call their mate back, and none of the half-besotted sailors was quick enough to stop the lad.

Crisp pulled his cutlass and leaped into the path of the wild-eyed madman, thrusting his blade in front himself. The Hollander was unable to check his momentum and impaled himself on the rusty length of steel, pulling the pistol's trigger in reflex as he slid up the length of the sword. The shot went wide and clipped the ballocks off a ram that had been brought up from below and left wandering about the deck bleating. Crispin and the dying sailor crashed to the planks in a bloody tangle of arms and legs. Crisp struggled manfully to get out from under the limp dead weight as the hilt of his own sword was pressing hard into his almost cracking ribs.

DeVaca and another of his crew helped pull the twitching body off Crisp and helped him get to his feet again. Crispin turned just as a sailor put his long-barreled German horse pistol to the head of the sheep and pulled the trigger. The ram was driven to the deck and tufts of smoldering wool gave off a faintly acrid smell.

"Fresh mutton for you tonight, Mr. Mull!" exclaimed DeVaca. "But first, let's show this Frenchmen our heels. Mr. McFadden, fire the Dutchman and throw her crew in the drink. We'll see if that slows the bastard frog. Load the stern chasers, and put some lads in my cabin with muskets to show him a hot time if he starts to close." He turned to Crispin again. "Gracias, Lieutenant. I'm afraid I would have been headed for the Davy's with a round shot tied to my feet if you hadn't stopped him. Afraid I was looking the wrong way. Let's finish the transfer and get under way lads!"

Crisp was busy wiping the blood off his blade on the shirt of the dead man when a series of splashes signaled that the Dutchmen were starting to tread water. Red Mike ordered a few planks from the ship's stores thrown overboard as floats for the crew of the *Guilderhoose* to share. The carpenters' axes fell with a near simultaneous thunk of iron biting into oak and the two ships began to drift apart just as the first flames started to lick above the hatchways.

The Frenchman was still several miles off but was closing with remarkable rapidity. It was an old axiom of DeVaca's that the other fellow always had a swifter vessel no matter what, and therefore, one never wasted sea room or time in giving the enemy his distance.

The *Matador* began to put sea room between herself and the La Revanche, which became even greater as the French warship slowed to examine the fiercely burning *Guilderhoose* and the stranded Dutchmen.

DeVaca had been crafty as well and had raised his false French colors on the burning brig to decoy the French captain into thinking it a ship of his own nation. Every ship carried sets of false colors in order to bewilder privateersmen and enemy warships. The Dutch brig had worn the colors of two nations this day, and neither was of her home port of Kampen.

The *La Revanche* checked her pace, but as they came alongside the swimmers, they tossed a line overboard and hauled two wet Dutchers on deck. In a matter of a few moments, the captain had ascertained that the vessel was not French and took up the chase again. The ruse had slowed the French only momentarily and had bought the *Matador* another fraction of a mile. With only five miles between them, it would be a derby finish.

As dark settled in, it was so clear and bright that Red Mike had nowhere to hide. It came to his mind that if he lowered his ensign and raised the British colors, he might enlist the help of the Royal Navy. With every inch of sail she carried taut and full, the *Matador* plowed her way south through the night. If DeVaca could bring the Frenchman within range of a British war ship, he would try to insight the Frenchy to fire, thereby warning any British man of war of her hostile intentions.

With each passing hour, the French gained on the privateer who slipped closer toward her waiting guns. It was a dangerous gambit but the only one left to Miguel Antonio DeVaca. As the wee hours wore away and dawn approached, *La Revanche* began creeping up almost within cannon range. Cape Anne was approaching off the starboard bow, and Red Mike knew he was coming near the station of several Royal Navy vessels. He had given them a wide berth only days before when he tried to stay out of sight of their prying eyes. If any of them were about and ready to make way, he might have a chance of shaking the snapping French dog.

The pace was furious, and the *Matador* had at most an hour before the speeding warship would catch her up, and then in a duel, the *Matador* would surely lose unless she scored a lucky hit early on either the main mast or dropped a hot round in the magazine. Without such success, the only other hope was to find a spot where he could run her aground and abandon ship, but the shoaling waters in these parts gave little likelihood of that. Like as not he would tear out her bottom before he was close enough to shore to bring off the crew.

As the morning sun rose to larboard, Crispin could see several sail dead ahead. The closest were clearly no more than fishing boats and of no help. The Frenchman was intrepid in pursuing an enemy so deeply into English colonial waters, and apparently, he hoped to beard the lion in his den.

The Frenchman opened with his bow gun, hoping to get the *Matador*'s range. The first shot fell several hundred yards abaft the stern lights, which indicated that Red Mike still had over a mile. Ten minutes later, the second shot came and fell just a scant fifty or so yards short and seaward.

The farthest sail that Crisp could see looming was substantial and seemed to be making sail toward the racing ships. Before the frogs could fire a third round, Red Mike had ordered the stern gunners to give the French a taste of their own medicine. The shot rang dully on the weather deck and Crisp was unable, at that great distance, to see what, if any, damage it did.

"Short by two hundred yards, Mungo!" yelled DeVaca. "Mister McFadden, go below and see what assistance you can give." It is worth recalling that the first mate was an exceptional gunner and more likely than any other to hit the enemy.

The third shot from the *La Revanche* passed close by the mainmast and pierced the main'sl. The ship of war now had their range. The *Matador*'s stern gun barked again, and DeVaca, watching through his glass, could see the geyser as the shot landed wide to starboard and short nearly a hundred yards.

"We can get no closer, Captain," said Socrates with a touch of frustration. "The gun's too light and has not the range." He added with irony, "I think the Frenchman will oblige us and come closer though and make himself a better mark."

Crispin Mull's uncanny luck held true. Captain DeVaca would have been grateful, except that he had no idea that Mull was especially blessed with good fortune, even in the face of catastrophe. The cloud of sail that had appeared on the horizon grew now, and Red Mike's spyglass showed that, indeed, it was bearing down on them. As she appeared hull up with Britain's colors snapping in the wind overhead, Mike prayed to the Almighty Papist God of his Irish mother that the vessel was a ship of war, forgetting, of course, that the French were also of the Catholic persuasion.

The French, having gotten their range, fired another round. Mr. Dodens put the helm over hard, hoping that any slight deviation would throw off the French gunners. The fourth ball had found a mark and smashed a stern lantern to bits. By the time Dodens had heard the gun's report and reacted, the shot had done its job. The near blind helmsman had saved them from worse though as the Frenchman would have to stay in the wake of the *Matador* in order to score another hit with his bow gun or else wait until they had gained so substantially on the schooner that they could luff up and bring their main batteries to bear.

Red Mike ordered the steersman to make a course straight for the oncoming vessel. If she was a British ship of war, then hurrah! The day was saved. And if she were a fat merchantman, then perhaps she would be an easier mark for the daring Gaul.

Crispin clenched his jaw tight and hoped for the best. If the Frenchman took the *Matador*, the best he could hope for was the gaol at Montreal or Quebec and the worst, death or another swim in Leviathan's deep.

The sails loomed ever larger in his glass, and DeVaca could see the British Naval Jack flying proudly. While he watched, the gun ports suddenly opened, revealing the wolf's teeth. With twelve guns down each side she was more than a match for the Frenchman.

The *Matador* heeled hard to starboard. As she leaned into the turn, the British warship put her helm over and presented her broadside to the French ship, which was now less than a thousand yards behind the *Matador*. The distance between the two ships of war was almost a mile, but the bold and disciplined British vessel, the HMS *Saphire*, decided to check the Frenchman's momentum and gave him a full thunderous twelve gun broadside. *La Revanche* presented little mark coming straight at them, but still two of the iron round shot found marks. England's tars were no mean chuckers of shot and their practiced aim told true. Geysers of water sprouted all about the bows and flanks of *Revanche*.

The French were now well aware that their situation had become perilous and that they needed to alter their course. They came about and began lobbing their own shots towards the British vessel. The race had reversed as the hunter now became the quarry. The *Matador* watched both of the vessels slip away to the north and the roar of cannons became dull thumps in the distance, slowly rolling across the water as *La Revanche* fled for Canadian waters and the protection of war ships near Louisburg.

The near-miss with *La Revanche* had signaled the beginning of the end for the *Matador*'s brief northern cruise. The brush had been too close for Red Mike. He had prayed to the virgin and to all the saints in heaven that he could remember, that he would escape the Frenchman's guns. He could smell his own demise if he didn't change his wicked ways.

As they cruised toward Boston Towne, DeVaca began to think upon the selling of the loot of the *Guilderhoose* and then turning command over to the crew. Let them choose who they would to lead them. Socrates was their best choice, yet there were others who were also capable. Mike would need to retrieve his own fortune from hiding and set himself up where no one knew him.

Perhaps, he considered, he could settle in the sugar islands and live the idle life of the planter. The idea of wallowing in clean sheets with a buxom slave girl under each arm and his every whim attended to sounded not at all unappealing. To Miguel's way of thinking, buxom slave girls seemed a prerequisite of the planter's way of life, accompanied by handsome boots, fine horses, and pretty silk scarves.

Of course, there was one bit of unfinished business that needed seeing to—the debt he owed the young lieutenant of Foot. His life had been spared by the quick thinking and actions of the Englishman. Red Mike was unaware that Crispin was of Scots birth and could have cared less. In his colonial thinking, all Britons were English if they were in the madder red uniform of the king.

A plan began to coalesce in his fertile mind. He would need an extra set of hands to bring off the treasure. That would be the lieutenant. Then, with the soldier's permission, he would return him for a ransom, and they would split the amount. DeVaca was quite sure that the young man was as keen on financial gain as the next fellow. Half the ransom, plus his horde and the accumulated wealth from this most recent cruise, should put him up well for many years and, if invested wisely, might grow to become a substantial fortune.

Socrates McFadden had shaken Red Mike's hand at the dock in St. Augustine and wished the Spaniard well. The former slave had purchased DeVaca's share in the ship.

There were many sailors who had bluntly refused to sail under a black and said that no good would come of it. First mate was one thing, but for a son of Ham to command a crew was an abomination against God. This was, of course, a rather odd bit of moralizing from men who regularly plundered the wealth of others and cut down innocents without reason and scant license. Sailors are a superstitious lot, and some believed the ship was doomed under the strong but tar-colored hand of Black Socrates. The remaining crew had already bestowed on him this name, befitting a tyrant of the seas, and had given their murderous pledge to obey. The dissenters were paid off the and left ashore to find another ship to crew aboard or to make their own through darker means.

Red Mike DeVaca and Lieutenant Crispin Mull had agreed upon the terms of Crispin's release and had divulged their plot to no one. They took a clean and fair run schooner for Charlestown and worked away as ordinary seamen of poor but honest means. The labor was light, and the little crew lively and merry, so Crisp passed the days quickly. His time aboard the *Matador* had schooled him well enough that he passed as an able seaman without a batted eye or questioning look.

Miguel had given his name as Roberto McDonough, a crossbreed of Irish and Spanish blood, which was, of course, the truth, and all of the tiny crew just called him Spanish Bob for jest, which suited him just as well. Crispin signed on simply as Crispy Mull and told the accepting fellows he was from Edinburgh and working his way home, hoping to see his parents before they shucked off the mortal coil.

PROVIDENCE

Providence, Rhode Island, was certainly not London, and Peggy Fairchild felt she had been cast into a drab and lifeless limbo. The lively life of the colonel's courtesan was countless watery miles behind her. Her present existence consisted of sewing and cleaning for Goody Harding, the wife of Captain Harding.

Gone were the halcyon days of late breakfasts, enjoyed in bed with Beverly, and the nights of gaming and unbridled passion. No longer would she be able to dream of being the mistress of Blanchard Hall. Peg had never been a religious girl and had, in fact, ignored the sinfulness of her young and hedonistic life with Beverly. Faced with life in a small colonial port, Peg began to scheme a new future.

Captain Harding had married Constance God Is Great Strong, the only living daughter and granddaughter of Puritan ministers. While the rest of New England was leaving behind them the horror of witch trials, Indian wars, and the severe strictures of religious law, the Strongs cleaved even closer to the teachings and beliefs of their ancestral fathers.

Constance, as you might imagine, had a pinched face and a boney frame that came from her shrewish disposition and constant labors. If ever there was a woman who spurned the pleasures of the flesh and saw men as nothing more than hornless pawing devils, it was she.

Isaiah Harding had married Constance for her family connections and respectability, and those had proved fruitful while Goody herself was anything but, being barren, and therefore unable to provide issue to inherit the loveless couple's thriving shipping firm, Constance grew even more distant from her husband.

Seamen are a hardy and debauched lot, and when they make port, they release their pent-up animal desires upon their wives and the unwed daughters of farmers, excepting of course those fellows who indulge themselves in the flesh of professional ladies. Captain Harding's loins were not exempt from the burning desires of carnality. With Peg aboard the *Indian Rose*, he had never passed a more pleasant voyage. Every morning and evening, the good captain had indulged himself with a sporting romp. Peg, of course, was not a foolish girl and realized that she needed a patron in the colonies, and as Isaiah owned her indenture and could protect her from the lusty seamen of the *Indian Rose*, she had done her best to make up for the many years of begrudging and lifeless lovemaking of Goody Harding.

By the time the *Indian Rose* reached Providence, Harding was completely in love with the object of his bullish rutting. It was out of the question for him to put his wife aside, so he planned to install Peg in his home as maidservant to his wife and an assistant to the cook.

Peg, by now, was not the trusting petite dame she had been with Beverly, and she was quite sure that all the whispered endearments would lead only to muffled moans of pleasure in the attic or the smoke house and not to a place in polite, if boring, colonial society. She was right, of course, yet as long as the good captain wished to spend himself with her rather than in Goody Harding's loveless iron trap, she had a card to play.

Goody Harding had made herself available to her husband one night of each month he was home, and he had seemed eager always. When the sweating and pain were over, she knew she had done her duty as God would wish. Two months went by, and on both occasions, he had pleaded either fatigue or ill health. On the third such occasion, Goody began to suspect that something more was afoot than mere coincidence, and she cast her angry and suspicious looks in the direction of the new girl her foolish husband had brought back from England.

Goody Harding was a wise, if sour and ill-tempered, woman, and she looked the situation over carefully before she accused anyone of anything. As her witch-hunting grandfather Goore had said, "Look first in your own house for evil, for the devil hides his wanton lust and his lies in the tabernacle of the family!" His other great admonishment had been "Strike Satan only in the open, for it increases your worth in the eyes of God, and your enemies will be diminished by the brilliance of your righteousness!" There was more wisdom of this pious nature and Grandfather Goore had even written a tract upon the hunting of witches, which received only feeble acclaim. The Reverend Goore had died in the wilderness of western Massachusetts when he was oddly set upon and devoured by a pack of wild squealing pigs. The swine were never seen again, and only his wooden mallet and a Bible were left untrampled. Grandfather had carried the mallet as his sole weapon, believing that he should smite his enemies with only the tools of the carpenter. Clearly, a brace of pistols charged and primed would have been of more use than the oaken hammer.

Goody Harding decided to bide her time and keep a careful watch on her husband and the girl Peg. If the young strumpet could satisfy the captain's animal desires and no child was begotten on her, then perhaps she, Goodwife Harding, would no longer have to dread the monthly visit to her sinful Eden parts. *On the other hand*, thought the righteous woman, *what would God think of my house when my husband copulated with the servants like a musky old goat?* The quandary was one she would need to ponder and pray upon.

If the town became aware of the illicit and evil affair, her reputation would be destroyed, and God forbid, the saucy harlot should bear a child of Isaiah's. There were always recourses to such problems if one had forewarning. Goody knew of several girls whose own families had remedied the sin of bastardy rather than bring shame upon the home. While the secret was rarely well kept, the families maintained their respectability in the community for having the propriety to attempt to hide the wickedness of their errant daughters.

It was not unheard of for a married man to father a child on a servant, but the whispers and glares in church were more damning than some could manage. One dear lady had hanged herself in the woods rather than face the consequences of her husband's indiscretion. Goody Harding knew that suicide was as great a sin as fornication and would never indulge her own grief and embarrassment in such a sacrilegious way. Conversely, Goody could not allow things to get so out of hand that her husband's behavior brought ruin upon the house and the family name. Not only would they be ruined in church and polite society, but no one would do business with folk who were so indiscrete.

※

Peg was safe from the prying hands and probing tongue of the captain for months on end while he was away at sea, and if Goody Harding was aware of his attentions to her when he was home, she kept her feelings well hid. The harpy woman was a strict taskmaster, and Peg rarely had a moment to herself from sunup till sundown. She sewed, and she cleaned floors and polished silver and pewter. When she was done with those things, she cut firewood and planted, weeded, or harvested in the vegetable garden. Even folk who lived in town grew their own winter and summer vegetables and herbs and usually kept some hens for eggs.

In the late morning hours, she would accompany Goody to the market to buy butter, milk, and meat, and then on to the wharf to buy fish. If a ship put in, Goodwife Harding would go to see what fabrics and other goods it brought, both to purchase and to keep her husband informed of what the competition was selling and what prices it fetched. All of Peg's tedious labor freed Constance to see to the good management of the family business. Naturally, the captain employed men ashore to purchase new cargoes and to keep the books, but all knew that their reputations were at stake if the captain's wife caught them sleeping at the wheel or dipping into stocks or coin.

When the captain was in Providence, he saw first to the business of his current cargo, then had a go at the books, and headed 'round to one of the taverns where the local merchants and traders met. It was in this convivial atmosphere, over a pipe and a tumbler of spirit, that he would begin to learn of all that had happened in his absence and what new goods were being bought and sold most briskly. Isaiah never made it home before the evening of his first day tied up, and when he did, he would question his wife closely for all she knew and had done and matched this against what he had learned on the docks and in town.

Peg's room was in the eaves on the third floor along with the cook, an elderly widow who was mostly deaf and racked with rheumatism. Here she would wait, patiently listening for Harding's arrival at the door, knowing that in an hour or two, when the queen of chores had gone to her sleep, he would take a stroll in the garden and expect her to join him in the shadows of the imported English walnut. He was a poor lover and knew nothing of how to satisfy a woman's needs, but at least, he was gentle and quick. One may rest assured that he always had some trinket or bauble in his pocket for her. A cheap piece of jewelry or a bit of fancy ribbon that he thought might take her eye. Harding had never inquired into her past, and so was unaware that Peg was used to more expensive notions; still, at least, he was thoughtful. If she had worn any of the things other than during one of their trysts, Mistress Harding would likely have taken it away and surely would have administered a caning across Peg's supple bare back.

For two months, Peg had missed her monthly effusions, and now she was sure that she was with child. At first, she thought merely that the hard work had put her off her cycle, and then, she suspected that the moonless cloudy skies were to blame, but finally, she had to face the rather harsh reality that fields well plowed and tended yielded the most wondrously bountiful crop. The good captain had tilled her fertile region with great regularity, and now a child of those moonlit garden trysts grew within her.

Harding had been away at sea for nearly four months and was not due home for at least another month; he was bound for Madeira, the West Indies and home via the southern colonies. Peg had no one to turn to and feared that as her belly began to swell, Mistress Harding's jealousy and suspicions would grow angrier and perhaps even deadly in the end.

She had heard that the Indians used herbs to weed out an unwanted future nursling, but she knew no one who could tell her where to find a helpful savage, nor, for that matter, anyone she could even share her secret with. The cook, Hattie Sikes, was as useful as a leaky bucket and as deaf as a post. Goody Harding had seen to it that Peg had made no friends and had no time over the past two years to speak with anyone alone for more than a few minutes. Peg had heard of girls who had rooted out their own unborn, but she hadn't the slightest idea how to begin. She had also heard tell of girls who had died of bleeding from clumsy and hasty ministrations. The time was soon or not at all, and that opened another line of questioning, which she was ill prepared to answer.

Goody Harding had never been fecund and was no more productive in the family sense than a pile of rubblestone—unfit for even a foundation. Peg could easily give to Isaiah the child he sought, but without a doubt, Goody would smother it before she would allow a bastard to sleep even one night under her roof. No doubt, she would reason that any child born of sin was outside of God's law and, therefore, the spawn of Lucifer.

Peg tried not to think on the subject for several days but was so scared and fatigued by the nagging monstrosity of her situation that she slept not at all. One day, while scrubbing the hearth, it occurred to her that perhaps she could strike a bargain with her mistress. If Goodwife Harding could be made to appear as the natural mother of the child, then perhaps Peg could buy her freedom for the price of the babe but only if the sharp tongued woman could be made to see the sense and profit in it. The frigid woman was prudish and pious to a fault but shrewd if she could see the gain in a thing.

Weeks passed as Peg thought on how to sell the woman her plan.

※

"Fat and lazy!" spat Goody in her clipped tones. "No doubt your sloth will bring ruin on me. You're a waste of good food and lodgings. Perhaps if I cut your wages and your potage you'll see your waywardness."

Goody Harding paid Peg a stipend as did all folk who held an indenture, for it was the law, and a stingy master could be sued in court for withholding the cash terms of the contract. Peg's contract, which had been written by Isaiah himself, was poor in the first place and withheld the value from her in the second place. It stipulated that Peg was to receive the cash in a lump sum at the end of the period of indenture, which was seven years from when she set foot on Rhode Island's soil. What's more, the cheap couple had deducted the price of her passage from the amount due and provided only the barest minimum for clothing and bedding.

Naturally, the captain made no mention of additional services. Isaiah himself likely would not have been so Scotch with his purse strings except that he knew he had to placate his marital partner if he wished to maintain the fraudulent propriety of his illicit relationship with pretty Peggy.

Constance was more than aware of Peg's growing stomach, and suspected that, in truth, it came from acts more carnal than slothful. The girl kept to her duties and rarely required more than a word or two as inducement to work.

Goody knew she could not accuse the girl without proof but was sure that time would out. The girl's hands and legs remained trim, from what she could tell, yet her breasts appeared to be swelling, no doubt with milk for her damnable husband's bastard. She would search the girl's clothes for signs of her monthly flow, and an occasional check of the privy house should turn up a moist red rag if the girl was innocent.

On the one hand, Constance would feel vindicated by her husband's mistake. She could then face him with evidence of his wantonness and debauchery. On the other hand, what she had feared happening in her home was most likely now a reality.

Sadly, by the time she had proofs against the girl, it was too late to root out Isaiah's evil, and her house would come under the doubly damned pall of adultery and fornication.

Goody's first slap was an insult, and Peg started to clench her fists; the second slap came quickly and nearly stunned her. She stumbled backwards as a fist landed squarely on her cheek.

"Slut! You filthy little harridan! You think to come into my house and cuckold me! Dirty, vile little b———!"

Alas, for Peg, no rag or stain had been discovered by the scold's inquisition.

By the time Goody Harding had reached the middle of her tirade, Peg was sprawled upon the floor. The pregnant girl rolled to the side as a square-toed, buckled shoe came straight at her stomach with much ferocity. The toe of the hard shoe landed painfully in her crotch, and Peg instantly and instinctively curled into a ball in order to protect the lusty captain's unborn vagitus.

"Goody, please stop!" begged the lass. "I told you only because I hoped you might wish the child fer yerself."

"Your bastard! You copulated with my husband under my very roof. This house has belonged to four generations of Goores, and never has anyone defiled it the way that you and my husband have."

Her hair stuck out at mad angles, and it looked as though it had been combed by a Dutch windmill. Spittle gathered at the corners of her mouth, and she alternately wrung her hands and shook her fists. A foot flew out again, this time catching Peg in the shinbone, barking the skin and making the blood flow.

"I, take in your whelp? I'd sooner drown the maggot in the rain barrel than let anyone know that my husband kept a whore!"

Peg threw her arms over her head, knowing that what she was about to speak might bring on a fresh rain of blows.

"Mistress, no one need know the child isn't yer own."

No blows came. Peg looked out from behind her hands. Constance was standing at a window staring out while her hands twisted her apron and spasmodically clenched and relaxed.

"If you hide me from eyes, Goody, and we pad yer belly. No one need know the babe isn't yours. I've thought it through. When enough time has passed, we pick a stormy night when the doctor could in no way come to us, and we say that is the night you bore the child. Hattie can see only a little better than she can hear. She can be the witness. Only the captain and you, and I need know. When the neighbors and such ask what became of the serving girl, you can say a fever near took me, and you are keeping me to home to recover. When visitors come, I'll hide."

Visitors were rare at Goore house as the Harding's had few friends. Constance's less than sterling personality had not been conducive to the making of friends; still, there was the odd cousin or relation that dropped by. When the captain was home, it was less rare for a messenger from his crew or investors to come to the deceptively gay yellow house with its fashionable black shutters.

Peg had thought it all out in great detail. She had even prepared a false belly from scraps of drab linen and duck down. The belly went on over the chemise and tied in the back with two cloth tapes. When the petticoats were put on over it and all was in place, no one would be the wiser. Women fawn over each other when they are with child, but Peg was quite sure no one would dare, nor care, to touch Goody Harding's womb.

Each day, she would tell Goodwife Harding what it was she felt and where she was uncomfortable, and in that way, Constance could repeat any of the information if someone were so bold as to solicit the cold woman's feelings.

The plan was intriguing, and Goody listened and grew somewhat more calm as Peg stood and dusted off her apron. Peg did not share all her thoughts on this arrangement—her plan was deep and deceptive.

"What of my milk? How will the babe be fed when others are about," questioned Goody, warming to the idea.

"Well, no one must know I bore a child," said Peg. "So we cannot run the risk that someone might see me nursing. And, as you will have no milk, we needs must find a wet nurse for the babe." Peg became bold. "After all these years without a child, it will be more believable if your milk doesn't come in."

"If I agree," snapped Goody, "then you do everything as I say. If this were to get out, I would be ruined and so would the captain. Your reputation may not be worth a hapenny, but ours is good, and don't you forget that!"

"Ma'am," whispered Peg, "that's not all. I want my indenture ended and fifty pounds to return home on."

Her hands were perspiring, and she wiped the palms on her apron but forced herself to look Goody right in the eye.

"Aye, I should have figured you fer the type to haggle over yer own babe."

Silence settled between the two women and stretched into a smothering eternity as they took each other's measure.

"I'll not haggle, Mistress Harding. If you don't agree, then I'll run away and have the babe in the woods if I have to, and then I'll turn up at meeting one fine Sunday, demanding that Isaiah greet his only child."

Goody, of course, acceded to the demands, as she had no choice, and it served her own purposes twofold. One, she would get the girl out from under her roof and away from her husband; the devil's concubine would be out of her house. Two, she would have a child to inherit the family fortune. The girl may be a harlot and a seductress, but she had a mind, and Constance had little doubt that, together, they could pass off the babe as her own.

She would see to it that Isaiah had nothing to say about it. In the end he would, no doubt, see the wisdom of it. In the meantime, if he balked, she had ways of making him pay.

"We mustn't waste any time," thought Goody aloud. "The more you are seen in public, the more likely one of these busybodies is to spot the swelling. Tomorrow, we will shop as usual at the docks. I want you to complain within hearing of wagging Davy Ross that you are feeling ill. I'll be far enough away that you'll have to raise your voice for me to hear ye."

"That is fine, Goody. I'll say I am warm and feel faint and that we must go home, or I won't have the strength to help cook with supper," added Peg.

Peg's diabolical plot was in motion. In six months, the babe would be free of her womb, and Mistress "Satan's Your Uncle" Harding would be lying cold in the ground, her nag's tongue stilled forever.

Indeed, what she had not told Goody was that she planned on slowly poisoning her for the next several months and that on the fateful night of the delivery, Goodwife Harding would get the last and most potent dose of the deadly potion.

Most likely, the insalubrious concoction was of the nightshade family. Savage herbal folklore had spread to the good people of New England decades before, and no doubt, Peg's brew was some perverse version of a sachem's tea intended to drive out bad spirits. It certainly would drive out Goody's spirit.

After a suitable amount of time had passed, no less than six months, but certainly no more than a year, Peg would marry Isaiah. She would, of course, adopt her "stepchild."

It would be easy to convince Isaiah that Constance had been weakened by the stress of the deception and caring for the newborn, and clearly, she had been unwell for many months, lending credence to that statement. There was no need for the good man to know that his serving girl and bareback galloper had been slowly killing his wife and that she was the cause of the pious woman's unhealthy and eventually lethal malaise.

Peg doubted that the captain would mourn his wife over long nor that he'd turn up his nose at being able to climb beneath her skirts wherever and whenever he pleased.

Peg had thought on this plan for many long nights over the past few weeks, and now that it was moving forward, she had no doubt that she could carry it out with alacrity and pleasure. There was more to her darkling script, but she dared not think on it until she had affected the sad and liberating demise of her mistress. Peg had been a victim of Beverly and his lackeys and then of Isaiah and his wife, and she planned to be a victim no more. Pretty Peggy Fairchild was taking her destiny into her own fine, porcelain hands. It never occurred to her that if she had kept her thighs well clamped and followed her mother in the dressmaking trade, she would never have found herself giving birth to a bastard while plotting murder.

The good captain found himself pinched between a rock and a hard place and decided that his return to the sea would be best for everyone, especially himself. Being gone from Constance was never a hardship, and now that she was aware of his "improprieties" as he called them, it went doubly so.

Her tirades had been unbearable, and now her scheme to pass off the child as hers was more than he could tolerate. Let her plan what she would. He would go along with anything if it meant she would cease her blameful rantings.

The only regret he had in leaving was that he would be unable to saddle Peggy at will, which was quite all right with him as he had no desire to mount her whilst she was with child anyhow.

He had not even lost his sea legs when the *Indian Rose* put out to sea, this time bound for Bristol, Amsterdam, and Lisbon, and due home only after the weanling was delivered and his wife suitably occupied with cradles and swaddling.

THE SILENT BLADE

It is worth recalling that there was a fellow aboard the *Matador* named Trepan and that he had a dirty black linen patch over one empty socket. It is no cosmic coincidence that the name and description matched the strangler from London who had attempted the death of the Right Honorable Douglas Barden, which as you may remember is how P. Peter Lane fell afoul of the law.

After having escaped the hangman, Trepan slipped his bonds with the aid of a cutpurse named Hubbard that he had known for years. Hubbard had a crippled elder brother who had lost a shank in a ship-to-ship battle when he was a lad. John was the brother that freed Trepan's hands, and it was his elder sibling Billy Indigo (so named because he was covered with tattoos) who helped the strangler find a ship for the colonies.

With his murderous and larcenous history, Trepan quickly found work in the West Indies. The assassin roamed the docks of Nassau, picking up spare coin collecting on delinquent bills owed by seamen. Usually, a whisper in the dark and the glint of the moon off a deadly silvery dagger blade was enough for even those hearty souls.

Not curiously, wiser merchants soon discovered that Trepan was quite useful in helping them balance the books.

Even the Royal Navy had employed him upon occasion. The admiralty was always short on sailors quite simply because no one wanted to join due to the poor pay, wormy rations, scurvy, howling hurricanes, red hot cannon balls, and heartless captains. His Majesty's uniformed representatives on the high seas hired toughs to go find able hands to fill out the crews.

Paid by the head, the press gangs clubbed any poor sod into submission and dragged him down to the ship where he was placed under lock and key until the vessel was far out to sea. Many a father and well-heeled gentleman, foolish enough to be out and about after dark when a ship was in port, found themselves swabbing decks and climbing rigging within the week.

Trepan, by himself, brought off six men in one night. He had spotted them drinking heavily after a wedding feast, and when, at last, they had passed out under a palm tree from too much punch, he had bashed them on the head with a leather wrapped lead cylinder and then gagged them and staked them to the ground. It took some effort, but with a borrowed cart and donkey, he managed, after several trips, to convey all of them to the docks by dawn.

The young swains awoke with the most abominable headaches and a lieutenant of the Royal Navy standing over them, informing them that they were now sailors in His Majesty's Squadron, patrolling the Leeward Islands keeping the waters free of Circe's misbegotten bastards "greasy Spaniards, counting house Dutchmen, and boy buggering French Privateers."

In due time, Trepan became a liability to low people in high places, and he felt that a change of air would do him well. Taking a dangerously leaky snow for St. Augustine one sultry and stormy moonless night, Trepan had finally come within the orbit of Red Mike, so he had signed on with the privateer out of self-preservation, not a love of the cleansing salt air. He had hoped that, in time, he might work his way to New York or Boston, where he was sure he could find employment plying his trade.

As Miguel and Crispin departed from St. Augustine aboard the schooner, Trepan was making preparations to shadow them. That denizen of the dark could smell conspiracy and gold and silver specie from a league away and knew that the former captain and the "kidnapped" officer were up to something that smacked of secrecy and large quantities of coin.

There was nothing to hold Trepan in the Spanish colony, and he was in no way eager to serve under Black Socrates. That ebony buck was too keen on mayhem and battle, and Trepan had seen enough of that already under the steady hand of DeVaca.

He had managed to eavesdrop on DeVaca and Mull as they sat one night in the captain's cabin, speaking about taking ship for Charlestown. Trepan would be a week behind them while he tried to find a ship, but since he was heading north anyhow, he concluded that he might as well sniff them out along the way. Perhaps, they would become careless and allow him the opportunity to slip a silk scarf tightly about their necks or slice a blade through a windpipe, provided, of course, that they had secured some form of lucre.

Murder was business, not sport, and he never worked for free or took chances just to seek satisfaction. One lethally passionate life-severing act in a career was enough. Trepan owed allegiance to no one and wouldn't give a second thought to sending a former comrade to his final reward for a price. Coin was coin, and the acquiring of it did not allow for emotion or sentiment, not that Trepan had either of these in many long years.

His mother had abandoned him to the care of his rum-soaked grandmother, who had beaten him well and often until he learned to pick at least two pockets cleanly every day, turning over all of the gains to her.

One night, she had beaten him a little too hard with the knotted rope she kept looped about her wrist, and the boy had fought back. In her mostly inebriated stupor, she hadn't been able to get out of the way of the jagged, broken knife quickly enough, and the groveling boy had cut right through her Achilles tendons. While she was wallowing about on the floor of the squalid Thames side hutment, he had whipped her mole and wrinkle covered back raw with the knotted rope, and then when he tired of his revenge, he strangled the life out of her but not before she clawed out one of his bright green eyes with her dirty old talons.

He had barely lived through the blinding experience, but being only eight, he was quick to heal. When one has to murder one's own grandmother in order to survive, it has a rather morbiferous tendency to harden the soul and extinguish the flame of hope and innocence altogether. Whatever the boy lacked in mercy on the one side, he made up for with a superb sense of timing and stealth on the other.

The middle-aged Trepan usually wore a packet of poison in a small flat waterproof leather pouch tied about his neck, a slick little rosewood handled dagger nestled in his right sleeve, and a red silk scarf tucked into the pocket of his well-worn greasy brown wool frock coat that smelled of coconuts, seaweed, and damp earth. A twelve-foot length of strong hempen rope was wrapped four and a half times around the waist of his dirty baggy linen breeches. The scarf, as previously mentioned, was a strangler's weapon, and the rope was handy for everything from second story exits to tying up drunken partygoers or for the occasional hanging by special request of a paying customer.

Perched in a hidden pocket under his crumpled, mud-spattered, three-cornered, beaver felt hat was a set of tiny steel tools and a selection of keys that would gain him entrance through most doors and into many a strong box. The tools had been fashioned by a clever, bald dwarf named Eben Octavius Drake who worked for Mister Galton, a contractor in London who produced musket locks for the Tower Armory. The little fellow snuck into the shop after hours to do odd jobs for friends with ready cash.

Trepan was a master of blending in, disappearing and gaining silent entry. As has already been noted, he moved like a dark shade through the ever-dusky underworld of London and later Nassau. Now, the naive colonials would face the subtle scourge of the assassin's trade.

※

As the shadows passed over the grass beneath the waxing moon, a night bird called softly from the copse of trees around the tiny barn. The building was constructed of squared logs chinked with a mixture of clay and fine straw. A coat of whitewash had thinly disguised the barn's frontier origins. Off the back of the little building was a chest high fence that enclosed what was clearly a pig wallow. One knew it was a pig barn before one saw the wallow by the particularly pungent odor of porcine manure.

Red Mike quickly scaled the fence and landed with a splash in a pocket of mucky water that almost topped his midcalf boots. He reached down and turned up the tops of the supple black boots so that his entire lower leg was covered.

Crispin's nose wrinkled at the stench. He passed the spades over the fence to DeVaca and then hopped the rail himself, being careful not to land in the most poachy part of the quagmire.

"Bloody reeks," hissed Crisp. "Couldn't ye find a better place to bury it, for heaven's sake?"

"And who would think to look for buried treasure in a pig pen?" queried Mike angrily. "Now shut your gob, and start digging where I show you. It's only about three feet down and right in the center here."

The two men got straight to work as silently as possible. The muck was heavy with water but easy to scoop out. It was well past midnight by the time their spades chinked against one of the iron bands that wrapped around the small oak trunk. A few moments later, the two men gave a heave and the small chest let loose with a sucking noise as it came unstuck from the muck at the bottom of the muddy hole

A lone figure stood in the blackness behind one of the ancient elms, keeping well back from the barn.

Crispin carried the two spades while Red Mike led the spavined, cow-hocked, old bay gelding that packed the chest on its back. The two men had only gone several hundred yards down the road when they heard a frightened squealing coming from the pen. They both cursed under their breath and hurried on their way.

Clearly, one of the nearsighted swine had come out to investigate after their departure and had fallen into the slippery hole, which they had failed to backfill in their rush to depart. The farmer, who had never known of the great fortune buried in his pig yard, was to awaken to the mystery of an indignant hog grunting in the bottom of a three-foot pit. All of the two men's tracks from the night before had been obliterated, and the farmer was never to know how or why his sow had come to this impasse. The blame fell on a neighbor noted for playing practical jokes, but he maintained his innocence right up to the hour of his death. The story was never forgotten and is still told in those parts with much laughter even to this day.

Trepan followed the two through the darkness, and even though he was quite sure he could eliminate one of them with the dagger, he was not at all sure that he was quick enough that he could take both men. They were, after all, men of arms and carried pistols and knives in their belts, which meant caution in the extreme. Liberating the trunk of coin would be no easy task, Trepan was sure, but he was willing to brave death trying.

DeVaca stood stooped over the trunk, which sat on the floor in the middle of his room. He had sent Crispin to fetch two glasses and a bottle of Madeira from the bar on the first floor of the inn, and instructed him to bring them back along with pipes and tobacco for a celebratory smoke and drink. Miguel also didn't want Crisp to see the contents of the chest. Of course, Crisp knew it was treasure, but Miguel feared that if anyone knew how much, they might not be able to resist temptation.

Over eight thousand pounds value in gold coin and jewelry sat heavily and silently, glittering warmly in the candlelight thrown from the pierced tin lantern that Red Mike held in his hand. At the sound of boots on the stairs, he let the lid down and refastened the wrought iron hasp with a new lock to replace the rusted one he had to knock off with a hatchet.

"Here's to yer good fortune and my swift return to the regiment!" toasted Crispin as he walked in the door with a bottle under one arm and the rest on a tray.

"Aye, here's to a bargain kept." Mike stuck out his hand. "What, with my half of the ransom plus this, I'll be able to take up a new life free of the sword. Tomorrow, we deliver your letter into the hands of a man I know who'll take it to the governor. He should be able to affect your transfer in a month at most. Tomorrow, you must go though. It wouldn't do fer the locals to recognize the 'kidnapped' officer as the fellow who was living with a shipmate at the Gordon's Tavern. Your story won't stay quietly in the governor's mansion."

"I ain't shaved since we put in and in these rags,"—Crispin gestured at his raggedy old uniform breeches, the torn bloodstained coarse linen shirt he had been given and the plum colored wool waistcoat he had liberated from a Dutchman—"I surely don't look like an officer, but I suppose yer right. Do ye have some plan as to where I might hide out though?"

"I have given it some thought, Senor Mull," said Mike with a smile. "I know of a camp not far from town where some of the local lads stay when they're hunting ducks in the fall. A bit of old canvas over a couple of broken spars is all, but you shouldn't need more this time of year. The ground is firm, and the bugs are tolerable, what with the breeze off the sea. I'll fetch ye food and drink, an' when the time comes for the exchange, I'll bring you a set of worn but respectable clothes. When the ransom amount is agreed upon with the government, I'll pay you your half out of this." He tapped the lid of the chest.

"How do we ensure the exchange and make sure the governor's men don't lay hands on you, Captain?" wondered Crisp.

"A good point, and one I have given some thought to." Miguel warmed to the subject. He clearly enjoyed sharing the plot. "We will meet near a woods that I know outside of town. You and I will stay back in the trees. Their man will place a sack with the ransom on the ground, in the open. They'll know that until I see the sack, you won't be set free. As you approach them, you tell them that there is a gang of us, and if anyone touches the bag to take it back, you and they will be cut down. Within an hour, my coin and I should be well gone. With your half of the kidnap money, plus the half share you earned from the Guilderhoose, you should be well set for uniforms and traveling expenses for quite a while, I should think, Mr. Mull?"

"Indeed, and I can hardly wait for fresh linen and a clean uniform. Not that I minded the treatment aboard the *Matador*, it's just that it was a bit more primitive than I'm used to. No offense intended."

Crispin had been on the beach for several days when Red Mike came to him with clothes and supplies.

The duck hunter's encampment was rustic in the least and barbaric in the extreme. There were certainly no fresh bed linens. Two old splintered spars, a broken hull strake, and some ship's rope made up the skeleton of a drafty lean-to, which was covered in rotting sailcloth. It served well enough in fine weather and kept most of the rain off in foul.

Miguel led the broken down gelding in with a pack and a demijohn of cheap wine on its back. The good lieutenant had subsisted for the first two days on nothing more than crabs and a small sack of cornmeal, without anything more potent than fresh water to drink, which was fine in the short term, but he had no desire to play Mr. Defoe's *Robinson Crusoe* on this windswept, sandy Carolina stage.

"Sorry to have kept you waiting, Mull" hailed Miguel heartily. "I thought it best if I made myself obvious for a few days after my 'shipmate' disappeared. No sense in attracting any undue attention. I told the innkeep I was going to fish and hunt for a few days. I imagine he thinks me a great sot, what with all of the wine I bought and the fact that I wasn't carrying a fishing pole or firelock."

Crisp stood up from the fire and went over to help the Spanishman unload the horse.

"I did begin to wonder if you had forgotten me. Any word yet from the governor?"

"Indeed!" smiled Mike. "I have word today from my man in the mansion that the Governor has sent a note to New York to enquire about the truthfulness of our claim. It will likely take several weeks or a month for word to reach him that your plight is genuine, and then I think things will happen with great speed."

The two fellows got roaring drunk that starry night and supped on cold chicken that Mike had brought along. Neither of them could walk a straight line, but they spent hours battering away at each other with dulled cutlasses as Red Mike tried to teach Crisp the finer points of close quarters fighting. Crisp received a bloody lip from the broad iron knuckle guard of the captain's blade, and Miguel carried a bruise between his shoulder blades where Crisp had thumped him with the pommel of his cut toe when the Latin grappled him.

They woke in the morning with the waves lapping at their feet and their notched swords still loosely gripped in their hands. They had dropped in complete exhaustion, and in spite of the drink, Crispin had learned a great deal in the hours of rivalry and instruction.

After a hearty breakfast of raw clams and boiled eggs washed down with wine, they had parted and agreed to meet again in a week, at which time Miguel promised to teach Crisp to throw both knife and axe. Throwing knives and axes is a futile tactic in combat because throwing away good weapons tends to leave one defenseless, unless one has an unlimited supply of blades; still, it is a pleasant pastime when life and death don't hang in the balance.

Included in the pack of foodstuffs and used purloined clothing was a worn copy of *Homer's Iliad*, translated from Greek into Latin, the latter of which Crispin had learned to read in his formative years.

His father had insisted that he learn it, and as he put it "a mun can no be a gentlemun or a larned mun of science without it, and I've every intention that you shall proceed, or you'll have no supper fer a month!"

At fourteen, this had seemed too much, and Crisp's stomach had overruled him. In the end, after a week of short rations, he had relented and attended his instructor. The Latin master was a skinny, pasty-faced young fellow who was always nibbling daintily at a piece of greasy meat, and who also was reading for the law and tutored Latin for much needed extra coin.

That night in the duck camp and for the rest of the week, the ancient Grecians would regale and entertain Crispin with their heroic adventures. Thanks remembered to the best efforts of Attorney George Cumberland Yaddaw.

Shore birds waded up and down the wetted sand, and pelicans stooped to dive for fish while the gulls called out raucously, and Crispin paused for a moment to ponder on things even greater than his own eventual rescue and advancement in the regiment. That lasted for perhaps a day, and then he observed two gulls squabbling over the head of a rotten fish and he remembered that the universe and dame fortune helped those who help themselves. His chance to rise above the flotsam and jetsam, to be other than an opportunist, had slipped away.

Alexander pleaded, Hannibal cried out, and Charlemagne wept, but Crispin was deaf to their entreaties. The spark of greatness had burned for a brief moment but had failed to ignite in the young man's breast, and more so than at any other time in his life, he had squandered the opportunity to seize something more. It is uncommon for an individual of low birth to rise above the shallowness of passing wealth and the hollow accolades of his peers long enough to hear and absorb the wisdom of the ancients.

It was near the end of the week, and while Crisp lay out on the sand sipping wine and reading, imagining his heroic return to the Fifty-Sixth of Foot, the first wisps of cloud began to invade the perfect French-blue vault over his head. In a matter of an hour, it caught his attention as the southern sky filled with ominous gray clouds and the waves began to build.

DeVaca was due tomorrow, and Crisp wasn't sure what exactly to do if the weather grew too stormy. The tattered canvas of the lean-to was flapping wildly in the rising wind, and as the rain pelted down in fat drops, he hurried about, tightening down all the guy ropes and stashing his meager supplies under cover. Finally, he wedged himself in one corner of the small shelter where there were fewer holes, and he prepared to wait until the storm had blown itself out.

From his vantage point on the sandy rise, he could view the waves as they turned an angry shade of gray green topped with foam. The surge of the storm began to bring them closer and closer to the foot of his lowly hillock, which elevated him little more than a man's height above the flood. The sky was growing blacker with each passing minute, and Crisp began to believe that the storm was not going to simply blow itself out until it had inundated his tiny prominence and washed him out to sea.

The sea, Crispin was beginning to think, had it in for him, and he was sure he would never return to the ocean again if he could once get away from it. The rapidly rising tide was threatening to cut him off from the little spit that led back to the mainland when the winds rose to a banshee shriek and his shelter became a sail once more.

He grabbed a sack that had previously held cornmeal and stuffed some boiled duck eggs and cheese into it and, grabbing his old Dutch cutlass, bowed before the gale and fought every step of the way, hoping that he would make it to the main shore before the dunes were completely awash and cutoff. He timed the waves and sloshed through the one low spot with the water swirling about his knees.

By the time he had reached relatively safe ground, Crisp could not see his camp when he looked back, even though it was no more than a scant hundred yards away. Moving quickly away from the shore, he swung around to the northwest, hoping to get into the lee of some trees as he worked his way back toward Charlestown and the dry comfort of Gordon's corner Tavern.

※

The separation of the two men had been precisely the ripe opportunity that Trepan had been waiting for. After a day of careful observation, he was sure that Lieutenant Mull was not returning to the inn immediately and that the chest of specie would still be in the room that the two men had shared at Gordon's Tavern.

Trepan continued his cautious ways around DeVaca. He knew his former captain was a more than slightly dangerous fellow and that any hasty or foolish move on his part could result in decapitation or a pistol ball in the belly or some equally mortal injury. Playing with vipers simply wasn't safe. Yet if one used the right tools and showed proper restraint and care, even the most deadly of creatures could be dispatched with ease. Fortunately for the strangler, neither of the men was aware that he was on their track nor that anyone else even knew of the presence of the treasure.

DeVaca locked himself in his room on the second floor of the inn each night and came out only occasionally during the day and never went to the same place twice. Trepan followed him to the docks where he was making enquiries about ships and their comings and goings, and upon another occasion, he followed him, at a safe distance, outside of the town to the encampment of the English officer.

Trepan recognized that in order to kill his former commander, he would either need to gain silent entry to his room or else ambush him spontaneously during the course of his travels. Miguel was mostly abroad during the day and commonly in the company or close proximity of others, making ambush a difficult proposition at best. The only sure bet was to gain entry to the room after the man had gone to his bed and kill him in his slumber.

This was one of the preferred methods anyhow, and the only thing mitigating against it was the troublesome entry into the room. Taking a sleeping man with a knife was like butchering tame rabbits—-both parted the eternal veil without a struggle. The tavern was locked at night, and entry via the main doors was not a sage act. Left with only the window, Trepan would have to gain entry by either using a ladder from street level or by a rope from the roof. The greatest difficulty lay in remaining unseen by bystanders and not waking the sleepers within the hostel. Awaking Red Mike DeVaca, and `so being caught dangling from a rope or standing on a ladder like a would-be suitor, was the last thing Trepan wanted to do.

DeVaca was, of course, the most physically dangerous man whose demise he had ever attempted. Certainly, he had sent a prison full of street toughs and sailors to their doom, usually with a finger of sharpened steel behind the left ear at the top of the neck where it joins the skull and on up into the brain case— instant, certain, and quiet death.

Trepan had slit several jugulars before he learned that they could still scream and fight for several seconds before they collapsed in a pool of their own thickening blood and expired rather noisily. Stabbed in the heart, a stout man could fight for nearly a minute, and only amateurs and butchers went for anything below the neck. Strangling was strictly out of the question with anyone larger than the average woman or boy of fourteen. He had once botched a job by trying to strangle an active youth of his own size, and in the end, he had to knife the lad numerous times before the stripling gave up the ghost. Thankfully, the lad's brother hadn't cared if the job was messy or not, and the wealthy brat had paid just as well as long as his elder sibling was eternally out of the picture.

If he could poison the Spaniard's drink before he went to bed, the job would be easy, but the innkeep always drew the drink himself and carried it up immediately, which left only polluting the entire half tun or barrel. Doing that would call for a larger quantity of poison than he had and would kill far too many patrons of the inn. While Trepan had no moral or professional objections to killing others, it simply would be too dangerous. The authorities would hunt exhaustively to catch the perpetrator of such a murderous harvest.

THE TWO STORMS

As Peg's belly grew, so too did her hatred of Goody Harding. Not because her mistress was any more cold and self-righteous than before, but simply due to the fact that she saw no one else. Other than Hattie, the ancient, deaf, and near-blind cook, Peg had no companions, and as they say "familiarity breeds contempt."

On the plus side of the ledger, she had more time to plot and plan the parsimonious, frigid woman's eventual end. In fact, that was the one activity that filled her days while she scoured and sewed in relative silence.

Bitterness began to creep into Peg's pores and under her skin, the way it had with the captain's wife. Ironically, Goody began to smile more frequently and had a quick in her step that had not been present, even in her brief and boring childhood.

The cold woman's childhood had been filled with catechism, drudgery, and fear of the Almighty and the papist French.

The good farmers and townsmen of Massachusetts and New York were in constant fear of a raid by Huron or Abenaki savages and Canadiens. After the second destructive attack on Schenectady in the wilds of New York, the Goores and Strongs, who had always had a mutual safety and prosperity alliance, decided to quit the fringes of civilization and move back to Rhode Island for the future welfare of the children.

Little Constance, age five at the time, had carried her infant cousin on her back over mile after wearying mile of forest track and post road.

"Move along, child," her father had chided. "Satan's minions walk in our tracks, and the slackards will feel the edge of their scalping knives!"

Goody hoped to give her child the stern love and devout teachings she had learned in her home. The unborn child already wore the sin of bastardy, and only an especially wholesome and pious child could overcome the promise of perdition that its mother had bestowed upon it.

Captain Harding had no godliness left about him and would not be allowed to come near the baby, lest his sinful influence infect the milk of wisdom that would flow from her by the grace of Almighty God.

The months had passed quickly for Goody; she had heard the whispers, of course, behind her back. Fishwives in town prattled on about a woman of her age daring to have a child, and others cruelly speculated about who the father was. In truth, no one believed that the stone-hard woman could have found anyone other than her husband willing to father a child on her. Some of the women laughed and vulgarly suggested that perhaps Goody had ordered one of the captain's sailors to do the deed, which the captain could or would not perform.

Autumn came on the heels of a plentiful and soft summer. The only happiness that Peg could find in her brood mare's existence had been the warm evenings enjoying the fireflies and the twinkling stars as she lay back on grass freshly cropped low by the sheep that were kept penned in the backyard. As the hours rolled off towards midnight, she would remember the intoxicating nights of faro and bagatelle, sipping punch with Beverly, and then her maidish thoughts would turn to the future she would share with Isaiah, which, of course, brought her back again to her plan for Goody.

The days grew shorter and the air more rarified with the promise of a fine ripe harvest, and Peg began to prepare for the day, which she knew was not far off, when she would push and sweat and bleed, forcing one life into the world while another was ushered to perdition's flame.

At regular intervals, she had dosed Goody's tea with the deadly herbs she had learned of from a half-breed granny woman that lived on the outskirts of Providence town. The old dear came into town once each week to peddle potions and poultices and the charms and baskets she wove from ash splints or anything that came to her knarled hands. She had shared her herb lore with Peg after several "chance" meetings in the market.

Peg had lied and said that they were having trouble with pests about the house and what could she poison them with? The witchwife had sold her a pouch of dried leaves and small twigs and berries and told her how much to use to kill a cat, rat, or other pesky but crafty creature. Naturally, Peg had calculated Goody's weight in cats and multiplied the dose. She smiled to herself when she thought of how many rats Goody weighed, and she imagined a great heap of the creatures monstrously making the shape of a woman.

Boiled or ground, the brew or powder was an efficient tool of destruction. A casual question had confirmed with the old woman that the poison had a cumulative effect, and that the victim did not need to ingest all the herb at once. The special blend had been decocted by the shamaness over many long years and had been tested on stray cats, barn rats, and even a neighbor's bull who was a notorious fence breaker and corn trampler. The rats expired quickly but the cats less so because of their finicky tastes.

The bull had eaten several handfuls mixed with corn and molasses before he rampaged about, demolishing a smokehouse, a haystack, and a part of an unfinished backhouse. The bull too had expired, but only after inconveniently damming a small creek with its carcass, which then resulted in the flooding of the neighbor's garden, destroying his onion crop.

The old woman had thought it a good way of eliminating an unwanted nuisance. Instead of ending one menace, however, she created another. The neighbor, unaware of the poisoning, was sure that she had put an evil spell on the bull. Angry and vengeful accusations flew about for months, and the old specter of witch trials began to flutter about, only to be extinguished in the end by the lack of evidence of evil and satanic deeds. The judge had thrown the case out and ordered the farmer to publicly apologize to the old woman.

Potent enough to level a bull, Peg had been sure that the poison would be adequate to still the clock that ticked inside the leather-hearted automaton whose jaws clacked on endlessly about piety, bastardy, and the clarity of righteousness.

Rain came sheeting in sideways and lightning lashed the skies; it was on just a night like this when Peg had planned to deceive everyone into believing Goody had given birth. Like all carefully laid plans, however, one can never account for the fates. Call it coincidence or serendipity, but on that storm-whipped night, pretty Peg's loins began to spasm, and her fluid broke. The lusty unborn was demanding exodus from the cramped confines of its mother's womb. The gods would whelp their pup when they pleased no matter what Peg Fairchild had plotted.

One part of her design had even improved; the *Indian Rose* had sailed weeks ago and wasn't due to return for even more, taking with her the stalwart Captain Harding. He had signaled his tacit approval of the plan by pretending not to notice that both women had bellies that were swelling, one with feathers and the other with his heir.

Fortunately, Peg had been alone in the backhouse when the babe made clear its intention to be born—not under a star, but a tempest. She quickly told Constance, who began to complain loudly and plainly in the presence of the old cook that she thought she was going to deliver at any moment.

For the past two weeks, Goody had been suffering from cramping of the bowels and dizziness and odd tremors and had mentioned it to the cook in passing. Little did she know that her midmorning tea had been tampered with and that she was now only a cup of tea away from the banks of the river Styx, where the silent boatman waited to ferry her over to the other side.

The elderly woman, under Goody's orders, began to prepare cloths for washing and swaddling the babe and washing the mother clean after the birth. A copper pan was fetched for collecting the afterbirth, and a length of jute string and a sharp knife to cut the fleshy tether that bound mother to child.

Goody headed straight up to her chamber, along with Peg, who did her utmost to look anything but pregnant. The old cook bustled about, making the preparations, oblivious to the fraud that had been perpetrated under her murky eyes for months.

Alone in the chamber, Peg stripped off her royal-blue-and-mustard colored petticoats, stays, stockings, and the pockets that tied about her waist. With difficulty, she climbed into the rope bed in just her chemise.

Hattie knocked at the door and started to open it but was caught up short when Peg barked an order to leave everything outside, warning her that Goody wanted no one else in the room. While this had been going on, Constance was peeling off her petticoat and fishing out the false stomach she had been wearing every day for six months. Stashing it under the immense bed, she rolled up her sleeves and then brought in the things Hattie had left as she heard the old woman descend the heavily worn and narrow back stairs to the kitchen.

Neither woman had an ounce of experience in child bearing, but both had heard it described and discussed in excruciating detail, and as they had nothing more to go on, they set to work. Goody kept Peg's brow well mopped and gave her sips of water from a wooden mug. Peg, meanwhile, tried hard not to push until she could stand it no longer.

As a girl, she had listened in while her mother and friends shared stories that had been enough to curl the young child's hair. Her mother had told a friend who was reaching her time with her first child, "Hold your breath, sputter, beat the bed, and curse your man, but don't push until you think your honey pot is going to rip in two, and then bear down with yer buttocks all the way to yer feet."

Peg screamed and clenched her dainty fists. Her damp, tangled hair framed her face and, all in all, it gave her the appearance of one of the furies. Thinking that she was being torn asunder, her caterwauling became a stifled, plaintive moan of agony, and then the pain kindly abated.

Goody stood stooped at the end of the bed. "There's the head and the shoulders! Push, girl!"

It was the shoulders clearing her Eden parts that brought a moment's respite, and then Peg took a deep breath and bore down one last time. The slimy wee frog slithered free of its maternal pond and lay writhing with a silent scream on the old gray blankets that Goody had put down.

Mistress Harding quickly tied off the cord and severed it, separating the little girl from the bloody afterbirth. Little did she know that the windpipe needed clearing and that a raucous squall was the sign that all was well. Fortunately, Goody's hands were deft at cutting, and when she realized the child wasn't breathing, she quickly plucked out a gob of caul that the babe had inhaled and had become lodged in the back of its tiny mouth.

Peg had begun to wipe down her thighs with a wet cloth; two hours of acute pain and then a final half an hour of pushing had left her weak and shaky. Slipping out of bed and nearly collapsing, she stumbled to the door and called out to Hattie to bring up a cup of tea. Goody paid her no attention whatsoever and acted as though she and the baby were the only two souls in the world. She gently rocked and cooed to the little red child who lay swaddled warmly in her arms as she wandered about the room.

A candle began to jump and flicker erratically in the cold draft near the window. The storm outside rose in roiling inky black intensity, split now and again by blinding blue flashes, followed by the crash and peal of thunder.

Again, Peg had to holler out to Hattie to bring up the tea. She pulled off her white chemise, which was stained about the hem with blood.

"Mistress, you must put down the babe and put on my chemise. We'll just take time for a cup of tea to restore us, and then you must smear some blood on yer thighs and get into that bed. Then, I'll let Hattie come in and witness the sight of you after the birth."

Peg was exhausted and weak, but she could see that the older woman was so engrossed and entranced by the child that she would be of no help.

The tea, of course, was about to be laced with the generous and final dose of the poison she had obtained. After carefully grinding the twigs and berries into a coarse powder with the brass mortar and pestle in the kitchen one late night, she had wrapped it in a page she had pulled from Goody's well-read Book of Psalms and then carefully sealed it with wax and stowed it in one of her pockets, which now lay in a tangle on the floor with her petticoats. She would retrieve the packet while she dressed, and then, when she stepped out into the hall to pick up the tray that Hattie had left, she would pour all the contents of the despicable packet into the teapot. Of course, she would drink none of it herself, but she knew it was the one pleasure that Goody enjoyed.

Goody had slipped the bloodied chemise over her head, and then laid back in the cherry wood rope bed to enjoy a quiet moment with the baby and a cup of tea before they brought Hattie up to unwittingly bear false witness. Peg had taken the baby into her own weary arms as Goodwife Harding arranged herself in the pillows like Bathsheba. She sipped quietly at her tea for several minutes with a content expression on her face, and it seemed to Peg that she was viewing something very far off and visible only to herself.

"What do you think of my beautiful daughter?" she asked Peg as though Peg were seeing the child for the first time and had nothing to do with it.

Before Peggy could answer, Goody's legs shot out ridged, her arms flew up into the air, propelling the cup across the room, and her body shook violently for several long breaths, and then her eyes rolled slowly back up into her head until only the whites could be seen.

Peg laid the baby down in a deep oval basket that had been prepared for just that purpose and stepped over to the cumbersome old Hadley Chest where the copper pan with the afterbirth and knife sat. Wasting no time, she slid the knife up into the dead woman's loins and twisted it about in an effort to create a flow of blood. As the cooling blood trickled out, Peggy dumped the afterbirth onto the bed between Goody's knees; she smeared some of the clots onto the woman's upper thighs and then backed away to survey her work.

At that precise moment, the child sent out a loud bawl and the candle, which had been guttering so feebly in the draft, flickered and went out, casting the room into darkness while the storm outside howled on in its madness.

※

Crisp slapped the sodden three-cornered hat against his leg and gave his worn oilskin greatcoat a shake as he mounted the narrow tavern stairs. It would be morning soon, and if he was lucky, he might catch a few hours in the land of Morpheus before DeVaca awoke, and he had to explain his presence and plan a remedy.

He turned the post in the thick, hand-forged iron lock with the ornate key Miguel had given him. Pushing open the cypress wood door to the room, he instantly felt a blast of cold wet air on his face.

Lightning flashed outside the open window and revealed a slightly built man standing in the corner of the room nearest the bed. Blackness dropped over the room like a burial shroud, but the ghost of the scene remained seared on Crispin Mull's eyes. A heartbeat later, lightning flashed across the sky again, and this time, the figure from the corner could be seen trying to make for the upraised window.

Crispin rushed forward, pulling his cutlass and thrusting it forward as he plunged into the darkness. Trepan heard the lieutenant's boots on the boards and spun around, dropping into a crouch with his dagger held up and out.

Again, blue light lanced through the room, and Crisp saw the strangler crouching in front of the dripping sill. He dropped the point of his sword and felt it flex a second later as it sank into wool wrapped meat.

Trepan cursed and slashed about wildly with his dagger but cut only the unblooding darkness. Crispin held the assassin pinned against the white painted boards of the wall and kicked out with his booted right foot, striking the murderer in the breastbone and stomach with rib-cracking blows.

He heard the knife clatter to the floor. A brilliant burst of lightning showed him the manslayer slumped against the wall, his chest heaving. Crisp reached down with his left hand and caught Trepan about the throat and began pulling him to his feet, even as he withdrew the sword from the wounded man's shoulder. He cast his sword backwards and grabbed the seat of the fellow's grimed breeches with his now free right hand, and then with a quick and mighty shove, he ran the killer out of the open window.

As Trepan's heels exited the portal, he grunted a foul epithet, and a second later, there was the sound of something very heavy and meaty landing in a very shallow puddle on the cobbled street two stories below.

Lighting the candle that sat on the stand next to the bed with his flint and steel, Crisp could see that DeVaca's blankets were soaked with copious amounts of blood. Pulling back the man's collar, he saw that Red Mike would never see the chance to make amends to his dear mother.

Turning back to the window, Mull could see as well that there was a large rope tied fast to the leg of the bed and that the length of hemp led out the window. Sticking his head out into the hurricane, he could just make out the treasure chest dangling barely above the window of the room below, swaying in the wind.

He was unsure how the thief had manhandled the treasure out the window, but in the next flash, he could see a cart and pony waiting in the street below. Trepan had missed striking the farm cart by inches and lay sprawled in the street behind the tailboard. Remarkably, the animal had not spooked and resignedly stood with its head down as the storm and death raged on above it.

Crispin knew at once that if he stayed put or alerted the innkeeper to the murderous events, it must come out that he was in league with DeVaca to collect the ransom. There was no way that he could maintain his anonymity or the ruse that he was the Spaniard's shipmate. No one had more right to the treasure than he, and there was no good sense in leaving it slung over the street, just waiting to be discovered by some passing carpenter or oysterman.

With all his youthful strength, and his feet braced against the wall, he was only barely able to lower the trunk the rest of the way to the street quietly. *The assassin was obviously much stronger than he had appeared*, thought Crisp. He was quite glad that he had not had to grapple with the lapidator.

He rooted about in DeVaca's leather covered sea chest and helped himself to the clothing and items he fancied. At last, slipping a brass-mounted pistol and his well-notched cutlass into the broad belt he wore over his waistcoat, he bid the dead captain a fond and final farewell. He was truly sorry that the bold man was dead. They had become good friends, but there was nothing for it now but to save his own reputation and, if possible, make himself deliriously rich with the same stroke.

When he got to the street, Crispin found the cart, but Trepan's broken body was gone. *Damn and blast*, he thought as he leaped up onto the cart and took up the reins.

Trepan staggered painfully toward the waterfront, his one arm broken and the other stabbed through and, dragging along as well, a badly fractured right leg. One side of his already less than handsome visage was hideously bruised and bleeding from several places. Every breath was agony from his ribs, which had snapped like twigs under the kicks administered by the English officer.

Of course, the rain was pouring down so fast that it washed away most of the gore, and he couldn't see his hand in front of his face in the darkness and rain, so he had to grope his way by memory. Occasional bolts sent down from Olympus would light up the heavens, allowing him to steer only a little more surely.

At last, coming to the pier, he crabbed his way up a stack of crates and burrowed under the tarp that covered the uppermost tier. Waves like small watery mountains smashed over the end of docks and threatened to inundate the entire area, including the customs house and warehouses full of goods.

Trepan, of course, was in such hurt that he cared little if he died in the night from his injuries or was drowned in the wrath of the deluge.

How, he wondered, had it all gone wrong so quickly? The storm had hidden his every movement, and DeVaca had only flinched but once as Trepan stabbed the dagger deep into the interior of the sleeper's skull. With the treasure halfway to the street, he had been as sure as the ebb and flow of the tides that by morning, he would be richer than Croesus.

The pain was excruciating, and in the morning, rather than being wealthy beyond his wildest dreams, he would be a soaked and battered wharf rat, huddled under a saturated canvass, licking his wounds like vermin that had fought a losing battle with an ill-tempered mongrel. The young blade would pay.

No one had administered a beating or kicked him like a dog in many long years, and Trepan was angry and hateful for the first time in the thirty-five years since Granny Scopes had gouged out his eye. The gold was still a goal worth following, but now the revenge he sought ran deeper and hotter than even his avarice.

THE GIANT AND HIS LOVELIES

Crispin Mull presently had two problems, not least of which was that the fellow he had pitched out of the window in Captain DeVaca's room was clearly not dead. Corpses simply don't get up and just wander away in the middle of a raging storm. Driving through the rain and wind had given Crispin little time to consider his options, yet he knew that in order to secure the coin and distance himself from the bloody deeds at the Gordon's Tavern, he needed to get free of Charlestowne and remain discreetly out of sight for a day or two.

He drove the pony through the floodwaters that rose nearly to its rear hocks, but finally had to admit to himself and the poor soaking beast that they could go no further. They had come to a creek that ordinarily cut the road without a bridge and could be stepped across by a tall man with a single stride in high summer. This night, it was a rushing torrent that would sweep away man, pony, cart, and gold to where Crisp least wanted to be—the sea.

Slowly and carefully backing the pony and cart away from the irresistible current, Crisp peered into the maelstrom and spied, not far off the road, a feeble glow. It was a barn on a slight rise where he prayed he might take shelter. A lantern glowed brightly through the crack of the closed doors, so surely, someone else was also sheltering within.

Off the left end of the small barn was a lean-to affair with a shake roof flanked on two sides by a rail fence and with a gate at the end nearest Crisp. Opening the gate, he could see that no animal resided there at the moment, but from the dung that floated in the several inches of standing water that had collected, he guessed it was commonly a horse stall. The pony gladly walked in, relieved to be out of the worst of the weather. No doubt that had the poor dumb beast been able to talk, he would have cursed Crispin Mull for a fool for being out on a night like this.

Leaving the back half of the cart sticking out into the storm, Crisp tied the reins off to one of the rails and slopped his way back out to the two large doors of the main barn. He pulled off his hat and put his eye up to the crack of the door, hoping to gain some insight into whom and what was within.

What he saw was something of a shock to his wits and nearly obliterated his grasp of the situation he was in, what with the treasure and the storm and all.

Sitting inside the barn comfortably ensconced in the soft golden straw with a lantern sitting beside him on a stump was a giant conversing quietly with six large slavering hounds arrayed in a semicircle before him. The giant was quartering broadside away from Crispin and was talking and laughing in moderate tones, thoroughly engrossed in telling a story to the enraptured pack. Crispin stood rooted to the spot with his jaw nearly scraping his boot tops. The deafening roar of the storm drowned out what the man was saying, but the hounds who sat up on their haunches seemed to be giving the giant all of their canine attention.

Finally, he tipped back his shaggy head and chuckled merrily and, reaching into his pockets, pulled out a handful of something, which he tossed to each of the hounds in turn. When he stood up and stretched, Crispin estimated his height at seven feet, and his girth was immense. The fellow must weigh as much as twenty-five stone or better.

He was wearing a greatcoat of spruce green wool and had on leather leggings gartered at the knee with strips of blue wool; the leggings went halfway up his thigh and covered his lower leg, protecting his red worsted wool stockings. Underneath the greatcoat, which was thrown open, he seemed to be wearing a natural linen wagoner's smock tucked into the deerskin breeches with a formerly elegant emerald-green brocade waistcoat over the top of it all and belted with a broad leather strap. Hanging from the belt was a superb bone handled hunting knife, a smallish pouch of bearskin, which hung hair side out under the buckle and next to a handsome Damascus steel war hatchet. His once flame red beard was shot with gray, and hung nearly to his chest. The backs of his massive hands were covered with a tracery of old scars and new scabs.

"Come on, my lovelies, time to bed down. Enough of stories. Tomorrow the bear wait for us, and if we're damn lucky, maybe a hugeous braw tom catamount."

The giant pulled on the ears of a big male hound. "Banquo, ye fool, don't be grabbin''im by the tail, or Meester cat will lay ye down fer gude."

He reached over and patted the heads of two lean black and tan marked dogs. "Juliet, Brutus, when ye hit tha track, ye let us know an' I swear by St. Andrew's holy robes, I'll not let ye down. I fancy a fine brawl tomorrow, an' I guarantee ye with one shot I'll lay out tom or boar an a feast ye'll have, but it's fer sartin that catamounts fight better and bears taste better, so I leave it to you which ye'd prefer. Good night, ma beauties."

Going around to the end of the barn, opposite the lean-to, Crisp found an open window without panes and heaved his sodden frame over the sill. He closed the rough board shutter after himself. He was standing in a tack room with harnesses and odd wagon parts; he could just see the lantern around the corner. As he was slipping quietly up to the doorway that led into the main part of the barn, Crispin stifled a sneeze that was brought on by the dust and chaff of hay.

The lantern winked out, and the whole barn was cast into darkness. Just before the flame had been extinguished, he had seen the ladder close at hand that lead to the haymow over his head. As quietly as possible, lest he wake the sleeping dogs, Crisp ascended to the mow where he shed his outer layers of clothing and burrowed under the fodder that lay piled deep about.

Throughout the night, he was awakened by the screech and snap of shingles being ripped loose and the rattling of the doors in the wind as they strained against the bar. At least, he was dry and reasonably warm. He thanked his lucky star that he hadn't remained on the beach, waiting for the storm to blow itself out nor that he had tried to brave the swollen brook. The chest full of specie would be safe from the storm and the giant until morning, and barring bad luck, he and the resolute pony should be able to pick their way around the flood once the winds and rain died back.

At dawn's break, the sun was well hid behind the overcast and muddy sky that drizzled still. The winds were gone, and the floodwaters slowly began to subside, and the world looked less like the stage of Shakespeare's *The Tempest* and more like the Carolina coast that it was. Crisp sat up and tousled the straw out of his hair and began to yawn loudly before he remembered where he was and who was below.

The giant stood leaning on his sizeable Dutch wall gun, looking up at Crispin while the hounds lay patiently and adoringly at his feet.

"You've naught to fear. I'll wait fer ye to dress yerself afore I cut loose the hoons," said the giant.

From the smile on his face and the relaxed attitude of the dogs, Crisp was certain that he was not about to be torn asunder. The priming in his pistol was soaked at any rate, and no doubt, he would have to pull the charge. Still, he didn't want to descend to the main floor without a weapon, no matter how friendly the giant and his pack seemed. He fished the cutlass out of the hay and made a show of sticking it in his belt before he gathered up his coat and climbed down the ladder.

Once he was standing on the main floor, Crispin cleared his throat and tugged at his sleeves as though, somehow, this were going to make his appearance more presentable. He was entirely unsure of how to introduce himself. Giving his rank might be an announcement to the world of his presence, and how would he explain why he was out of uniform and in possession of an absolutely fabulous fortune? The problem was solved for him.

"Hector Bohemund Griffin at yer service!" The giant, still holding his oversized musket, bowed at the waist and swept the floor with his cocked hat. "Ma friends an' I have few ootside of these braw hoons. Call me Griff, an' in case yer wonderin' where I hail from, I'll till ye. I was born on the side of a ben, what ye call a mountain, in Sutherland Scotland in seventeen and seven, but I come here nine years ago after Prince Charles Edward Stewart was driven oot of Scotland in wimmen's petticoats. I come to Maryland with Alexander Buchanan. Fer the last seven years, I been chasin' bears, catamounts, an' wolves. An' there is no match fer maself an' this howlin pack of lovelies."

Hector stood silently, waiting for a response. Unused to long conversations with others of his own kind, he had a tendency to come on like a great hairy, untidy explosion, often leaving the other party with little to say. His immense bulk by itself left most folk stunned as it was rare for a healthy specimen of a man to exceed six feet and some few inches, and clearly, Hector was way beyond that measurement. Coupled with his sudden loquaciousness, it was daunting in the least, and it often left the recipient standing with his jaw flapping in the breeze created by the wind of Hector's mighty lungs.

Hector Bohemund Griffin was the largest and only son his mother had ever had. His six sisters were all of normal size at birth and had given their mother no more trouble than is to be expected when life is eased into the world through the portal of self-awakening.

Hector's mother was gathering wool from thistle heads on the side of a mountain when the jolly lad made it known that he wished to enter the fray. Before she could make it back to the stone cottage high in the misty heather, the lad had begun to breech. Knowing that both her life and the bairn's were forfeit unless she did something quickly, in a shallow squat, Rose Griffin reached down between her thighs and pulled the silent child from her own womb. The cord was tangled all about the grand bloody bairn, and she feared both she and he would die. Taking the cord in her teeth, she bit it through and unwound the fetters, tying it off with a bit of thread she had unraveled from her own woolen petticoat.

Lying back on the heather with a stone for a pillow and the silent boy upon her chest, Rose Griffin gently crossed the boundary between this life and the next, and as her clay chilled, the boy nuzzled and rooted at the cooling teat. Rose Griffin had saved her boy, and both would be found just after sunset when her husband and the older girls went searching with torches, fearing the worst. All Ian Griffin's clansmen were sure that his boy was the biggest they had ever seen, and word went out that Rose Griffin had died giving birth to a champion.

"I see," said Crispin a bit doubtfully. "Since we are being completely honest upon our first meeting, let me say you are the largest fellow that I believe I've ever seen."

"Ah, that is likely true enoof. I've niver met ma match. Well, ma hoons an' I have an appointment with a bear, so I'll leave ye ta yerself. The farmer that owns this byre is in towne. He was trapped there by the storm, nay doubt, as he did not return in the evening as he told me he would. I'm sure he'd no mind yer stayin here, but he has the tendency to be a bit rash, an' he might just shoot or send fer the sheriff afore he thinks ta ask what yer aboot. I dinna mean ta horn in, but if ye dinna mind dried bear meat, we could mayhap break our fast together?"

"Yes, well, you see, I'm heading up the coast. I've a pony and cart outside, if he didn't drown last night," replied Crisp. "And I'm rather afraid we would only slow you down in making your appointment."

"Ah," said Hector again. "I see it's to be that way then. I should've known when ye didna give yer name. Is it ma size then? Most wee men are that way—a bit sketchy aboot bein' with a great heap like maself, I mean. I'd no hurt ye. I haven't eaten a man in at least two years. The small bones were always gettin' caught in ma teeth, and I give up livin' in caves and waylayin' travelers when I left Scotland."

Hector's attempt at humor was not lost on Crispin, and after a moment's reconsideration, he agreed to eat with the well-armed giant but only after they had found someplace more private than the soon-to-return farmer's barn. Crispin feared anyone learning his identity before he could secure the chest and sort out how best to report himself free of his "captors."

The pony had indeed survived the night, and Crisp gave it a drink from the trough along with some purloined hay from the mow, and then he and Hector mounted the seat. The poor pony was dragging nearly seven hundred pounds through the mud, and in places, Hector had to get down to help push the cart through the morass that was left in the wake of the storm. The hounds trotted happily along behind, mostly staying off the road and ranging alongside through the brush and trees, hoping to pick up a stray scent.

By midmorning, the light drizzle had stopped, and they were well clear of the outlying farms that gathered around Charlestowne for the sake of business. The woods grew more mature, and by noon, Hector advised a halt. Both men had gnawed away at the dried bear meat and had forgotten to stop earlier.

The conversation had revolved mostly around the hurricane, the road conditions, and the hunter's hounds. Crispin had introduced himself while ruminating on a large piece of flat, wind-dried meat, remembering, of course, to leave off his rank. The leathery flesh was tough but settled well on his empty belly. He had remembered, after several mouthfuls, that he had some boiled eggs and cheese in his sack, and these he shared with the giant. Hector threw each dog a handful of the dried meat when they broke from their travel and labors, and he pulled a flask of rum from his canvass knapsack, which lay under the seat.

All in all, Crispin was in better shape than he had hoped the night before. Without Hector, he could never have driven the roads until the sun had been out for several days to dry up the mud some. Certainly, the provisions were nothing to sing about, but his belly was full, and Charlestowne lay behind him, and with this latter-day Goliath and his dogs accompanying him, he had little to fear from even the most desperate man or beast.

"I must needs tell ye," said the highlander as they sat on a log at the side of the road. "I am old enoof to be yer da. So I've no fear of insultin' ye when I tell ye that yer a liar and, no doubt, runnin' from the law."

Crisp was quite taken aback at the bluntness of the giant and at the astuteness of his guess. He jumped up from the log and stepped back, afraid that Hector meant to lay hands on him for some sort of ill perceived reward.

"I may be young enough to be your son, but that gives you no right to basely insult me, and as a matter of fact, I am not running from the law. In fact, I am seeking out the law after I have taken care of several things. What exactly do you think I've lied about?" rebounded Crispin, putting his hand unconsciously on his cutlass and backing away from Hector.

"Take yer hand off a yer blade. There's naught to be afeared of. The only reason I say yer lyin is that yer fine speech does no match yer." He gestured up and down Crispin's person. "Well, ye look rather like a highwayman or a pirate. And while I'm not a gentleman maself, I am somewhat careful the company I keep, lest ma throat is slit in the night."

"Well, jolly good for you!" Crispin was beginning to feel the heat rising in his blood. He hadn't been near a looking glass in some time and was not aware of his state of dishabille. "I am no cutthroat or vagabond, and if anyone has pause to think here, I should think it was me! After all, you're the giant with a bloody rampart gun and pack of bloodthirsty killers, and I'm only a lonely traveler!"

"I knew it! I knew it! I knew ya'd hold ma size against me. It's alwas tha way. Everyone thinks because I'm big that I'm either goin' to eat them whole or I'm too stupid ta do simple sums. By tha way, ye've naught answered fer why a gentleman is wearin grave digger's clothes?"

Crispin explained that he could not explain at the moment as he was under a secret oath and that his sartorial statement was a bit care worn due to his clothes being lost in the storm. Hector asked why he didn't have a spare set in his trunk, and Crispin divulged that the trunk did not belong to him, but that he was guarding it and delivering it to the owner and that it contained nothing more than family mementos and books.

This, of course, was a ridiculous fabrication, as any nitwit could guess that family momentos didn't weigh half enough to sink the cart in the mud, and why would they need guarding in the first place? Luckily for Crispin, Hector was gracious enough not to press for a more plausible answer.

They spent the rest of the day trundling northward, and while the ground conditions were too plashy for the hounds to pick up a scent, it was not for lack of trying. The two men agreed to remain traveling companions for the next several days, at least, or until Hector's four-legged companions struck a hot track. Each man had his own reasons for letting their disagreement rest without further debate. Crisp reasoned that he was safer with the giant than without, and Hector craved companionship and was willing to suffer the younger man's reticence and equivocation.

Their progress was slow. The road was poor in condition and had turned to a sticky mass, necessitating occasional stops to rock free the cart or to push the cumbersome vehicle past particularly nasty stretches. Crisp managed to convince the huntsman on several occasions that the chest did not weigh enough to merit its removal. He was simply terrified that, if it were dropped or jostled, Hector would learn the true nature of the contents, and that he would then have to confess the truth or be made a victim of robbery from the very man whose protection he was hoping for.

During the night of the first day on the road, Crisp had pulled the charge from his pistol and reloaded it while Hector looked on. Ironically, Crispin thought that there was no harm in letting the fellow see that he was armed and able to defend himself though Crisp was unsure if a pistol ball was capable of felling a giant.

The lucky shot that had brought low Shep Wells (who was no Lilliputian) was just that, and in the years since that encounter at the Black Dragoon, Crisp had come to realize that, although he had successfully killed two men, in both cases, it had been sheer luck. His most recent combat in DeVaca's room had made him even more aware of the resilience of the human form. The pistol was a deterrent, but unless he managed to shoot Hector in the head or heart, he would likely be smashed to flinders by those massive paws before the giant succumbed.

As long as the treasure remained under lock and key, he and Hector were unlikely to come to blows; and if Hector had to smash anything to smithereens, it would hopefully be a bear or a catamount. Crispin was quickly learning that the price of great wealth was distrust of your fellow man. Any fool who trusted in friendship, to say nothing of mere acquaintance, when over eight thousand pounds sterling was at stake, was more simple witted than the average lump of sod.

The travelers were no more than forty miles north of Charlestowne at dawn when the hounds struck a track.

Hector blew the halloo upon his horn and bellowed out, "Cry havoc, and let slip the dogs of war! It's Shakespeare ye know" as he piled out of the cart and crashed through the brush and trees, fast on the heels of the last two dogs, Ajax and Cleopatra, who were running neck and neck.

Crispin was unsure what to do. The giant had left his canvass pack, so he couldn't just go on and deprive the man of his goods, and besides, without Hector, he was far more prone to attack. He pulled the cart off the track into a palmetto grove that was less dense than the woods surrounding it. Then, tying off the pony, he traced the wheel ruts back down the road where he found a welter of dog tracks and what was clearly a bear track as it differed in both size and shape from the footprints of the hounds.

Crisp had seen a bear once being led about on a silver chain in Edinburgh. The poor creature was part of a traveling act and entertained the crowd with its antics, rolling about atop a gaily-painted ball. His only other experience with bears had been the furry bearskin mitered hats worn by the Grenadier Company of the Fifty-Sixth.

Finding the spot where they had left the road, Crisp plunged into the undercover, and then paused to listen when he found a small clearing where he could stand upright. The giant's hunt horn sounded several hundred yards to the right front, and the hounds could scarcely be heard in the distance, hundreds of yards beyond where the horn blast had come from.

Crisp had foolishly brought along his cutlass. Having no notion of the forest or of bear hunting, he had thought it a fair substitute for a hunting sword. He was completely unaware that in bear hunting with hounds; the huntsman went as unencumbered as possible so that they could traverse the rugged countryside and keep the pack within hearing until the bruin either treed or was brought to bay. As he dashed through the trees, dodging deadfalls and pools of standing water, the old blade kept getting caught in the creepers and deadwood. His hat was knocked from his head so often that he finally gave up and carried it in his hand.

At last, he could see Hector a few hundred feet ahead of him, standing quietly to listen to the pack give voice. They had been slowly climbing until they were on a low ridge covered with white oaks, and the brown nuts were already thick upon the ground, even though it was only late September. Coastal Carolina could boast no great mountains, but its swamps and waterways were an endless labyrinth capable of confounding even the most experienced woodsman.

Hector stood with his head cocked, listening intently to the music of the hounds. He had leaned the enormous musket against a stump and was lighting his stub of a white clay cutty pipe.

"Ma compass and the sun agree. They've turned north from west, and by the way their choppin', I'd say that they're gonna tree any time now. As I told ye, each dog in the pack has its own special purpose." He drew long on the pipe, pointing the stem of it towards the sound of the dogs before he continued.

"Juliet and Brutus are the strike dogs. They only run a hot track. Banquo runs cold nosed, and if the track gets thin, he can keep with it when they lose it. Ajax and Cleopatra are fearless at the kill. Banquo has a notion to get in the way of tooth an claw. Now, Friar Lawrence should be barkin' tree any minute. When ye hear a choppy mouthed dog that ye think will never hold his tongue, that's Friar Lawrence, and he lets me know to come on fast, 'cause they've bayed up or treed a bear or panther, an' it's up to me to git there straight away an shoot it dead, or there'll be hounds to bury in the marnin. I planted Julius Caesar two months ago. He got too close to a cornered catamount an' the beast tore him wide open. He was a brave hound."

Hector picked up the great weapon and started trotting in the direction of the hounds, not waiting or looking back to see if Crisp was coming, all his attention now on the cry of the dogs.

PLANS RIPEN

The mourners had gone to their homes, what pitiful few there were, and Isaiah dropped wearily into a wainscot chair pulled before the banked fire. Gone for months, he had sailed home to find that Constance had "perished" in childbed. He, of course, knew that Peggy had borne his child, but the community and the family had believed Constance's death normal and hadn't been in the least surprised that a woman of her years should die giving birth.

Standing before her captain like a servant awaiting orders, Peggy had explained to him that the poor woman had simply been overtaxed and unwell, as he well knew, and that the strain of it all had weakened her, and that she had collapsed the night of the birth in the midst of the deception.

She had no choice but to carry out the plan. Only now, everyone must believe that Goodwife Harding had sadly died, unable to even know her own child. The reputation of the family was at stake, and Goody Harding would not have wanted the truth known by the community, and after all, Peg was only looking after the captain's future and the future of their child, and protecting his dear wife's untarnished reputation.

"Rot! I'm too damned tired for this dancing, Peg. The woman died because she had a heart of stone and blood of ice water. I'm sure she despised you more than I, and I am sure she bore me no love. If you, of all people, think I shall miss her overmuch, then you are greatly mistaken. I came to you all those nights because you made me feel welcome in your presence, and you are far more fetching than that hatchet faced shrew ever was. I'm going to bed. Are you coming or not?"

"I am flattered, sir, but what will people think if they know you are making merry with your maid?" asked Peg with mock demure.

"Take yourself to my chamber," he said imperiously, pointing to the stairs. "Hattie has gone to her sleep already. I heard her finish the cleaning and climb the stairs near an hour ago. Tomorrow, you may fix my breakfast before she awakes, and no one will ever be the wiser." He winked roguishly and was quite unsure whether he should order her again or coax her.

"Is that what you think of me then? I bear your child and hide your sins from the world as well, and all I get is to make his 'lordship' breakfast and to cool his sword?" She spat out the last part with venom of sarcasm.

Isaiah looked shocked that Peggy would speak out like this. In his experience, she had been a willing filly who curtsied coquettishly, showing a daring bit of bosom and who waited upon him slavishly.

"Damn me! You think you have a right to more, don't you? Mayhap you do. I will think on it after you have cooled my sword. Otherwise, you can go to the eaves with Hattie after I've givin you a hiding." He said this last with mock ferocity, but Peg was not at all sure he didn't mean it in some other more brutal way.

"I'll hold this out," said he, straightening the fronts of his waistcoat. "Tomorrow we can talk about your continued future in this household."

The wet nurse happened to live several streets over from Harding House and had offered to take baby Caroline to her home each evening to be suckled. She would then return with both her own infant son, Thaddeus, and the captain's daughter in the morning. Without the obvious presence of a wet nurse, the truth would be known about Peg and the captain. Not only was it imperative to the deception of the town, but Pretty Peg's milk had dried up in a matter of days without a babe supping at her tender breast. Patience Ackerman spent her days watching over the children and helping Peg and Hattie perform the menial chores.

Before the captain's return, one of Goodwife Harding's dour cousins, Samuel Goore, had come to stay and watch over the estate until the master of the house should return. During those weeks, Patty and Peggy had become friendly and shared in the chores equally, but when Isaiah returned, Peg had become uppish and played the part of mistress of the house, ordering about Hattie and the nurse and doing less than was typically her share. If Isaiah noticed or cared, he didn't show it; and for all purposes, it appeared that he approved of the situation. When he had been settled in for a day or two, Peg even began to take her evening meal with the captain.

"You have mastered the crew," commented Isaiah wryly as he cut into the hot, juicy roast. "And they seem unlikely to mutiny. Where do you intend to take your ship?"

Peggy pointedly ignored the metaphor. "I do not know what you are talking about, sir. You have filled a void whenever it seemed it fit to you. Am I not to prosper by your example?"

"Aye! That you are, dear woman!" He stood at the end of the long maple trestle table and pushed back his plate and cleared his throat. "I had prepared a better plan last night in my head. I know I promised you several days ago that we would talk about your future in this household, and we did not. That is because I had to decide for myself what was best to do for little Caroline and the future of Harding house."

Peg looked like she wanted to speak. She too put down her fork, pushed her staffodshire plate back, and started to open her mouth to speak. Isaiah quickly waved her silent and gestured abruptly for her to remain seated.

"I have observed you taking things in hand and have decided to set aside your indenture and take you to wife. You're beautiful, and you have more grace about you than my wife ever dreamed of. You make an excellent hostess, and I'm sure you could give me a son or two. What do ye say, Peggy?"

Propriety and decency demanded that Isaiah wait a year and allow blooms and grasses to grow over the final resting place of his wife, but with little Caroline to think of, relatives and the town would likely forgive him if he took a wife before the lengthy period had passed. Waiting months and slowly making clear his intentions towards Peggy public would smooth the path and make her life less troubled. Polite society would accept, if not forget, that not long before, she had been his servant. It was not unheard of for men to marry women in service, and in time, some few women would even carve out their own place amongst the dames and misses of Providence. Maintaining the charade of decency meant that Peg must go each night with Hattie to the eaves and then wait until the poor old bird was snoring soundly to sneak silently down to the second floor and crawl, naked as Venus, into Harding's bed.

Of course, Peg wanted everyone to think that she was devoted to and in love with the captain so that when she acted on the second half of her devilish plot, no one would think her guilty in any part.

Trepan's wounds had healed admirably, with the notable exception of his right leg, which remained stiff and caused him to limp painfully. His pierced shoulder and broken arm had neatly healed in a few weeks under the care of an old ship's surgeon whom he had to pay handsomely for both services and ensured silence.

Days after he had reckoned himself nearly healed and running short on funds, Trepan had sneaked back into the doctor's home and stole back every last tarnished penny he had paid the unwise old fool, along with a tidy profit snitched from the physician's palsied fingers while he slept.

Aware that the thieving lieutenant would likely travel northward, the assassin decided upon a plan that would place him in the van with a chance to head off the bullying officer who had so bluffly relieved him of DeVaca's gold. Having learned something of their scheme to enrich themselves at government expense, Trepan suspected that the young lieutenant's next move would be to report himself to his regiment. Never one to undertake a complicated plot without ample planning and desirous of an enriching resolution, Trepan enquired into the disposition of the Fifty-Sixth of foot.

Their temporary cantonments, he learned, were at New York until the weather broke on the far end of winter. The flank companies were posted to a battalion that would undertake a fair weather campaign in the northern marches of the old Dutch colony. The string of wooden forts along the Hudson River was woefully undermanned and provided the only protection for Albany and the lower districts of New York. The stalwart red-coated regiments of the line, combined with the brave, but rustic, provincial militia, would stand guard against the incursions of the sneaky French Canadian irregulars and their wildly painted savage allies, wrapped in the furs of the lynx and wolf. The flank companies of the Fifty-Sixth would march northward and take up their vigilant watch along the Hudson while Barley Blanchard and the balance of the regiment would remain in the environs near Fort George in lower New York, trying to remain warm and reasonably well distracted.

Trepan took a brig to Philadelphia, paying for his passage with a garnet ring he had "borrowed" from the doctor. Leaning heavily on his walking stick, Trepan had roved about the city of friends, trying to pick a pocket or two or three in order to add to his account. Coach fare from Philadelphia to New York was quite dear when one factored in lodgings, and he had no wish to arrive broke.

Careful that nothing of the goings on in Charlestowne should be attached to him, Trepan decided not to take ship from Philadelphia to New York on the simple wisdom that word of the murders could reach there before him and that he might be detained, along with anyone else coming from the southern colonies. Nothing good would be gained from a lack of caution.

The walking stick, on which he now relied, like all his accoutrements, had more about it than outward appearances gave away. The hardwood shaft hid a secret surprise for meddlesome officers or any that made the mistake of thinking that the one-eyed gimp was a soft target. Concealed within was an eighteen-inch triangular dagger that came to a needle sharp terminus. The figural handle of the dagger and the cane were one and the same, a vicious fanged snake's head carved from ivory with yellow glass beads for eyes.

Trepan had "borrowed" this also from an innocent; however, the poor fellow had not fared as well as the doctor. A gurgling sound from the throat of the traveling actor had signaled his more than quiet discomfort. He was discovered a day later in the Charlestowne alley, where he had gone to relieve himself of the previous night's bread, behind a stack of empty brine barrels. Apparently, the wraith maker was no infatuate of the theater, or else, he coveted the cane more than the theaterian's performance of Hamlet's soliloquy. The actor wore a bloody smile on his neck that went from ear to ear and allowed his head to fold back at an obscene angle. The cane, which had toured with the mummer on three continents and an even half-dozen island ports, was missing along with his pitiful purse and his badly worn peach-colored sateen breeches.

Two murders in Charlestowne in one month's time had the sheriff and the powers that be in a proper turmoil with questions being asked on all sides and people afraid to go to their beds or out into the streets after night had fallen. Everyone knew an assassin haunted the shadows. He had struck at Gordon's Tavern and had murdered a hapless thespian, and it would be weeks before anyone went abroad after dark, most especially those who wore fancy breeches.

Trepan eventually found he could put the stick to more than one good purpose. He had inadvertently twisted the head of the stick, daydreaming about what he planned to do to

Crispin Mull when he caught up with him, and out popped the gleaming blade.

The trip from Philadelphia to New York consumed only several days, and when, at last, New York lay at coach step, the winded team stood heads down, with foam gathering about their bits, blowing steam from flaring nostrils. Trepan began his explorations by taking a deep breath, ripe with the many smells of the city. He tucked the walking stick under his arm and limped about the municipium, ignoring the pain in his leg and poking into every alley, basement, and courtyard he could.

The odor of horse dung commingled with the haze of wood smoke, and the stench of slop jars bred with the aroma of the sea (which was itself a blend) created a distinctly urban potpourri that whisked his blackened soul back to London for a moment.

A cacophony of sounds issued from the damp cobblestone streets. The strains of mongers calling out their wares, the staccato bleating of sheep in the middle of the Broadway and away off to the west, the hammering of a mallet knocking up a new building could all be heard on the cold misty morning air. The creak and rattle of wagonloads rumbling in with the day's supply of produce and firewood for the hungry citizenry and the lowing of oxen added to the clamorous din.

Long ago, the finest and most convenient forests had been felled to build stores, homes, and churches where the bells tolled and called the dutiful to worship, and also for spindly fences to keep out the wild animals or for fat, splintery chunks of fuel to burn in the great brick and stone fireplaces.

The woods now were far out of town, away beyond the green pastures and verdant fields. Nearly all the residents of New York had to pay to have firewood brought into the burgeoning city unless, of course, they were wealthy enough to own a country house and a town home, in which case the wood was sent in from the country house. Only a smattering of old Dutch Patroons and Crown officials could afford such extravagance.

While the provincial town was only a tiny fraction the size of mighty London, it served as a temporary but adequate replacement for what Trepan liked to think of as his old hunting grounds. Charlestowne had been little more than a backward village by his grimy, malodorous standards, but at last, he was back amongst the haze and bustle that veiled an underworld that he called home.

※

The sign that hung from a rusting wrought iron bracket, above the double door, read, Hermann and Werth—Ships Stores and Carters. A small single door had been cut within the large left-hand side of the twin portals. Clearly, when the two large gate-like doors were opened, a wagon could be pulled within for the loading and unloading of materials.

Trepan had gravitated towards the waterfront as usual, knowing that there, he could find work and information and that his presence would go unremarked amidst the motley collection of sailors, dockworkers, and fisherman.

He slipped into the dim cavern of the warehouse and then, stepping to the side into the deeper shadow of a great chestnut beam, waited for his eyes to adjust. Voices could be heard talking off toward the gloomy back of the building, but many piled coils of rope, some as thick as your wrist, and wooden buckets of tar, along with barrels of oakum and two empty freight wagons, lay between the assassin and the source of the conversation.

Every sneaking fox requires a lair, and Trepan was no exception. A door opened at the opposite end of the warehouse, allowing daylight to stream in and pierce the darkness, and just as quickly, it was smothered as the door clapped shut, and the voices ceased. Alone in the grayness, he began to search about as only vermin can with considerable stealth and amazing accuracy and attention to detail. Within an hour, Trepan had decided that the mezzanine loft overlooking the main floor gave him the most security with the least likelihood of being discovered.

Climbing the lone ladder, he had found great heaps of beige canvass carelessly piled about, covering the entire narrow platform, and in no time, he had selected out a sizable scrap and designated it as his future pavilion. While the loft provided only one exit, it was conversely quite simple to defend from a frontal assault.

Roaming the docks by both day and night, Trepan was assured that he could earn a wage plying his trade; and if Lieutenant Mull hove into sight, he was just as sure that the news would reach his ear quicker here in the mariners' world than anywhere else.

Herr Hermann had come to the colonies twenty years earlier, and while no great seaman himself, Hugo had a natural knack for seeing the value of things. He and his brother-in-law, Adolph Werth, had gone into business scavenging the shoreline for materials washed up from wrecks, and then that had gradually evolved into the purchasing of any hulk that they could before it sank into the harbor, salvaging everything of use and reselling it at considerable profit. Every hinge, pulley, and nail was retrieved, repaired if necessary, and resold to shipwrights and captains who found their products serviceable and cheaper than their competitors.

At last, the two frugal Rhinelanders had acquired enough wealth to build a new warehouse from their store of salvaged ships lumber. In their expanded chandlery, they added a forge for the making of all manner of wrought iron ships fixtures as well as selling new ships materials from anchors and chain to sail cloth and spars. Typical of the Teutonic race, the two men were at work by dawn and often stayed until late, burning the midnight oil.

Trepan found their comings and goings unpredictable as they bustled about the docks, frequently bringing guests back to the warehouse to share a glass and examine the inventory. Their employees were somewhat more predictable as they came in the morning at cockcrow and left before sunset unless the smith stayed late, working on a special project for a customer with an emergency.

Existing in his shadow world, Trepan was outwardly unaffected by his lack of a plain home. While he made no friends (as he trusted no one), he did have his cronies and informants with whom he shared a companionable tankard now and again. Staying late at the taverns frequented by sailors, he was often one of the last to leave. If he spied a light burning at the warehouse upon his return, he simply loitered in the darkness until the light was extinguished and the Germans had retired to their hearths. Using his key (you will recall he had a collection), he let himself in, whereupon he mounted the ladder to the loft and nestled into his Bedouin palace, using a pair of "borrowed" boat hooks and the wall to create a tent effect.

Men who practice the assassin's trade do not sleep soundly; no doubt their dreams are troubled by the quiet tread of revenge. While the lack of sleep assuredly adds to their general fever of ill will towards the world at large, it serves as a useful ward against justice and vengeance.

Hours before dawn, Trepan was up and about, slipping out of the warehouse before anyone could arrive in the morning. After performing his meager toilet (relieving himself and splashing cold salt water onto his face and hands) under a dock, he tarried near the bakers, waiting to buy the first hot brown loaf to come out of the brick ovens. More cautious than ever, Trepan was unwilling to practice the blade-for-hire trade, which had, for so many years, been his principle source of coin. Instead, he fell back on the old standby, which Granny Scopes had taught him so well under her cruel rope.

As a cutpurse and pickpocket is how he now kept himself in bread and ale with occasional splurges on meat and Madeira. New Yorkers were not as wealthy nor as numerous as Londoners, and as a rule, he limited himself to a purse every other day, lest he attract too much attention and the constabulary be forced to locate the perpetrator. Naturally, the city had its own local adherents to thievery, and he had also to be careful lest he anger them sufficiently that they take it upon themselves to eliminate an interloper.

After several weeks of acquainting himself with the regions around the waterfront and leading into the heart of the town, Trepan began hanging about the encampment of Beverly Blanchard's heroes. He pretended the part of a crippled veteran of George's War, down on his luck. For hapennies, he would hobble about the city, running errands for the officers or any of the men who could afford his toadying. Most often, he was fetching creature comforts for the gold-laced officers. While the pittance he made helped purchase libation, it also didn't prevent him from picking a single pocket, but most especially, it allowed him to listen in on the most recent crop of gossip to be making the rounds of the gathering army.

He had it from a sergeant that the colonel had been contacted a week or ten days previously by the governor of Virginia, regarding the existence of a Lt. St. Crispin Mull, bearing a Crown commission in the Fifty-Sixth regiment of foot. The sergeant, who served as Blanchard's orderly, said that the colonel had responded to the governor with a note sent by special courier, and that it was all "bloody amazing" as the young lieutenant had been "gived up for lost" when the *Wampum Belt*, the transport he had been aboard, was sunk by "a divilish storm."

Trepan, naturally and subtly, inquired as to when the courier was expected back, and whether or not there would be a celebration when the lost officer was returned as he would like to watch just to lay eyes on a fellow as lucky as all that. Did the sergeant think he might be able to get a fellow "sojer" a place to watch from, "comfortable like."

Of course, the young sergeant had taken a liking to the partly blind old gimp and agreed that if there were such an event, he would do his level best to help the former marine to watch the proceedings. He thought it was bloody terrible that a fellow who had given his eye and a piece of his leg for Crown and country should be begging pennies under the fluttering of the Union Jack.

CHASING THE PACK

Crispin was thoroughly winded when he finally caught up with the amazingly agile giant and his baying pack of courageous, foolhardy hounds. The bear had come to bay on a tiny hummock of land, amidst a riverine backwater on the far side of the ridge from which they had last listened.

The bear, a largish boar, running better than thirty stone (over four hundred pounds) had backed himself up against the roots of a cypress tree, and the foolish dogs nipped in and out, trying desperately to anger the animal more than it already was. Dodging the scythe-tipped paws, it seemed as though the dogs each dared the other to greater extremes of carelessness and insanity. The bear popped its teeth and roared into the faces of its darting and harassing tormenters.

As Hector waded through the murky waters toward the melee, the bear became even more agitated, sensing, perhaps, its own impending doom. Trying to charge out of the bugling and chopping cordon, the bear, its hackles raised, took swipe after swipe at the crazed hounds. Finally, just as Hector gained a shooting position, Banquo, the strong, braved the bruin one too many times, and a full swing of the powerful bear's awful right paw caught him smack on his ribs, staving them in and sending the dog spinning across the hummock and out into the fennish water.

Crispin watched all from the bank and stayed as clear as possible, not daring the brackish flood nor willing to wet his feet in pursuit of what was clearly a suicidal sport.

For whatever reason its poor piggish brain could summon, the bear decided that this was his best chance to break clear and put an end to this plaguesome bother. As Banquo lay wallowing and yelping in the shallows, the other dogs gave back before the ferocious king, and the bear, taking advantage of their new found wisdom, charged into the water. Whether he meant to do Hector harm, or whether the man merely stood in his path, shall never be known, but whatever the brute's motivation was, he bore down on the giant like a coal-black comet.

Hector calmly shouldered the wall gun after removing the leather frizzen cover, and slowly applied pressure to the trigger. The bear was within only a scant few yards when the massive musket roared and spewed a load of heavy shot and a great one hundred caliber ball into the bear's face. Unfortunately for Hector, the lethal ball only penetrated the thick, slack hide of the bear's withers after passing harmlessly between its ears. The scatter shot peppered its face and blinded the beast in one eye, but slowed him not a whit. Before he could even bring the huge firelock down from his shoulder, the bear had crashed into him, driving him down into the thigh deep water.

The hounds were not far behind and, in only a few seconds, were swarming over the bear's back, shoulders, and rump. The bear had planted its front feet in the giant's chest and the mountainous Scotsman was now fully submerged with only a foot here and a hand there breaking the seething surface of the water. The monster shook and twisted, trying to shake off the dogs but never took its forepaws from the hunter's chest.

Crispin, seeing all from the edge of the mere, knew that he was the massive man's only hope. Drawing his pistol from his belt, he brought it to a full cock; and then hauling forth his old Dutch cutlass, he waded toward the fray, cursing under his breath and with horrible knee-knocking trepidation. When he got within several yards of the brawl, the enraged bear became aware of his reluctant presence and, shaking its head at him, let out a defiant roar. Crisp took another step forward and then, crouching toward the water, pointed his pistol upwards to the underside of the bear's jaw, and pulled the trigger. The pistol barked and jerked, and Crisp instinctively turned his face away from the acrid smoke as the hammer fell.

Looking back toward the bear out of the corner of his eye, Crispin could see the animal sit back on its haunches and then wobble over onto its side, flopping into the water with a great splash. The hounds continued to nip and bite at the half submerged forest king, worrying it and daring it to come back from the beyond.

Crisp, realizing instantly that the bear was dead, scrambled forward and shoved his arm down into the water and, grabbing Hector's beard, pulled him to the surface, which was no mean feet because of the fellow's great size and the fact that he had been pressed into the muddy bottom by the immense weight of the bear. From the time the bear had broken out of the ring of snapping hounds until Crisp hauled forth the waterlogged giant, took far less time than it does to tell it.

Hector spluttered and coughed up mouthfuls of the brackish dregs of the swamp and finally managed to find his wits and the strength to grope about the squashy bottom until he found his musket. Calling the hounds to him and leaning on Crispin's shoulder, they staggered back to the shore, leaving the steaming corpse of the angry fat bruin lying in the swamp for the time being. Even the broken and bleeding Banquo somehow managed to rejoin his half-drowned highland master.

At last, the great black hide, heavy with water, hung dripping and steaming from the branch of a pine. A toothsome roast, sliced from the powerful hind quarter, oozed bloody juices and sizzled with little spurts as the fat rolled in greasy droplets into the fire under the spit, making the flames sputter and flare.

Hector, being a kind and gentle giant, tenderly wrapped brave Banquos's ribs with strips of linen torn from an old porridge-colored hunting smock that the hunter carried in his canvas pack. The brave hound lifted his head and licked the hand of his "braw hugeous" master as the Scot deftly swabbed the blood and bound the cracked bones.

Crispin, meanwhile, wrung the dank water from his threadbare stockings and had upended his boots on two sticks set in the ground near the fire so that they might dry by morning. He reloaded his pistol from the small gray linen bag of supplies that he carried in a pouch in the pocket of his greatcoat and checked to see that all was in order.

The other hounds—Ajax, Cleopatra, Friar Lawrence, Juliet, and Brutus—lounged about the fire, spent from the battle, their heads resting on their tails or on each other's backs.

Fortunately for Hector, his thick woolen greatcoat had kept the claws of the bear from doing more than puncturing the skin on his chest.

The remaining portion of the carcass, which was unbutchered, hung from a lone pine tree like a grisly hairless demon of the underworld. When the hunter had skinned out the head of the bear, he had also peeled off its lips and nose, leaving behind a leering snarl. The paws too had been hacked free of the body as a part of the skinning process so that the finished hide bore the weapons of the once living bear. The pelt would fetch a goodly sum, but because of its weight and size, it was quite necessary that the enormous nimrod scrape and dry the skin before transporting it any great distance. If the hide were left as it were, the process of decay would wreak havoc on the fur, and the pelt would begin to rot in a matter of days with the hair sloughing off in thick wads.

Hector had fashioned crude scrapers from thin pieces of split wood using his handsome Damascus tomahawk with its figured maple handle, and both he and the somewhat more squeamish Crispin Mull began to remove the great lumps of fat that clung to the hide. The pelt was staked to the ground in a little clearing near the fire that the giant had swept free of forest debris using a bough cut from a bush that overhung the nearby water. Sweating through the morning, they gouged and scraped, occasionally using their belt knives to separate a difficult piece of muscle until the entire hide was free of flesh and fat.

As Crisp removed the last bits of membrane, the Scot began erecting a frame of poles near the fire. Crispin threw the last of the hide flesh to the hounds and sat back to watch the Highlander at work. He tied four stout poles together in a square and then connected them with an X-shaped frame of smaller poles tied on with jute cord he carried in his pack. After an hour or so of labor, the frame was ready to receive the hide, and Crisp helped to lay it across the poles and stoke the fire to smoke and slowly dry the skin. The proximity of the hide to the fire pit had a chimney like effect, causing a draft that drew the smoke towards the hide, helping to dry it and keeping off the egg-laying flies that still buzzed about even on warm fall days.

The pony, who had been left for more than twenty-four hours, had pulled free of the sapling to which Crispin had tied him and had gotten the cart well wedged between two larger trees and stood patiently waiting for someone to rescue him. At last, they had returned to the proximity of the road with Crispin packing the hide on his back and Hector carrying the wounded dog cradled in his arms like a beloved sickly child.

Crisp admitted to the hunter that the chase had its merits as a diversion and was most assuredly a manly sport not for the meek or faint of heart. To himself, Crispin thought it also the sport of madmen and fools. It seemed to him no less dangerous than privateering, and perhaps even more so and yet, it certainly appeared less lucrative. In hindsight, he thanked the gods that the bear's hide lay in the back of the cart rather than his lying deep in the belly of the brute. It is a rare event, indeed, when a green hunter shoots an enraged bear with a single shot from a pistol and lives to tell the tale, but Lieutenant Crispin Mull was nonplussed, for, to him, it was no great feat. After all, Dame Fortune had followed him all his days.

The morning dawned cold and clear on the following day, which happened to be Crisp's twentieth birthday, though he was unaware of the auspicious occasion as he had begun to lose track of time weeks before. It was an unusually brisk day for this time of year in South Carolina, and he was completely ill attired for the frosty temperature.

Hector stamped his feet and slapped his mittened hands together as he waited for the fire to rekindle. The hounds had huddled together for warmth, and they slowly yawned and stretched in the milky dawn light. Crispin beat his thighs in an effort to warm his frozen flesh and then crouched near the feeble but growing flames to heat up his stinging cold fingertips.

He looked away with disgust as the unabashedly ill-mannered hounds began to urinate, worry at their gonads, and scratch the last of the summer's pestiferous fleas. Cleopatra alone sat like her queenly namesake, watching every move that Hector made, no doubt, unlike her namesake, waiting for a burnt scrap from the previous night's half-cooked haunch of bear venison.

"How long do you suppose it will take us to reach Williamsburg going overland now that we've no road? I don't fancy trying to live in the woods during the winter, if it's half as savage as these swamps. I reckon I am no man of the forest. Eating berries and 'possum' is fine if you're a redskin, which I am decidedly not, unless one counts the color my nose turns in this blasted chill. Does it snow much in Virginia?" asked Crispin, blowing into cupped hands and wiping his nose on a raggedy old scarf.

"It'll take weeks even if we don't do any hunting."

Hector's Scots burr seemed thicker somehow in the still morning air.

"Tha chances of us not crossing paths with a bear or catamount between here an' Wilmington, like as not, are no very gude. I fancy the hoons will pick up a scent without lookin' fer one before the next couple of days are oot. By the time we reach Williamsburg, like as not, we'll be celebratin' the birth of the Holy Child. As far as snow, it would be uncommon in these parts. If ye climb into the Bens and Crags of North Carolina or Virginny, ye'll see some snow, but ye'd be better served to worry about protectin' yer hair than keepin' yer gems warm."

Hector paused for a moment, thinking, then continued, "If ye wish, ye could take yon pony and head north by east an' ye'll make Williamsburg in a score of days if yer lucky, or ye can treble it and stay with me and hunt. If I shoot enough beasts alone, then I'll drag them on a travois maself until I have to build a cache. I can come back fer the hides with packhorses later. That pony will be carryin' a great load just bearing your mementos, but he might haul a travois with a few hides, and then with what you and I can each bear, well, I'd be more than willin' ta split seventy-thirty with ye as suitable inducement and ta save maself havin' to come back."

Crisp looked aghast and stood up, putting his hands on his hips indignantly. "What! You mean you want to give me a paltry 30 percent, and I'll be carrying your stinking furs and using my pony?"

"It's just that you've no offered me a share in yer mementos, and ye'll be needin' me an' tha hoons ta git ta Virginny, and as ye've noted, yer no a lad fer the forests, an' I doubt ye'd make it more than a week before ye got lost," said Hector smugly, feeling that he had the upper hand.

Crisp countered coldly, "Fifty-fifty or you and your lazy, ravenous, damned hounds can bark up another tree."

"Sixty-forty, an' that's as fair as ye'll git from a fellow Scot, an' ye know it!" grumbled the giant, starting to ruffle at the remarks about his beloved dogs.

Crisp knew he had best take the deal proffered by the Scot. Hector, of course, was quite right that Crisp had offered no share in his treasure, and of course, he was also correct that Crispin would require his skills to journey to Williamsburg, so the young officer had little or nothing with which to drive a bargain. Partly out of an effort to maintain the fiction of the mementos, and partly out of Scotch pride, Crisp had felt that he must drive a deal with the hunter. It was quite clear already that Hector Griffin had no delusions about the true nature of the contents of the chest although Crispin was quite unsure how or when the man had learned this. So while both men knew the truth, they continued to refer to the gold as mementos, and Crisp maintained the failed fiction that he was some sort of wandering laborer, carting mementos to a mysterious customer in Virginia's capital without knowledge of the roads or the obvious lack thereof.

Now the road had given way to a track and the track to an Indian trace. Crispin and Hector had unharnessed the pony and, using Hector's tomahawk, had disassembled the thills between which the pony stood. Using a few of the boards that made up the slatted sides of the cart, they constructed a useful travois upon which they could place the trunk and the bear hide and still have room left over for poor old Banquo.

As the days progressed and autumn grew on with the frigid nights more of a regular occurrence, Crispin and Hector became better acquainted though the fraud concerning Crisp's current situation still stood between them.

Hector, of necessity, taught him the finer points of bear and panther hunting, and Crispin quickly became an expert at distinguishing the direction the chase had taken and which hounds were giving tongue. While he began to appreciate the excitement of baying up the prey, he still shied away from the business of the skinning out of the carcass as it reminded him too much of some of the grisly sights he had witnessed as a lad growing up in Edinburgh.

His father had oft times taken him along on his many nefarious and grotesque missions that involved acquiring things like the left hand of a felon or the kidney of a fresh killed dog or once even he had watched as an associate of his father had boiled the flesh from the bones of a little fellow from Aberdeen who had been crushed against a building by a freight wagon full of rotten fish. Crisp preferred to see his meat cooked well and lying on a charger with a garnish rather than quivering and spasming at his feet or dripping blood from a game pole. It bothered him not in the least to know from whence his supper came as long as he didn't have to soil his hands with the gore of its making. Of course, rather than seem a milksop in front of the giant, he had choked back his bile and closed his eyes when it came to eviscerating or butchering his share of the game.

Panther meat is a greasy, rancid flavor, and great Hector only chopped it up for the pleasure of the lean and ribby hounds while he and Crispin subsisted largely on roasted bear meat with the occasional viand of raccoon or deer. Hector tried to shoot as little as possible in order not to frighten the game in the neighborhood or bring down the wrath of the local red men.

PLOTS THICKEN

Barley Blanchard threw the note from the governor down on the small oak table. First, they had found the damned lieutenant, and then, according to this latest message from the governor's secretary, they had lost him again.

Months had gone by, and the colonel had quickly gotten over the damning loss of a third of his regiment in the storm but had managed to find suitable replacements for only a portion of the men, and the loss of his steadfast and daring lieutenant was a stinging blow. Upon careful reconsideration, however, he realized that all the men with firsthand knowledge of his peccadillo with the Fair Peggy had been lost with the Wampum Belt, which was not altogether a bad thing.

Still he had shared the information about the brave lieutenant's forthcoming return with his staff, and now, he would have to tell them that it was all a hang fire and that, apparently, the governor was either mistaken or an idiot or both.

The sergeant filed the wax sealed note along with the rest of the colonel's correspondence, which, naturally, Old Barley was carefully saving for his substantial and heavily edited memoirs, which he would write following his singular and fantastical victories over the French in the savage reaches of these colonies.

Sergeant Collward was careful with whom he shared his juicier tidbits of gossip. Tittle tattle, especially the kind that was true, was the currency of the army and, if doled out sparingly, could buy a smart fellow a tankard of ale or, if given to the right officers, foodstuffs and favors. Invitations to work at the officers' soirees were also not out of the question. The leftovers were doled out to the servers. Collward was in the enviable position of being privy to every aspect of the Fifty-Sixth's business, along with every last detail of Old Barley's personal transactions. In all the ranks of the Fifty-Sixth, there was only one individual who knew more secrets than he, and that was Sergeant Major Spurling, who had returned to England, along with Captain Kinnaird, to raise replacements for the men lost aboard the Wampum Belt.

The sergeant knew one man who would be truly downhearted to find that the hero of the regiment would not be returning as expected, and no doubt, the patch-eyed veteran would be glad to share a bowl of Yankee pipeweed and an ale for this information. While the young fellow acutely felt the soldier's loss of sight and nodded sympathetically at his crippled gait, he was not about to give away the information for nothing. After all, he had lost his own ale money in a game of dice just the night before, and he had a powerful thirst on.

What had the bloody lieutenant done? thought Trepan. Did he get himself lost, or had he decided to take his substantial fortune and begin a new life somewhere else beyond the Crown's reach? It was a puzzle and one which perplexed the strangler no little bit.

He had been certain beyond a doubt that the young officer was too vain to give up his station in the regiment when he foolishly thought he could have it all. The assassin was torn. He could not afford to hire someone else to be his eyes (or eye as it were) in Charlestowne, and he daren't leave New York unattended for fear the lieutenant would show up in his absence and that the treasure would be secured before he could lay hands on it or the officer.

Sergeant Collward's information had been a blow to his plan, which had seemed to be progressing quite well. He had thought it only a matter of time before he laid hands on both the lucre and the white throat of the dashing young man.

As the weather grew ever colder, Trepan could feel the raw air through his threadbare coat and the dead actor's sateen breeches, which stood as both a constant and bitter reminder that had he managed to spirit away DeVaca's coin, at this very moment, he would be living a life of wealth and leisure in London. Instead, he shivered beneath his coat and slept like a stray dog unnoticed in a cluttered corner. If it took him all the rest of his days, Mull would pay for the assassin's current ill comfort. He cursed the lieutenant's family for a thousand years for the insult, injury, and penury that he had brought down on this rapidly graying middle aged head.

With little else to do but wait and plot for the day when eventually the lieutenant must return, Trepan turned his good eye toward securing a more reliable income than that which he could make almost honestly as an errand boy to the Fifty-Sixth. While the Latin peoples and the Gallic mob thought nothing of employing assassins, it has always been a point of honor amongst the Anglo Saxon race that a dirk in the dark is simply not fair play, and so it is to be avoided and should never be used except as a last resort failing war, diplomacy, and of course, marriage. Trepan never entertained for more than a moment the thought of applying to the commander of His Most Britannic Majesty's Land Forces as Pale Death or, as the Romans fashioned it, Pallida Mors. Lurking in the alleys and roads of New York, waiting for a fat purse, was certainly no better, and it no longer satisfied his needs anyway and would perforce bring down the wrath of justice sooner rather than later, and so he sought new employ.

If the friendly Crown would not or could not use his services, then he was left with the only obvious alternative. So with careful questions and properly applied quantities of spirituous lubricants, Trepan managed to locate a broke, nameless woodsman who, for a price, would deliver a message to the commandant at Fortress Niagara, built where the River Niagara issues into Lago Ontario. The woodsman, who was a half-breed Seneca, shared ancestry and sentiments with the popish French and had absolutely no qualms about returning to his familiar haunts and, for the right price, would carry along as well a brief message. No doubt, the commandant would also reward his diligence in delivering the note, and after that, he was free to pursue his own aims which consisted primarily of gaming, hunting, and loafing—three past times for which he was well known. The woodsman's brief stay in New York had been purely accidental as he had accompanied a delegation of Mohawks journeying with Sir William Johnson, the Baron of the Mohawk, friend to the sauvage, faithful servant of George the Second, and the Adam to many a fair or dusky Eve.

Trepan had got it in his evil and greedy mind that he could sell information to the French in Montreal regarding English troop dispositions in the Hudson Valley and the environs around Albany and New York. Keeping a keen eye open (for one was all he had) and a ready ear cocked would of themselves net him many salient facts. If he lacked for information to peddle, he could always cook some up and spice it with a few of the juicier stories being whispered about regarding the high command or sprinkle in a bit of the ever present gossip swirling around outside the governor's house. The Frogs had no way of checking the accuracy of the information or of testing Trepan's veracity. He would even be willing to wet his blade in Abercromby's spleen, if enough coin were available, which, of course, there was. Blood money could be sent via the commandant at Fort Niagara and his corps of runners and scouts who lingered about in the villages and isolated dens of the Iroquois, seeking information and alliances.

General Abercromby, the interim English commander, was typical of his self-indulgent ilk, completely lacking in common sense when it came to the art of war. He wished to conduct it more as a gentlemanly chess match than as a titanic struggle between two great nations bent on dominating the wealth of North America. To the general, this was a chance to earn accolades and favor at the Hanoverian court of King George the Second, and he was completely unaware that the French had employed one of his own countrymen to spy upon him and skulk about his headquarters and the governor's manse.

Montreal had responded with favor to Trepan's traitorous proposal and had authorized a pouch be sent from Niagara with a few gold Louis and a note requesting information regarding the disposition of troops in the districts around Albany. Contrary to what Trepan believed, the French governor was no fool and no novice in the art of deception, subterfuge, and deeds done à couvert. The governor, Vaudreuil, would compare Trepan's reckoning of troops, cannon, and baggage against the tallies sent by Canadian partisans who provided his field commanders with information. If the new spy's information were accurate, then there would be more assignments and perhaps even General Campbell the Earl Loudoun and supreme English commander in North America would not be safe when he arrived in New York to take command.

Trepan passed along his information to a fisherman from Sandyhook, who handed the secret communiqué to a greedy Connecticut fisherman whose brother-in-law was a Basque codman living on the bleak and frigid Gaspe Peninsula. He, in turn, gave it over to a one-armed Canadian trader, who sent it on to Montreal with a bateaux full of cheap trade goods destined for the tribes on the upper lakes. It was hardly an efficient method of communication, but it served the governor's purpose, and it took no more than two or three weeks for the dispatch to make its complete journey. However, more than a month would pass before Trepan could receive a reply and payment. This situation could render the response dated, and he unable to carry out the directive of the governor's man in the shadows.

Vaudreuil never signed or even penned a message to his agents but had, instead, a mysterious secretary carry out this dark business. The fellow was quite astute and was often able to exert influence or make suggestions to the royal appointee.

The payment for this information came to Trepan by another route altogether, which was nearly as twisted and tangled as Medusa's serpentine coiffure. A Recollet father from Fort Niagara secretly gave the pouch of coin to a warrior who lived on the idyllic stream banks near the southern source of the Genesee River (Chenusio in those far-off days). The brave then walked and ran for two days and gave the pouch to an aged member of the Tuscarora nation but not before he had removed one of the gold coins for his trouble. The old Indian then rode a broken down dapple gray mare to a point near New York where he was met in a cornfield by a local hatter who carried the coin into the city and deposited it at the bottom of a rain barrel outside a tinsmith's shoppe. The hatter's mother had been a Frenchwoman, and he had silently turned his narrow crooked back on his father's people after an English officer had horsewhipped his drunken father once for disparaging the king's troops within hearing of said officer.

None of the couriers knew where the coin was destined for, nor for whom it was meant, and none ever saw Trepan, yet, every six weeks the delivery would be made with obvious adjustments for extenuating circumstances such as the hazardous nature of winter travel, ambushment, and the unreliable character of several of the couriers.

※

Isaiah Harding at last had found what he thought was his share of the hero's reward. Though he had never practiced a heroic act in his life, he fancied himself an intrepid mariner without peer. In truth, the sharp-eyed captain had weathered a storm or two and had a voyage or two where he only broke even on poor cargoes, but it goes without saying that he rarely risked a loss nor braved all on a toss of the bones. It is honestly spoken that taking to the waves is to cast one's future into the hands of the fates, but if ever a captain was cautious and meticulous in his planning, it was Isaiah Harding, master of the *Indian Rose*, owner of the *Indian Maid*, and part owner of the *King Philip*.

Now that the self-styled, latter-day Ulysses had his Helen, he was loath to heed the ocean's siren call. Still, he trusted few with his business, and feared that, if allowed, his crew would rob him blind while his back was turned and engaged in more pleasurable entertainments, and it was likely true.

Peg, of course, encouraged the captain in his trading voyages as it meant that her silken petticoats spent more time about her ankles and less about her ears, and of course, successful cruises meant ever more money and an even finer lifestyle for the Harding's. With her babe well cared for and a wardrobe full of handsome gaily-colored gowns, Peg rather enjoyed her peaceful days while Isaiah was away at sea.

Hattie still prepared the meals and spun quietly by the flickering fire. The new Mistress Harding was not so stingy with her wealth as was the first Goodwife Harding. Peg had hired a slow-witted girl to help Hattie with the menial chores like fetching the firewood, scrubbing pots and pans, and beating the rugs.

The girl, Ruth Pettibone by name, was the niece of a neighbor and had, since her sad and untimely birth, been more simple than dull. Ruth came at half the cost of a witted child, and Peg had naught to fear from her and was quite sure that she could not conspire with the deaf and infirm old cook to steal the silver nor would she gossip about her employers at market. Ruth's eyes had a strange oriental cast about them, and the girl tended towards dumpiness but was always cheerful and happily hummed a little ditty to herself no matter how onerous the chore. The tune never varied, and most thought her eyes were vacant, but her family knew those orbs saw something far away that was unseen by others, and it brought Ruth great peace and joy.

Peg was far too consumed with maintaining and improving her circumstances and appearances to give even a moment's thought to the girl. As long as the work progressed and the sounds of domestic happiness emanated from the kitchen, she cared not a wit what transpired under her nose.

Patience Ackerman still nursed the baby Caroline, and she it was who kept order in the house when pretty Peggy was out. Peg, for the most part, left the care of the baby to Patience, but when she took the time to recall little Caroline, who was no more than a suckling, she would dote on the child for hours or until her own thoughts distracted her and reclaimed her attention. Suddenly, she would call sharply for one of the dowdy women to come and take the whimpering babe, and she would plunge back into her schedule like a child bored with a toy it had played with over long and in which it was no longer interested. Forgiving little creatures that babies are, wee Caroline could not have cared less if her mother cooed and teased her with a bright ribbon or if Patience allowed her to crawl about on a blanket in the kitchen. Peg, of course, would have been momentarily appalled if she had ever seen her daughter playing like a common brat, and then she would have resumed her composure when it occurred to her that someone else was seeing to the child's needs, and she was free to pursue her social ascent amongst the small elite clique of Providence. It was not even a daily occurrence for Peg to poke her carefully coifed head into the kitchen. Instead, she focused her attentions on shopping, having tea, attending upon the dames of town, and appearing socially acceptable.

Domestic quietude and an air of civil tranquility were all that Mistress Harding sought. From her days of rearing her unruly siblings whilst her mother sewed to her more ardent wine filled days and nights with Beverly, Peg had never had a calm and confident moment in all her young life. As supreme ruler in her husband's absence, and with all his financial resources within her gentle reach, the demure murderess sat back in her gaily colored gowns and reveled in her new found sense of superiority. Patience and old Hattie had not failed to notice the new way in which she carried herself and the tone of her voice was plainly seen in her upraised chin and the firm set of her mouth. Simple Ruth Pettibone could not be insulted even though she was brushed aside without the notice one gives a stray cur.

While Peg had settled into her new role, there still remained a darkened corner of her mind that murmured a reminder that all would not be complete until her husband was moldering in his best suit of clothes while his eternally shuttered eyes took survey of his own damnation.

It was in the days, not long after Isaiah took his leave, that Peg also heard word that Beverly Blanchard's regiment was freshly arrived in New York and that her darling colonel was guiding them. The one man's absence and the other's nearby presence after two years of separation were, of course, the very prod that would drive her thoughts down that fatal avenue.

It would be presumptuous to assume an intimate knowledge of the mind of the fairer sex. Those males acquainted with pretty Peggy had oft found that it was more than mildly perplexing to try to understand why the woman continued to love and cleave to the man who disposed of her while she plotted the end of the one man who had ever given her what she desired. Whether it was her unbridled Salome-like lust for power or the addled thinking of the female mind in love, one can only hazard to guess. To date, her thoughts had been precise and cogent, and observers can only surmise that her thoughts continued so, and that Peg suffered more from the desire for privilege and authority than the near dementia of the distaff penetralia mentis.

WILLIAMSBURG

Crispin crawled out of the crude but solid lean-to, intent on giving back to nature that which he had so stoically ingested the evening before. The ground was covered with a thick hoarfrost which turned up the edges of the brown leaves and made the entire forest floor sound as though it were covered with egg shells at every step. While the lean-to was certainly neither a palace nor even a cramped and smoky barracks, it had offered a modicum of insulation from the penetrating cold. With his pale bare buttocks stinging in the snapping air, he began with his mind's eye to count the hides that he and Hector had collected.

The giant had agreed that when they had amassed twenty-five combined bear and catamount pelts, they would begin to work their way toward Williamsburg. With nearly that many bear and panther furs, as well as a smattering of deer hides and bobcat pelage, Crisp began to allow his mind to wander toward the vague future and what plans he should make for the disposition of his fortune and how best to rejoin his regiment. He used a handful of moss to clean himself up and then blew into his cupped, rapidly numbing fingers and walked briskly back to the shelter.

They had built the lean-to a week before when Hector had pronounced the surrounding region as, "So full a sign, the hoons'll ha' three panthers treed at once!" They had located a gigantic tree that had fallen and scooped out an elongated shallow pit close by the log and then filled it with pine boughs, bracken, and moss. At last, they had propped poles against the side of the massive tree, which was well over six feet high lying on its side. After covering the poles with more moss and the dirt that they had scooped out, they constructed a fire pit at one end, just outside the shelter, surrounding it with stone and building up the back of it several feet with mounded dirt so that it would reflect heat into the interior of the den. Hanging a bear hide over the other end completed the hidey hole and provided a reasonably warm and soft bedding area. The hounds, as is their wont, weaseled their way in and curled up between the gargantuan huntsman and Crispin.

More and more, over the past few days, the ribby hounds had begun to take quite a liking to the young officer. Lame Banquo, most of all, seemed to have grown attached to the lieutenant. The bony but graceful russet-colored canine naturally shared not only his warmth and offered himself as a pillow but also freely shared his tiny passengers.

Crisp was rather glad that there was no looking glass where he would have to confront the barbaric, flea-ridden, sun-creased ruffian whose nails were caked with a combination of dirt, ash, and bear fat. His breeches especially were stained with a palette of bloody juice of roast bear, pony lather, dirt, and grease of dog. In a rowdy, smoke-filled, waterfront tavern or native wigwam, he would be just another frontier adventurer. In the salons, chocolate houses, and clubs of London, he would be unable to find work holding a gentleman's horse or bearing his sedan chair. In gentle company, one preferred to be announced by a servant rather than a pungent odor. Here in the wilds, not only was there no one to smell, there was no one to care if the stink belonged to the master or the hound. Crispin turned his mind away from the thought that he was currently so debased that he could not even pass for a servant and bent his thoughts rather toward that moment when he would make his triumphal return, and he would not only smell like a new man, but he would be able to hire all the servants one could desire.

"I dinna suppose there are many more beasts ina these parts!" Hector paused and threw a piece of cold meat to Crisp. "An' I must confess, I'm in sore need of ale an' bread. Man canno' live on meat alone!" He grinned and tore into a piece of char black but juice dribbling muscle, the rosy fluids running into his beard.

"I was hoping you would say that," replied the younger man. "I'd begun to think we mightn't make it in time to celebrate Christmas. Do you suppose we could take enough furs to finish the job as we make our way to Virginia?"

Crispin knew better than to hope that the giant would give up the chase before he had met his goal, but hoped in his heart that the Scot could be convinced at last to begin heading in the general direction of their ultimate destination.

Avoiding contact with the savages had been a great preoccupation of the lengthy Scot. Necessary and effective woodland diplomacy required lavish gifts and interminable congresses with sachems and wise men, all of which consumed both money and time, neither of which Hector had in great supply.

Trespass was the chosen method by many, most of whom were unscrupulous, and a few of whom were out and out Indian killers bent on rapine and thievery. Uninvited incursions only worked well provided one had the skills to circumvent savage scouts and hunting parties that were constantly ranging across the mountains and wandering the traces.

The frontier, of course, was rife with tales of adventurers and traders who had angered some local chieftain with false dealings or "accidental" homicide. In the end, they would be tied up to a post in what passed for the town square, with their toes slowly roasting, while women and children jabbed at their blistering flesh with pointy sticks and hooted out incomprehensible insults in their local gibble-gabble.

Hector gave ground whenever he came across native sign and taught Crisp also how to identify Indian spoor. With four good eyes, the men managed to travel without incident; however, their journey was made none the shorter for the occasional detours and the obvious natural obstacles they confronted daily.

The two hunters were woefully under armed, with only the wall gun and Crispin's pistol and cutlass, to say nothing of being deprived of supplies and in no condition to continue the long hunt on into the colder months. Powder had begun to run short, clothes that were already inadequate were wearing thin, and the men themselves were tending toward a pinched leanness.

The almost exclusive diet of meats was taking its toll. Tea made from white pine needles kept their teeth from loosening up with the scurvy, but their bowels began to gripe from the distinct lack of roughage, and without bread or cereal, they both had begun to lose weight and had little left to spare or to keep the wind from playing a baleful tune on their ribs.

Snow was an uncommon event in these climes, but as the frigid days advanced, it became clear to Hector Griffin that the winter ahead might well be more severe than typical.

As North Carolina slowly slipped behind them and Virginia lay looming on the horizon, Crisp began to solidify his plans. Trusting that he would arrive in Williamsburg in one piece, he had decided to forgive his share in the proceeds from the peltry and let the highlander keep it all in payment for bringing him safely across the wilderness.

If he could locate a good tailor, he even planned to commission a new woolen greatcoat for the Scot to replace the tattered and frayed one he wore. The constant wear and tear on clothing brought about by primitive forest living, along with the bear attack, had rendered the giant's coat little better than rags.

Crispin, himself, eagerly anticipated the opportunity to soak his scratched and bruised limbs in hot water to draw out the chill as well as the grime, and then change into a fresh new linen shirt and a woolen frock coat and breeches. Civilized discourse and a bumper of brandy by a roaring fire would satisfy his immediate needs.

Before he could enjoy these simple prerequisites, however, it was all-important that he decide upon his tale and how and when to go about divulging his true identity if, indeed, he should even let on who he really was. He had never given thought to not returning to the Fifty-Sixth regiment, lately called the Cheviot

Guards; after all, it had been his plan now for several years to be the youngest colonel in the army and to find a fitting bride who could help him secure a dignified and responsible position in society.

For so many months now, he had been preoccupied with his survival at the hands of DeVaca, and then later in carrying off their joint conspiracy and following that in merely crossing and surviving the frontier with the giant huntsman that he had never considered the obvious alternatives. With eight thousand in specie, he could go where he wished and be whom he would be, given he was careful and didn't attract too many questions. This also seemed reasonable until he realized that he could never return to England lest he be recognized nor could he risk a run in with anyone from his old regiment.

He could live in the sugar islands or on the continent or here in the southern American colonies. But he would hang for a pirate and a deserter if he was ever caught, and with a little digging, it might come out that he had kidnapped an officer's concubine and sold her to a smuggler, and then he fancied he would be lucky indeed to only be hanged. The British army was not notoriously lenient on gentlemen who defamed the madder red coat or brought shame upon the colors.

On the other hand, if ever he returned to the regiment, old Barely Blanchard would see to it that he was well taken care of for the sake of silence and loyalty, and he could still carry out his original plan and occasionally draw on his secret wealth to supplement his meager pay.

The greatest difficulty for the hunters had been in crossing the many and various rivers that bisected their path. Without ferries, it had been necessary for them to find the shallowest fords and then swim the pony while floating the hides on a clumsy make-do raft. Crisp had kicked furiously, propelling the raft with all of their goods, furs, and naturally, the weighty oaken chest while the hounds swarmed about paddling madly alongside.

Crisp had never been a great swimmer, and lately, to his chagrin, he seemed to be spending an unusual amount of time in or on water. While still in South Carolina, Hector's tale of a monstrous ivory-colored bull alligator—sixteen feet long, catching a grown buck in mid-stream and pulling it down before the noble animal even knew its peril—had provided Crispin with ample reason not to tarry during the crossings.

The giant thrashed along, his head bobbing up and down as he walked along the uneven bottom against the powerful currents. Occasionally, he let fly with an oath as he tripped on a submerged snag or stubbed his toe on a sharp rock. Once, Crisp thought he was gone for good when the Scot disappeared for nearly a minute, but then he emerged from the flow two hundred yards downstream, sputtering and gasping Gaelic curses.

On making the far bank, Crisp would disrobe and ring out his clothes while Hector and hounds shook vigorously. The giant stamped his feet into his boots, clamped his sodden Grendel-sized three-cornered hat onto his head, and turning to Crispin, blithely asked if he planned on pressing the wrinkles out of his stockings?

By the time they had reached the Cape Fear River in North Carolina, their skills in raft building had risen to such a level that they were able to ride that flood atop the raft only barely damping their feet.

Hector was a natural navigator, using the sun as his guide and only rarely on heavily overcast days stopping to consult his compass. Marching north and turning obliquely and trekking north east by north upon occasion, they came into Virginia as a gentle snow began to fall. Of course, Hector had no way of knowing they were into Virginia until they came to the southern extreme near the Roanoke River, whereupon he headed them into the westering sun for two days.

At last, they found an adequate crossing and built their last raft; and upon gaining the far shore, they faced starboard and, after a careful consultation of the compass, trudged in a northerly direction, hoping to make the James River in a week's time.

Lands about them became more civilized and fields opened up around the pair as they entered Tide Water, Virginia. Characters of their apparent ilk rarely received little more than momentary notice from the stooped and sweating blacks who labored in the tobacco fields or who fished along the languid creeks and rivers. Hunters, explorers, and rustic riffraff came and went with some regularity, often towing a string of pack horses with rawboned hounds trotting alongside. It was already an ancient American tradition for the solitary hunter to be accompanied by at least one hound and a pair or pack was common as well. The soon-to-be famous long rifle and a sharp-toothed dog did yeoman service in driving back the wilderness and keeping the campfire safe from marauding savages in search of worthy scalps.

Being the oldest colonized region in British North America, it is not hard to imagine the wealth and bucolic gentleness that had settled over those counties. For nearly one hundred and fifty years, generations of English country folk had been delving into the soil and bringing forth that golden weed that, when dried and smoked, brings hours of relaxation to many a hardworking fellow in Britain and on the continent, and for which the southern colonies are so famous. The blacks that toil in the sun tending that valuable crop do so without complaint, but it defies common sense to think that in their breast the same yearning for freedom does not beat that drove brave Spartacus to throw off the cruel shackles of Roman slavery. Crispin was fascinated by the happy songs he heard rising up from the throats of a people held in a state of bondage, enforced by the lash and gun.

His father had once gone to great lengths to secure the head of a blackamoor footman, tragically smashed by a coach that rolled over on its top and its retainers along a barbaric excuse for a road in some almighty forsaken, high mountain glen. The buyer had boiled the sad, uncracked skull clean with the objective of eventually making a comparison of the volume of water a Negro head could hold vice the volume held by the average Scotchman's pate. The theory he hoped to prove was that the Negroid brain was smaller, and therefore inferior, to the occidental European brain. Unfortunately for the gentleman, the opposite proved out, and he had to reluctantly abandon his theory of Caucasoid superiority based on brain case volume.

Several years later, the same gentleman tried to prove a connection between blindness and the consumption of tomatoes. He was challenged by an elegant Italian duelist (the notorious fop Rafaelo Edwardo Marini of Florence) who, after eating a bushel of tomatoes over the course of a fortnight, extinguished with a single shot from a pistol at ten paces, the flames on twenty tapers set in a row. Not a trick for a blind man.

The would-be scientician gave up his investigations in disgrace, paid the wager, and returned to a life of upper-class leisure. And so William Paris Maynard, a failed experimenter, expired many years later while overexerting himself, unashamedly cavorting, leafless in a Roman fountain with a fourteen year old French nymph named Lilly Munier. Lilly had run away from her groping stepfather, the Sieur De Mott, straight into the arms of another morally delinquent old debaucher—Maynard. The Florentine duelist continued to derive a living for several years by practicing feats of marksmanship throughout the European continent until he was arrested for disturbing the peace in a hamlet in the German principality of Schleswig-Holstein. The poor fellow caught the ague in prison and never again saw his beloved vineyards or the extensive collection of ancient erotic statuary that surrounded his immaculate hillside villa.

Williamsburg was no Glasgow or Edinburgh, but it was the most respectable town that Crispin had seen in the months since leaving Charlestowne. He was careful to choose a modest tavern and not to be too obviously lavish with his coin.

He had parted company momentarily from Hector as the giant patently refused to be separated from his pack of fanged companions. The hounds, of course, were allowed in the cobbled stable yard or the muddy front inn yard where they could lay peaceably about or snarl and snap with the local curs and leg lifters, but they were under no circumstances welcome in the taproom, dining room, or in second story lodgings. It was without shame (A man as large as Hector Bohemund Griffin is never ashamed unless he chooses to be.) that the giant headed off to the mow above the stable with a warm loaf of bread under one arm and the fist of his other tightly wrapped about the handle of a wooden bucket full of ale.

Beds in most taverns were woefully inadequate for a man the size of the Scot, and it was not uncommon for travelers to share a bed with their fellows. No one had ever volunteered to sleep with Hector, and he had found it less than comfortable to share the slats with some reluctant itinerant German tradesman who shivered and squeaked every time he rolled over in his sleep. The little fellows invariably stole the covers and left him cold on the one side, and with the footboard digging sharply into his calves, it was anything but restful.

Crispin had purchased, for a few pennies, a large piece of beef that had started to turn, and this was his gift and thanks to the hounds. Hector had chopped it into equal shares, and while he pushed back into the straw, luxuriating in the rich yeasty flavors of bread and beer, the dogs each lay scattered about, worrying at the tender greening meat and growling quietly in their throats if their companions even looked at them sideways.

Cleopatra's teats had begun to swell, and Friar Lawrence proudly stretched and allowed the others to pay homage to their new chieftain. Banquo's day had come and passed, and while the old hound still had hunts left in him, he no longer possessed the unquestionable strength of tooth and claw necessary to challenge the younger dog for the lady's favor, so Hector anticipated the day when he would be the godfather of a new litter sired by the good friar. All in all he was happy with the end of his journey. It had come as a pleasant surprise when his young partner had declined his cut from the sale of the peltry. Now, with the proceeds jingling in a purse and the knowledge that he would have a half dozen or more fine young hound pups to sell in the spring, Hector gangleshanks prepared to settle down to a restful winter of smoking sleeping bears from their dens and of filling catamount bounties.

Lieutenant Mull concluded his successful interview with the governor by bowing low at the waist before making his soldierly exit. The governor had sagely promised to send a missive off to the governor of New York and the Earl Loudon, announcing the emergence of the long lost Lieutenant of the Fifty-Sixth.

Crispin, as it turned out, was a liar of the first water. He had vaguely explained to Governor Dinwiddie that he had survived alone in the wilderness for a month after escaping from mysterious cutthroats. He finally trudged footsore and weary into Williamsburg. He didn't think the fabrication all that great; after all, he had killed wild beasts and had hunched about the frontier for over two months. Dinwiddie was too busy to question the young Ulysses and hadn't a care for some lieutenant gallivanting in the forest.

Crispin sipped at his coffee, his legs civilly crossed. He felt inwardly self-conscious in his simple brown woolen suit with its large pewter buttons and plain black linen cravat. He went on to explain that he had decided to make himself presentable and well rested before reporting his return from the dead, but here he was now, and did the governor think he should have to wait long before completing his return journey to the regiment?

"We must wait and see, young man," replied the royal appointee. "I fancy you should rejoin your regiment in time to begin the spring campaign season at the latest."

The governor's mansion was without compare in the provincial town and beyond a doubt, the most inspiring structure Crispin had seen since leaving England. He reveled in the orderly and civilized atmosphere created by the rich paintings, voluminous drapes, elegant English walnut furniture, and the Sheffield sterling coffee service which the silent slipper-shod servant had brought into the office to serve them. Slipper-shod servants were one of the obvious signs that one had attained a high level of wealth and authority. After all, most colonials couldn't afford servants; and of those that could, only a tiny fraction could employ slaves who were often dressed better than the somewhat rustic colonial middle class.

Once again out on the frost-covered lawn, Crispin smiled smugly and silently congratulated himself upon the deception. He thought returning to the regiment was surely the proper thing to do, and well-mannered Williamsburg had recalled to him the extent and superiority of English culture—even if it was only a colonial town on the far edge of the growing imperium.

Hector, however, was another kettle of fish that needed taking care of before the lieutenant could safely return to the martial fold. The Scot was far too intimately informed of Crisp's wanderings and actions of recent months, and it was necessary that the lieutenant secure his silence before the giant blathered about his traveling companion. If the governor were ever to get the scent of the truth and compare it against Crispin's accounting, then there would be embarrassing and perhaps even dangerous questions.

Now that he had committed himself to a course of action and could not bolt to either side like a fleeing hare, he almost felt relieved. Hector's silence would still need to be assured, yet he cared far too much for the giant to see ill done to him and certainly knew he personally was incapable of doing the man physical injury in any case. Having established a friendship with the hunter, Crispin was quite certain that his loyalty and silence could be acquired and guaranteed for very little. If he had learned one lesson from his father, Lane, and DeVaca, it was that every man had his price, and in his own brief experience, every man could be corrupted.

Upon ordering a great coat in a rich deep-green wool lined in a royal blue and emerald-green stripe and sporting magnificent brass buttons, Crispin stopped around at the gunsmith where he purchased a fine used brass-mounted horse pistol of seventy-one caliber along with the mold for the lead balls. The smith quickly installed a shining steel belt hook at Crisp's request so that the giant could wear it suspended from his girdle. These gifts, coupled with a small purse of Spanish silver, were, Crispin was certain, more than adequate to persuade his friend of the absolute importance of discretion.

"What da ye take me for? Some breed of fickle savage who canno' be trusted without buyin' his loyalty? Did ye think if ye told me tha' truth that I'd run to the law and tattle on ye?" Hector threw his hat down in the street and began stamping on it with his right foot. He looked for all the world as though he was dancing an angry jig or trying to put out a fire.

"Fer the love of Saint Andrew mun, we're from the same country an' we've froze together and sweated through fen an' forest together, and on top of it, ye proved yerself a brave companion when ye killed the bear back in the beginning. Do ye think me so poor that I'd sell ma friendship?" He ceased all movement and stood with his shoulders slumped and his head hanging like one who has just heard of the death of a favorite son and is crushed to the marrow with grief.

The discussion had begun over a tankard as Crispin told the hugeous Scot a true portion of his odyssey. Naturally, Crispin had omitted references to the "mementos" and also the fight with the greasy assassin at Gordon's Tavern. After a lengthy description of his interview with the governor, Lieutenant Mull had cautiously edged up on the delicate nature of the favor he required of the hunter and how he planned to show his gratitude to his friend and deliverer. He slid the bag of silver across the pine plank table. And there began the great bit of trouble.

Crispin stood silently for a moment or two with his arms tightly crossed before speaking, his voice dripping with arrogance. "Had I but known that my gifts would have so offended you, I certainly would have spared myself the expense and you the offense."

As he warmed to his diatribe and his anger grew steadily, he began to imagine somehow that he was the insulted party. Standing ramrod straight now with his hands clenched at his side, he went on, "If you feel that strongly, then I will take back the gifts and hold you to your word, Mr. Griffin!"

Passersby turned their heads to watch the argument but politely kept walking rather than become embroiled in a fight that had obviously spilled out of the noisy tavern and into the street. Crispin took the enormous coat and, draping it over his arm, turned to stalk off, the paper wrapped pistol and mold tucked under his arm.

THE CORSICAN SAILOR

The *Thankful Shepherd* rode at anchor like a half-filled bowl of soup in a washtub. Two of the crewmembers were always kept at the pump to keep the holds from filling with seawater to such an extent that the poor old vessel settled by her stern and sank into the soft mud of the harbor.

Her master had been too penniless to make better arrangements, so he dropped his anchor in the harbor while he was rowed ashore in the ship's leaky jolly boat. Ashore in Providence Towne, Captain Samuel Welch hoped to sell his tiny cargo of molasses and mahogany lumber and then auction off the ship for scrap. The *Thankful Shepherd* was nearly thirty years old and had seen far too many furious nor'easters. She was weak in the knees, and her planking cracked and leaky. In the most recent storm, she had lost one of her yards, and the bowsprit had been badly battered. When all was said and done, she was a dying creature of the waves kept afloat only by the tireless and valiant efforts of her largely Corsican crew, whom Captain Welch had hired when he purchased the ship in Porto Vecchio four years earlier. Pasquale and his cousin Berto had labored exhaustively at the pump and managed to keep the leakage from rising much above their knees. In the forward hold, much of the mahogany was under water, but the barrels of molasses, which had been moved forward when the aft hold flooding was at its worst, sat atop the piled lumber, now safely clear of the dirty harbor brine.

At last, the mate had come below and relieved the two swarthy, mustachioed men. Two of their shipmates took their turns at the hand pump while the cousins changed into clean wearables for the trip into Providence. The captain had sent back the jolly boat with a message for the mate that the men could begin coming ashore as the cargo had all been sold and would begin transshipping to a lighter in the late afternoon, and all hands were not needed aboard for the time being as long as the gasping and wheezing pump could be manned.

Pasquale's thirst was greater than it had ever been, and while he had mechanically slaved at the pump, he daydreamed of quaffing a great mug of rum and mounting some spirited colonial filly for a sporting romp.

Berto knew his black-souled cousin's weakness for the drink and had dragged him out of many a tavern in their fortress-like island homeland. The rum was no great evil by itself, but Pasquale was one of those bitter fellows whose mind was always dark of normal, and when he imbibed, which was frequent, he became nastier than Old Nick's hoof.

They both had donned clean canvas slops along with brightly colored shirts and had tied silk scarves about their necks. Berto had also pulled on a pair of canary yellow stockings and then his buckled shoes while Pasquale wore only a pair of worn brogans and bare shins as his stockings had been washed overboard one day while doing laundry on the weather deck.

Pasquale Penciolleli had a streak of meanness in him like no other in his clan. Before he had reached the age of twenty, he had murdered several poor sods that had tried to court his bereaved and widowed mother. Even on the bloody island of Corsica, Pasquale was considered a dangerous fellow, and finally, the law reluctantly, and with some trepidation, decided it was best if he were brought to heel. Another cousin of his from his extensive group of relations, was a bloated and balding magistrate married to Pasquale's prettiest and eldest of eight sisters, warned him of his impending apprehension. In consequence, he signed onto the crew of the *Thankful Shepherd* and convinced his younger cousin Berto to come with him and see something of the world.

✵

After Peg had enquired into the status of the three ships that the Harding's owned or had an interest in, she proceeded down to the fisherman's wharf to purchase a cod. Slow-witted Ruth Pettibone had trailed along and would serve as the packhorse for the sizeable fish.

Peg was used to navigating her way through the human flotsam and jetsam that orbited the waterfront. The most unsavory place in the neighborhood was just back from the docks. The sign had seen better days but was not without some couth even if the clientele was. Symples Tavern was serving its fourth generation of mariners, and clearly, a few of the customers had been there when the first round was splashed into crudely glazed clay tankards seventy years before. Of course, in those far off days, these bleary-eyed old topers had been but young lads, stopping in to drag their fathers home for supper. The odors emanating from the interior advertised the tavern's wares and the filthy habits of its patrons. The savory but overpowering aroma of a fish stew mingled with the stench of stale urine and the scent of pipe smoke mated with the fragrance of tar.

Normally, Pretty Peg would have passed directly beneath the sign and thought nothing of it. While the persons within were of a rough and tumble caste, many of them had worked for her husband once upon a time, and she was recognized as Isaiah's fetching new wife, whom everyone felt was a thousand fold improvement over her predecessor.

On this day, however, Peg was still a dozen paces from the threshold when a bearded scalawag in a dingy gray frock coat came reeling out of the front door backwards, screaming like a scalded monkey with his right hand clamped over his bleeding ghastly empty right eye socket. Pasquale followed close on the fellow's heels and punched the half-eyed dockhand deep in the belly, and then tripped the fellow up, pushing him down into the gutter where he forced the man's mouth open and crammed in it the gory and cruelly out of place eyeball. Giving the beaten and partially blinded roustabout a sharp parting kick in his cullions, of course, caused the pathetic sheephead to gasp and swallow his own orb.

The Corsican spat a gobbet into his enemy's pain-wracked face and then wheeled about to go back into the rowdy darkness of the tavern. The now half-sighted laborer was helped to his feet by his boon companion, a coward who hadn't dared to step between his friend and the Corsican. Together, they staggered off down the street in search of a doctor.

Peg had witnessed the whole barbaric event and found herself flushed with excitement and admiration for the hearty Arabesque sailor who clearly would brook no insult. To her eye, he looked the part of a dark and dangerous warrior, hammered and forged in the flames of Vulcan. She had never been attracted to the likes of rough working men; she found them, by nature, coarse and dirty like her father. But this fellow was bronzed, hardened, and mysterious, like some sacrificial dagger of the ancients, and while she could not envision herself embracing him, the idea of being in the presence of so much furious potential was heady and left her trying to catch her breath.

Beverly had given in to her whims and made her feel important in a world in which social standing was everything. Isaiah had laid before her the wealth she so desired. But this fellow, while she had no intention of giving herself to him, excited in her the thrill of danger and violence. Pretty Peggy had seen many handsome rakehells in her day, but for some inexplicable reason, this fellow was different. He was turmoil, pain, and riot, waiting to be unleashed. He recalled to her a storm with its jagged lightening and claps of thunder. Mistress Harding commanded Ruth to put down the fish and go into the stygian tavern and find the man. She gave the simple girl a Spanish dollar and told her to give it to the man and ask him to come out and have converse with her mistress. Pasquale had taken the shining coin and agreed to come round to Goore House long after dark and await the signal of two candles burning in the kitchen window. Peg had described the house's layout and told him which tree to tarry under until the signal came.

When Hattie and Ruth went into the attic room and Caroline was sound asleep, Peg lit the second candle and placed it in the window. The fire in the kitchen hearth had burned down to a dull orange glow, and Peg took a seat in the chair that Patience usually occupied and left free the three-legged stool from which Hattie and Ruth would stir the bubbling copper pots used to cook supper. The sailor had been sitting on the stool for several minutes, listening intently to Pretty Peggy's plans for Isaiah without speaking. The firelight played faintly on Peggy's fine face, and while he absorbed her words in his mind, he imagined ravaging this lady while her husband's lifeless corpse hung still in the forest.

Peg had outlined a plan for the Corsican to ambush her husband late at night and kill him with a knife, which she would supply—the very blade which had loosed the flow from Goodwife Harding's loins. She had lied to Pasquale, weaving a tale of beatings and drunkenness whenever Isaiah returned from the sea. She had even gone to the extent of bruising herself on the arm earlier in the day and then rolling up her sleeve to show the sailor. In his willingness to believe, he never thought to ask her how the captain could have done this injury while he had been away at sea for weeks.

Peg flirted shamelessly, touching the islander on his knee and leaning forward so that she could display her wares in the dull glow of the smoldering embers. She pressed another Spanish dollar into his damp palm and told him to please consider her plight before he said no.

Pasquale was taken with the young English woman and had already decided to slay the Yankee captain for the sheer joy of feeling the life slip away from a man who could beat such a beautiful girl and for the fair amount of coin she offered for the deed—and for the chance of comforting and distracting the beautiful signora after the beast was dead. In his deep, gravelly Mediterranean (He was descended of Arab slavers, Carthaginians soldiers, and Greek traders to name a motley few.) accent he explained to her that he would not need to think on this thing, but he pocketed the coin just the same. The dog would die just as she asked, and when it was done, he would come to her with proof that this was so.

His mind was already turning over the possible proofs he could provide. The captain's clothes or his watch were possible, but no, he thought that of those items that remained undamaged and without taint or stain, he would keep all for himself as an additional reward. Fingers, hands, and ears had been popular at home in Corsica, but he did not want this poor woman to ever doubt his courage, so he settled rather quickly on bringing her the entire head. A head was the perfect evidence as it could not be faked or substituted. *Perhaps she would show me her gratitude*, he thought with a leer.

The embers were nearly extinguished when Peg escorted Pasquale across the room. As she led him to the darkened portal, she brushed his hand with hers and took a deep breath, letting him have one last glance at her gently heaving and tantalizing bosom, and told him to return in a week at the same hour when she would give him a special knife and his final instructions. A jet of flame spurted up in the fireplace, hissing like an adder. Pasquale looked into her eyes just briefly and then bade her good night, slipping off into the starless, inky night. Penciolleli told his cousin nothing of his meeting with Peg, and for the next week, they spent their evenings aboard the *Thankful Shepherd*, waiting for the auction to sell her. Along with the rest of the crew, they helped in keeping her afloat, which became somewhat easier after her cargo had been transshipped, unburdening her and allowing her to ride higher in the water.

Berto had found a ship for them to sign on to—one that would be leaving Providence in a month's time, bound for the West Indies with a bulging load of pig iron, gunpowder, and broadleaf tobacco. The Corsicans would move aboard the brig,

Sally Adair, in two weeks' time to help bring the cargo and stores aboard and make the vessel ship shape and ready to sail.

Harding and the *Indian Rose* were expected in Providence any day now and were already a week overdue, which gave no one alarm as deep water vessels seldom arrive on the appointed date and are almost never early.

Three weeks passed, and still there was no news of the *Indian Rose*. Peg began to hope that Isaiah's ship had gone down and taken him with it. Perhaps a storm had sunk her, or her crew had mutinied, or she had caught fire and burned. Heaven knew what luck or, as others would have it, ill fate might have found the *Rose* between swells. While Peg silently hoped for the worst, she showed a grave and concerned face to the wives of the crew who irregularly stopped in at the Harding's offices to inquire if word had been heard from any other ship as to the whereabouts of the *Indian Rose*.

Alas, Peg sighed. "We must wait and pray, ladies, as is the duty of all wives who send their husbands out to sea." Looking forlorn but stoic, she passed down the wharf with Ruth in tow. Two days before the *Sally Adair* was due to sail, the slightly tardy *Indian Rose* gracefully slid into her berth and disgorged a happy crew, glad at last to be home after a successful voyage.

As the hour was late, with it getting on toward supper time, Isaiah had a perfunctory look at the books to see what had been sold and purchased in his absence and then went on around to his favorite tavern where many of the older captains, who had since retired, went each evening. The *Royal Mast* was a far deal cleaner and less rowdy than Symples and, of course, was another block back from the waterfront. Warmly welcomed, he ordered a glass of claret and filled his pipe and asked the fellows what news had happened while he had been away. Pasquale heard almost immediately that the *Indian Rose* was home. He had concocted business ashore before she had even finished tying up, so he was already lingering in the vicinity of the *Royal Mast* when the captain arrived an hour later. At their second meeting, Peg had given Pasquale the knife and then had shown the Corsican a painting of the captain that hung over the long polished sideboard in the dining room of the big yellow house. As Isaiah went into the *Mast*, the Corsican checked beneath his own waistcoat to see if the hand axe he had "borrowed" from the ship's carpenter was well secured. No one thought anything of a sailor carrying a knife in his belt but walking about with a hatchet made little sense at night. Sailors always needed a knife for line work and a thousand other chores that they did every day aboard ship.

The hours passed slowly, and Pasquale stayed hidden as the shadows deepened, and a blanket of stars appeared in the sky. In twos and threes and singly, the patrons of the *Mast* reluctantly began to head for their own hearths, leaving behind the rosy glow and sociable chatter.

When they had arrived in port, Isaiah had one of the mates take his trunk home for him, so with empty hands, he rolled down the street, enjoying the sight of the lamp lighter going about his business and the chimneys puffing up little columns of blue smoke that spoke of cozy quarters and happy homecomings. Those who had never been to sea could not appreciate the simple joys and scenes of life ashore. As he strolled along, he examined the information he had learned in the tavern and added it up with the tally of profits and losses from his latest cruise in order to get a picture of the current state of his financial affairs. The Corsican sailor had left his brogues in the alley outside the *Royal Mast*, padding along in his bare feet so that the Yankee pig wouldn't hear him coming from behind. They left the waterfront and passed through the mercantile and residential neighborhoods, the Captain's steel-trimmed boot heels clicking crisply on the cobbles. Goore House, for such was it's name, as you will recall, sat on the edge of the town, and the gloam became deeper, and the trees became more closely spaced as they neared it.

At last, they reached a stretch along the lane where there were no neighbors within sight, and Pasquale was determined that this was where the ogre would meet his end. He had sneaked along, hanging back forty or so strides, and now he picked up the pace, closing to within a few seconds of a quiet sudden rush. Isaiah's feet crunched along in the gravel and dirt, unaware of the danger creeping up from behind.

The sailor began his final dash but could not have accounted for the shooting star, which passed brightly over their heads at precisely that moment, causing Isaiah to turn and follow its path, which of course allowed him to see the wild-eyed murderist bearing down on him. With a startled yelp, Isaiah dived into the bushes at the side of the road and, instantly coming to his feet, pulled out his ever-present screw barreled pistol from his coat pocket.

Pasquale, anticipating the victim's route of escape, leaped in midair and changed direction, landing imprecisely but directly in front of Isaiah, coming to a halt with the knife raised, his forehead lightly touching the muzzle of the gun. Realizing that his fortunes had changed in a heartbeat, Pasquale dropped the blade and remained absolutely motionless. "If you move, I'll kill you where you stand," said Isaiah nervously, trying to sound courageous and in control. Pasquale acquiesced and showed his conformity by not uttering a sound.

The captain began, after a few seconds, to regain his composure and ordered the Corsican to take one step backwards and to explain why in the name of Jehovah he was attacking him.

Pasquale, of course, was loath to tell his intended victim a thing. Harding assured him that if he remained silent, then he would kill him and report it to the sheriff in the morning.

The islander took him at his word and began to reveal the tale, leaving out only the parts where Pretty Peggy flirted with him, thinking this would surely incite the abusive and now angry husband to murder. While Isaiah had never before killed anyone, he had seen his share of narrow by a hairsbreadth escapes in his reckless youth and that, coupled with his sense of absolute superiority, made him a reasonably dangerous man.

The Corsican told him how he had planned to slit the captain's throat and decapitate him, followed by hanging his headless, naked corpse in a tree in the forest (perhaps not the wisest confession ever given). Naturally, he bore ample witness against Peggy and told the captain how much he was to receive for the murder, adding that she had even provided the knife. Pasquale was a violent but pragmatic man and was not about to sacrifice himself so that she could continue on in her big house. After all, the brute was only home one month out of four, and certainly, she could tolerate the occasional thrashing.

Isaiah became incensed at the lies Peg had told and had no forgiveness in his heart for his would-be killer, a man who had more murder in him than gallantry and conscience, so he fell back on his original threat and shot the olive-skinned fellow squarely in the mouth, blasting out a largish hole in the back of his head and sending him reeling back into the bushes at the side of the road.

Isaiah was shaken by the finality of what he had just done, but with only a minute's pause, he knelt at the side of the corpse and felt beneath the waistcoat for the hidden hatchet. After hacking through Pasquale's strong meaty neck with his shaking hands, Isaiah looped the long black queue of hair around his fingers, retrieved his hat that had fallen in the road, and proceeded to walk the remaining half mile to his home. The blood from the ragged stump of Pasquale's neck dripped silently in the dust. The minutes spent in walking allowed him to slow his hammering heart and to formulate a plan of surprise for Pretty Peggy. Reaching his own yard, Isaiah paused beneath the trees and removed his boots and stockings, doffed his hat, calmly pulled off his waistcoat and shirt, and then put his waistcoat back on. He thought he looked reasonably piratical, which is how he judged Pasquale to have looked in the darkness. He pulled the brass hoop earring off the limpid eyed head, fastened it to his own ear, and then, wrapped the bloody noddle in his shirt and started for the kitchen door.

Peering in the window next to the door, Isaiah could see no one at the hearth. The fire had been banked for the night, and the kitchen seemed deserted. He thumped loudly on the door, knowing that Peg would want to answer it herself and would forestall the other women. Likely, Hattie wouldn't hear it, and Ruth could not make water without explicit instructions. A moment passed, and he heard her muffled voice through the door, calling up the back stairs, and then the soft glow of a candle advanced swiftly down the hall leading from the dining room as she raced to reach the door.

He drew his head back from the window and averted his face as she pulled open the thick, painted oak door. He forced his way by her brusquely, and she gave way before the looming form of the sailor, silhouetted against the indigo night. Once in the room, he stood with his back to her, screening her view as he placed the severed head on the worktable and peeled away the now crimson shirt from the Corsican's bloodless face. As he stepped back and turned toward his wife, he moved to the side, revealing the gory object on the table to her gaze. Holding her candle high, Peg saw first Pasquale's face staring blankly back, part of his lip shot away and his front teeth missing. A dribble of blood formed on the table beneath the butchered flesh, and too late, she realized that the man standing before her was not her Corsican deliverer but rather his now enraged would-be victim. Peg waited for the blow to fall, but Isaiah just stood there, the candle gleaming brightly in his eye. Drawing the knife, she had given the sailor from his own belt, Isaiah stabbed it roughly into the table where it stuck at an angle, the sound of its vibrating blade the only noise to break the silence.

A long minute passed, and then with tiger-like quickness, his right fist shot out, landing with a sickening crunch on her nose.

His left fist flew right behind and landed on her neck, knocking her to the floor in a heap of twisted petticoats. "Beat you, did I? Apparently not enough, my love!" roared the captain. He reached down and grabbed her about the throat, choking off any word of complaint or protest. Isaiah handled her roughly, kicking and pushing her up the stairs toward their room. Upon reaching the bedchamber, he gently picked up little Caroline's cradle and removed it to the hallway without waking the sleeping child. Returning to the room, he quietly closed the door and placed the candle he had carried upon the stand. Peg huddled in the middle of the bed.

He had his way with her quickly and for one last time. Rising from the bed and drawing up his breeches, he looked down at the frightened and bleeding woman.

"If you dare to speak, I will cut out your tongue. Caroline will stay with me, and you will leave this house tonight, and if you ever dare to darken my door with your sluttish form again, I will kill you like the scum you sent to do me murder."

Going to her armoire, he removed the oldest and most drab of the many and mostly gay and pretty gowns within.

His rhetorical interrogation continued. "Did you give yourself to him? Don't answer. I don't care to know." He threw the clothes at her and watched as she pulled them on. "You are nothing more than a murderous whore, Peg, so you might as well look the part." For her part, Peg could think of nothing to say. She was shocked, terrified, and now felt ill-used, which indeed she was, yet she knew if she spoke, it might only serve to set him off again. She was well aware that, with her plan dashed by the Corsican's incompetence, unless she did as her husband said, he might, in his rage, murder her out of hand like he was some wrathful medieval lord and she an offending churl. Once she was robed again, Isaiah took her roughly by the arm, squeezing tightly without a care for her discomfort or pain and forced her down the stairs and out again into the kitchen wing. Pushing her into a chair, he warned her not to move while he rummaged about, finding a sack and placing in it a loaf of bread and a bottle, which he filled with water from a bucket near the fire.

It briefly occurred to her to snatch up the knife and try to finish the job Pasquale had bungled, but she knew that she was neither strong enough nor fast enough to accomplish the deed and that in the end, Isaiah would only thwart her attempt and kill her for certain. Men, it seemed to her, always abandoned her just when she began to rely on them. Unfortunately, Peg could not see the irony inherent in her own thoughts.

Harding grabbed a drab shortgown jacket that hung from a hook inside the door and then propelled her out across the lawn, past the privy and into the barn. Once inside, he lit a wooden barn lantern from the candle he had carried and carefully blew out the exposed candle. Grasping her firmly by the back of the neck, he forced her about the dark interior, finally shoving her back up against an upright beam. He snatched a piece of rope from the tack room and tied her hands behind her, lashing her to the post by means of a leather strap about the throat. He then set about harnessing the diminutive black mare to the chaise. The two large wheels of the graceful cart spun crazily as it tore down the road. Isaiah had only hours to spirit his wife away from the neighborhood of Providence and return to his home and do away with the mangled remains of Pasquale Penciolelli.

Peg lurched about the seat, unable to maintain a constant balance with her hands secured behind her back. Isaiah cracked the whip over the mare's rump and called to her, urging the horse on.

He hoped to take pretty, broken-nosed Peg at least twenty miles from home before abandoning her and turning around. He had left a brief note on the cradle telling Hattie to go and get Goodwife Ackerman and tell her that Mrs. Harding had run off, and he was in search of her. They were near the Connecticut line when, at last, Isaiah pulled up and let the mare cool out.

"Stay away from here—far away, if you understand my meaning," threatened the captain. "I want to hear no word of you. If I chance to hear gossip, I will visit upon you the portion you sought for me. Mark me, Peg! Now, get out," he barked, cutting her bonds with a clasp knife and then viciously slashing the blade across her cheek.

Peg reached for her stinging, bleeding face as Isaiah placed a boot against her ribs and kicked her out of the conveyance. He threw the sack containing the bread and water at her and turned the mare around and, calling to her, trotted back up the dark and narrow road toward Providence.

Pretty Peggy stood disconsolately in the middle of the lane, the sack hanging limply at her side, and watched as the chaise melded into the lowering gloom of the trees overhanging the road. It was three in the morning or thereabouts, and the retreating clip clop of hoof beats grew more distant, finally ending in silence before Peg could rouse herself from her sense of shock at the ill-fortune she had inherited upon the death of the Corsican.

She would have collapsed in the road and wept if there had been anyone to watch or to care, but alas, there was no rescue at hand, and she was too frightened to give into tears just yet. She tugged the shortgown tightly about herself and hugged the sack to her chest as she shuffled up the road, away from Providence. Her tears stung the scarlet gash that started high on her delicate jaw, and she knew her only hope lay in making it to New York and, perhaps, in finding Beverly before he went off on some damnable campaign against the French. After returning to Goore house, the heartbroken and angry captain still had to tidy up his home and his affairs.

Naturally, the Corsican's body still lay in the shallow ditch as the dawn broke, and the birds began to sing. Isaiah grabbed the headless sailor's shirt collar and, with great effort, dragged the body back into the woods several hundred yards until he came to a bog. Taking off his stockings for the second time, he waded out into the muck and pushed the body down and then laid upon it several flat rocks that he had found lying about.

After cleaning up and returning to the house, he dug the head out of the dung and straw in the mare's stall, where he had stashed it as an afterthought. Dropping it into a hole in a hollow oak tree in a copse of trees behind the barn, Isaiah left it for the bugs to clean and for a family of field mice to occupy.

Captain Harding put on a brave but saddened face for the household and the town in the days following. The story he told was that he had come home and found a note from his wife, stating her intention of running off with the Corsican, and further, he said that the thieves and adulterers had absconded with a secret cache of coin that only he and his runaway wife knew of. Isaiah said he forgave her indiscretion and told a few friends that if she returned repentant, he would take her back. No doubt (he said with a lie), the strain of raising the child and his long absences had taken their toll, and her thinking had become addled. Everyone felt his pain, and most only blamed the silly woman who would leave such a fine man and take up with a common seaman and him a papist to boot.

In the years following this tale, after Goore House had passed out of the family and the Harding name was long forgotten, it became commonly believed that a spirit haunted the lawns of the Goore manse. An angry dark-haired man, dressed as a sailor, is seen to stride out of the barn on moonlit nights and walk down the road towards town—perhaps, hoping to find his way back to the *Sally Adair*. The kitchen door will sometimes open slowly of its own accord and suddenly slam shut with an ear-splitting bang.

Hunters claim they have seen the same revenant, standing by the side of a pool in the stunted, lichen covered woods nearby, and they say also that when the ghost is approached, it becomes as wispy as pipe smoke, and this is followed by the sound of a gunshot, which will echo in the woods just before the apparition disappears entirely. If you doubt their veracity, ask anyone who has come home from town late of night and passed down that shadowy stretch of lane. The last half-mile between the town and Goore house is still reckoned a brave man's journey on a moonless night, and it is not uncommon for horses to become skittish and even refuse to go on. No doubt, this frightful work is the doing of Pasquale Penciolelli's shade, restless in death, wandering this side of the veil as a result of his evil ways and his untimely parting.

FAT ANNE AND CAPTAIN PIPE

The rude, intrusive thumping at the door stopped as Crispin crossed the floor to answer. Standing in his stockinged feet with his shirt untucked and his hair unwigged, he did not feel suitably attired to greet guests, but still, the visitor had been insistent and had refused to accept his silence as absence. As the door swung inward, Crispin was not in the least surprised to find the giant standing on the other side with his hat in his hand and his head bowed. "I've acted shamefully, and it were ill words for a parting of friends," Hector said with apology. "I've brought ye a present."

He pulled his hand from behind his back, and in it was a leash made from the leather of an old harness, and attached to the other end was Banquo the Strong.

"He's far too lean and old fer the hunt, and he's most attached to ye, or so he told me last night while we were yarnin' in the byre." Hector held out the leash toward Crispin. "Please take 'im."

Crisp readily accepted the leash. "You great fool you, you know they don't allow hounds in the inn. Are you trying to get me thrown out?" He stepped aside, gesturing for the Scot to enter. "I will accept Banquo, only if you will accept the gifts I have for you."

Banquo immediately curled up next to the small brick fireplace, and Crisp offered Hector a chair by the blaze. Furniture usually groaned under the strain of the giant's rather immense weight, and so he politely ignored the empty comb-back Windsor chair and instead sat on the floor, Indian style. Crispin, not wanting to offend his friend further and wishing to pet the dog that he had unconfessedly missed for the last several days, likewise sat on the floor in the native fashion, staring into the flames. "I'm glad ye've found yer way back to yer kind, but I'll confess, I'm gonna' miss yer prissy ways and yer fine lowland tongue," said the big man, also staring into the fire. Crispin looked at the hearth in front of him. "I'm sorry I questioned your friendship, and I shall miss you as well, and you cannot know how fond I am of this hound."

It goes without saying that the matter of the "mementos" was still unbroachable, but at last, Crispin could share stories surrounding his separation from the regiment. He allowed Hector the opportunity to believe that the trunk contained secrets belonging to the government, which, of course, Hector politely ignored. Crispin was totally unaware that Hector had peeked in the trunk one night. Crispin had been deeply asleep, and the giant had carefully and gently removed the key from Crisp's coat pocket. Hector had no use for great wealth and had seen much honesty in Crisp's actions, so he forgave the young man his deception. While he was glad to be back in good graces with his giant, Crispin was equally heartened by the very fact that his time in the wilds would remain known only to them, and Governor Dinwiddie would be none the wiser. In the coming days, Crispin paid a visit to the tailor who, of course, fashioned the coats of all the colonial militia officers; and after taking many and seemingly arcane measurements, the old fellow quoted the English lieutenant a price on the coat, waistcoat, and breeches. It might take several weeks, he explained to Crispin as he was waiting for a shipment of fabric, which included in it the lace that was a requirement on Crispin's coat.

With additional shirts and silk stockings, Crisp was out a small fortune; and while the wait seemed a bit inconvenient, he understood that things sometimes took longer on the edges of the empire. In London, a good tailor with help could have produced the needed garments in half the time and for a little less, but then, the English tailor didn't have to wait for ships to cross the Atlantic to stock ample materials.

After making rounds of the hatter and cutler, he managed to procure a passable small sword with a silvered shell guard and a lovely black tricorn. He had thought half a moment about purchasing expensive knee buckles and buttons but decided he did not wish to appear too profligate with his wealth, so instead, he settled on a stunning pair of boots and adequate shoes with plain silver buckles.

Inventorying his treasure took several days and only presented future problems concerning the sale of the numerous pieces of jewelry. Crispin supposed that most of the stones were real and assumed that DeVaca would not have included them in the horde unless that was the case. Disbursing the treasure would require assistance and expertise, which he did not have.

The young officer idled his time in his room, reading two-month-old news contained in papers from London that he had borrowed from a local planter, whose acquaintance he had made in the taproom. He engaged, of course, in drinking and gaming with members of the provincial gentry, losing modest amounts and gambling no more than would be seemly for a lieutenant.

With his eyes always open for a pretty ankle or a rosy bosom, Crisp soon learned the names of every suitable young lady in Williamsburg but found none to his liking from the small collection available. After Christmas and New Year's, the dun brown of winter was broken up by a series of dinner parties, shooting parties, and dances. As the only English regular officer of marriageable age and one who was romantically unclaimed and not involved in fighting the French and the sauvage, he found himself invited to a number of social events. Water fowling on the James occupied at least one day each week, and at least two nights were spent in gaming at the tavern. Often, on weekends, he found himself the welcome houseguest of some wealthy planter with a cross-eyed daughter or a spinster sister he hoped to pawn off on the unsuspecting swain.

Many of the supposed gentry had, no more than a generation or so earlier, been little better than small holding farmers, grubbing about in the rich Virginia soil themselves instead of employing nimble, work-callused black hands. Good breeding would demand at least several more generations in order to eliminate the obvious defects from the bloodlines of many tidewater families. Crispin, of course, conveniently forgot his own lowly beginnings in his pursuit of beauty and station.

Fox hunting with horse and hound was the eye around which the gay weekends spun, and Crispin's riding was becoming greatly improved. He had momentarily considered buying his own mount at auction but decided that, again, that would be a manifest expenditure, which he could not readily explain. Winning the horse at cards, however, would put a saddle under him with no explanation needed.

There were several other officers in the colonial capital, one in particular who rode a handsome Virginia hunter. The dapple grey horse with a jet-black mane and tail belonged to a militia major who constantly bragged of his connections in England and, in general, bored most of the company at the tavern with his incessant tales of conquest among the ladies during his recent visit to London and Birmingham. It was generally accepted, and accompanied by knowing chuckles, that the fellow could not have coaxed a single, penniless slattern into a tumble. It was said that his first and last conquest had fallen asleep during one of his interminable stories, and the poor wench died of old age before he finished the race.

Crisp, of course, gently edged the blustering fellow into a game of cards and, knowing the man's pretentiousness and pomposity, egged him into betting the horse against a stunning pigeon's blood ruby ring, which Crisp falsely claimed had belonged to his late mother. Losing the hand, Crisp begged for the opportunity to win back the ring as it was a family heirloom and was worth far more than a used saddle and a hunter. Once again, he slowly lured the fellow into betting the horse. Only this time, Crisp held the winning hand.

Lieutenant Mull then promptly insulted the fellow by condescendingly suggesting that a militia officer could ill afford to lose such an expensive mount and saddle. The Major, true to form, sneered at the loss and said he could afford to lose a half-dozen such hunters and reminded Crisp that it was he who had begged for the chance to win back a family bauble, and Crispin need not worry as he would not ask for the animal back.

Those who had watched snickered politely out of sight and thought Crispin was very clever for getting both the major's horse and his goat. The posturing colonial stalked off, muttering about insolent youth which he followed with the tossing down of numerous bumpers of imported wines until such time that he stumbled out of the tavern unevenly and borrowed a bony nag to trot home on. The tavern echoed from the smoky rafters to the well-scoured floorboards with toasts to Crispin and gales of laughter as one of the other fellows sat astride a bench and did his best impression of the major riding off, elbows flapping and heels kicking.

A wax sealed note arrived at last one day, confirming Crispin's story of the sunken transport and of his personal description as a young, handsome, middling-sized Scotchman. Colonel Blanchard ended the communiqué by urging the governor to put Crisp on the first boat available and that any expense would be covered in returning the brave lost man to the Fifty-Sixth Regiment. Crispin partook of a glass with the governor, toasting British arms and his own future, and then accepted the thick packet of dispatches and bowed his way out of the official presence.

It had taken no small bit of convincing, but Crispin had finally prevailed upon Governor Dinwiddie to allow him to undertake the journey to New York overland on his new mount. He explained to the governor that, given his recent experience with ships, he preferred to keep both of his feet on dry land for some time and went on to say that only a direct order or a chance of return to England could induce him to set foot on a ship at this juncture. The governor had understood Crispin's sentiments exactly as he had had a less than pleasant voyage himself when he crossed the water to take over Virginia's highest post. Dinwiddie had kindly offered Crisp an escort to the common border with Maryland so, in the company of two mounted privates of the Virginia Militia, Crispin proceeded to meet with his regiment once again. Now, obviously, he could not carry with him the chest of lucre, so he filled to the brim two coarse flour sacks with coin and jewelry, and these he tied tightly and placed in his saddlebags. The rest of the treasure he removed from the tavern in the dark of a moonless night, spiriting it away and carefully burying it where he could find it again but where no one else would ever think to look. What he carried in the well-padded sacks would take care of him in very fine fashion for years, if he were cautious with his spending. Someday when he had the freedom of movement, he would return for the balance of the Spaniard's horde.

Naturally, he was expected to buy the private's their drink at the end of the day, but they carried their own rations, and each night, they encamped in the April air under a canvas they carried with them. Crisp either recompensed some modest householder with a few copper and silver coins, or when available, he stayed at an inn.

Neither of the privates had a clue as to what Crispin carried with him, or it would likely have been a sore temptation to them that might have landed Crisp in an early grave.

Old Banquo trotted along beside, and when he seemed winded, Crisp would have one of the privates take the hound up before him on the saddlebow. His parting from Hector had been brief and heartfelt, and the giant had wished the young officer well and commented on what a fine figure he cut in his new uniform, and how he could barely imagine that the same fellow had helped him scrape hides. The great man pumped his hand and smiled warmly before stepping back and watching as Crisp wheeled up the road to meet his escort. April in Virginia is mild and pleasantly green with the dogwood in bloom and the creeks and streams burbling merrily down the forested hillsides to wet the fields and orchards in the fertile valleys. Crispin enjoyed the ride and conversed very little with his escort, but instead, either thought about the bright future he had arranged for himself or simply breathed deeply of the cleansing air, enjoying the ample sunshine.

Unlike many of his peers, Crisp was becoming more attuned to the wilds and was less of an indoorsman. Most Brits found the colonies savage and untamed and suspected it was full of ill humors waiting to kill the unsuspecting gentleman. It is, of course, true that there were many fevers and that often the fever season was a time to leave the city and seek bucolic pastures, but Crisp increasingly found the land not at all savage but rather more adventurous.

It stands to reason that Crispin found the colonies more hospitable, in large part, due to his outstanding luck and his unerring compass, which seemed to lead him out of danger and into wealth and station. Simply put, he began to believe in his own indestructibility. Naturally, when one has always enjoyed these advantages, it is reasonable to presume that it will continue forever, and Lieutenant Crispin Mull was no exception to mortal ambition as you have seen. They were on the ninth day of their travels and would soon be more than two hundred miles north of Williamsburg when Banquo whined a little and trotted off the road into the forest verge that bordered the narrow track. Crisp pulled up and ordered one of the privates to fetch him back, post haste. The surly fellow refused the order and just at that moment, Banquo gave full tongue, bawling loudly.

Crispin damned the recalcitrant militiaman roundly and quickly dismounting the grey, headed into the woods in full pursuit, knowing that the catamount or bear must not be far ahead. If he could catch and leash Banquo quickly enough, Crispin's progress would not be too upset.

The woods were neither dim nor thick, so Crisp could see Banquo climbing the side of a hill many yards ahead. The lieutenant drew back the cock on the pistol he had pulled from the saddle holster and carefully reprimed the gun, easing the cock back to the first notch of the sear in its inner works. Reassured that it would only go off if and when he was ready but most especially then, Crisp clamored upward, following the hound's cries. The trees were enormous, and the footing among the roots and rocks occasionally treacherous in riding boots, but Crisp safely arrived at a bench on the side of the mountain and paused to catch his breath and await the dog's urgent calling.

❋

All discussion had ceased when the hound gave voice, and the three members of the abbreviated war party scattered to the nearest trees to check the priming in the pans of their fusils. The bear shambled along until it neared their hiding place, and when it caught wind of their scent with its keen nose, it turned right and proceeded along the side of the mountain. Five minutes later, a dog, panting heavily, limped into view and snuffled about before turning to follow after the skinny bruin with its patchy spring coat. The party's leader lowered his French trade gun and watched as the dog moved out of sight. The other two members of the trio emerged from their hiding places, and once again, the conversation resumed in undertones. The largest member of the group shifted her massive breasts with her strong upper arms, clearly trying to adjust the straps of her elk skin shooting bags and the tumpline that held her bedroll. Fat Anne, as the English called her, disagreed with her paramour, Captain Stone Pipe. The captain (so named by the Brits because in his younger days, he had been a great war captain of the Delaware tribe and because he smoked like a chimney) wished to move quickly away from the area, afraid that the hound portended a party of white long hunters. Anne, however, thought that they should wait in the trees and see what came after. Perhaps there was a chance for easy guns and scalps, and she reminded him, if he wished to leave, she would fight them alone as she had the frontier householder two weeks earlier. The white settler had thrown up a hasty stockade around his pathetic cabin; he seemed well armed with several manned loopholes in the walls. Stone Pipe had suggested finding other easier prey when the big squaw had suddenly laid aside her firelock and stripped off her shirt and bravely walked out of the forest into the stump-filled clearing with her great bare pendulous breasts swaying. When she had reached the center of the clearing, she sat down before the crude gate. Pipe stood back in the dark of the trees, stunned by the woman's courage.

The foolish settler had opened the gate and approached the curious scene with his rifle cradled in the crook of his arm. There was no way that the farmer could have suspected that a half-naked Indian wench portended danger. The sight of her would have been a curiosity to the most seasoned frontiersman.

Stone Pipe shot him through the heart from the cover of the trees. Fat Anne, rising up nimbly, rushed into the cramped ox and sheep-filled enclosure and ferociously struck down a seventeen-year-old boy and his sixteen-year-old cousin, along with the man's wife, using just her tomahawk. Before the painted Amazon could fell her though, the white man's wife had gotten off one shot with the musket from the open doorway of the cabin, grazing Fat Anne's thigh.

In a flash, the two women were locked in mortal combat, the white woman swinging a large English Brown Bess musket and the savage wench wielding her bloody axe. It was a one-sided fight that ended with the Indian widow warrior blotting the bloody grey and blond scalp on each of her huge bosoms and screaming at the top of her massive lungs—an altogether sobering sight. In the several years they had been together, Pipe never ceased to be simply amazed at the woman's bravado and strength. It was more than unusual for savage women to take the warpath; it was almost unheard of in every confederation. While women might control politics in some tribes and have great influence over the war chiefs, they never themselves took to the warpath. Fat Anne had taken the bloody trail against the whites when her husband and children had been murdered by white hunters. She alone had survived the harrowing experience and had been cruelly ravaged and then thrown into a river to drown. When she finished tamping flat the sod over the grave of her mutilated infant daughter, she had promised herself revenge. She had taken a well-worn Spanish miquelet firelock from a settler after she had plunged a deer antler into his pale, fat belly. With those weapons, she had gained more tools and experience. Captain Pipe had found her two years later; she then had four stretched scalps hanging from her shooting bag and was holding a musket muzzle to his naked, paint-daubed chest. Fat Anne's story does not begin there however.

The daughter of a great warrior and a strong, broad-beamed German girl who was taken captive in a bloody raid, Fat Anne understood the Englanders, as her mother called as all whites, and knew in her broken heart that they would not be glad until they had slaughtered every ochre-colored babe and copper-skinned youth. With her own tear-stained eyes, she had watched helplessly as the Pennsylvania hunter drove his bitter hatchet into her little daughter's beautiful face. Her original name amongst her people had been Strong Mother, and she had been a genial woman, quick to laugh and tender with all the village's children, taking special delight in making corn husk dolls for the little girls. As a dutiful wife, she had served her husband well and always made him proud of her strength and her wit, and he was most pleased with her prowess between the blankets.

All that happiness had ended when the white hunters walked into their family's winter camp, seeking to trade guns and powder for furs and hides. Her esteemed husband, Fast Otter, had welcomed the trade and, after feasting the whites, had brought out his bundles of fur for trade.

One of the men fetched some shining steel traps from his horse packs along with a jug of rum, but the bargaining had become heated when Otter said he would not trade for the steel traps and asked instead if the men had ruffled shirts and red blankets for his wife. One of the hunters called him a damned heathen thief and, pulling a pistol from his wide leather belt, shot Otter in the stomach. Then the two had quickly clubbed down the family's eleven-year-old son, breaking his back and staving in his skull as the lad tried to scramble for his father's weapons.

In their drunken savagery, they pinned Strong Mother down and had their way with her for many hours, then made her watch the mutilation of her beloved baby before throwing them both from a wooded bluff down into the Monongahela River.

"Best to kill the nits before they grow to be lice!" said one of the murderers.

The third member Pipe's party, Broken Toe, a slender quiet warrior who permanently limped and spoke but rarely told Stone Pipe he would follow Anne. She had powerful medicine and would not be struck down in battle until the spirits were finished with the destruction of the whites.

War chiefs lead their followers by courage, strength, wisdom, and coup de main, not the exercise of power through legal authority, and Captain Pipe had lost his command of men many years ago when he suffered an ignominious defeat. No longer was he a truly respected war leader. Broken Toe and Fat Anne deferred to him out of honor for his past deeds and his knowledge but did not feel that they were bound to him or owed him any strict allegiance.

The three were a loose but effective group of misfits, attacking only those they knew they could easily overwhelm. For years, the frontier had been sporadically suffering from the grim and gory depredations of much larger parties, so their crimes often times were ascribed to more sizable companies of marauding natives and thus, the three went unnoticed in many cases.

Captain Pipe eschewed the use of the torch, which was a common tool with other war parties. Pipe knew that a column of smoke on the horizon, more than anything else, signaled a settler's neighbors to a war party's presence. Gunshots often rang out on the frontier, but when they accompanied a burning, it could mean only one thing in those cruel days of treachery and revenge. Leaving the crude homes open to the forest's slow destruction and the vagaries of the weather rather than setting it ablaze, the threesome thus often found an unprepared white just over the next ridge or around the shoulder of a mountain. Never had they strayed so far east as this, and at last, they had decided to loop north and west, avoiding major settlements, and perhaps, with a bit of luck, they might hunt down a lonesome traveler or a foolish farmer or two.

Crisp rested briefly on the bench where the Indians lay in wait. Banquo gave tongue far off to his right, sounding as though he may have dropped into a crag or vale. He turned and began to follow Banquo's cry. He had not gone more than several hundred yards, however, when suddenly, stars leaped before his eyes, and a dull ringing, like the distant sound of a hammer at the forge, filled his ears. He lost all sense of up or down and felt himself falling sideways into a dark well that spun like a slowly turning wheel.

Fat Anne was stooping over Crispin's fallen form, removing his hat, preparatory to removing his scalp, when Stone Pipe calmly stayed her vengeful hand. In his quiet, guttural tones, he explained to her that the English officer was worth far more alive than dead. Broken Toe slipped the carved wooden war club back into his belt and put the lieutenant's tricornered hat on his head while the other two argued about the white's fate. Plunder had been sufficient at the homesteads that they had raided but lacked the pretty finery so dear to the savage heart. Strong Mother considered Pipe's words and thought about the danger of conducting a prisoner across the frontier to the French at Fort Duquesne.

※

The warrior woman led an ancient bay plow horse by a rope that had once hauled a wooden bucket from a well as she trailed along behind Broken Toe who, with his fusil slung over his back, prodded Crisp along ahead of him with a stick. The horse switched its tail, glad it no longer pulled a plow or drew a wagon.

Captain Pipe scouted the front of the party by some three hundred feet or a little more than a musket shot. The load of booty on the horse was carefully distributed and made not a sound. Pipe's advance hopefully forestalled any ambush or, at worst, gave adequate warning to those that followed.

Crispin had been stripped of his small clothes except his red breeches, which no self-respecting warrior would wear. His coat, which was too small in the chest for either of the men, was stashed amongst the other loot while his expensive shirt had been cut down the front and was being worn by Pipe like a sleeved weskit. Broken Toe had pulled a bloody, torn wagoner's smock from his pack and told Crisp with signs to put it on. His riding boots also had been taken, and instead, he was given a pair of worn but serviceable moccasins.

He had been stumbling along with his numbing arms and tingling fingers tied to his sides for several days. Upon occasion, Broken Toe and Fat Anne would switch places, and she would drive the lieutenant, only her stick was sharpened to a needle point, and she delighted in poking and jabbing with it every time Crispin stumbled. To the woman who had warmed Fast Otter's bed and loved his children, Crispin represented the worst aspect of the Englishers. Strong Mother knew that it was the royal governors and the British military establishment that had rarely pursued the punishment of traders who had robbed or hurt the Indians. To be sure, Sir William Johnson did what he could to protect and champion the red man's cause, but his complaints and petitions took months and often fell on deaf ears. Once in a great while, some despicable trader would be punished, but taken as a whole, most whites cared little what happened out of their sight over the vast mountain spine that runs from Bay Colony (now called Maine) to Georgia. As long as they were safe to carry on business as usual, then the devil takes the heathen and the hindmost. It was because of this attitude and the tragedy of having her former life stolen that Strong Mother took satisfaction from Crispin's pain. He didn't understand a word of their gibberish, and while Crispin had tried to tell them that he had coin to buy his own freedom, they had only scowled, and Captain Pipe boxed his ears again painfully. He, of course, did not know their names and found everything they said a jumble of guttural utterances, incomprehensible and ugly to his ear. After a day of pleading and begging and attempting to find the words which they would understand, Crisp gave up at last. To his mind, they were like children with no concept of money or wealth, content with some new trinket or toy like his pistol. Only a foolish child would greedily grab a redcoat over a sack bursting with gold.

Captain Pipe had understood enough of what Crispin had to say but was not willing to risk his companions' lives in trying to parley with two militiamen who, most likely, would themselves know of and covet the coin. So he feigned complete ignorance and pretended that he neither spoke nor understood the king's English. Pipe was sure that if Strong Mother were aware of both the gold and the soldiers, she would drag Broken Toe off, and the two of them would attempt to ambush the escort. Though it might work, the captain was afraid that sooner or later, Fat Anne's luck would run out; and while he wasn't married to her, he was very fond and respectful of the younger woman. Keeping the information to himself, he boxed the officer on the ear every time he was near and thought the Englishman might be getting close to making himself understood.

Pipe was sure that if he could get far enough from the mountain where they had captured the white man, they would be safe, and he would no longer have to worry about the other two turning back. The bounty the French would pay for the Englishman was not insubstantial and a degree of Pipe's old respect would be restored and warriors would once again wish to take to the war path with him. Crispin lay by the fire each night with a rawhide halter about his neck, which was tied loosely to a tree. His hands were still bound in front of him with another tether that was lashed to Pipe's wrist. Any movement would awaken the old warrior, and Crisp would receive a round of abuse one would reserve for a hound that had rudely lifted its leg on your best boots. By the third night, Crisp learned to sleep without moving and he began to fall into a rhythm of jogging during the day and resting motionless at night.

He found that if he moved quickly on the trail and didn't complain, the natives ignored him. They kindly stopped once each afternoon for him to evacuate himself, and they fed him dried meat and parched corn in the mornings and evenings but gave him only tepid water from a gourd canteen in the mid-afternoon.

The first day, Crispin had been in constant fear; but by the middle of the second day, he was sure they were not going to kill him outright, and he felt quite certain that they were still many miles from their destination. Until they reached their goal, he would do his level best to gain their respect and try to learn some of their savage patois so that he might bargain with their chiefs and sachems when he was given the opportunity.

Crispin was woefully ignorant of how the process worked and truly believed that the Indians would boil and eat you (which they did upon occasion, but not always as Crisp believed), but he also ignorantly imagined they were intellectually simple and could be tricked or bought. While there had been a time in the near past when the red people had not fully understood the twisted laws of the white man, by this time, they were well aware of the unfair rules and deceptions that many whites considered normal humdrum business practices when dealing with the copper skinned children of the forest. Crispin suffered from the most common form of Anglo arrogance—that of supposing his intellectual capacity was somewhat superior because of the snowy quality of his skin.

Captain Pipe was familiar with the baseless arrogance of the whites and was terribly insulted and galled by the idea that such a weak-spleened people could possibly believe they were better. If they were so superior, he asked himself, then why did they come here at all? If their kings were so strong, why then couldn't they feed all their people? Their goods were cunning, he granted, but they were a loud, ungainly race, and his people could only benefit when the whites gave up their arrogance and meekly stayed by the sea.

He thought that the French were a little better, but even they were better only for sometimes living with the Indians and sharing their hardships. The French king's goods were not so good as the English king's, and neither of the monarchs had ever come to council but instead sent lesser chiefs, and this rankled in Stone Pipe's heart. Simply stated, the Frenchman wanted to make other Frenchmen out of the Indian, and the Englishman only wanted the land and the animals and didn't give a thought to what became of the Indian. *In either case, the true people are the losers*, thought Captain Pipe. He had no intention of becoming a Frenchman and was not interested in selling the land to the Englishmen at any price.

AT THE YELLOW WASP

No longer comely, Peg had made her way to New York after several weeks, and during which time, she stopped often and performed menial chores for simple fare and a dusty hay loft to sleep in. Once she had cleaned herself up and her cheek began to scab over, she looked less like one of the Furies, and she lied, of course, to explain her disheveled and scarred appearance. No one would take pity on a murderess, but a woman who had been beaten and set on the road by her heartless "brother" demanded some sympathy from even the most stony hearted of New Englanders.

By the third week, she began to recover from her broken nose and the swelling left her face. The bruising about her eyes faded, but her once pert olfactory organ now was hooked hard to the left and had a pronounced hump in the middle, marring her formerly lovely profile forever. The scabrous wound to her cheek flaked away and left behind a livid scar. Peg's sporting figure made up for her now rough appearance though, and men began to notice her rather than look away as they had when she was newly cut, so she found that she had yet another source of income as long as she was discreet.

One night, she had entertained two youths in the mow of a barn while one of the lad's parents slept in the house next door. He and his handsome friend had paid her well and shared the hard cider they had purloined from the family's stock. The very next night, the resident boy's father paid her a call long after the moon had set while his wife snored loudly in the bedchamber. Leaving before cockcrow, the farmer placed a coin in her sleeping hand and slipped back into the house before his wife arose. Adding what she made off her amorous visitors to that which the wheezing Goodwife paid her for chores and sewing, Peg had enough to make her way into New York at last.

Sergeant Collward reported to the colonel that there was a camp drab or washerwoman outside who insisted on seeing him. She claimed to have personal communications for the regimental commander, and she could deliver them to no one else she said. Collward sighed as though bored with the whole inquiry and was quite sure that the colonel would order her sent packing, except for one curiosity. "Oh, one more thing, sir, I found this queersome. She said Lieutenant Mull sent her? I don't understand it though. He's not due from Virginia for another fortnight." Old Barley's head snapped up from the victualling report he was perusing before signing. "Send her in, Sergeant. Perhaps there is more in this than a whore looking for a handout."

Peg had covered her head with a scarf, like an Irish peasant woman, and looked down at her worn shoes so that none could get a clear look at her face. If she were to find her way back into Beverly's bed, then she wanted no connection to the lowly washerwoman she currently appeared to be. She, of course, had no fore knowledge of Lieutenant Mull's adventures but had thought that by mentioning the name of her abductor, the sergeant would get Beverly's attention without her having to give away her identity or more information than she was willing to. As the sergeant escorted her into the tent, she didn't see the one-eyed "veteran" who was lounging about across the street near the fort's wall, within easy ear shot of Old Barley's tent. Colonel Blanchard sat back in his chair with his hands folded in front of his growing paunch. If the visitor had been a lady, he would have greeted her standing and perhaps even have offered her refreshment from his ever-present bowl of punch. Blanchard's idea of punch was a liberal amount of rum with a lonely lemon slice floating in it, a dash of water, and just a pinch of sugar, just so that he could call it punch.

The drab was no lady, however, and he had no intention of getting to his tired feet. The woman clumped in her brogans and removed the cloth from her head and slowly lifted her chin. "I don't know why you sent me away," she said quietly but bluntly. "But I have come to beg you to take me in and help me, Beverly."

Old Barley leaned across the table peering into her face. "Good God! It can't be. Damn my eyes!" His brain raced and stumbled as it twisted through the labyrinth of emotions that ran the gamut from fear to joy and finally ended in consternation at the return of an old problem he had long thought safely put away.

He rose and peered over her shoulder to the front of the tent, hoping that the sergeant was napping or outside smoking. Collward politely appeared to be engrossed in cleaning one of the colonel's other uniform coats. Coming around to the front of his table, he fetched a folding chair from nearby and indicated that she should sit. Barley opened his mouth several times as though to speak, and nothing came out but little haws and stutters because he clearly could not think of what to ask first. Finally, after many long seconds, he again became the master of both his mind and his tongue. "What on earth are you doing here, dear girl?" he asked in complete puzzlement.

"If you mean why am I in New York, you would know better than I how I came to the colonies. If you mean what am I doing in your pavilion, then I have already told you. I have missed you for years and have been brokenhearted since you sent me away," she said pettishly, her eyes on her hands which lay in her lap. Old Barley was gullible enough to accept that statement, and also Peg had become a very accomplished liar, specializing in playing to male vanity. Barley walked slowly back around the table to his banister back chair, his chin resting on his chest and his hands clasped behind his back. Sitting down, still with his chin resting on his breast and with his hands again before him, he seemed deeply lost in contemplation. Peg chose to stare at the floor, and her hands nervously twisted at her scarf, which lay in her lap.

After many long minutes, Barley finally and slowly raised his head from his apparent reverie. Reaching for the blue china inkpot, he picked up his quill and began to write. Peg was unsure what to say or what to think. At last, the scritch and scratch of the pen stopped, and he dusted the paper with sand and set it aside to dry for a moment.

"I'm afraid, my dear Peggy," said he "that we can no longer be together. Our liaison reached an end two years ago. I am truly sorry to see that you have fallen upon lean times and regret that your previous beauty has been so badly marred as to make your condition pitiful." He reached over to pick up the letter. "I have here a letter, which will allow you to draw bread and meat from the regimental kitchen when you leave, and here are a few guineas to help see you through while you seek a situation more suitable to your current station. I would appreciate it if you would inquire after work with one of the other regiments. Perhaps in Albany," he said coldly, taking the coins from a drawer.

The conversation was clearly at an end. Peg had remained quiet throughout, but finally, a small and genuine whimper escaped her lips. She plucked the coins from the desk and dropped them into her pocket and then, picking up the letter, looked it over briefly and then she slowly tore it down the middle and, leaning over the table, deposited the pieces in Beverly's lap. Before straightening up, she reached out and gave his nose a great and violent tweak, twisting it on its side. The colonel leaped to his feet and gave out a bellow of pain as she released the fleshy protuberance, turned on her heel, and breezed past the sergeant who came running at the sound of his leader's discomfort.

Blanchard said nothing to the sergeant, and they both watched out the open tent flap as the woman stalked across the camp. Barley rubbed gently at his snout and prayed that he had seen the last of Margaret Fairchild but was quite sure that he should have had her strangled when he had the chance. He briefly contemplated hiring out her demise but was far too afraid of getting caught, and so the matter rested for the moment.

Trepan was entirely unsure what had just taken place in Blanchard's tent but was assured from the woman's apparent pique that it had not gone her way. Valuable gossip could be traded for secrets or in some cases sold directly to his masters in Montreal. The strumpet almost certainly had a story to tell, and with any luck, he could extract it for free and make a tidy profit. She clomped up the street in her brogans, oblivious to the lethal shadow that slinked along behind. Peg had no destination in mind and walked onward without goal or aim in a fit of anger. She plotted old Barley's violent demise in a dozen different ways. She had entered the city the night before and had slept the night in a haystack on the edge of town, eating a crust of bread to break her fast at dawn. She had picked the straws out of her hair as she walked the remaining miles, hopeful that her travails were at last at an end. Peg had dreamed of resuming her life of idleness. Living the last few weeks like a starved mongrel bitch had been worth it until the fateful meeting. The rude and insulting dismissal from Blanchard had been completely unsuspected on her part as she had believed that Beverly would welcome her back into his bed with his wife and clubfooted daughter far away in old England.

Trepan followed her to a dram shoppe on the waterfront where no one would think twice of serving an unaccompanied woman. Her coin was as good as the next slatterns and willing wenches kept the regular customers happy. Of course, she knew this only by instinct and not through experience, but it seemed that the lower she slipped, the more naturally she understood the rules. Of course, in Peg's case, it was not as though she had slipped, but it was more as though she had come home, the prodigal daughter returning. While she despised the malodorous clientele, she had a strange affinity and sympathy for them that defied explanation. Their rules were simple and in accord with her own. Despite her many years with Beverly and her time as the good captain's wife, Peg still had not purged herself of her lower caste notions which were to her as was nakedness to the savage, that is to say as natural as drawing a breath.

Only in its here-to-fore brief incarnation as a cobbler's shoppe had the Yellow Wasp tavern ever been anything more than a sinkhole for sailors and dockworkers, a place of endless iniquities and countless deals with the devil. Trepan himself was now a reigning resident and was well-known to the after sunset crowd who huddled in the dark recesses, sullenly lapping up their spirits and shunning the elbows and laughter of honest folk. He could not have been more pleased when she chose its gaping maw and without hesitation vanished into the smoky murk. He paused to light the stub of a pipe he carried and to allow the woman to make herself comfortable before he began his stalk. Peg had eased herself into a dark corner where she sipped at a dirty tumbler of rum and surveyed the fumy den while her thoughts wandered back over the futile conversation with Beverly.

There was nothing more she could have done, and she concluded that her prospects were sparse. The few guineas she had to her name would carry her for a time if she lived sparely and obtained work soon. Having performed all the necessary chores at Harding House, there was little that Peg could not do if she chose. Surely, she thought, there were easier ways to earn a living than by gathering hens' eggs and scrubbing floors. As her eyes adjusted to the dim light, she saw an enormous form, like a giant toad sitting in the farthest reaches of the Wasp's belly. While she strained her eyes trying to make out the face of the bloated man, he reached out and pulled a candle closer so that the light reflected off his taut, waxy skin. Peg drew a breath. He was staring right at her with a glint in his dark beady eyes and just the faintest hint of a grin on his wide mouth. O. Nicholas Nero Magoggle was known for nothing good and, more often than not, had his chubby fingers with their pointy nails dabbling in something unsavory. Few, if any, ever knew his whereabouts at any given moment, and those who sought him rarely found him on their terms. Magoggle summoned the seekers, and they came. No one knew the full extent of his business but he, and only a few even dared to guess at how he earned his portion. Those who knew or suspected rarely even blinked and never spoke—if they thought to keep their tongues when the truth was near at hand.

Smuggling was whispered by some to form the center of his trade while others said it was slavery, and still, others thought he was a money lender. In truth, it was all three and more. Magoggle had not met a vice he didn't like nor one upon which he could not turn a profit nor a man who did not need his services at some time or other. To tie his name to any crime or trade was an impossibility. Persons in the correct offices had received their wages, and threats had been uttered with a foul-breathed hiss.

Trepan was vaguely aware of the wide net that Magoggle cast, but out of professional respect and a refined sense of survival (that some would call fear), he had so far steered clear of the fat spider's web. He had thought it was no sense getting entangled in the affairs of others. Now, here was Magoggle, leering at his strumpet and she looking back like a bird entranced by the cobra's dance. "Ye've the look of a girl down on her luck and in need of an introduction," said Trepan to Peg. He had slipped onto the worn plank settle near her hip while she was busily returning the basilisk's stare. She startled a little and looked down to see who had spoken.

"If I was in need of an introduction, you hardly seem the type to whom I'd turn." Peg looked back up, but the candle on his table had gone out, and she could see nothing in the blackness that surrounded the corner where Magoggle rested.

"I suppose ye'd like to know who the great man is now, wouldn't ye?" tempted Trepan, nodding towards the shadows.

"I could walk over and ask him myself if that were what I was after!" rounded Peg. She shifted her weight to her other foot and sipped at the tumbler, ignoring Trepan again.

"Now, what does a lass of the regiment want with the likes of him?" He kept his hands on his walking stick and pointed to the darkened recess of the tavern with his chin, beyond the drink dead faces that hovered nearest them.

"I've nothing to do with any regiment. What is his name, if yer so all knowing?" she asked, leaning back and resting one foot up against the uneven stone wall.

"I'll tell ye his name if ye'll tell me why you were in the camp of the Fifty-Sixth of foot. His name is Magoggle." He winked, trying to seem impish.

"To see my man," Peg said plainly, her tone implying she would say no more. Trepan sensed like a cat stalking a mouse that the time was not yet ripe and that he must wait. He hoped that her information was of more interest than she let on. *Not of the regiment and to see her man, aye, that's queer*, he thought. Her guarded answers suggested to his twisted mind a more complicated story lie just out of reach. If she were of a mind to trade, then he would oblige her with an introduction. Rising from his seat and bowing low at the waist in the manner of a gentleman, his hat swept the floor, exposing his thinning greasy hair.

"Allow me ta introduce ye ta Mister Magoggle, and then perhaps, ye'll entertain me with yer tale—or yer front," he said with mock gallantry and a leer. You will recall that because of his less than dashing appearance, Trepan had never had a way with the fairer sex and had always relied either on the point of his knife or on favors from the likes of the late P. Peter Lane to sate his lust. If she had no story worth telling, then the wench had other wares with which to repay him. He ushered across the room into the waiting shadow.

Magoggle raised his bulk from the table and, reaching out, took Peg's dainty hand in his own pudding soft paw. He gestured for her to sit next to him and, with a flip of his hand, waved Trepan off while he dispatched a skinny, dirty young scoundrel, whom he called Pretty Danny, to search out a taper to brighten the gloom. The owner of the Wasp wasted little on candles and less on wood for the fireplace. Several boys fetched drinks—and a tapster remained safely caged—filling tankards and pitchers behind the bar. The boys dodged the hungry clutches and caught the shining coins flipped through the air by wolfish customers on the prowl.

Trepan moved off into the crowd, seeking anonymity in numbers. He didn't wish to talk to anyone but, instead, discreetly observed the by-play between the slut and Magoggle. *Little did she know*, he thought, *that once Magoggle had gotten his talons into her, there was likely no way out until the fellow was through with her.* Women, he had long ago decided, were a mercenary lot, attaching themselves to the fellow who could give them the most and then abandoning him as soon as a better prospect came along. As he pondered the predatory behavior, he saw Peg begin to flirt with the massive reprobate. No doubt, she imagined herself gaining the ascendancy. Instead, she would be lucky if he didn't crush the life out of her in his copulative embrace.

The rotund villain stood up and, taking the "offering" by her arm, escorted her through a curtained doorway in the back of the shoppe toward a fate which Trepan could only guess at. If the wench came back, then perhaps he could induce her to tell her tale. Waiting for the cursed young lieutenant was an exercise in patience and in resourcefulness. He was beginning to run out of information to sell to Montreal, and the lies would begin to become transparent if he didn't have something near genuine with which to spice them, and of late, there was nothing that the frogs did not likely already know. No doubt, Magoggle would be grateful, and perhaps, he would send a minor reward to Trepan for the introduction. Trepan knew that significant rewards carried a price that he was unwilling to pay at the moment. Never in his existence had Trepan ever worked for someone else unless he was assured that it was to his overwhelming benefit. Working for Magoggle could be to no one's benefit but the fat man's.

The curtained doorway had led to a backroom full of empty oak casks, and that in turn had let out into a cobbled courtyard strewn with litter, which they crossed before going into the building on the far side. Passing through a heavy iron-trimmed wooden door, Peg's eyes adjusted to the faint light coming in from two-leaded windows set high in either end of the narrow, oblong room. The floor was stone like the rest of the house, and the only pieces of furniture in sight were a large antique wainscot chair and a rope bed with a dirty wool blanket on it. The door slammed shut behind them, and Magoggle settled his girth into the chair and looked at Peggy standing dumbly before him. He took a drink from the deep green bottle he had brought with him. Placing it between his blubberous thighs, he held it gently by the neck.

"Dance for me," he said quietly with a menacing tone.

Darling Peggy had thought she knew what was expected of her, but this was quite unusual and beyond her ken. "Excuse me?" she asked.

"You said you wished to make me happy," stated Magoggle flatly. "That will make me happy."

"There is no music," Peg said, pointing out the obvious.

Magoggle began to hum quietly. To the provincial ear, it would have been dissonant and foreign. To an experienced ear, had there been one, it would have sounded mysterious like a gypsy dance or perhaps even a Corsican lament. It was many sounds and none, changing and shifting, and at times sad and then erotic, by turns exciting and frightening like a song of war.

Peg found the rhythms and began to step and sway to the music, her hands struggling to untie the stays that bound her upper body, her face flushing with an excitement that she could not even explain. She moved like a dervish, her auburn hair whipping her bare naked shoulders like a lash. Minutes or perhaps hours later, she awoke, lying spent and chilled on the damp flag stoned floor next to her tangled clothes. Hearing a titter of laughter, she looked up, and Magoggle was nowhere in sight. In his stead, there was a redheaded boy of a dozen years or so sitting in his chair. The lad was clearly excited by her state of complete undress, and when he saw she had spied him, he jumped up from the chair and scampered out of the door and presumably back toward the tavern.

※

"When ye dance for the devil girl, don't expect a shilling," said Trepan, coming in a few minutes later. He threw her chemise at her as he openly eyed her bosom and rump like a butcher assessing the best cut from a side of meat. *She definitely had wares*, he thought, his appetite growing with each feminine movement.
"Where did he go?" whispered Peg.

"I don't know. When the fat man came back without ye, I sent one of the serving boys to look in and see that my new lady acquaintance was safe an' sound," Trepan replied cockily as he unwittingly caressed her petticoats while she pulled the chemise over her head and retied the drawstrings on the soiled sleeve cuffs.

Peg could remember very little of the afternoon with Magoggle. The first round of dance had made her tired, and she was wetted like a mare fairly run. She had drunk from his hand after he poured it full of warm, spiced wine, and then she had danced some more while he sat humming in his chair, his cheeks flushed with excitement or wine—or both. For certain, she had not conjoined with him, and she had no recollection of any embrace or other intimate contact. What puzzled her was that she was as weak and sore as though she had just risen from a long night of amorous congress.

"Come with me, lass, an' tell me yer tale, and I'll buy ye a supper, fer it t'is that time, and if ye've a mind, ye can tell me what passed between ye an' Magoggle." Trepan held out his arm in a companionable way.

Peg, feeling weak in the knees and in need of strong drink and food, knew she could overcome her initial revulsion at his grimy, scarred, one-eyed face. Knowing nothing of his murderous background was something of an advantage as well, even though she could not appreciate it at the moment. While Pasquale's volcanic temper had been exciting, Trepan's mathematically calculated violence would have put her off considerably had she but known it, even though she and he had a great deal in common since she, of course, had done away with Goody Harding in a like manner. The oysters were rich and filling, and they washed down well with a stolen bottle of Canary wine.

Trepan had spent richly from his miserly savings, hoping that the wench would give him everything he sought. It was not without trepidation, however, that he hosted and toasted the crooked nosed beauty. First among his considerations was the expense, and secondly, he had nervously decided to divulge his hideout in the loft of Hermann and Werth. Peg, of course, was too tired and hungry to care where he dragged her, and once she had swilled half of the bottle of Canary wine, she became sleepy and pliable—her answers came without guile. "Since it's no great secret that ye went to talk to Barley Blanchard, would ye mind tellin' me why? Out of nat'ral curiosity, of course," asked the assassin as he lay back in a couch of loose sail cloth.

Peg, sitting like a savage with her limbs crossed, popped a plump oyster into her mouth and chewed the juicy morsel with great relish as a contented smile crossed her face. "In another life, he was my lover," said she matter-of-factly. Her fall was nearly complete. She took a deep breath and stretched, her ample bosom straining at the binding of her dirty stays.

Trepan's eyes widened, and he took a hurried tug at the bottle of wine. Seeking buried treasure, he reached out his dirty hand toward her petticoat. Peg, in her tired and semi-inebriated state, responded as though she were under a spell and sat still and uncaring. In her mind, the thought occurred that she owed the man for the meal for his consideration; and if she closed her eyes, what was a few moments dalliance in the scope of her existence after all?

The tortured iron gates screeched open, and as she fell backward into a pile of canvass, the fire-blackened jaws swallowed the grappling couple whole. Peg let out a plaintive cry somewhere between pain and pleasure, and Trepan threw back his head, his eyes furtively darting left and right as if he were seeking The Watcher. The iron twins crashed shut behind them. Somewhere near the wharf, a stray dog howled with glee. O. Nicholas Magoggle had gotten his way, Trepan had gotten his desire, and formerly pretty Peg was about to get her reward.

RANSOMED

Captain Pipe pushed Crisp down the heavily wooded shale and clay slope toward the Indian village below. Children playing in dun colored fields of last year's corn stalks and squash vines saw the group descending the slope toward the river and ran to tell mothers and fathers of the war party's approach. Cheerful shouts and raucous cries greeted the ears of Fat Anne and the others, and Crispin was quite sure that things were about to change, and he was not at all satisfied that the changes would be to his liking.

Crispin's time with Hector had, however, prepared him for this better than not at all. The Scot had told him numerous blood-curdling tales of savage kidnappings and scalpings. After overcoming his initial disgust at the descriptions of the horrendous tortures, Crispin had listened like an enraptured schoolboy to the stories—most of which were true and had only the barest of embellishments added. Hector had told him how men who were meek and pliable rarely lived long after capture as most natives supposed this to be a sign of weakness, and in their culture, which lauded personal bravery, the weak and cowardly were useless and deserving of little respect. Tortures were meant to allow a fellow to explore the horizons of his own inner strength before entering the Happy Hunting Ground and, if well met, were sometimes occasioned by proud applause and even more rarely by acts of mercy.

An honored warrior was one who cursed his captors, boasted of his prowess in battle, and silently and stoically faced all trials of pain, no matter how gruesome. The savage warrior was quite clear that those who screamed and cried out in a cowardly manner brought on even greater tortures, usually to the hoots of laughter and derision from savage onlookers. Inevitably, the cruelty ended in a grisly and agonizing death, the corpse defiled by old women and children, the execution relegated to stories told over a gnawed venison bone and which were repeated for a month at the most. White captives too often presumed that if they begged loudly and protested long enough, someone would take pity on them and relieve them of their agonies. Nothing could have been farther from the truth, and sadly, those craven enough to plead for mercy invariably sealed their own fate. The brave would be remembered, their remains honored or sometimes consumed like meat in order that the diner should take on the attributes of the deceased. The savage warrior was quite clear that when and if he was captured, his life was most likely forfeit, and he had best make a good show of it and meet his creator with his head held high. If good fortune should be his and his captors adopted him or enslaved him, then he could still hold his head up in brave company.

Tender Christian mercies were unknown in the woodland castles of the Red Indian and, sadly, are as little known in many of our larger and more civilized cities and towns. I am sad to relate that much mischief and injustice to the savage was practiced in places populated by prelates, clergymen, and members of the Christian community who are supposedly practitioners of compassion and pity. Pulpits and hallowed halls of learning and the law echoed with demands for justice at the muzzle of a cannon. This should come as no surprise though as some of our very own Pilgrim fathers drenched their hands in innocent blood in the fighting with that estimable sachem—*King Philip*.

Fat Anne jabbed Crisp with every stride, for she hoped that this would be her last chance to take revenge on this white man while he was still alive, and poking a charred corpse with a stick was not to her taste. Women and children often times were allowed in the gauntlet line, and this was their one chance to participate directly in the jubilant tormenting. Elder wise women would sometimes be consulted regarding adoptions and women who had lost a son or daughter could speak up and lay claim to some likely specimen. Weanlings that had survived the hardships of the trail were invariably taken into the tribe while for youths and adults the future was much less certain.

Crispin did not know that Pipe had planned to ransom him, so afraid to show his cowardice, he squared his shoulders and stuck out his chin defiantly. Fat Anne saw this and drove her fist into his kidneys, and as he stumbled, she clouted him between the shoulder blades with the butt of her fusil. Children with hickory whips cut from saplings, and branches swarmed towards him, and the women, many of them carrying hoes and clubs, joined in. Pipe, not wanting undue harm to come to his valuable prisoner, stepped between Crisp and the buzzing mob, holding up his musket and speaking loudly in his native patois, brusquely ordering the women to do the Anglais no great harm. The children swept around Pipe like a furious tide flooding passed some ancient stone guardian and began striking at Crisp's legs and midsection with their springy switches, raising welts with each lash.

Holding his head high once more, sure that he was about to be massacred by enraged savages, he broke into song, belting out the chorus of "Rule Britannia." Shortly into his concert, Crispin let out a profane oath and, acting out of instinct inspired by pain, swatted a boy of ten summers or so squarely on the cheek and sent him sprawling into the dusty path that lead down the center of the village. Thinking that he needed to bluster some more in order to preserve his own life, he summoned up what courage he had left and added to it a large dose of righteous indignation. "By God, I am an English officer, you bloody stinking heathens, and if you have an ounce of civility in you, you'll drag off your ill-mannered brats before I snap their necks!" While he most rabidly desired to grab several of the children and shake them like rabbits for the pot, he knew this would be unwise and also his hands were tied together at the wrist, making rabbit shaking just the slightest bit difficult.

The fog that had enveloped his thinking on the trail had passed, and Crispin was possessed of a clarity of mind that men rarely experience, except when facing the ivory gated realm of eternity. The riotous crowd laughed at the boy he had struck, but Crisp was sure they would draw the line at infanticide, and there would be no guffaws if he broke a child's neck.

Fat Anne struck him again in the kidneys, and this time, Crisp stumbled and fell to his bloodied knees. A girl of no more than five stepped up and struck him across the mouth with her wooden scourge, leaving a red streak across his cheek and cutting his lip. Pushing himself up, he thrust the tiny girl out of his path and continued to stagger along behind Captain Pipe. Ahead of him was a group of young warriors swinging war clubs and testing the keenness of their hatchets. Crispin was desperately afraid he was about to soil his breeches but was even more frightened of what the devils would think and do if they knew he couldn't control his own bowels. Clenching his buttocks tightly, he began to pray silently, which he had not done for himself since he was taken by DeVaca.

Pipe was warmly met by the young warriors who showed great deference for the older man. Captain Pipe would soon reach the sixtieth autumn of his age, yet he still took the warpath, and this time, he had returned with a valuable prisoner who would bring prestige upon the village, not just the hatchets and gunpowder they received for the scalps of hapless farmers and their fat German wives. When they paddled the Anglais up the river by canoe to Fort Duquesne, the French commander would pay them in guns, blankets, mirrors, and copper pots, but he would also have words of high praise which would be spoken in front of all the attendant Indians, traders, and of course, the soldiers of the garrison. Keeping a gun for himself would be Pipe's only reward. The rest he would distribute to his two companions and to the other members of the small village. Captain Pipe's wife had parted the twilight veil many years before, and he had never found a suitable helpmate to replace her. His one surviving son had been crippled in a tree-felling accident and was no longer able to take the bloody trail but could still hunt and trap with the aid of his strapping wife and two young boys. With them, Captain Pipe would rest through the winter, but there were still many months until then, and now he wished to share the glory and the wealth. In a few weeks, after resting and conferring with the French, he would decide whether or not he should depart on another foray into scalp rich English territory.

Many of the young warriors would now desire to follow his lead rather than choose an inexperienced war captain from their own ranks. In his village, there were at least two dozen young fellows (forty summers and under) of the age to take to the warpath and another four or five who lived up the creek in single family camps. With a real warband, Pipe's village would count for more with the French at the Fort at the river forks, and he could soon pass off the red hatchet to a younger man, and he could rest easy, fishing in the Monongahela, trapping rabbits in snares with his grandsons and hunting deer and elk. Perhaps with his honor restored, even Strong Mother would join him when he rested from his labors, and he could hold her tightly beneath warm thick blankets of French wool. All this had passed through his mind by the time he shoved Crisp's head down and pushed him through the hide-covered doorway of the council house.

The men entered silently one at a time and sat on the woven rush mats that lay on the sandy floor surrounding a small, almost smokeless fire of oak bark, which was carefully maintained. The warriors, young and old, each brought out their pipes, stuffing them with tobacco, and began smoking and talking softly amongst themselves. Crispin was lead to the rear of the lodge and lashed fast to a supporting post by means of a halter looped about his neck, and then his hands also were tied behind the pole and a rawhide gag was slipped between his teeth and knotted around his head—all in all, a very uncomfortable position to be in, and one which was not likely to increase intestinal fortitude.

After checking Crispin's bonds, Pipe moved toward the front of the lodge and took up his place amongst the warriors. It had been over a year since he had sat with the men of his village, and then he had not had the respect for his abilities as a war leader that he clearly enjoyed today. Broken Toe and Strong Mother joined him in the circle. Broken Toe also was from the village, but Strong Mother was not even of his tribe, yet her size and her evident standing with Captain Pipe had precluded anyone objecting to her presence. The matters under discussion would be the disposal of the worthy prisoner and a report from the other war party that had gone out from the village in the early spring.

Crispin listened to their guttural chatter but could make out none of it. When their calumets had been laid aside, one of the men had risen and spoken of the larger war party's depredations. They had been gone for many weeks and had themselves just returned, he explained for the benefit of Pipe and his companions. Returning with a dozen scalps lifted from several families, they had brought home no prisoners but only some horses and guns looted from their victims. Barking Fox, the speaker, who also had lead the expedition, knew his business and had traveled the warpath with Captain Pipe in the past, but he did not have control over his young men and had been unable to stay their murderous hands. Twice they had taken prisoners, but then they had become roaring drunk on looted spirits, and they had unwisely butchered perfectly good captives. Fourteen-year-old twins, a boy and a girl, had been tomahawked and scalped before Fox could stop the riot of anger and blood lust.

Barking Fox did not tell it this way in the council, but all who were there, even those who had raised the hatchet in their drink addled state, knew that it was his weakness as a leader that allowed these things to happen. While they were proud that a man of their small village had captured an important prisoner, the men of the other party were also embarrassed that they, with more men, had returned with less. In the future, Barking Fox would be consulted, but it was clear the men were not impressed with his command. The village was too small to have a war chief, but the men would always choose one from their own tiny ranks to lead them and represent them to the French and to speak for them when they joined with larger war parties.

This was the position that had belonged to Stone Pipe many years ago when they took the path against their traditional enemies to the south. In those distant years, the village had been larger, and Captain Pipe had lead upward of three score warriors, but on his last raid, he had walked into an ambush and nearly half of the men had been killed in a single fusillade of arrows and musket balls. Those that had survived knew that it was Pipe's over confidence that had cost them so dearly. After his wife's death, Pipe had taken to wandering far on long hunts, visiting neighboring tribes and joining with them on raids against their enemies. The village was used to his long absences and occasionally heard words of him from travelers. They knew also that it was his loneliness and his shame and the subsequent loss to the village that kept him away.

Pipe waited until after Barking Fox had been seated for a minute before he rose to speak. He did not linger long on the capture of the Anglais or take the credit for it. Instead, he told of Strong Mother's bravery and the swift but careful blow struck by Broken Toe that had felled the prisoner. It was a gentle chastisement of Fox. Clearly, Pipe's tiny band could control themselves and could think of the good of the village rather than sating their own bloody lusts. Pipe said that all would benefit from selling the Anglais to the French and told the young men that the entire village would go up the river to turn over the Anglais to the Commander at the Fort. All of the village would enjoy the fruits of the capture. In two days' time, they should all be ready to leave. Only the very old and a small guard of older boys would stay behind, mostly to keep the rabbits and other rodents from raiding the newly planted gardens. The village chief nodded in agreement and the attending warriors seemed impressed with Pipe's magnanimity.

⁎

The flotilla of canoes glided upstream with Crisp seated in the middle of the lead canoe, which held just four occupants. Broken Toe sat in the bow of the craft with the Englishman behind him while one more space back, Fat Anne was guarding Crisp, and Captain Pipe kneeled in the stern and matched Broken Toe stroke for stroke, skillfully guiding the craft ashore.

The possibility of a strategic fortification at the junction of the rivers Monongahela, Ohio and Allegheny had made the piece of ground rather hotly contested. The English, of course, were there first, but before they could erect a defensible position and man it, they were driven off by a larger force of French soldiers. The French had laid claim by right of some foolish metal plaques that had been distributed throughout the region by Captain Pierre Celeron de Bienville some years earlier. The plaques had been a Gaulish assertion to ownership of a property to which they had no greater right than their enemy, the Hanoverian dynasty of British monarchs. They erroneously believed that the tablets would establish their legal rights to the Ohio country and vindicate them in case of a dispute.

Naturally, both nations had lied to the savages, asserting that they only wished to build the fort to protect and assist trade. Naturally, the Indians were not as foolish as the great powers presumed them to be. The natives, however, were foolhardy enough to think that they could demand or enforce the removal of forts and trading posts if they became offensive. It is plain as day that the presence of the fort under the control of either power was a war just waiting to happen. Control of river ways was control of the interior and, hence, the fur trade—neither party was likely to take the loss of the site sitting down. It was from Duquesne's log walls that issued the force that drove off Colonel Washington and also a year later that mauled and routed the brave but ignorant General Braddock of Britain who had come to take revenge on France for the insult of defeating a Virginia militia officer (Colonel Washington).

It was in this wood and earthen bastion of French arms and courage that Crispin got his first look at the enemy. Pipe handed his end of the prisoner halter, along with a score of scalps, to the young dark-haired sergeant of the guard, who, along with two privates, marched Crispin into the fort, stopping in the middle of the tiny parade ground. Crispin had never heard of Fort Duquesne and could not fathom its importance in the events about to unfold. A large body of Indians, Canadian bush lopers, and a small but effective force of French Marines of the Forty-Fourth Regiment had massacred the aforementioned General Braddock's column the previous summer. That story of the war is for another time though.

At this juncture in the current hostilities, the commander, one Captain Dumas, was currently occupied with encouraging and organizing irregular raids being carried out by his copper skinned allies, primarily of the Shawnee and Delaware nations, but also of the Potawatomic, Wyandot, Chippewa's, and others. Pipe, along with his companions and Barking Fox, waited quietly and respectfully for King Louis XV's representative in the wilds of New France. The parade ground, which was no more than fifty feet to a side, was well graveled with a mixture of small stones and crushed clam shells and was barely adequate to hold all of the participants in the morning's solemn business. The guard detail stood stiffly at attention, and another fifteen white-coated marines with their broad blue coat cuffs and knee high white canvas gaiters remained motionless with their backs close along the squared log wall of the commander's office.

Crispin dared not look about lest he draw unwanted attention from Fat Anne. Little did the young Scot know that he was about to be luckier than he had ever been in his life, including even his promotion or the temporary possession of DeVaca's gold. Most captive men would, by now, have been nothing more than a smoldering heap lying at the foot of a charred and smoking post of green wood in the middle of some heaven forgotten collection of wigwams deep in the wilds. Not only had he escaped torture, but he had also been swiftly taken to the nearest fort to be traded for a small cartload of useful but hardly valuable truck.

Captain Dumas, not wanting to offend by keeping Pipe and his village waiting, emerged from his office, ducked his head to clear the low lintel, and placed his black tricorn with its gold lace trim carefully on his head. "It is good to see my Brother Stone Pipe whom I have not seen in many months. I see he has been busy and indeed very courageous to have captured an Anglais right from under the nose of the governor of Virginia," said the French officer in a formal congratulatory tone.

"The people of my village and this woman,"—spoke Pipe as he gestured to Strong Mother, who stood behind him with her short musket with its repaired stock in the crook of her arm—"bring you this soldier of the Anglais as a gift. The French King has sought our friendship and asked us to help him in driving out the English from our lands so that you and we may share peace." Pipe gestured around the fort with outstretched arm, his palm turned up taking in the people and the land with a single articulate gesture.

With his craggy face, shaven head, and a creamy white blanket thrown over his naked shoulder, he looked for all the world like some bronze senator of a woodland republic. Caesar Augustus himself would have known him by action and appearance and would have welcomed him as a warrior statesman, seating him at his right like a favorite.

Dumas issued an order to a young ensign to go and bring pipes and tobacco for his Delaware Brothers. Then, the elegant Dumas, along with Captain Pipe and his party, left the fort, and passing through the strong wood and iron gate, crossed the drawbridge and exited to the broad plain east of the fortress where many hundred natives were camped, including those of Pipe's village.

The commander had caused a great bark and pole lodge to be erected there for the purpose of entertaining the large numbers of savage allies with whom he must treat. Like the small council house in Pipe's village, a fire was always kept burning, and the air was purified with dried sage placed on the glowing embers. Taking their seats, the group, now joined by many of the men from the village, sat and shared the tobacco provided by the French. When the smoking was finished, which took some time and preceded all official ceremonies and councils, the two leaders got down to business.

The Frenchman had discreetly sent for the goods to be brought, and these were laid before Stone Pipe's feet. A small mountain of goods began to build as privates from the garrison set down armfuls of trade items. Pipe took in the contents of each delivery and made a mental tally, comparing it against the things he desired and knew were needed in the village. Colorful silk scarves, silver brooches, ruffled linen shirts, wire for snares, a small keg of gunpowder, a large iron pot, long plumes from exotic birds, and a dozen other items piled up. Lastly, the ensign brought to Dumas two fine French fusils made in Tulle France.

Dumas stood and walked around the fire and held out the weapons to Pipe, who rose from his mat and took the weapons from the French officer and examined them closely, grunting with approval before placing them on his mat. Grasping each other by the forearm, the two men embraced, and then Pipe motioned for one of the dusky warriors to begin the removal of the loot, excepting of course the guns, one of which Pipe would keep. The other he would give to White Eyes, the War Chief of the Delaware. His aged fusil he would give to Strong Mother, replacing the battered old piece she had always used. For her part in the bloody and daring raids, Fat Anne would also receive many colorful strands of beads, a new tomahawk and much of the loot that was taken from the homes and cabins they had decimated, and Pipe would also let her keep the old bay plow horse. In the years to come, many a settler's last sight would be of a bare-chested Amazon wearing a dirty tricorn, swinging a spiked war hatchet.

Strong Mother would die many years later, lovingly surrounded by all her daughters and granddaughters, her ancient body covered with the tracery of battle scars earned on the warpath with her now future husband. Broken Toe did not survive the war but was drowned in icy autumn water, trying to escape from a rabid she-wolf that had staggered into his camp one night on the banks of the Beaver River.

The meeting between Dumas and Captain Pipe had begun in the midmorning, and while they oversaw the exchange and receipt of payment, another of Dumas's officers was quietly interrogating Crisp back inside the fort. The gentleman quickly determined that Crispin had little of value to tell and knew nothing of benefit to the overall French strategy, and indeed, they actually knew more about the disposition of English troops than he.

A party was leaving at midday to carry messages to Fort Niagara and to bring back supplies. Crispin would be sent with them, and if he were lucky, he would be in Montreal by autumn where he would await exchange. Crisp was game for anything as long as it got him out of this blasted wilderness and away from Fat Anne, her pointy stick, and her murderous gaze. Other than his brief respite in Williamsburg, Crispin had so far found the colonies to be a disgusting, filthy, and painful experience, and he wanted nothing more than to retreat as quickly as humanly possible. Despite his distinct aversion to ships and water, at this point, he admitted to himself that he would crew aboard a stinking, leaky fishing boat if it would take him home to England. He was given bread and a cold slab of boiled venison, washed down with a poor excuse for wine that might better have been called vinegar, and then was lead out of the fort. Unsure of his future and unable to speak with either the natives or the Gaulish regulars, he looked about himself like a country lad making his first visit to the great city of London.

At last, he was led stumbling down the riverbank to a spot where a number of canoes had been drawn up. Two bush lopers, or coureurs de bois, and two marines threw their packs into a largish bark canoe and, then cutting off Crispin's rawhide halter, pushed him out into the water and gestured for him to get into the boat. It was perhaps midday, and Crisp was back in a canoe after only having gotten out of one a few hours earlier. He looked up from his spot in the boat, and there stood Fat Anne on the bank above, all alone. Taking her knife from her belt, she pointed at Crisp and made slashing motions in front of her belly and over her head. It was quite clear to Crispin that if he had remained at Fort Duquesne, she would have found a way to kill him, and it was equally clear that she meant to stab him to death if they ever crossed paths again. He could not fathom her depth of hatred for someone she did not even know and who had never done her an injustice. All the same, Crisp was quite sure he would make a study of not returning to the frontier. He waved and smiled, pretending he did not understand her motions. In her frustration, she threw a perfectly good scalping knife at the canoe, which was now fifty yards from shore. The blade, of course, fell many yards short and sank quickly in the dark water.

The vulgar bush loper in the front of the canoe yelled at her in Delaware, saying, "Crazy woman, you waste a good blade for nothing, bah! Now go home to your husband, and make the two-backed beast!"

Strong Mother turned and toiled up the bank, her head hanging like a hound that losing the quarry has let the master down—only her harsh master was the memory of her wickedly murdered husband and children.

The four Frenchmen alternated paddling upstream as they ascended the Allegheny River toward its juncture with French Creek where they would stay over a night at Fort Venango. The ascent, however, would take several days, and Crisp was also put to work paddling so that in all, they made good time against the current, and no one was overtaxed.

In the evenings, Crispin's feet were bound tightly and also his hands, but mercifully, he was given a palatable meal of jerked bear meat and a handful of corn meal. This was better fare than he had received from the savages, and it was a great relief that no one was pricking him in the back with a stick. His lower back was still painfully bruised from where Fat Anne had struck him. Despite the abuse and poor eatables, he was in remarkably good shape, which could only be attributed to his time with Hector the previous fall. Youth, a rugged constitution and raw strength, kept him going.

None of the four men spoke to him in English, and when they occasionally addressed him in French, it was cursory. To them, Crispin was only a piece of clumsy baggage.

After spending a night at Fort Venango, the party would proceed up the French Creek to Fort Le Boeuf, finally taking the portage trail from there to Fort Presque Isle on the south bank of Lake Erie. At each of the forts, they exchanged news and left personal messages for the commanders from Captain Dumas and received official correspondence and personal communiqués from the commanders that would be carried on to the principle fort at Niagara. At each fort, Crisp was carefully locked away in a jail or store room but was given a slightly more toothsome meal than that which he had got on the trail, so the light work of paddling and the improving conditions combined to put him in better rig than he had been in the score of days since he was made captive.

※

Ham Winsor, christened Hamilton Gilead Winsor in 1714, watched the Frenchmen from behind the smooth silver bole of a towering beech tree twenty yards from the portage trail that lead to Fort Presque Isle. Winsor himself had been on the trail, but hearing voices speaking in French, he had dived into the bushes and taken up his current position cautiously watching the path.

As the men rounded the bend and hove into sight, he dropped to his belly, pressing himself flat against the ground, quietly lining up an opening in the underbrush that would allow him to chart the party's progress. From this vantage point, he could only see their legs from the knees down, but that combined with the noise of their passage would let him know when they had safely passed his covert.

Winsor, now in his early forties, had been earning his living on the frontier on and off again for the past twenty years as a cunning master of the forest, second to none in tracking and shooting skills. Working as an assistant and interpreter to fur traders, he had never desired to be anything other than what he was—a long hunter and a woodsman. He owed not one shilling and had always managed to keep himself in enough cash or kind to purchase the things that he needed. While not a young man, he was not prone to the mistakes that get young fellows scalped, and he could still run for four miles and better fully encumbered with a rifle and a pack and shooting bags without taking a rest or pausing to catch his wind.

Several non-Quaker members of the Quaker dominated Pennsylvania Assembly had engaged his services and ordered him to spy out the situation on the frontier and keep them apprised of the horribly tragic developments. The assembly consisted largely of a group of religiously pacifistic gentlemen who were trying to keep the colony from becoming embroiled in a war against the French and the Indians. In particular, the Quakers objected to war with the Indians as they had long championed the cause of the red man.

Naturally there were a few non-Quaker members of that rustic parliament in Philadelphia who were aghast at the complacency of the colonies' founding sect. Hundreds of good people from the colony had fallen under the scalping knives and war clubs of the Indians. The French had whipped the tribes into a bloody frenzy of murder and arson. With calmly related accounts and perhaps the recaptured scalps of a few blond-haired children, it was hoped by Winsor's employers that they could force the assembly into taking appropriate action to defend the innocent folk of the back country.

As the prisoner escorts passed Winsor's leafy hiding place, Crispin stumbled and, stubbing his toe on a root growing in the trail, cursed loudly. Ham had caught only a glimpse of the legs belonging to the man who cursed, but he could tell from the tattered stockings and the English voice that the fellow was not likely a willing companion of French marines and sly bush lopers.

Once the party had passed, Winsor decided that here was just the sort of thing that his employers were looking for. No doubt this man would have some knowledge of what the Indians and the Frogs had been up to in these parts, which, if he could manage the fellow's rescue, would save him a trip deeper into dangerous country. Gaining the fellow's freedom, however, might be even more dangersome than sneaking into enemy territory, and then there was always the simple question of morality. Even if the man knew nothing, could he rightly leave him in the clutches of the French?

Hamilton G. Winsor silently argued with himself for several minutes, taking both sides of the issue and finally reached a wise decision. He would trail the party from a safe distance, and if an opportunity arose to secure the prisoner's freedom without placing his own life too much at risk, then so be it. *On the other hand*, he thought, *if the French guard is too tight, he couldn't jeopardize his own hide and the scouting mission on behalf of his employers and the people of the back country.*

The two bush lopers in their long hunting shirts and deerskin leggings set about gathering wood and building a fire while the two marines erected a canvas lean-to. Crispin sat with his back to a tree, his hands still bound, but he was in no other way restrained except by the fatigue of a long day's travel over rough trails.

Ham Winsor watched carefully from the lower limbs of an oak that grew a safe distance from the encampment. The bush lopers' movements were easy to follow as they both wore the red knit caps so favored by Canadians. The marines, on the other hand, frequently blended into the background of the white canvas they were handling. The fifth fellow, he could just make out by his grimy red breeches. The man seemed to be sitting under a tree doing nothing, which would add to the notion that he was being held against his will.

Winsor would be unable to attack them during daylight hours and was certain that he could only kill two of them with the rifle before his location was determined exactly by the two remaining. The two survivors would be able to flank his position, and there was little chance that he could kill both of them before they got a ball into him. If he waited patiently until the four men settled down for the night, he might, if he were lucky, be able to brain them in the head with his belt axe before they could awake and give him much of a fight. Sneaking up and killing white men in their sleep did not much fit with his notion of a fair fight, but he also knew it was likely the only plan upon which he could place any reliance. If he was swift and silent, Ham was sure he could dispatch the two coureur de bois while they slept. With only two marines to deal with, both of whom would be groggy and frightened, he was quite certain that given the element of surprise he could shoot one and fight the other to death without too much undue risk. Only an intrepid long hunter would consider grappling with the sharp toys of war a reasonable risk.

Winsor was certain the frog-eaters were overconfident. As they finished their simple supper of salted cheese and dried venison and smoked their pipes, they began preparations to bed down. It became clear from their actions that one would watch while three slept. Had they been duly cautious, they would have split the night with two watchers and two sleepers. Clearly, with their proximity to the little log fortresses and the friendliness of the natives in the region, they believed they had little to fear. To their way of thinking, one guard was simply common sense even if it was unnecessary.

The snores of three men deep in exhausted sleep carried even to the tree where Winsor rested. The fourth man, one of the bush lopers, struggled to stay awake. Crispin Mull, with his hands tied behind him and a lashing about his middle belting him to the tree, could find no sleep because of his physical discomfort. Nodding off for minutes, he would be reawakened by the ever-present pain in his shoulders and wrists.

Winsor crept to within a little more than a dozen yards of the fire, staying in the shadows and keeping a tree at all times between himself and the drowsy French woodsman. At last, sometime after midnight, the coureur de bois nodded off and his long-whiskered chin rested on his chest, a slight puffing noise emitting from his slightly parted lips.

Ham brought his maple stocked rifle to full cock and checked the keen edge of the knife in his broad belt. He shifted the rifle to his right hand and then, drawing the hatchet from its snug carrying place in his belt at the small of his back, rose up off the ground and, in a sudden burst of deadly speed, charged quietly into the camp, his moccasined foot falls, making little noise.

Reaching the guard, his axe fell straight and sharp, cracking through the top of the bush loper's skull with a soft crunch. The fellow never even flinched but fell forward with Ham's tomahawk stuck in his head. Winsor stepped back and gave a sharp upward wrench to the handle, pulling it free.

The other coureur de bois reached for his fusil, and his eyes popped open just as the brain smeared steel wedge parted his view and drove his head back down onto the pack he used as a pillow. The third man, one of the marines, was now fully awake and was rising to his feet, which tangled in his blanket. Hamilton let free of the axe handle and brought the rifle to his hip. Swinging the long slender barrel that swelled just a bit at muzzle even with the Frenchman's belly, he pulled the trigger. The rifle barked, and the marine was jerked off his feet as the round ball bored through his spine, buckling him in half and propelling him backwards where he landed on his comrade who was just coming to life.

The weight of his dying friend and the crack of Winsor's rifle left the last Frenchman disoriented and confused as to where the attack was coming from, and he was unable, with a dead weight on him, to do anything. Suddenly, the mostly dead weight of Private Harvieux was lifted from him, and before he could roll out of the way, Ham Winsor's rifle butt was slamming down on his cheekbone. The pain was blinding, and his right eye was destroyed. His hands instinctively flew up to protect his face from further blows, and he tried desperately to throw himself to the left, away from his assailant, when the next and final blow fell. The knife's long tooth of steel bit deep into the bottom rear of the Frenchman's head where the neck bone fits neatly into the skull socket. The marine spasmed with a lurch just once and then lay still as a dead man should.

The camp was quiet except for the crackle of the fire, which had been stoked by the guard just before he fell asleep. Crisp sat riveted and likely wouldn't have moved if he could. Hamilton Gilead Winsor just stood there looking around him as though he was daring one of the still warm corpses to move. A log on the fire hissed and popped, and Crispin, at last, found his voice, overcoming his fear of this firelock and axe wielding berserker.

UNION OF ROGUES

Hook-nosed Peg had risen lazily and found the dim loft deserted. Trepan was gone, and the only evidence of the previous night's diversion was a drained bottle of claret. As she rearranged her petticoats, she thanked her lucky star that the vermin was gone, and she wouldn't have to face him. What she had done with him, she told herself, was a matter of courtesy in the way of paying a debt, but now it was time to begin a new chapter in her life.

At the moment, the fat man at the tavern was her only opportunity for creature comfort, yet she was puzzled by and fearful of his strange spellbinding ability.

She descended quietly to the main floor of the warehouse of Herrs Hermann and Werth and let herself out into the busy morning bustle of the riverfront. Fishermen were bringing in the morning's catch, and wagons rumbled up and down the wharf carrying cargo just arrived from far flung ports. Terns and gulls wheeled sharply over head and a half-drowned dog floated by clinging to a log to no one's care or notice, most especially Peg's. The water was littered with refuse and flotsam, and a cracked chamber pot bumped up against the dog who gave it hardly a notice.

To the best of her drink bleared recollection, the Yellow Wasp was not far from the ship's chandlers.

Trepan, in the meantime, had been out and about acquiring them a lovely breakfast and pilfering a trinket for the lady. Never in his sinful, murderous, and filthy life had Trepan ever done a woman a good turn nor had he even the briefest flickering of a romantic thought—until now. As the years marched forward, and with the aches and pains that he had earned becoming more troublesome, he began to ponder his lonely future.

That damned lieutenant had added sorely to his list of pains and woes, and he was certain that in the years to come, he would need a partner he could trust. In his lustful and sinful mind, however, fidelity and trust were not synonymous. He was more interested in finding a buxom crony with whom he could occasionally have a roll, but not one to whom he was required to say either *yea* or *nay* nor *by yer leave*. Trust itself was a novel notion to him, for he had never given that most valued treasure to anyone and thought the rest of the world fools for blithely giving another person power over one's self. The previous night's indulgence had, however, begun his slippery gears turning. In the course of his morning rounds, he had turned the idea of an alliance over in his mind and decided that if she were game, the regimental trollop (He didn't even know her name.) was as good a start as any. If she didn't play out, he could always dispose of her. And then, on the other hand, if things did work out, well, it might be the first time in his mostly evil life that he had shared more than one evening's amusement with the same wench.

Scaling the ladder to the loft after he had assured himself that the coast was clear, Trepan poked his head into his hidey-hole and was shocked to find it abandoned. To say that he was crestfallen would be a significant understatement. For Trepan had, in the very moment in which he decided to share a trust, been spurned.

Sitting in a pile of canvas, he gnawed the warm loaf of bread he had bought after liberally smearing it with the purloined butter. He washed the whole down with his favorite ale but did not even taste the rich yeasty flavors as his mouth was filled with the bitter bile of revenge. He cast the cheap necklace aside and, wiping his mouth on his dirty sleeve, decided then and there that the grisette would pay. No army slut would ever turn her back on him. It never occurred to him that he had not even indicated to the woman that he had social intentions beyond an evening's entertainment, nor did it occur to him that she may merely have stepped out to make water or upon some other equally innocuous errand, which, of course, we know she didn't.

In Trepan's mind, their evening's coitus had implied an arrangement that being successfully consummated, she had then backed out of at a crucial juncture, just as he was willing to let someone peek at his shriveled soul. In his felonious and depraved mind, she was honor bound to openly decline his offer rather than slink off. Trepan, of course, had no way of knowing how recently she had come to his world nor could he have known that only a month before she had been a lady of some means. His relationships with the fairer sex had been limited to his cruel and painful grandmother and moments stolen with poxsy whores in greasy beds. If and when he found her, he would cut her well. A slattern of her stripe had no recourse through the law, so with little or nothing to fear, he reasoned it would be more interesting to see her fetching looks marred rather than to kill her out of hand.

Magoggle rested in his dark corner, leaning back in the Windsor chair, its spraddled legs straining against the gravity of his weight. He spent most of his days in that house of iniquity. The owner owed him many favors, so he was repaid with a grave dark corner and a table of his own by the only feeble fire from which he could survey all that went on. He saw Peg enter as though bidden. Sending Noddy Cope to fetch her, he poured his own glass full of his favorite spiced wine and then filled her already waiting glass as well.

They communed throughout the later morning, and Peg often tipped her head back and laughed at Magoggle's debauched wit. Her formerly lovely hands, now red and pinched from rough farm labor and coarse lye soap, touched his thigh lightly, and she leaned in and whispered depraved nothings in his ear.

At last as the noon hour neared, Trepan came in and espied the pair sitting in the corner. The assassin ordered an ale and then secured a place on a bench near to the door where he could observe the couple, but he himself would go unnoticed by most of the already drunken patrons, and where he presumed the fat man could not see.

As he reached the bottom of the leather tankard, Noddy Cope approached and in a quiet voice told Trepan that the great Mr. Magoggle requested the honor of his presence at his table as they had business to discuss. Trepan was not surprised that the fat man knew he was present, but was professionally disappointed in himself that he had not gone unnoticed.

"What can I do fer ye, Mr. Magoggle?" asked Trepan as he stood before the table. He nodded toward Peg, acknowledging her presence only in order not to offend the poisonous toad.

The fat as bacon villain slid a large silver coin across the table toward the assassin, giving it a last little flick of his pudgy forefinger in order to slide it all the way across the sizeable, round, butterfly table. The disc teetered half over the edge and hung there. Trepan, without looking, opened his purse, which was suspended under his coat, and swept the coin into the waiting pouch.

"There is no need for introductions here as my companion tells me the two of you met last night," said Magoggle without obvious rancor. "That little reward is for directing this fine lady to my table yesterday." He nodded toward Peg and went on. "I have an extensive business here in town and about as ye know, Mr. Trepan, and I am ever in need of solid partners upon whom I can rely to the last extremity. I believe ye had an interest in this fine young lady and I am willing to help ye both reach yer desired ends."

Turning to Peg, he smiled at her and patted her hand with his. "My dear, I have enjoyed yer company immensely this morning and am sure we will have many opportunities in the future to spend a great deal more time with each other, but at the moment, it would serve me well if ye would explore yer heart and see if there isn't room in it for the attentions of this gentleman."

He gestured dramatically toward Trepan who remained stoically quiet almost as though he were at attention. The patch-eyed strangler never glanced at Peg and didn't remove his eyes from Magoggle, possibly fearful that if he flinched he might be gobbled up like a fly. He cautiously released the sword within the cane from its hiding place, his thumb pressing against the glass eyes of the serpent's head his wrist giving a slight twist. The triangle of steel waited with deadly potential.

Peg pulled back and seemed on the verge of complaining most strenuously. Her jaw began to work, but then Magoggle just grinned impishly at her and winked, and she decided that it would be unwise to defy the wishes of the huge fleshy pink toad who sat beneath the ancient greasy powder-blue wig. The filthy hair covering reached its coiled locks to his shoulders where it lay twined in a matted mass.

"Here now, we all desire the same thing, don't we? Wealth!" said the fat one, uttering the last word in a very loud stage whisper. He resumed in normal tone, "I am quite good at acquiring it but have never found that I have enough, so I find that it is mutually rewarding to encourage others in new business adventures."

"What did ye have in mind?" queried Trepan.

Peg sat very still with her hands in her lap and her eyes darting back and forth between the two men.

"Well now, it is said that Trepan has light hands and is a fair picker of pockets, but others whisper that it is his blade that is light and quick. It is also said that he constantly inquires after the whereabouts of a certain Lieutenant Mull of the Fifty-Sixth regiment of foot." Magoggle leaned across the table as far as he could and placed his hand against the corner of his mouth as in a screen and hissed conspiratorially. "Some say the wench here"— he jerked his other thumb at Peg—"has an interest in the fair soldier lad as well."

Trepan took a step back from the table. "Fat lot ye know!" He was concerned no little bit with how Magoggle had learned this and that and with what else the mountainous miscreant was familiar.

"Oh! Ho, ho!" chuckled O. Nicholas Magoggle. "I know, my friend! I also know ye fancy tumbling the strumpet here! You'd like to share yer loot with her too, but she made ye angry, didn't she?"

The legs of the chair creaked again as he leaned back in his spindly throne. The feeble fire in the stone fireplace behind him leaped up as the fat from a saddle of mutton dripped onto the embers. The two villains ignored Peg and locked eyes, Trepan with a sneer on his lips and Magoggle with a gleeful grin that stretched from ear to ear.

While the two men were engaged in a battle of wills, which Trepan was destined to lose, Peg thought it wise to attempt an exit, so she slowly slid her chair back and quietly stood, thinking to step into the shadows and then bolt for the back door which was only steps away. Trepan's arm shot out from his side, and his hand possessively clamped around her wrist like an iron claw. Her hand came back to take a swing full on at his rat like face, but before she could follow through, Magoggle's chubby paw grabbed her petticoats and pulled her back down into her chair.

"Tis a simple offering I have," Magoggle started out, calmly ignoring Peg completely. "Tell me what the lieutenant has, and share it with me, and I'll let ye live and keep the woman." His pique began to rise. "Hold yer tongue, and I guarantee I'll burn the breath out of ye. I don't quibble, and I rarely bargain! It is all in my favor little man. Everyone in this town works fer me in one way or another."

All trace of humor and condescending patience were gone from his voice. Instead, he took on the tone of a man who fears nothing either side of the eternal curtain and who is in total control.

It was largely true that a good many low and nasty folk worked for him in one way or another, but of course, there were many more who had no connection what so ever with The Beast of Water Street.

Trepan had heard tales that several of Magoggle's enemies had been found staked out, facedown, several feet off the ground in a spread-eagle fashion with a small fire just under their chins so that they had been forced to inhale both flames and smoke but not before their faces had slowly roasted and their eyeballs had dried up like raisins. In more than one instance, the head had been oddly and quite unnaturally burned away while the collar was scarcely scorched. In another instance, a small green pumpkin on a stick was queerly substituted for the missing head. Strange powders and charms were most often found tucked into the victim's coat pockets and cuffs, and it was rumored that Magoggle employed red Indians to do this hideous torture.

The truth came out many years later when a mulatto slave named Nero Faith confessed on his fever bed to being Magoggle's secret executioner. The fat man had promised the servant his freedom in exchange for his dark African magic. The brown magician was a fourth generation medicine man on his sire's side and a second generation drunkard on his Welsh mother's side. When Nero was born, his sluttish mother had sold him to a Dutch Patroon for a barrel of rum and a worthless string of crimson paste beads, thus ridding herself of a bastard and gaining months of drunken debauchery. Nero Faith died as a chattel, and Magoggle's promise went unfulfilled, and the slave's mortal remains were placed in a shallow grave in the Negro burying ground without mourners or even a friend.

Doing some quick calculations without a flinch or a blink, Trepan decided that he dared not antagonize the arch villain. Half the loot and power over the woman was far superior to having his lungs seared and his remaining eyeball toasted to a nugget of char. It took only seconds for him to reach this decision, but to Peg it seemed an eternity before the small dirty fellow answered.

"I'll take the bargain and shake," said Trepan, holding out his dirty hand. "But how am I to keep the woman? She'll run the first chance she gets!"

Magoggle shook on the deal and then leaning back in his chair once again, sighed deeply. "If I will it, it happens." He turned to Peg. "My dear, if ye run or raise a hand against my good and true partner, brother Trepan, I will find ye and give ye to men infinitely more hideous and dangerous than our one-eyed bench fellow here." He waved his hand toward Trepan. "If ye do as he asks and help him in every way, then I will see to it that ye are rewarded justly." He winked and went on. "Think of him as the junior partner and of me as the almost silent senior partner, and think of yourself as a valued employee in our little triumvirate."

Peg nodded, knowing at that moment she had no other alternative if she wished to continue amongst the living. Trepan stepped back and grabbed a wobbly but empty chair from a neighboring table and sat down without awaiting an invitation.

"It's treasure," said the assassin plainly. "I don't know how much as I've never'd the luck to count it, but I'd hazard at least five thousand guineas."

The strangler had wittingly lied, which was, of course, no great feat for one so accomplished at sin. Trepan was aware from handling the chest that night in DeVaca's room that there was at least eight thousand and perhaps twice that. Magoggle wasn't the only schemer, and in the few moments he had been given, Trepan had already begun to lay out a plan in his greasy, fumy head that would allow him to cheat the obese blackguard.

Magoggle, for his part, lay before Trepan Peg's involvement with the young officer whilst Peg sat quietly as though under some spell. Trepan silently surmised that the fat man had got the information from her when the two had disappeared the day before. Peg added nothing to the story, occasionally sipping from a dirty tumbler of rum that Noddy Cope had brought to her.

The two villains discussed the likely future of the young lieutenant if ever he reappeared. Crispin's health was paramount to their success because only he could lead them to the treasure. How willing he would be to do this and what sort of "encouragement" he would need were unknown, but both vermin thought it improbable that the young swain would hand over the specie without a fight. Magoggle had his own plans for the officer and placed a higher priority on those than on the gold. But this was information he did not share with the cyclopean back stabber. Bringing Crispin within his grasp would give the wigged monster just the access he sought to polite society.

P. Peter Lane and Magoggle had never known each other, and that was just as well for civilized folk on both sides of the Mer Du Nort. Lane, as you have seen, was less dramatic and prone to homicide than Magoggle, but it must be said that had the likes of them ever joined forces, the rest of the good citizenry would only have been safe if well-armed, indoors, and near the glow of a homely fire. Trepan, while far more deadly, was interested only in expanding his own wealth and increasing his position.

Magoggle would never cease his pursuit of power until he controlled all the wealth in the city and possessed all the people. Nibbling tiny bites from the rotting blackened regions of the town no longer sated him. He wanted to rip open the entire carcass and devour the city whole, where festering in his great belly it would become a seething pile of corruption, sin, blasphemy, and hypocrisy. Needless to say, a glance out a window at Broadway today will confirm that this did not come to pass. Good and decent folk still dutifully troop off each Sunday to their respective houses of worship, and life in the bustling city goes on, but there was a time unbeknownst to most when that was in jeopardy—an earlier time when New York was only mere steps from becoming the Calcutta of the New World by the design of one hideous being. Like many other tales, that is better left for a rainy windswept night and another merry blaze.

FROM THE FRYING PAN TO THE FIRE

"I do hope and pray you are an Englishman?" Crispin asked, trying to sound calm but with a definite trace of genuine terror creeping almost imperceptibly into his tremulous voice.

Ham Winsor stepped well away from the fire and circled the camp anticlockwise in the darkness, coming up behind Crispin's tree, and still, he didn't utter a sound. Using his knife, he quickly cut Crispin's bonds.

"Don't say nothin'. Just do as I tell ye," he said in a whisper. "Fetch the best musket ye can find and all the cartridges. If ye need any clothin's, take whatever ye want, but be quick about it. Do it now."

He cut the cords binding Crispin's hands, and then he quickly rooted amongst the corpses, coming up with a knot of tobacco and a flask of brandy from one of the bush lopers and a gold ring from corporal Boudreaux, the last to die. Taking a canteen that had belonged to one of the marines, Ham doused the fire as Crisp yanked on a hat belonging to one of the two French soldiers.

If possible, Crispin looked more piratical than he had when he was in company with DeVaca. Wearing his torn red uniform breeches, a stained and torn hunting shirt, a powder blue waistcoat that had belonged to a marine, and a dusty black tricorn, he looked more the part of a bandit than a prisoner, what with the bayonet belt and cartridge box en suite with the belt knife taken from one of the coureur du bois.

Ham grabbed him by the elbow and dragged him away as a column of steam rose from the soaking embers.

The frontiersman spoke in a whisper. "I told ye to be quiet, and I mean fer ye to keep at it. There's a fair chance that there's Delaware, Seneca, or some other nasty Injuns about. Ye seem to be a smart enough fellow, so just do as I say an' we won't have any surprises tonight, understand?"

He checked Crispin's musket to see that it was loaded and then reprimed it and handed it back to Crisp, who was rather embarrassed that he hadn't had the presence of mind to do the same. He pushed Crisp's back against a smallish tree and then shoved him down into a squat and motioned for him to stay put like a dog. Winsor went back to the fire and, pausing for a moment, listened, then he stooped over and, pulling his knife from his belt again, quickly scalped all four men, stepping from one corpse to another. Holding the four bloody topknots by the hair, he held them out and gave them a violent whip-like shake to free them of blood. He walked quietly but surely back to Crispin and led him off into the darkness of the unending forest.

Crispin had spent a good portion of the murkish night, holding tightly to Ham Winsor's belt and stumbling through the darkness up hill and down dale. Splashing across stony creeks and toiling out of deep gullies, they put many miles between themselves and the scene of the previous night's attack. Towards sunrise, which was directly before them, Hamilton began to slow the pace; and as the sky had begun to brighten, Crispin no longer had to hold so surely to his belt. The brightening forest lay all about them, and Crisp had no idea where they were or where they were bound for, so he finally decided he must break the silence and ask.

"Where the devil are you taking me? And do you mind if we stop for a moment and sort some things out?" he asked in what he thought was a polite voice.

It occurred to him not for the first time that someone else was constantly herding him about, tying him up and taking him places he did not want nor intend to go. He had started out on a simple voyage from England to New York, and so far, he had seen far more of the ocean than he had intended, and any view of the frontier so far was more than he had planned for or desired. In spite of his new found love of nature, he found himself loathing fresh air, majestic trees, and musical birds, and instead, he longed for a smoke-filled barracks or a deliciously aromatic coffee house.

"Philadelphia. You're gonna tell the general assembly everything that's happened to ye since yer capture—after ye tell my employers," answered Ham. "Ain't no damned time to stop now! We'll take a break in an hour or so an' have a bite."

Clearly, the conversation was at an end. Ham picked up the pace, jogging down hills and creek beds, making no effort at stealth. He knew he was off the beaten track, even for savages, and wanted only to put many miles behind him.

By the time midmorning had rolled around, the rawboned long hunter and Crispin had climbed the steep side of a hill and found a nice large maple tree on a grassy bench that overlooked the creek bed they had just been splashing through. From this vantage point, he could see up the stream for several hundred yards, where as anyone on their trail coming down the creek would not see them breakfasting above.

As they sat down, Ham pulled a long piece of jerked venison from his pack and, splitting it half wise, handed over a strip to Crisp and then fished around in the pocket of his waistcoat until he found the flask of brandy.

"I'm Hamilton Gilead Winsor. Some gentlemen in the assembly asked me to poke my nose into Frenchy affairs out here. It'll take ten days er so before we make Philadelphia. Take yerself some sleep. I'll watch," said the hunter, staring down into the gully below.

"I'm Lt. St. Crispin Mull of the Fifty-Sixth of Foot, if you care! I was captured by ill-mannered, half-naked savages in Virginia and was turned over to the French at Fortress Duquesne after being abused by a large nasty squaw woman, and I have to report to my regiment, Mr. Winsor," replied Crispin, trying not to show his heat at the fellow's truculence. He knew he owed this man his freedom.

"That's good, Lieutenant. You can go to New York right after you tell the Pennsylvania Assembly 'bout what ye saw. Now get some sleep." Winsor lighted his pipe and sat with his back against the tree and the rifle in his lap and Crisp's French musket near to hand.

Crispin was caught between exhaustion and outrage at the peremptory treatment. In his fatigue, he was truly beginning to hate the colonies and everything and everyone in them beyond all sense and reason. Torn between tears and rage, he wanted nothing more than to shout out loud until some band of bloody handed savages came and killed him and put an end to all of his woes and troubles, and so he did.

When he awoke, he tried to roll over but realized to his dismay that it was quite impossible as he was tied upright to a tree with a large scrap of dirty cloth (likely his own filthy shirt) shoved into his mouth to keep him from cursing and screaming anymore. His eyes darted about, and he silently (as he had no other choice) wondered whether he had been left alone or if they had been captured by natives.

Ham Winsor stepped around to his side of the tree and, before pulling the rag from Crispin's mouth, told him that a single sound would be his last. Winsor pointed down to the creek bed and quietly told Crisp that a lone Delaware warrior had just passed down the stream only an hour before, despite his best efforts to keep them away from Indian roads and routes. He added that if Crispin made one more sound, he would cut out his tongue and leave him tied to the tree where, undoubtedly, it would take several days for him to die. Crisp nodded to show his understanding, and Ham took the rag from his mouth.

Winsor disappeared behind the tree where he began loosening the bonds. Crisp noted for the first time since waking, his head hurt; and as his arms became free, he reached up and found a nasty little nut swelling out of his head. The restraints around his ankles fell free at last, and he dropped to his knees.

"I've heard of men going mad before, but I swear this is the first time I've seen it," said Hamilton in a frank whisper. "Ye got quite a collection of curses fer a gentleman. I apologize about the knot on yer noggin, but I had to stop ye before ye had called in all the savages in these parts. It was just a tiny bash with a stick. If ye are still thinking crazy like, I will kill ye, just so's you know."

The sun was beginning to set, and Ham shoved the brandy flask between Crisp's lips and instructed him to stretch out and rub the soreness out of his legs. They had miles more to cover that night. Once again, Crispin held onto a tether on Hamilton's belt, but this time, the Pennsylvanian carried both of the weapons. With this precaution observed, he felt more assured of his continued safety with the unstable young officer.

They had been on the trail for five days and were in the middle of the Allegheny Mountains when Hamilton turned north and followed a small stream up into a cleft that ran deep into the side of a substantial hill. As they climbed upward, the ground began to grow less steep, and finally, it ended abruptly in a towering cliff of shale. Between them and the cliff of damp fern-covered stone lay a small green area about forty-five paces deep and sixty long. On the left, the creek they had been following burbled out of a lush flower rimmed spring that was shaded by an immense red oak, and the clear water cascaded down a shallow trough in the rocks, widening as it tumbled down the side of the hill. On the right, the clearing ended in a jumble of boulders.

Nestled up against the cliff in between was a crude little cabin chinked with moss, sprouting a mud and stick chimney and having a horsehide for a door. There were no windows to speak of, but there were two convenient rifle slits flanking the skin-covered opening. The cabin was no more than seven or eight paces across the front by three or so deep, and its steeply pitched, shingled roof looked high enough to dry herbs and hang smoked hams of venison high in the rafters. The front wall was covered with hoops and stretchers made of wood and used to stretch and cure the hides of animals. Standing next to the door was a waist-high length of upright maple log hollowed on the upper end with a wrist-sized stone pestle sitting inside. Clearly, someone had recently been pounding corn with it, which was evident from the kernels that lay freshly scattered in the dirt. A crude half log bench was pulled up next to it, and a gourd dipper lay on its side on the ground, leaking water. Separated a few yards from the cabin was a corral made of sapling poles, and inside it were three fine chestnut horses who, with their perked ears, watched the approach of Hamilton and Crispin with curiosity.

As soon as Crispin and the hunter had reached the outer edge of the clearing, a musket poked out of each of the two slits, and a voice called out loudly in Delaware, telling them to come no farther.

Hamilton called back in clear English, "It's me, Ham Winsor and an English officer I saved from the Frenchies!"

The voice answered, this time in good king's English. "I'll be right out."

The man's voice lowered and was clearly joined with another in the cabin in conversation, but it was unclear what was said. The bay-colored horse hide curtain was cautiously pulled aside and out stepped a black man wearing a coarse beige linen hunting smock and well-worn sand-colored buckskin breeches and bare brown shins. On his feet were Indian moccasins, and around his neck hung a strand of handsome cobalt-blue beads with a silver disk suspended from it. In his hand, he held a British Brown Bess musket taken as plunder at Braddock's bloody defeat and traded to him in exchange for a fine unbroken gelding.

Lord Church Hardaway had runaway from his master Thomas Hardaway Bills, a no account horse breeder and lawyer from New Jersey some twenty years before. Hardaway had gone to live with Indians, finally moving in with the Tuscarora of lower New York and Pennsylvania. It was amongst the junior most voice of the Iroquois empire that he had met his petite and gracious wife, Molly, a member of that esteemed and judicious tribe that had sagely become the sixth nation of the famous woodland society.

"Lord, I need two fast horses. Not a couple a nags, but real runners."

Hamilton explained his mission and promised to bring back the horses when he returned to the woods. He went on. Could he pay for their use in two months' time?

By the time they had fallen to haggling on the price, Molly had gone into the cabin and come back out with cups made of horn filled with cold spring water and fortified with spirits. Crispin stood back and quietly drained off his measure and listened to the deal making.

The handsome Indian woman silently returned to her grinding, paying no attention at all to the proceedings or to the visitors. At least once a week and sometimes twice, visitors came on foot or riding nags and then left with new horses. It was a scene familiar to her coffee-colored eyes. It was most common for the customers to be bronzed, savagely coifed, with pendulous shells or silver rings dangling from their noses and wearing the colorful and outrageous garb of the native warrior. Delaware, Seneca, Tuscarora, Cayuga, Shawnee, Wyandot, and others all came to them.

When finally the two men had reached an agreement, they began to follow a narrow, winding path through the boulders toward Lord's primary horse pens, which were higher up the mountainside. Lord and Molly had settled upon the mountain several years before and did a brisk horse trade with the red people of the forest and the few border whites that lived throughout those regions, and they generally enjoyed the respect of all about them. Lord knew though that while they had avoided the present nastiness to this point, it was unwise to build an indefensible abode. Likewise, he felt that keeping his herd too close to the cabin invited attack. If some marauding band bent on thievery wanted the horses bad enough, then it's best to be out of the line of fire.

The three mounts he kept next to the house were his own. It was not at all uncommon for his pens and pastures to have horses stolen from whites or raided from savages, some from as far away as the Carolinas and a good many pack and saddle horses passed through his hands each year. He paid well for the animals he had, and no one knew where he came by the hard cash nor where he kept it. Discretion was paramount in those tumultuous and bloody years and was often the virtue that kept a fellow alive.

Hamilton had known Lord for all those years and more, and the two had become fast friends and hunting companions, often sharing the bibulous hospitality of John Barley Corn in the evening by the fire. Despite Lord's chocolate-colored complexion, the hunter found him one of the most intelligent and well-read fellows he had ever encountered on the mountainous frontier. Hamilton dearly loved the sparsely settled mountains and valleys west of the Susquehanna, partly because a man was judged by his words and deeds rather than his lineage or the hue of his hide. Lord had unknowingly taught him much, sharing the wisdom he had learned from the bible and his wife's people as well. Lord knew what the Good Book expected of him, and he also knew when to pull his muskrat traps. He knew what dyes to use to disguise the color of a stolen horse, and he had even read another pair of books. All this combined with his personal experience in the state of slavery and of living freely on the border had made a frontier philosopher of him.

Of late, while Hamilton had no room in his heart for many of the murderous savages, he also had little sympathy for the unwanted, uninvited, and unwashed Germans and Irish who were constantly encroaching on native territory, carelessly building dirty cabins where they had no right to be and where the Crown law should have wisely forbade them from being. They were a willful rustic lot, only one-step from outlawry themselves and as unlettered as Tartary peasants. In their crudely simple logic, if the savages and their industries were not in evidence, then that was proof of native indolence, and hence, they (the savages) forfeited their right to possess that which they could obviously not fully utilize in their pagan state.

Hamilton returned with Lord from the mountain top pastures, and they each lead a fine stolen horse. Crisp's, led by Lord, would be a small delicate-looking seven-year-old bay mare of a little over fourteen hands, and Hamilton's was an old black stallion of better than fifteen hands. The horses wore bitless Indian bridles and, for saddles, had only a small blanket pad. The hunter accepted a dinner invitation from Lord, so Crisp and he idled the rest of the day with the Hardaways, supping on roast grouse stuffed with cornbread and roasted chestnuts, and then as the moon rose over the trees and the stars came out, the two men mounted and began their ride for Philadelphia. With a bit of luck, they would make it in four or five days if they pushed their mounts to a lather and took out only time to rest and water the horses, and at the very latest, they would arrive in no more than a week.

Crispin had no desire to visit Philadelphia nor to report to the Pennsylvania Assembly, and it was only his reliance on Winsor that stilled his tongue and kept him from spewing invective directed at the long hunter. His horse was lively but pliable, and if he had known the way to New York, he would gladly have sneaked off into the night and given the mare her head, but of course, Winsor would have awakened before he was beyond the firelight, and Crispin had no wish to be tied up again or worse. He was little better off than a prisoner. Hamilton had returned his musket to him but that meant nothing as he could hardly threaten the fellow with it if he had any wish to see his regiment again.

The trees lay all about them and were rarely broken by the very occasional meadow. Oak, basswood, hickory, maple, and a dozen other varieties crowded about, looming overhead conspiring to keep out the sun and hold back the azure vault. Here and there, Jacobs Ladders would pierce the canopy, reminding Crispin that there was a world beyond the leafy boughs.

For some reason, the wilderness in spring with all its leaves was more suffocating to him than the bone fingered forests of winter and fall. Hunting with great Hector had seemed more hospitable. There were no biting bugs then, and even on overcast days, the sky was there as an assurance that the world Crispin knew lie just beyond reach. Now in the spring, tiny flies nipped and pestered at the riders and horses, setting Crisp to coughing when he accidentally inhaled and swallowed several of the obnoxious creatures. His morning's rest was often interrupted in the predawn by the insistent mating calls of wild turkey cocks gabbling from their roosts.

Three days of hard riding had brought them to the far edge of civilized country, still a long day's hard ride away with its well-plowed fields and cozy, neat farms. Naturally, Crispin was altogether unaware of the nearness of folk who understood the use of a fork and did not wear animal skins to cover their nakedness. He was also oblivious to the fact that most of the natives he had met wore clothes made from the white man's cloth and rarely covered themselves with furs anymore. What he could see was the occasional rutted track that turned off the western wagon road and wandered back into the woods toward what he thought was most likely some settler's cabin. Here and there, a distant dog bark or the sound of an axe reinforced this theory, and Winsor seemed less concerned with stealth and more consumed with speed.

That night, rather than make their own cold camp, the woodsman turned them up one of the wheel rutted trails and lead them a mile back into the woods to a clearing. There, in the middle of a clearing that abruptly and providentially interrupted the forest, sat a tight, cozy cabin with a small crude barn made of barked logs and an even smaller crib for drying corn. Between the riders and the cabin, on either side of the path, was planted wheat and Indian corn in small neatly fenced but separate fields punctuated by the fresh stumps of trees. A wisp of smoke curled up from the cabin, and in the dusky twilight, the closing of God's golden eye threw the trees into an inky silhouette. A faint but warm candle glow shone behind a waxed paper window.

Former schoolmaster and inventor Jonathan Alerdyce Hollingswort and his family had cleared away the wooden bowls and cups they ate and drank from, and the four youngsters had just obediently climbed the ladder to the dark loft. The settler's close-mouthed wife, who was also the children's stepmother, sat beside the fire, mending work worn clothes while their father, in the one good chair, sat at the trestle table beside the lonely candle, drawing up plans and lists of materials for the mill he proposed to build during the coming summer. The massive grinding stones would arrive in a month's time, dragged westward by oxen on a lumbering, rattling wagon at great expense.

The sound of horses in the cabin's lane brought the gangling Hollingswort to his large, booted feet in an instant. He grabbed his slender firelock and called softly but firmly to his only son up in the loft. The twelve-year-old hopped down quickly and silently and went straight for the corner where Jonathan the elder kept his shooting bag and powder horn.

Matilda, the dowdy, taciturn wife had risen and dropping the clothes where she stood, stepped into the opposite corner and trundled out a cunningly made tripodial stand constructed of brass and wood with a blunderbuss clamped in a yoke at its summit, which was no more than chest high. Small wooden wheels allowed the contraption to be rolled over the packed earth floor. The woman stopped in front of the door and quickly attached a string and tiny pulleys to the wooden door latch and to the trigger of the stubby gun. Cocked and loaded with broken nails, two musket balls, three very round stones, and the shards of a broken stoneware tankard, the short gun would produce grievous effects on whoever opened the door from the outside without disarming the infernal device, which, as you can see, could only be done from the inside. She blocked one of the wheels with a chunk of firewood and then turned without a sound and, grabbing a wooden bucket of water from next to the fire, climbed the ladder to the loft where she joined the three silent faces peering down from above.

All this was done in absolute silence and in a matter of less than a minute as though carefully rehearsed. Hollingswort, meantime, was closing and latching a thick interior shutter, barring it in place with a stout branch of hickory. At last, he pulled a loop hole plug and, putting his mouth to it, called out into the darkness. Jonathan the younger, meanwhile, was removing the loophole plugs from the three other walls. Buckets of rainwater sat on the shingled roof painstakingly balanced by forked sticks all along the roof's ridge. Matilda removed several strategically located shingles and drew in the coiled ropes that went out the hole to the pails, allowing her to pull them over in the terrifying event that fire arrows set the roof ablaze.

"Come one step closer, and by Christ's blood, I'll blast ye straight into the forgiving presence of the great Jehovah!" Jonathan pulled his mouth away from the hole and then slid the muzzle of his musket out the port and peered down the barrel. The younger Hollingswort snuffed out the candle and stood ready by the fire, prepared to douse it too if his sire so instructed him.

Hamilton stopped dead, and Crisp reined up behind him, his mare bumping into the stallion's rump as the householder's voice echoed out across the small valley. Winsor knew he was in the man's sight as the firelock emerged from the small square hole.

"We are only two white men. We are heading for Philadelphia and thought mayhap you might have a mow where we could rest till morning when we'd be on our way," called back Hamilton very slowly and clearly, knowing the man inside was quite scared and liable to be jittery in the least.

In point of fact, Hollingswort was quite calm knowing that he had taken ample precaution and that if things became hot in an attack, the boy was instructed to load for him while he shot. They had spent hours practicing and could fire four well-aimed shots in a minute. He had also a brace of long-barreled pistols and an old snaphance carbine that had belonged to his grandfather Alerdyce, and if the savages were so brash as to rush the cabin, he could add them to the hail of balls issuing from the little fortress. He was well informed that natives rarely pressed an assault if the place were well defended and the householder resolute.

"Step down and come forward where I can see you better, and leave yer firelocks be."

Grandfather Hollingswort had taught him many things, and steadiness in the face of danger was perhaps one of the most valuable, along with "never underestimate an angry woman's ability to throw chopping knives." His final lesson had been, "Never be courageous in the face of overwhelming odds," which was, he said solemnly, why he bore no scars from cannon balls or chopping from kitchen knives.

John Hollingswort spoke clearly and firmly, making it plain from his tone that if the travelers didn't do exactly as he indicated, they were likely to be the recipients of his deliberate and lethal hostility.

Upon verifying their peaceable intentions with the inventor-farmer, Crisp and Hamilton tied up their horses to hitching posts near the barn and waited while the family disarmed the house and replaced the shingles. Winsor, with some sensitivity to the hour and of the inconvenience to the lady, declined an offer of leftover potage and, instead, politely asked permission for him and Crisp to dine on the jerked meat that they had brought in a linen bag.

Crispin had of late partaken of more than what he felt was his just share of dried meat and would gladly have accepted the offer of a bowl of boiled down rabbit, barley, and leek soup. Instead, he sat sullenly on the half-log bench and gnawed at the leathery meat. He disliked his coarse rescuer and had grown more despondent with each passing day. He was dismal over the prospect of going to Philadelphia and feared that he would never rejoin the Fifty-Sixth Regiment, whom some infamously recall as the Cheviot Guards. The treasure was never far from his mind, but more than anything, he wished to be with others of his kind—soldiers and Englishmen. His old companion, luck, he feared had deserted him.

The long hunter and the would-be farmer shared stories and details concerning the depredations along the frontier. Hamilton carefully committed the tales to memory, knowing that much of this was just the sort of information his employers sought.

Several of Hollingswort's neighbors had abandoned their crude steadings along the frontier and had moved closer to civilized country, and one family, less than a half-dozen miles distant, had been attacked. The family hunting hound had been killed, the horses had been stolen, and the family had been forced to hole-up in their cabin for a day while the Indians looted and burned everything in sight, driving off the bullocks and eating the murdered hound and fouling the well. It had only been the presence of a spring in the kitchen that had kept the family alive. Every fire arrow the savages shot was snuffed out in a moment by the unflagging settler.

Winsor told Hollingswort that the inventor's preparations were amongst the best he had seen, but that unless the man maintained an around-the-clock watch, they were no better than a half-baked loaf. Hollingswort agreed but could see no way that he and the boy and his wife could keep up with the watches and still work the farm by day, so he would take his chances after nightfall hoping that the savages bypassed his farm.

After sharing the last remaining stories and old news, Crisp and Hamilton finally went out into the barn and climbed up into the loft to rest, warm and secure for a night.

Just before dawn broke, Crisp was awakened by the sound of soft footsteps padding about in the stable below, and by the time he was awakened enough to realize that there might be some peril, Hamilton had clamped his callused, dirty hand over Crisp's mouth and whispered almost imperceptibly for him to remain silent.

Their horses out in the barnyard could be heard moving about, and then suddenly, there was a flicker of light that Crisp could see arc across the open mow door—a fire arrow. It was almost beyond irony and straying into the realm of bizarre coincidence, but he realized that the house was under attack by natives. As the fiery arrows thunked into the roof of the cabin, there was a loud explosion that could only be the blunderbuss report as some hapless warrior foolishly attempted to break into the interior of the Hollingswort's home.

Winsor had warned Hollingswort that if he wouldn't stand a guard every night, then he must, at least, bar his doors and windows at sunset. Clearly, the former schoolmaster had taken him at his word and had restored the deadly device to its previous location, and it had done its fell deed admirably.

Hamilton, rifle in hand, poked his bare head down through a trapdoor in the mow floor and then quickly pulled it back and threw the rifle to his shoulder, taking swift aim through the hole and fired into the darkness below. At the same moment, Crisp crawled quickly towards the mow door with his French musket and, spying an Indian trying to lead their horses off into the woods behind the house, pulled up and shot him squarely in the back. The savage soldier let go the horse's bridles and, stumbling sidewise, crawled and dragged himself by his hands under the cover of some nearby trees. The horses turned and fled back down the forest road, making it clear they wanted to have no more of this.

By now, the homeowner had joined the fray, and the war party, which was substantial, realized that they were under fire from the house, but were still in the darkness and confusion, unaware of the defenders in the barn. As the red warriors took up positions of cover that allowed them to shoot at the house with impunity, several decided upon climbing into the mow.

This all happened in the short while that Crisp was still struggling to reload, and he watched in horror and fascination as the first man up the ladder tossed his firelock into the loose hay and began hoisting himself up through the hole in the second floor. As his gun landed softly and he turned to dismount the ladder, Hamilton's belt axe crashed into the side of his mostly shaven head. With his legs and fat belly blocking the hole, his companions couldn't tell what was transpiring and only thought that he was having difficulty with the ladder. Hamilton hauled the lifeless form into the mow and waited, crouching just outside of the frame of the trapdoor.

Crispin had stopped ramming the ball down the barrel and stood rooted, his eyes riveted on the ladder as a second painted horror came up through the hole, only this one saw Crispin first and in his hurry to get down, the painted soldier didn't see the axe descending on his head from the shadows behind him. The tableau in the bloody mow began to brighten as the roof of the house now caught blaze. The body of the second fellow had fallen straight down, and the two savages at the bottom waiting their turns recognized the situation and fled the barn until they could return emboldened by reinforcements and fire.

The long hunter shouted at Crisp to move, and together, they quickly descended the crude ladder and moved cautiously toward the open door of the barn. Shots banged out, and suddenly, the blaze on the cabin roof fizzled, and Crisp knew that Matilda had pulled her ropes and upset the water buckets, drowning the flames. The savages yowled and shrieked in impotent anger, and Hollingswort cracked off a shot in response.

"Go back to hell, ye howling demons!" he added, hollering into the loophole.

The Indians cursed back vilely in their own vulgar tongue, none of which resembled the king's English, but their meaning was plain. From the left of the barn door, Crisp could see a group of about five Indians, one carrying a torch and all charging recklessly toward the barn. Realizing that the reinforcements had arrived and that their peril was imminent, Crisp leaped forward and sprinted toward the cabin, yelling for all he was worth for the owner to open up.

Hamilton was not far behind, but seeing that they were about to be cut off, he turned hard to his left and running full tilt, accurately fired his rifle from the hip, felling one attacker. He then melted into the tiny mob of reinforcers. One of the savages suddenly reeled backwards, the side of his head oddly staved in. Yet another heathen fell backwards onto the ground, clutching his manhood while the remaining two fought valiantly to drag the ferocious white man down.

Of the remaining two, one staggered back with his bloody hand spurting purple fountains from the stumps of two of his fingers which Winsor spat out onto the ground, but the woodland legionnaire wasn't out of the fight for good. Pulling a gleaming knife with his still good hand, the wounded warrior stepped forward and plunged the wicked blade into Winsor's belly. Mrs. Winsor's eldest boy crumpled in the cabin yard, and the savage who had delivered the mortal wound spat in his face and kicked him viciously in the ribs.

Crisp saw all this as he crouched terrified yet defiant in front of the cabin door waiting for Hollingswort to open up. The sage homesman had barred the way rather than expect the enemy to stupidly confront the blunderbuss again. Not unexpectedly, Crisp came under a hail of fire, and musket balls smacked into the logs all around him. Desperately shouldering his firelock, he fired into the retreating darkness, aiming at one of the muzzle flashes. The side of his arm suddenly felt afire, and he knew a ball had grazed him. The door swung outward and knocked him over. Reaching down, Hollingswort grabbed him by the shirt and dragged him back into the cabin and slammed the thick door shut just as several balls struck the thick planks, beating out a deadly tattoo.

Crawling on all fours over to the window that had previously been covered with wax paper but was now just tattered strips, Crisp raised himself up and barely peeped over the sill. Hamilton Gilead Winsor lay facedown in the dust, his head smeared with a crimson gore left from the raging war club blows that had ended his life. The few wisps of clotted hair that still clung to the sides of his head waved forlornly in the gentle breeze that blew just as the bright warm sun cleared the tops of the trees. The bloody-handed woodland Janissary who had stabbed Winsor completed the grisly deed by slicing the hair from the top of the dead man's head. After robbing the body of any useful truck, the three surviving warriors daringly shook the bloody scalp and Winsor's rifle at the stubborn little cabin and then carefully removed their own fallen dead from the battlefield of the cabin yard.

Matilda deftly wrapped Crispin's bleeding upper arm tightly with a wad of tow and bound it about with a strip of linen ripped from the hem of one of the shirts she had been mending the night before. Sitting on the floor and leaning his back against a bench, Crispin caught his breath and slowly calmed his racing heart. The gunfire aimed at the cabin had now nearly ceased and became no more than an occasional shot.

"Shoot them, in the name of God!" screamed Crispin on the verge of hysterics as he watched the devils who had killed Winsor fade back into the smoke hazed dawn, disappearing in moments under the forest curtain.

"No! Perhaps if I let them be with a scalp and a rifle, they'll leave us here in the house alone."

As if on cue from some demoniac playwright, the barn exploded in fiery tongues, and the corncrib began to smolder. War hoops greeted the conflagration, and in the fresh born light, Crispin could see the remaining savages—some almost gleeful and others angry, darting about with dead chickens dangling from their belts or waving some garden tool or piece of tack stolen from the dying barn. One of the garish savages, painted boldly in ochre red and hells hall black from head to toe, streaked by wearing an apron that had been left out to dry. As the flames rose higher, the musket shots became less frequent; and as the minutes ticked by, the barn crashed down, sending up a pillar of sparks and smoke, and no more shots or devilish yelps were heard.

More minutes and then an hour went by. After double-checking to see that all the firelocks were loaded and having eaten a crust of bread and downing a wooden cup full of buttermilk, Jonathan warily opened the door and stepped out onto the porch, and still, nothing transpired. As the schoolmaster began to cross the yard, Crispin stepped fearfully into the open doorway and, with great trepidation, inched out, knowing that he ought to cover the fellow and help him to investigate and secure the few undamaged tools that were left scattered about by the rampaging marauders. Of course, there was also the matter of burying the long hunter for which Crisp felt personally responsible, after all the man had saved his, Crisp's, life by delaying the party that was attacking the barn and for his rescue from the French. Crisp owed the man a debt of gratitude, that he could now only repay with a Christian burial.

Late in the day, after packing a few needful household goods and sufficiently salvaging all that was left, Jonathan and his son, both armed with firelocks and knives, went off in search of the horses. The natives had succeeded in fetching off Hollingswort's one good horse and in killing both of his oxen along with a trio of milk cows, which lay half burned in their stanchions under the smoking rubble of the barn. It had taken great courage, but the father and son had tracked down both Crisp's and Hamilton's mounts, which had eluded the savages, who, in their hurry, had overshot the animals' track. Unsure what the forest held, the father and son had ventured heroically a half mile into the woods, tracking the mare and stallion. Every tree seemed the likely hiding spot of some lurking Indian, waiting to leap out screeching and brandishing a gory axe. By the time they returned, it was nearly dark, and they had the terrifying night to endure.

Now, when the sun set, there would be no peace and repose from a day's honest labor. Instead, the family would sit by the reassuring fire, watching the crowding forest closely and praying that the Indians did not return to finish the job. The nearest neighbors had been struck down and lay in pools of their own blood, their farms burned to the ground by the same war party, so no one remained to come to the Hollingswort's aid.

While Hollingswort had searched the woods for the horses, Crisp had buried Winsor. Rolling the mangle-headed body onto a woolen blanket, he then dragged the stiffening woodsman in back of the cabin and, after locating a shovel that had survived the barn fire, dug a final resting place two feet deep and gently eased the cooling clay of Ham Winsor into the ground. He found many rocks lying about in the fields and placed them on the flatbed of the wheelbarrow, which he sweated to push back to the cabin. After building a cairn of stone over the grave, Crisp fell to the ground exhausted, his bandage was leaking blood, and the pain was overpowering his will. He recited the twenty-third Psalm through pain-gritted teeth and then staggered into the house where he collapsed again, this time falling into a deep sleep until the Hollingswort men returned in the early evening.

Winsor had never been a churchgoing man, and doubtless, his immortal ghost cared little for what prayers were read. In the years that followed, the shape of the farm changed and grew, and his eternal couch was lost amongst the weeds and second growth that rioted in the rear of the pigsty that had formerly been the Hollingswort cabin, erasing all earthly remembrance of the long hunter and the only proof of the deadly battle that had once been fought.

Crispin had agreed to stay with the Hollingsworts until they reached civilized farm country, which still lay two days walk to the east. Hamilton and Crisp, of course, had expected to reach it in a day, but with all of the adults walking and the Hollingswort girls taking turns riding upon the gentle mare, the journey would take longer. After hacking strips of meat from the dead oxen and salvaging everything useful from the house and packing it upon the stallion's back, the newly destitute and terrified family began fleeing eastward.

Their pace was rapid as Hollingswort feared attack at any moment. Taking the lead many yards in front, Jonathan the elder kept up a constant roving gaze of the thick woods on either side of the grassy, rutted track, desperately hoping to espy an ambush before it was sprung. Then came sturdy, brogan-shod Matilda in her drab petticoats and apron, and next to her was the lean, freckle-faced boy, each armed and leading a horse with one of the younger girls atop while the eldest girl walked between them.

Lastly came Crisp bringing up the rear. He bravely and constantly circled the main group, venturing a hundred feet into the ancient forest on either side of the road, hoping to force any assassins to fire on him and give the warning before the family could be assailed. For every fearful mile the others trod, Crisp walked five. In the past, selfless acts of bravery had been no specialty of Crispin's, yet he knew that if they did not all work together now, then there was little hope that any of them would reach safety, so he steeled himself to the task much as he had when he had inexplicably gone wading to Hector's rescue in that fetid Carolina swamp.

It goes without saying that they started no fire on the night of their hasty retreat, and they suffered horribly in the darkness because of the damp and the biting bugs which kept them slapping at themselves incessantly, nearly driving them mad and making it difficult for the men to concentrate on defense. The two youngest girls hid their heads beneath their mother's petticoats, and then Jonathan finally mixed a concoction of horse water and mud and daubed it about his arms and face as did the others. The odor was less than pleasant and in no way resembled anything goodly but did seem to ward off some of the bugs.

Late on the second day, with exhaustion etched in every begrimed crease in their wild-eyed faces and with their weary feet dragging in the dirt, Crisp and the Hollingsworts at last came upon carefully tilled fields and pastures full of fat cattle, and in the distance, a pretty white-framed house with its chimney huffing out friendly puffs of blue-grey smoke. The smells of civilization alone were a balm to the exhausted family—freshly tilled earth, ripe with spring's promise blended gently with the scent of cow dung and mixed pleasingly with the faint odor of wood smoke. Altogether, it was quite a different fragrance from the stench of burnt corn, immolated oxen, and the acrid stink of gun smoke.

If he had been a religious man, Crispin would have sunk down upon his knees, clasped his hands together with a show of humility, and thanked the LORD for his deliverance. Instead, he combined a profane oath with his maker's name and slung his musket over his shoulder, glad at last that he no longer had to beat the brush for wild Indians.

BLIND MEN AND JUSTICE

After a day and a night of recuperating by the fire and at the table in the farmer's kitchen, Lt. St. Crispin Mull had decided to put the frontier and the Indians behind himself as quickly as possible. The Hollingsworts had thanked him deeply and profusely for all his aid and had returned the stallion to him, keeping the mare for themselves. He did not bother to inform them of the agreement reached between Lord Church Hardaway and Winsor, feeling that the deal had nothing to do with him or with Hollingswort.

He accepted the gift of a pair of plain brown wool stockings from Hollingswort (to cover his scratched and naked shins) and did his best to shave his beard and comb the knots and tangles out of his hair, which had grown quite long during his captive's sojourn in the wilderness. His locks he tied back in a queue with a piece of red ribbon given him by Jonathan's eldest daughter who was practicing her coquetry.

Looking somewhat less terrifying, he at last bid the family good-bye as they stood in front of the neat farmhouse that they had come upon the night before last. With two night's sleep in deep golden straw and several good meals of beef roasts and smoked hams under his belt, compliments of kind farmer Woodruff, Crisp took to the road with a nod and a wave, making his way toward New York, penniless and looking not one wit like a British officer but more like a well-bathed scalawag.

With a bedroll slung from his back upon a rope and a small coarse linen sack with a few eatables tied about his waist, he was not at all sure of how he would make the journey. He was without guide and had only the directions given by the occasional traveler or householder. His rations would run out in three or four days' time and other than shooting game with his musket he had no hope of provisioning himself for the trip, which would likely take a week or more.

Crisp remembered well the Highland Rebellion from his own youth. When the fighting in the north near Inverness had ended and the portly Duke of Cumberland sent Bonny Prince Charlie scurrying like a hare in the heather, a great many of the Prince's brave highlanders had taken to the highways seeking work. They, of course, had surrendered their weapons after that bloody day on Drumossie Moor where they were soundly beaten by King George's Regulars. They hid their kilts in the rafters alongside their great pipes, which had lead them into battle, and looking entirely out of place, they wandered the roads with their great shanks and shoulders tucked beneath ill-fitting coats and hastily made breeches. Even Crispin's father, a devout lowlander (He despised fresh air and held that the bens and crags of the highlands were fit only for wolves and fairies.) and an outspoken supporter of the King and the Campbell's, said that seeing those broken men beg their bread was like seeing a war horse hooked behind a plow.

Crisp was sure that he looked as poor and downtrodden as those penniless highland Jacobites. Of course, it goes without saying that the Jacobites would have been glad of a musket and four legs under two to carry them. By comparison, Crispin was truly a rich man, but that is little consolation to a man lost and without tuppence or meat.

Crispin's father had profited after the war taking in a wee Jacobite drummer boy whom he'd lent out daily for all sorts of odd jobs, some savory and some less. In exchange, the lad had received his potage and a thin straw tick to sleep upon. The arrangement had lasted until a year or so later when the boy grew courageous enough to run away to America and left Ezra Mull cursing his ill luck. Crispin had known the lad only a little, but the older boy had taught him a Jacobite tune and an oath or two. Ezra had cursed the stripling papist for hotfooting it and told Crispin that was what came of showing kindness to a Catholic. Crispin, of course, had thought some on that and decided for himself that if his father had paid the lad a bit more and called him a traitor a bit less perhaps he wouldn't have run away; naturally, he didn't share this opinion with his father.

It was upon the third day after taking his leave of the Hollingsworts that Crispin found himself eating the last of his biscuit by a small fire with the darkness closing in and no idea of how he would eat on the morrow.

※

In the annals of fibbery, there are many tomes dedicated to the great liars and deceivers of the ages, but in the volume given over to colonial American days (one of the smaller editions), there is one page devoted especially for Thomas "Bedlam" Eaton. Eaton was born into fair and comfortable circumstances in the year 1729 and, by all rights, should have prospered honestly. By the age of fourteen, he had mastered Latin and astronomy and was making tremendous progress in mathematics. University was on his horizon and clearly Thomas had the makings of a physician or an apothecary at the very least.

A useful life was however not in his stars, for it was noted when he was still a youth that he was a bit over fond of cards and drink and no matter what his parents or the minister did or said he would not relent. Thomas Eaton had already learned that he could earn a handsome living without soiling his hands or exerting himself whatsoever. At the tender age of fifteen, using charm, guile, and wit, he swindled an old widow woman of modest wealth out of her coin and the silver coffee and tea service given her by her father on her wedding day. Wearing a rich brown velvet coat and breeches and a cream-colored brocade waistcoat, which the poor woman had given her late husband before he passed away, Thomas Eaton disappeared from life in Philadelphia. With her heart broken and her pockets robbed, the old dear set the sheriff after Eaton, but the lad had slipped free and was nowhere to be found.

Cards and dice remained his primary income for some years, along with the gleanings connived from unsuspecting ladies. Bedlam Eaton was of middling height and weight with brown hair—he was as unpresupposing a fellow as has ever gone unnoticed. He calmly blended into any crowd without a moment's notice. His eyes however were his most effective tool in fleecing the innocent, along with his great skill at disguise. Thomas had long before learned to smile and make merry eyes in the presence of the fairer sex, and he utilized his charm and wit (which was substantial) to the utmost.

It is worth noting that it was also at about this time that he received the label Bedlam. Some say he carried this over from his youth, asserting that his father had angrily dubbed him such after Thomas had noisily returned home late after an evening of debauchery. The word *bedlam* is derived from the word *Bethlem*, the name of the London hospital for addled droolers.

Others claimed that he had earned the name for his performances when he was caught cheating at cards. When caught out, he would leap to his feet and begin capering about and singing at the top of his lungs, which he madly interspersed with children's rhymes. If this failed to illicit pity or to distract his accusers, he would roll his eyes about and drool profusely, shouting at the top of his lungs, "I am the king of Spain! Bow before your liege!" or "I am the most beautiful man ever to have slept upon Vespasia's silken sheets. Look into my emerald eyes, and weep for the whore of Antioch!" and other such queer nonsense.

Still others say that his name was originally Bedthem, an allusion to how he gained the confidence of grieving widows. After several close scrapes, Eaton had decided that he needed to be less conspicuous, so he placed more emphasis upon fraud and deceit and less upon cheating at games.

There was not a card game or parlor in Maryland, Delaware, or Pennsylvania where he was welcome, so not long before this chapter of our story begins, he had again cheated a poorer man than himself out of his horse, cart, tools, and stock, so he took to the road in the guise of a blind, lame tinsmith. The odd robbery combined with schemes to deceive and cheat the unknowing, now made up the foci of his corrupt trade.

There were several sheriffs who had tied nooses for him, and no few wealthy and powerful gentlemen who had been cheated at whist and faro also sought his capture. Many of those who had dealings with Bedlam Eaton knew him better as Isaac Tew or Hiram Pease. He often presented himself as a physician traveling to visit cousins some distance away. If he were in Delaware, for instance, then the visit was in Fairfax, Virginia. All that was in the past, however, and now he was living life a bit more desperately, at least until the memory of his gaming days had faded from the minds of wealthy men.

Sitting up on the seat board of the covered cart, he dozed behind blue-tinted glasses in the fading afternoon sun while the numerous lanterns, candle holders, and nutmeg graters gently clinked and jangled. His head was cocked as though listening for distant sounds, but in truth, all he heard in his dreams was the solid chink of good coin, not the dull clank of coffeepots and sconces. His pockets were full for the moment, and Bedlam Eaton had decided to take a break from his "labors" to visit Princeton in the Jerseys. He had never before visited the town, so he was confident that there he could find pleasant lodgings and relax in the taproom of the local inn with no fear of being recognized. Drinking flip and making merry with farmers' daughters and pinching the butcher's pert and saucy wife would suit him fine. He planned to secure the cart and horse in a grove or a woods well outside of town and only visit to feed and water the horse but once a day, being careful that nobody should see him doing so and make a connection between he and the sightless white smith who gamely hobbled about on a crutch. He still had many miles to go before he reached Princeton, and in his mind, he would enjoy debauching all the local ladies and swilling punch and flip until he couldn't even stagger to his room.

As he bumped along in his dreams, he smiled drowsily at the memory of the settler he had tied up and robbed and of the exorbitant prices he had gleefully charged for the tinwares he had sold to the rustic farmers in the back settlements. When the last of the wares were sold, along with the cart and horse, he would acquire another disguise, but in the meantime, he enjoyed profiting from the labor of another man. Waking as he approached a fork in the road, he saw a fire burning just beyond the point of woods that split the two paths. The sun was almost set, and the fire was so small that he could not make out who or how many shared the warmth of its flames. If nothing else, he had found a fire ready for his pot, and coals upon which to toast his bread. If he were lucky, perhaps some tinker or itinerant tradesman had paused for the night. If such were the case, then he could already feel the bulging purse in his pocket swelling to the point of bursting.

The principle advantage of being blind and stumping along on a crutch was that no one ever suspected him of robbery or mayhem, so his victims revealed everything, and foolishly turned their vulnerable backs as though they were in the confines of their own cozy kitchens. Truth to tell (Bedlam almost never told the truth.), he had been a blind, lame beggar; a blind storyteller; a lame veteran; a deaf and lame veteran; and a blind, lame itinerant weaver suffering from the ague.

Nineteen innocent men in sixteen counties in three colonies had been robbed over the past three years, and the only thing they all had in common was an unsound stranger, often a fellow who seemed affable enough despite the sickly burdens the lord had placed upon his weary travel worn head. No one had yet connected him to the four failed businesses where he had absconded with the life's earnings of his four different partners before the stores could be bought or the stocks ordered. Word traveled slowly over bad roads, and so, few were the victims who knew or suspected that they had met with the likes of Bedlam Eaton. In truth, there were likely not more (at that time) than a dozen men alive who knew who Bedlam was nor that he was a one-man crime frolic. Mostly, he was just referred to as the blind robber.

Bedlam hailed the fire with a hearty "Hello, friend!" and prepared to put on the blind and lame act. Crispin "hallooed" back and squinted into the gathering dusk from his seat by the fire and saw coming around the bend toward the fork a one horse cart with a crude canvas canopy and a lone driver sitting up front waving to him. He hungrily wolfed down the last of his biscuit before he could be asked to share. He stood, mouth full and dusted the crumbs off his hands and, smoothing out his waistcoat, waited for the cart to stop. His musket was within easy reach and his hand rested lightly on the Frenchman's keen knife, which was tucked into his belt.

The driver brought the cart to a standstill in front of Crispin, and it wasn't until then that he could see that the fellow was blind. Eaton, of course, could see Crispin as well as you and I see the face of the man on the moon, but he looked off to his right and kept his chin tipped up with the aspect of one trying to locate a distant sound. It never occurred to Crispin to ask how the sightless fellow knew he was there. The tradesman, for Crispin could see that the poor fellow was such, wore a grey wool frock coat with stained cuffs which was worn thin at the elbows, and for breeches, he sported gray linen, the latter badly patched at the knees with blue-striped ticking. His plain white shirt was buttoned to the throat, and over it, he displayed a waistcoat of dirty white linen with pewter buttons. On his apparently middle-aged head (You will recall he was actually younger.) sat a shapeless dove-colored slouch hat turned up just a bit in the front. His stockings were baggy, and his shoes were tied on with short scraps of twine in lieu of buckles. All in all, the man appeared to be a penniless nomad, or perhaps the effect was such that Bedlam looked like a battered and dented lead figurine. Whatever it was, Crispin's eyes went quickly and pityingly to the crutch, which leaned on the seat next to Eaton.

Standing up, Eaton spoke gently to his white, sway-backed horse. "Whoa! Stand ye fast Bomilcar."

Taking up the crutch, he carefully began to dismount the cart. Upon reaching the ground, he groped his way forward along the harness and thills with the crutch tucked under his right arm. Reaching the horse's head, Bedlam stopped and balanced himself upon the crutch; he deliberately faced the wrong way. He held his right hand out to his right rather than to his left where Crispin stood.

"Medad Buck," he said by way of introduction. Crispin coughed politely to give away his location. Turning his head toward the sound, Eaton smiled, "Blind Buck most call me."

After exchanging names and pleasantries, Crispin invited the fellow to his fire. Clearly, he believed he had nothing to fear from the tinsmith. Given his most recent experiences, it is likely he would have been a far more wary host had the traveler been a sound specimen. Crispin was mistrustful of most of mankind and understandably so. After all, he had been kidnapped and beaten by Indians only to be rescued by an ally who refused to grant him his freedom, but he reassured himself, the hobbling, sightless tinsmith hardly seemed to pose a threat.

※

"Can you believe it! He felled the tree right onto his own house and with his wife in it! She survived, of course. Come out pullin' leaves and twigs outta her hair and cursin' like a trooper—so they say. Well, Mister Williford stands there and, with a straight face, and tells her that tree is fine wood, and he can make her a lovely set of chairs from it." Eaton paused from his story and, withdrawing his toasting fork from the fire, pinched the bread to see if it was done. He turned the slice over and then held the other side over the coals while his little copper pot of turnips and carrots burbled warmly over the fire.

Crisp had lost interest in the story from the outset and was far more interested in the cookery that was going on. *This Williford fellow is obviously gifted with no great wit*, thought Crispin. The colonial sense of humor seemed lacking in sophistication, and Crispin wondered what at all was amusing about a fellow who smashes his own house to bits and flinders.

Bedlam stirred the delicious-smelling pot with a wooden spoon and then took a taste. "Wants salt," he said. "Would ye mind fetchin' some from the locker in the cart lad?"

Bedlam was slowly bringing Crispin around to the point where they "could do business." Doing business, of course, meant something entirely different to the rest of the world than it did to Bedlam. Bedlam would lull his mark into a sense of false security and ease before he sprang the trap. Crispin returned with the salt and stood next to the would-be robber.

"Lad, ye've the look about ye of a man who's hungry as a hunter and is dreamin' of a feast. Would ye care fer a bite of soup?" He sprinkled some of the precious fine snow over the little kettle.

"Why yes, thank you." Crisp walked round the fire to his meager pack, rummaging in the bag for the wooden bowl. "Provisions have been a bit scanty. I really must thank you. This is the first hot meal I've had in days."

"Never leave a fellow traveler in want I say," said Bedlam as he held the small pot and spoon up towards Crisp, who scooped out several chunks of turnip and then poured off some of the strong broth into his bowl.

Having no spoon, Crisp blew on the turnip and cooled it enough to pick up with his fingers. Bedlam kept his seat and placed the warm pot between his legs on the ground where he sat and began to partake of the simple fare himself. They ate quietly, and after wiping and scouring out the bowl with a wad of coarse grass, Crisp laid back on his blanket and rested his head in his hand and listened a bit more contentedly to the humorous back woods tales of Bedlam Eaton. Perhaps the stories weren't as dull as he had first judged.

Eaton pretended the part of the rustic itinerant well. Being a natural mimic, he had quickly acquired the mannerisms and speech of the people around him. "Did you ever hear the story of that cabbagehead Giles Sherwood?" Eaton began to regale Crispin with another tale of a foolish farmer. This one had traded his neighbor a fine litter of piglets for a dying cat.

Crisp roused enough to throw another thick chunk of brushwood on the fire, and Eaton, with his story finished, pulled a penny whistle from his pocket and began to play a slow thoughtful tune. Crispin's eyes grew heavy while Bedlam's blind orbs swept from side to side behind his glasses, taking the campsite and everything in it into account. Breathing evenly, Crispin at last lay back and shook hands with the king of nod.

Beyond the fire, some night creature bustled through the leaves in search of its dinner, but Bedlam was in no hurry and was not about to give up a good musket and horse due to impatience. Normally, he avoided victims that carried anything resembling a weapon, but this fellow seemed young and inexperienced. Sure enough, the lad went to sleep and foolishly left the firelock leaning against the tree where it had rested all evening. After a half an hour or so had elapsed, Bedlam ceased his playing and arose, going to the rear of the cart to fetch some rope and a stout cudgel. It was time to do business.

Crispin had located his bed by the fire poorly. One small gnarled root kept poking into his back and at last he woke up, deciding he had to move. As he opened his eyes, he saw above him the blind smith with a stick in his one hand and a rope dangling from the other. *Odd*, he thought to himself before he could clear the sleep from his head. *He's not wearing his glasses.*

"Blast!" said Bedlam. "I really had hoped you would stay asleep. It's always more ugly this way." The cudgel descended with stunning force straight at Crispin's gentle forehead.

Without thinking, Crisp rolled swiftly to his right. The polished stick thumped into the dirt where his head had just been and he sprang to his feet.

"Damn you!" yelled the frustrated robber. He hauled back and prepared to swing at Crisp's knees.

The officer stumbled backwards and, seeing the musket next to him, snatched it up. The robber shoved the barrel to the side and brutally drove the round head of the stick into Crispin's stomach. As he doubled over in pain, Crisp heaved upwards with the butt of the gun and caught the tip of his assailant's chin, sending him reeling backwards toward the fire where he tripped himself up in the firewood and sat down hard in the orange embers. Eaton let out a birdlike screech and rolled out of the fire pit. By now, Crispin had recovered enough to wildly point the musket and croak out an order.

"Don't move!"

"I have to!" Eaton screamed back. "My breeches are on fire!" The robber writhed about, trying to kick off his shoes and strip off his pants.

Crispin sat down and rested the firelock on his thighs, gently rubbing his sore belly. The gun was cocked, and Eaton was presently more absorbed with the intense pain in his hindquarters than in resuming the attack, which was clearly over now that Crispin had acquired the upper hand.

"You're not blind, and I'd hazard to say that crutch is a ruse as well," spat Crisp.

Bedlam at last freed himself from his maliciously grasping trousers. "You're a quick fellow," he answered sarcastically. "I suppose they could use your type in Parliament!" He rolled around craning his neck, trying to look over his own shoulder at his bare and lightly seared buttocks, so concerned by the rapidly increasing pain that he gave not a thought to his nakedness. "How bad does it look?"

Crispin looked up and gave a cursory glance. "Blistered, bad I'd say, a bit of black, but that might just be ash." He got up stiffly and picked up the rope that had been dropped. One end was glowing from where it had fallen in the fire. He stamped out the smoldering end and threw it to Bedlam. "Tie yer feet together."

Bedlam protested loudly, complaining that with his hams well cooked, he was unlikely to escape or attempt Crispin harm. The officer firmly insisted, and after the robber had tied his own feet together, Crisp stepped forward and quickly bound his hands. Eaton had found a small pot of spermaceti lubricant in a locker in the cart and presumed that the real white smith had used it to maintain his tools. He had told Crisp where to find it and had begged him to apply it to the cooked skin. Crisp rolled the thief from his side to his belly and then kindly dribbled whale oil onto the wounds. Without a source for tallow or unsalted butter, it was the only grease they could think of for the roasted flesh. Crispin rolled the prisoner in his blanket and then left him to lie on the cold hard ground. The sneaking bandit deserved no better, and Crisp slept fitfully, sitting with his back up against the hard wheel of the cart. Waking now and again to toss wood on the fire, the musket rested heavily in his lap with the lock at half cock. Eaton groaned and pounded his fist in agony, and occasionally, Crispin would throw a stick at him and curse him to silence.

In the morning after dousing the fire and picking up the camp and preparing a monkish breakfast of dry toast (just for himself), Crisp loaded Bedlam roughly into the back of the cart and made him lie facedown on the hard planks. With the stallion trailing behind on a rope, Crisp headed the cart down the left fork of the road while Eaton protested that it was the wrong way and, in general, groused about his ill treatment and, in the next breath, complimented Crispin in an attempt to make friends and restore his freedom.

"A daring capture, Mr. Mull. You are obviously a man of parts and not the half-starved callow youth I took you for. I apologize if I've used harsh language. You are obviously a man of breeding and parts. I know you are only doing your duty, and if you knew the true circumstances of my penury, you would undoubtedly see the justice in restoring my liberty."

Eaton had given up all pretenses and no longer played the part of a rustic. He gritted his teeth through it all as the burning on his posterior was fierce.

Crisp now understood how Ham Winsor must have felt when he, St. Crispin, had suffered his bout of madness in the forest. The man's flattery was annoying in the very least, and Crispin needed quiet in order to concentrate on formulating a plan. Reaching around behind the seat, he found some tools wrapped in an oily rag and dumping them out, he shoved the filthy cloth into the silver-tongued robber's mouth. At last, with some peace, he could devote his attention to what needed being done next.

He had driven eastwardly without incident and without seeing or passing another soul for a day before he finally came upon the tiny community of Englishtowne, just a few miles north of Pottstown in Pennsylvania. There was no sign telling him where in the world he was, and the crossroads were nothing more than a forge, a ramshackle excuse for an inn and three houses huddled about the crossing of two tracks. The squire of the hamlet, if such he and it could be called, was of course the smith who owned both the busy forge and the sorry inn, along with the best of the three stone houses.

In troubled times, like the current crisis with the savages, the local population, which included a dozen farmer families up and down the roads, converged upon the stockade and blockhouse which lay a mere hundred yards rearward of the inn on a dimple of a rise. The little fortress could hold more than fifty adults and two score of cattle for upwards of a week. In recent years, it had seen little use and so was not in the best of repair; but in the past few days, the yeomanry of that neighborhood had been as busy as bees restocking it and patching the worst of the holes in the roof. This they did under the watchful eye of the smith, who not surprisingly was also the captain of the local company of militia.

These intrepid warriors belonged to a regiment of colonial soldiery commanded by a brewer from whom, it goes without saying, the captain purchased his ale. The local band of rum-courage soldiers was currently gathered at the "Big Tree Inn" and were tossing down copious amounts of liquid bravery to slake the thirst they had worked up repairing the Englishtowne Fort. Word had been passed down the road by retreating settlers that the savages could not be far behind, and if the Pennsylvania assembly did not take action quickly, then Philadelphia itself would come under a hail of fire arrows and perhaps those blasted Quakers deserved it!

Captain Elisha Maythuse had bought his happy lads the first round and drew the tankards himself while his eldest daughter served them up with a saucy flip of her pretty striped petticoats. Some months past, she had rested her roving eye on handsome young Filey Bush, the company drummer, a strapping sixteen-year-old with bulging muscles and a thick mop of curly brown hair. Filey was poor at sums but could run faster than the wind and could stroll to the fair with a fat calf over each shoulder, not to mention he could beat the cadence and call the men to arms with his drum. He was just to the young ladies' taste—strong arm and a weak head.

Crispin reined up Bomilcar in front of the shabby establishment and tied him to the tilting sign post which hung over the slanting gate, which itself was centered on the waist high broken slatted fence that had once neatly enclosed the front yard of the inn. Maythuse had a habit of doing things up nicely and then never touching them again in the belief that there was no sense in his possessions lasting longer than himself, especially as he had no sons to leave them to. Crisp noted the peeling and flaking whitewash and the sloping front step, which had settled low on its right. A man in his cups had best be sure footed if he wished to make it out the front door without doing himself serious injury.

Laughter greeted Crispin's ears as he paused in the doorway and allowed his eyes to adjust to the feeble light.

"Excuse me, is there a justice or a sheriff about?" queried Crispin, stepping in and addressing himself toward the counter.

"I'm the closest thing there is to law here in Englishtowne," answered Maythuse from behind the plank and barrel bar. The short round smith wiped his hands on his dirty white apron, which he presently wore over the top of his blue and red regimental coat. "Captain Elisha Maythuse, in what way can I be of help to you, sir?"

"I have captured a ruffian, a sort of highwayman to be a bit more exact, and I should like to be rid of him," replied Crispin, politely but directly.

The rest of the patrons leaped to their feet and charged the door in a race to see who could get out first and look into the back of the cart. Crisp stepped aside to avoid the crush and waited for the hubbub to quiet before he continued.

"Could you take him off my hands, Captain, as a favor from one military man to another?" Crispin knew he had to establish a friendship with this fellow if he wished to divest himself of Bedlam Eaton.

In reality, a lieutenant of regulars was the superior of a captain of militia, at least in the eyes of the Crown. He was sure, however, if he ordered the captain to assume custody that the officer would balk. Most colonials, it seemed to Crispin, were more interested in personal advantage than in the maintenance of a just and lawful countryside. It never occurred to him that he had spent most of his time in the army pursuing his own advantage more selfishly than perhaps any of the backward Americans he had met. He presumed correctly that the smith was no different, and it was true that Elisha Maythuse was more inclined to sell ale than he was to sweat over his anvil, and he was more inclined to fix a plow or make a hinge than he was to play the jailer, which is to say he did not fancy himself a representative of the provincial court.

"And to what unit do you belong, sir?" asked the barman officer skeptically, looking Crisp up and down.

"I am Lt St. Crispin Mull of the Fifty-Sixth of Foot, attempting to return to my regiment after my capture and barbaric confinement by savages and papist Frenchmen. My story is long and tiresome, sir, but I would be glad to share it with you later over a glass of port once we have secured the prisoner." Crisp turned and went out, praying that the hotelier captain would follow him.

The crowd about the cart seemed disappointed to have found an ordinary looking fellow, gagged and partly naked who was seemingly asleep. In truth, Thomas Eaton was so mortified at being seen this way (with his breeches missing and his fundament pointed skyward) and was also terrified that he would soon be hung. He was feigning sleep in hopes that they would all go away and that his bonds would magically melt.

The sometime soldiers were deflated at having not found a growling, booted, and spurred highwayman, complete with mask and pistols. They began to mill in pairs and threes, murmuring about hangings they had witnessed and the merits of hemp rope over jute and whether or not the Crown shouldn't just bring back beheadings like in olden-times. Standing back talking softly behind their hands, they politely waited for the captain to render his judgment upon the situation.

"I've got no fancy port, Leftenant. Men around here are used to simple fare and simple drink. Just where do you propose I would hold this knight of the road?" The provincial officer was starting to sound worried and slightly perturbed. On the one hand, he grew concerned as he had never before had charge of a red handed robber; and on the other hand, he was slightly irritated at the arrogant presumption of the Englishman.

"A draught of ale will do nicely," said Crisp offhandedly. "And I'd say your cellar or chained to a tree would do as well as any dungeon unless you have some better place?" They had reached the cart, and Crispin gestured towards the supine form of Eaton. "There he is in all his glory, Captain. I propose he might be made to confess the name of the fellow he robbed the cart from. I had little desire to speak with him, so I left the interrogation for more experienced authorities such as yourself. He had a pouch on him, brim full of coin, no doubt from other victims. I half considered keeping it for myself for all the trouble he has given me but decided that his jailer and I together could better decide its disposition."

Not to mention that Crispin was afraid that if he kept the tainted silver Bedlam would tattle on him. He finally decided that he could split the purse with whomever he turned the thief over to and still be the hero for capturing a rogue. Sometimes, doing the right thing had its own rewards, he had thought. In his mind, he had spent the coin already on clean clothes, a razor, and a saddle of mutton dripping with juice and surrounded by onions and turnips washed down with a nice bottle of port. The moral separation between Bedlam Eaton and Crispin was so narrow one could barely slip a shaved guinea or the name of an apostle between them.

"I'd say we must hold the coin along with the cart until the sheriff can get here," said the stocky smith, seeming a little less concerned now that he had seen the countenance and demeanor of the prisoner.

Crispin tried heroically not to show his disappointment and anger at being told the coin should be held so that some backward sheriff and this Falstaffian excuse for an officer could divide it up between them the minute he was down the road and over the hill.

The root cellar beneath the tavern's kitchen was cold and cramped, being little more than a hole in which to place bushels of root vegetables. Bedlam looked about for a seat and seeing none, he cast a glance over his shoulder up the ladder and was just about to lodge a protest when the captain slammed shut the trapdoor of his subterranean prison. Sergeant Crowley of the militia rolled a large, untapped barrel of ale across the floor, and stood it up smack on the center of the trap, weighing it down heavily. The darkness was complete, and Eaton could hear the other men walk away, their footfalls sounding hollow on the floor boards inches above his head.

Bedlam now was sure he was in a bad spot. These farm folks lacked sufficient sophistication and would not be manipulated once they saw things plainly, not to mention his buttocks still burned and, at the same time, his feet were freezing as the cold dirt sucked the heat out of him. He was quite sure that the justice here in Englishtowne would be swift and most undoubtedly violent. He had not been deaf to the muttering in the tavern yard, and it was clear that these sods would revel at the sight of him dangling from the gibbet. It was often easy to gain a farmer's confidence as they tended to be a trusting and naive lot, but Bedlam had also spent enough time in their company to know that they were not nearly as merciful as their city cousins and were mostly unwavering in their Old Testament sense of justice.

The captain had dispatched a man from his company, none other than young Filey Bush, to ride hard and rout out the magistrate and the sheriff of the county, both of whom lived some distance away. While Filey leaned low on the horse's neck and squinted into the darkness, Crispin and the captain sat down to enjoy a bowl of stew and a tankard of ale. Their conversation revolved mostly around the war and what units were posted where and what the French and their arsonous savage allies had been up to.

As Nancy Maythuse cleared away the bowls, she made sure to bend forward sufficiently to allow Crisp an unspoilt view of her pleasingly white, unsuckled bosoms. Filey Bush was miles away, and while he was a strapping lad, he never would be an officer of regulars, thought the foolish girl.

Crispin politely requested a room and warm water to wash up with, and since he was without funds, he wrote out a promissory note and pledged his word that when he was reunited with his regiment, he would make good upon the debt, which satisfied the innkeep-captain-smith.

Shortly thereafter, he had been shown to his room, and a fire had been laid in the room's small fireplace when along comes young Nancy to his door with a cracked redware pitcher and a basin half full of steaming water. Entering quietly and placing the bath items on a small table, Nancy lowered her eyes and, facing the bed, asked Crispin if there was anything else she could do for him.

"Thank you, no. That will do for the moment. Come back in a half an hour and fetch them away, and I'll see if there is anything else that needs your attention." Crispin smiled pleasantly at the girl and then turned away, dismissing her with his back.

Young Nancy had fancied she could capture the officer's attentions, and she thought him handsome enough that despite his rough appearance, she looked forward to ministering to his manly wants. Fooling her father about her absence from the kitchen was quite another matter. While the captain knew his daughter for a coquet who trifled with the attentions of young men, he had no fore knowledge of the true state of her lily garden, and had he been aware that Filey Bush had been sowing clover there for many months, he likely would have taken the strap to her and an axe handle to young Filey. Nancy enjoyed the attention men showed her and was always on the lookout for the best husband. She was also quite aware that she needed to make a good and final match in the next few years, and after all, she would soon be sixteen, and most of her family and friends had been married by eighteen.

※

Crisp used the last of the now cold water and the linen towel to wash himself clean of the scent left from rutting while Nancy straightened her chemise, smoothed her rumpled petticoats, and combed out and tied up her tangled blond tresses.

The lieutenant lowered his voice like a conspirator. "Miss Maythuse, I must say, I haven't enjoyed myself like that since I was in Williamsburg." He reached out and pinched her firmly muscled posterior.

The girl squealed with delight and spinning around and slapped the lieutenant on the cheek, but it was more a playful thing than a scold's rebuff. "And you, sir, are the most dashing gentleman I have ever seen in Englishtowne." Standing on her tiptoes, young Nan gave him a kiss on the lips and then, grabbing the tray with the wash items, swirled out of the room like an innocent flirt rather than a strumpet who knew how to satisfy a randy man's desires.

Had Crisp known that she plotted to capture his heart, he would have had a hearty laugh. He thought her merely a girl of loose habits who fancied being tended like a filly pastured with a prize stallion. He assumed, and not incorrectly from her apparent "skills," that she had shared her affections with many a young swain. What Crispin was unaware of and what he would never learn was that the one union they shared had resulted in the planting of a Scottish Bluebell in her patch of cowslip and snapdragons. The lily garden so regularly tended by Filey Bush, which Crispin saw as little more than a patch of wild flowers, was soon to burst into bloom and would in the ensuing months bring forth a little bud bearing a remarkable likeness to the "English" lieutenant.

The magistrate and sheriff arrived early in the morning of the following day, and Crispin, well rested, cleaned up and, looking more himself, gave testimony against Bedlam Eaton in a makeshift courtroom, which was none other than the taproom of the inn. He swore his oath before God while Eaton stood silently, pantless and with his shirttails dangling raggedly just above his red knobby knees, looking like a man resigned to the fate of the gallows. Captain Maythuse had kindly produced a pair of old wooden shoes which offered some comfort but which gave Bedlam a look of both the melancholy and the hilarious. Standing contritely before the bar, he hung his now foul-haired head while the sheriff read the lengthy list of charges. A packed gallery that consisted of every man for miles about sat quietly sipping at their tankards of ale or tots of rum, attentive to every word.

Seated in a plain straight-backed chair, Crispin looked the wigged magistrate in the eye and, taking a deep and dramatic breath, exhaled audibly. "He came at me while I was sleeping, apparently with every evil intention of smashing in my head and robbing me of my horse and weapons." He swore this soberly and with obvious care as to the choice and clarity of his words.

One of the rare truths that Eaton had ever told, Crispin never believed. Bedlam had never killed anyone and was sorely dejected that anyone would think him a cutthroat murderer. Indeed, his very plan had only called for knocking Crispin upon the head and trussing him up loosely so that he should be able to free himself in a few hours. This explanation had been lost upon Crispin and seemingly would be lost upon the jury of stolid agriculturists.

After Crispin had completed his tale and the judge had interrogated the prisoner, the dim smoky courtroom was adjourned at midday for what the portly "Justiciar" called "a bit of lunch." After an hour or nearly thereabouts had passed, the men all gathered again and his honor wiped the remnants of a pork roast on his brown wool coat fronts and allowed Bedlam to declare his innocence and then finally empanelled a jury of rustic farmers to hear the remainder of Crispin's testimony.

Sadly for Thomas Eaton, there was no lawyer within a reasonable distance and so the judge ordered his jailer, Captain Maythuse to act as his counsel, and again, they adjourned until the following morning, thus allowing the captain a chance to prepare whatever defense he could muster. It goes almost without saying that the captain had no intention of defending the robber, and after giving him his dinner of salt pork and stale, moldy bread (The colony paid only pennies a day for the upkeep of the prisoner, so why waste good victuals on an unrepentant villain?), he spent no more than a few minutes in the root cellar listening to Bedlam's feeble lies. Sergeant Crowley stood by, the hole with his gleaming musket at the ready, prepared to shoot in case the malefactor should attempt a desperate escape or try to lay hands upon his captain.

"Guilty!" The verdict was rendered in less than two minutes of deliberation, immediately following the trial, which itself lasted no more than one hour, most of which was spent listening to Crisp's story yet again. Captain Maythuse had explained briefly, and without even the vaguest trace of conviction, that Eaton had no intention of killing Crispin and was only set on robbing him.

Sadly for Bedlam, no one else believed the truth when they heard it. The robber knew that there was little he could say in his own defense, and for a minute or so, he regaled the judge and jury with a lie about a villain to whom he owed a debt that he could never hope to repay unless he turned to thievery. The stone-faced jurors seemed no more interested in his lies than the truth and so in the end, he just stopped talking. Acting upon behalf of the Crown and colony, the sheriff lay before the jury the list of charges once again and presented to them "the likes of this vile and miserable creature who has attempted murder upon the brave heart of Lieutenant Mull, a king's officer returning to the bosom of his regiment after his imprisonment by the popish enemy."

It was a far cry from a regular court, but the participants attempted to show a modicum of decorum and fairness, and while they all accepted Crispin's word verbatim and would have hung Eaton upon that alone, like free Englishmen everywhere, they believed the accused deserved counsel and a chance to speak on his own behalf before being sentenced. While it may seem perfunctory and irregular at this future date, it was the best that could be provided in those dangersome and far off days.

"Having heard the jury's verdict, Mr. Isaac Tew, do you have anything you wish to add before I pass sentence upon you?" intoned the judge in his most imperious voice, trying to sound as though he were seated upon the highest bench in his Majesty's Court instead of in a darkened taproom in a no account Pennsylvania tavern.

Bedlam Eaton had, of course, lied from the very beginning even to the point of providing Crispin with an alias in hopes that he would not be connected to his other misdeeds, which, of course, he was not. Unfortunately for him, the judge required only the crimes he was currently charged with to sentence him to be "hanged by the neck until life no longer resides within." Eaton had seen one fellow strung up on the gibbet and it had taken long minutes for the poor sod to faint away, all the while his face had swelled and blackened from the effects of strangulation, and he kicked his shackled feet in a most disturbing fashion. In the end, the black headed corpse had hung awkwardly with his tongue protruding and his eyes bulging out to stare at eternity.

As the sheriff took Bedlam firmly by the elbow to escort him back to the root cellar, a small puddle of yellow water could be seen collecting about his wooden shoes, and a lone tear trickled out of his left eye and rolled down his mournsome cheek. Taking no more than a few steps, Bedlam Eaton collapsed and lay pitifully upon the floor sobbing and clinging about the fat ankles of the sheriff. Unlike his past performances, this one did indeed appear to be sincere, and it even softened a few of the cold stony hearts in the taproom, including Crisp's, but in the end, the affected individuals reminded themselves of English justice and the importance of law and order.

The neighborhood's parson had visited Bedlam in the evening, but the robber had been uncooperative, and in the end, the minister had left shaking his head and frowning because he had been unable to salvage the thief's soul.

Later on the following morning, Filey Bush sat disconsolately in the back corner of the Big Tree Inn while Nancy fawned over the English lieutenant and stood eagerly by his table waiting upon his every whim. Crisp, in an effort not to break the young girl's heart unduly, had promised her he would be back in two months' time to pay his bill in person. Of course, he had no such intention. The post could carry his payment, and Crispin would not need to visit the backward little burg except in his memory. While Crisp was packing his bedroll, Captain Maythuse had kindly restocked his empty sack with enough provender to see him several days down the road and well on his way to New York.

Less than an hour earlier, Crispin had taken one last look in on Bedlam and had told the robber that he had no one to blame but himself, and Crisp added that he hoped Eaton would face his end like a man. Further explaining that he was damned sorry, he had to play a role in his downfall. Eaton begged him to intervene, and then just as Crisp reached the top of the short ladder, he cursed Crisp for a meddler and said he would pray to the devil that the lieutenant would find a miserable death of want and disease, forgotten by his friends and even his enemies.

Sergeant Crowley tested the rope and inspected it carefully for signs of fraying or weakness. At last, he tied the prickly noose and secured the loose end to a yoked ox, who, with the dumbness which only a beast of burden can exhibit, stood patiently and innocently chewing its cud while Bedlam took his last walk out of the inn, through the crowd of at least three score and ten and down to the large tree in the front lawn.

Most well-meaning folk would not want a felon hanged in their front yard and would think it some kind of ill omen, but Elisha Maythuse knew that the corpse would bring everyone in the neighborhood back again and again to see the grisly trophy of justice. And while waiting, they would undoubtedly indulge in an ale or a meat pie or bring him a plow for mending. Innkeepers in small hamlets are constantly on the lookout for any method by which to increase patronage, and acts of violence are bound to create much hub-bub and excitement in the remote outposts of civilization.

Crispin sat his horse nobly, ready to depart the instant that Eaton was gone to his rogue's reward. Nancy, standing next to Crispin's mount, rested her hand lightly upon the iron stirrup. Young Filey stood up on the porch at the rear of the assemblage and tossed down the last of his cider, scowling at the Englishman, going completely unnoticed by the object of his scorn. All in all, it was a dramatic tableau suited to the brush of Rembrandt or Hogarth.

There was little fanfare and the magistrate, along with the sturdy captain and the sheriff, stood off to one side and finally, the "Right Honorable" merely inclined his head toward the straw-hatted farmer, signaling that he should begin.

The ox ambled forward as its owner tapped it upon the rump with a light willow switch. The weight of Bedlam Eaton was insignificant to the mighty bovine. While it strode forward without a care, just before the felon's wood shod heels lifted clear of the ground, he let out a pitiful wail. "God in heaven don't do this to me!" and in a moment or two, he was hanging just beneath the limb, and the muttering and whispering crowd fell silent. Eaton's feet pedaled frantically at the air as though he were insanely driving Baron Von Drais's walking machine, which, of course, would not be invented until many years in the future. Perhaps more appropriately, it appeared as though he was trying to find some miraculous purchase for his weight. Eventually, his soot-smudged spirit would find solid footing on a set of cold stone steps that lead only downward.

The ox backed a step as the countryman brought it to a halt and thus Eaton slipped a notch, jerking and swaying before the ox again stepped forward, banging the robber's head on the underside of the stout branch. Bedlam's mouth worked spasmodically, but nothing came out, not even a gasp or a wheeze. As his lips darkened and his face turned the shade of royal purple, his thoughts became muddled, and he found himself less concerned with what his feet were doing, and then, he altogether forgot what had happened to him and where he was and he just smiled to himself. Outwardly, however, his contorted lips appeared to snarl, which satisfied the jurors that he was a desperate man and that they had done the righteous thing.

The heartless rustics who turned out for a morning's rare entertainment held their silence as the movement became less desperate and more pathetic. At last, Thomas Eaton's mortal husk hung empty and unmoving, suspended between heaven and earth by means of a homely thread normally utilized for more peaceable employment- like dragging logs or hoisting hay. Without breeches or trousers, there was nothing to catch the man's last earthly act, so in the end, Bedlam's soil fertilized the grass beneath the tree and that was perhaps the only unselfish public act he ever performed.

Crispin's heart had skipped a beat or two, and he had to remind himself that the man was a detriment to society and that British officers never displayed their emotions or perhaps he would have been prone to shedding a tear or two on the robber's behalf. Taking a deep breath, he reminded himself that justice had been done and the world was rid of a would-be killer and that he had honestly performed his duty as befitted a Crown officer.

Nothing half as interesting as the hanging of Bedlam Eaton happened in Englishtowne, Pennsylvania, for another fifty years, and by then, few were the folk who even remembered the robber or the English officer who had brought him in. The inn tumbled down a few years after the captain's timely death when a cracked ridge beam gave way. The lumber was auctioned off, so the Big Tree Inn became chicken coops, a garden gate and a number of other odd and useful things, including a privy for the new church, which replaced the old church after it had burned down from a lightening strike in the autumn of 1761.

Nancy Maythuse, finding no better prospects (The English lieutenant had never returned.) and with her belly swelling in a most embarrassing fashion, married Filey Bush five months after the hanging. Filey, somewhat later during the colonial rebellion, became a sergeant of the Pennsylvania Line, and afterwards, along with his ambitious wife, moved his fruitful clan of straw-haired children and grandchildren onto the Phelps and Gorham Purchase in the wilds of western New York. The eldest boy, George, looked nothing at all like the father who had reared him, but his handsome good looks and uncanny luck stayed with him all the way to the New York legislature where he made quite a name for himself in his elder years by opposing the construction of the Erie Canal. After being defeated in the next election, he never again held office, but ironically, he became fabulously wealthy shipping wheat on that "grandiose ditch!" which excavation he had tried to block.

THE PRODIGAL RETURNS

The first sight of the pointy church spires and gray-slate roofs of New York had been a balm to Crispin's waning spirits. He had not seen a collection of more than a dozen and a half buildings in one place since he left Williamsburg unless one counted the impermanent wigwams and crooked longhouses surrounding Fortress Duquesne. He had run the horse the last mile to the river, careless of his own safety and thinking only of reporting his return to the Fifty-Sixth and of the "good to have you backs" and "tell us all about it, mans" his return would engender.

As he embarked upon the ferry, his mind again leaped joyously at the thoughts of creature comforts and of civilized companionship and discourse, something he had dreamt of upon many an occasion and at last the hour had come. The boat crawled across the water as he dragged his dirty fingers through his unkempt hair, and vainly conscious of his own monstrous appearance, he tried to straighten his wrinkled and stained waistcoat.

The island of Manhattan neared, and the water behind grew while the water in front diminished, and all the time Crisp's thoughts became more serious as he tried to think of just the words he would use when he walked into the camp of the Fifty-Sixth of Foot. Surely his long disappearance and his sudden and dramatic reemergence from the wilds would be cause for an uproar and would create a good degree of speculation as to his whereabouts in recent weeks, and he would need to be mindful of clearly explaining his actions and adventures since leaving Williamsburg. If he played his cards well, he might parlay the fight at the Hollingwort's farm and his capture of Bedlam Eaton into a promotion. With any luck, and we must remember he had been born with it in large doses, he could cover the weeks and months following the sinking of the Wampum Belt cavalierly, passing it off as "a boring, but manly saga of survival at sea hah-hah! eh what?" and "a confusing but adventurous walk in the woods—of course, I tried to evade the clutches of murderous Indians."

The rickety, leaking boat bumped the muddy, graveled shore and Crispin, leading the now cooled stallion ashore, inquired of a waiting tradesman as to the whereabouts of the cantonments of the Fifty-Sixth.

Returning to the bosom of the regiment was as great a comfort to St. Crispin as the curve of a mother's breast is to her sleeping babe. Of course, his reappearance had begun with curt questions from the sentry followed by a soldierly welcome from the sergeant of the guard, which in turn was followed by a seemingly hearty and sincere greeting from old Barley himself when Crispin at last was ushered into his presence. The aging flaxen-haired officer had toasted him with port as Crispin reported his actions over the last weeks.

"Glad to have you back in the fold, Mull! You look quite a sight, and I must say the stink about you rather reminds one of an uncovered grave, but the ordure [He liked giving things their French accent.] shall wash off and a pair of breeches without holes should damn well do miracles! Allow me to drink your health again!"

Several bumpers of port later and after being lead to a nearby home where another lieutenant rented rooms, Crispin made himself comfortable and presentable in a borrowed uniform which fit too snugly in the shoulders but was at least clean and respectable. His now spare frame was firmly muscled and his once gentlemanly complexion was nearly as bronze as a quadroon's.

Barley, meanwhile, was perplexed. Should he be glad that a trusted junior had returned, or should he rue the return of a fellow who was far too familiar with his own sordid affairs? He decided to await further developments before making his final judgment.

Dinner the following night in honor of the return of the conquering "hero" was held under a cloud-like pavilion of canvas bedecked with greenery and the gay whites and yellows of early summer blooms. It had started off quite solemnly with the regimental major offering a prayer of thanks, trailed by the clink of sterling cutlery and crystal glasses and with every red-coated officer afraid to intrude upon the prodigal's quiet mien.

After silently consuming his dinner, Crispin had somberly invited their queries, slowly building to his audience as he embellished and recreated every event for his own glory and their edification. The gravy boat became the Wampum Belt sloshing about the table, so by the time he reached dry land, dribbles of meat juice were splattered on the table cloth, and he was bravely defending himself from catamounts and bears with jabs and bold strokes of a butter knife. With a self-deprecating and-there-you-have-it smile and casually tossing the knife aside, he delivered into being his own legend complete with feats of daring-do and hairsbreadth escapes. Barley applauded loudly, and the officers stamped their feet and cheered in approval.

He had learned from his father the art of expanding upon the truth in order to give the impression one desired. Crispin's father had never advocated lying but had tutored Crispin at length in the art of telling the truth. With a more sober face and simple humility, he told how he had saved the fetching Hollingswort daughter, a veritable princess of the back country, from certain death and rapine when he grabbed her dusky attackers, one under each arm, and leapt into the raging river, which inexplicably ran by the girl's window, drowning both of the warriors in the torrent before he scaled a cliff to return to the fray. Because he had indeed lived through the screeching, dirty, bloody horror of the Indian attack and could not envision his acts as heroic, Crisp was certain that no one else could see him thusly either, so the only way to elevate himself to the level of a Ulysses or an Atlas was if he grappled the enemy with his bare hands or a steely blade. Shooting a retreating raider in his naked back and watching him drag himself under the forest boughs was anticlimactic and might even be thought of by some as a craven act.

With this in mind during the subsequent telling, Bedlam Eaton was pursued and subdued with a flaming brand snatched from the flames of the campfire. The desperate rogue had fought tooth and claw, he explained, but in the end, Crispin had parried a particularly vicious thrust of the robber's blade and disarmed the snarling highwayman. Cooked bottoms, sore jaws, and barked shins did not make as riveting a tale as parried thrusts, quick thinking and deadly slashes. Crispin related how as the fellow had mounted the gallows steps he had blessed and thanked Crispin for saving him from a wasted life of crime and villainy. And so it was that Crispin raised himself (even in his own mind) from felon and wilderness pilgrim to knight errant, rescuing damsels and capturing bloodthirsty felons. Of course, most of the officers would have been nearly as envious of the truth had they but known it. With the campaigning season about to begin none of them had yet had the chance to test their mettle against the French and their savage confederates.

St. Crispin was assigned to a company within the week and assumed his duties with zeal and greeted each day fresh and eager. He reveled every morning in the luxury of toast and tea after rising from his night's slumber, wrapped in fresh linens like some decadent emperor. The only thing that intruded upon his refound sense of utter contentment and superiority was, of course, the puzzle of how to regain possession of DeVaca's plunder. He was at the moment penniless as his name had been stricken from the regimental payroll when he was presumed lost at sea. It would likely be some months before the paymaster straightened out the tangled mess, and he was once again able to receive his portion of the king's war chest.

It seemed that by turns, he was either rich beyond belief and unable to openly spend the coin or he was reduced to a state of paupery and unable to obtain coin. Writing home to his mother, he pleaded for the loan of whatever she and his nefarious father could spare after, of course, he had reassured them that he was hale and hearty and not lying on the ocean's bottom. He recounted his adventures for them and concluded with the belief that he would return to England draped in laurels and able to repay his parents every cent they graciously gave, along with a tidy nest egg for their dotage. This amount he knew would be a tiny fraction of the hidden fortune that awaited him in Virginia.

The last part he did not share with them, but instead, he led them to believe that he would grow rich on war booty and land speculation. He drew them a map of the area around Ft. Duquesne and said that he and several other gentlemen (who remained unnamed) were forming a land company to buy the confluence and surrounding lands at war's end. He did not bother to mention that the lands in question were hundreds of miles inland, unreachable except by Indian trace and currently under French control. The map was rudimentary at best and reflected his complete lack of knowledge of the regions through which he had traipsed as a prisoner and a reluctant refugee.

His mother would have sent him whatever funds she could spare from her plump, jingling little purse without him needing to weave the fiction about land speculation, but his father, on the other hand, never considered money a proper gift, and to his thinking, loans were for fools. The return upon investment was the only factor worth weighing in Ezra Mull's scheming, counting house, tomb robbing mind, and even Crispin's commission had been seen as a way of improving upon the family's station, and hopefully, their prospects for the future as well. Were he to know the truth, he might think Crispin's situation more a liability than an asset therefore Crisp had decided the best course was to dangle the chance of a rich return under his father's prominent nose.

Crows cawed back and forth, calling harshly to one another in the gray early morning light as they skimmed over chimneys and flocked toward a tremendous oak that stood just back from the water, which lapped quietly at the shore. Crispin's room was on the third floor of a neat brick house that stood several streets back from the river but which still had a fine view of the channel through the white trimmed dormer.

Trepan grabbed Peg by the arm with his dirty but nimble claw and dragged her back around the corner and out of sight of the house.

"He'd not know me in the daylight," he hissed. "But I'm certain still that he'd be s'picious if he clapped eyeballs on me. You go an' tell 'em inside you heard Leftenant Mull was lookin' fer a washerwoman. If he don't come down, then we'll have to find another way, but you'd best pray he comes down 'cause it'll save us all a lot of bother. Now spruce up, an' try not to look like a whore who's laid fer Magoggle and a king's man o' war."

Indeed, she had not entertained the crew of a man o' war, but for the last several weeks since Magoggle had pronounced them strumpet and thief, Trepan had been getting even with her for walking out on him by insulting her at every turn.

"Listen, you dirty little thief," she railed at the strangler. "I'll do this my way, and you'd better not interfere. That's the last time you'll tell a lie of me or insult me! You'll not get near that treasure without me and without the cursed coin. Magoggle's got no earthly use for ye." She crossed her arms and stared hard into his lonely bright-green eye, bravely hoping he'd back down.

Trepan was not about to be cowed by a strumpet and knew that if he lost this round, then she would begin to think she was his equal, like a dog that fed up with the whipping turns on its master. Her timing was most inconvenient, but this was a situation he felt he must remedy immediately before she got out of hand. His foot shot out, and he stamped down hard on her instep. Peg's foot came up quickly, and then she instantly forced the pain from her mind. Reaching forward, she grabbed a handful of his greasy hair while her thumb groped for his one good eye. Trepan drove his right fist into her stomach, but Peg held on for dear life, and as she collapsed towards the paving stones, she dragged him downward.

Just then, the front door opened and an aproned servant woman stepped out and walking to the gutter, upended a slop jar, adding the reek to the trickle of dirty water that ran along the shallow course. Peg let go of Trepan's hair, and he straightened up and held a finger to his lips, glaring at her while his foot kicked her sharply in her buttocks. Peg stifled a yelp and scuttled backwards out of reach before she stood up.

✯

Trepan still lurked thirty or forty paces away around the corner. His hands unwittingly played with the red silk strangler's scarf he always carried in his pocket, twisting it tighter and tighter. He'd kill her in a heart's beat if she turned on him again.

"We do the leftenant's wash. All of his washin'," emphasized the saucy cleaning girl.

Peg quickly stuck her brogan-shod foot in the slamming door and commanded loudly, "Tell him it's his cousin Peggy from Blanchard Hall, fallen on hard times. I know Crisp'll see me." She placed special emphasis on his first name, implying a familiarity that allowed her to ignore his rank and call him by his Christian name.

A few minutes later, Crispin having arrived in the doorway, looked the scar-faced woman up and down, searching his memory without uttering a word before it suddenly hit him like a solid shot who she was. The scar, the unkempt hair, and the plain hum drum petticoats had sufficiently disguised her former comeliness, such that it had taken several moments before he recognized her as his first successful encounter with one of Aphrodite's acolytes. The cleaning girl delivering him the message had left out any reference to Blanchard Hall and a cousin, so without a clue, he had little to stimulate his memory, and the common wench before him bore scant resemblance to the colonel's coquet.

The memories of that rocket-like coach trip came tumbling back, and it was then that Crispin noticed that about her eyes she had the same look of prettiness and helplessness she had back yonder despite her presently drab appearance and the marring of her cheek and twisted nose. Her shapely figure also seemed much unchanged, and he recalled how then he had marveled at her tiny waist as the coach lurched about while she clung to him like a hunter to the mount. As they had cleared the last fence, she had risen high in the stirrups and cried out the "View Halloo!" Certainly the bloom was fading from the rose, but he'd no doubt she was still a spirited romp.

He decided to take the woman into the cobblestoned backyard behind the house for an interview. It was unseemly to conduct personal business on the front step. Servants and peddlers used the rear entrance, and if he was to speak to her without causing raised eyebrows in his host's home, then he could not take her to his rooms, much as he might wish to saddle her up for another outing, so they stood beneath an elm, and Peg began to spin a tale of woe sure to break the steeliest of hearts.

Crispin couldn't help but feel that he was in some small way responsible for her present troubles (Of course, it was more than a small way.), so he offered to let her return in a few days to wash his clothes and do some shopping for him, but he reminded her that the work would last only until the regiment moved out in a few weeks' time. Naturally, he omitted any mention of his present finances. Surely, he thought that he could borrow enough to pay her a few pence. It would assuage his sense of guilt, and mayhap she would provide him with sporting services.

Formerly pretty Peg played her role admirably, keeping her eyes downcast and seeming grateful for the scraps he had kindly tossed her. She was quite certain that given a few moments alone with him, she could shape him to her will like a bar of red-hot iron wrapped around the horn of the smith's anvil. The only question in her scheming mind was whether she should carry out Magoggle's plan or secure the Lieutenant's affections for herself. After all, she thought, Mull alone knew the hiding place of the treasure and he was a far sight handsomer than the one-eyed assassin. If she must attach herself to a man for security, then there were worse choices than the young Scot.

It was no accident that she neglected to mention that she had been to see Beverly first, nor did she offer to explain how it came to be that she had known where to find Crispin. His reputation firmly secured within the regiment and spreading throughout the army and the city, Crispin, in his arrogance, assumed she had merely picked up idle tittle tattle and had tracked him down.

※

At last, Beverly Blanchard had received orders instructing him to embark the Fifty-Sixth of Foot by ship and whaleboat for Albany. Upon their arrival at said town, his flank companies were to rejoin the regiment for a week and then by forced marches were to unite with Colonel Bradstreet whose troops were assembling to reinforce Forts Oswego and Ontario. The weakling stockades were situated on the southern shore of Lake Ontario where they stood a shabby guard on either bank of the Oswego River.

The flank companies had spent the winter locked up in a stinking stockade guarding the Hudson and now were headed off to even worse. This was their portion for being part of the elite forces of Georges Rex. Fourteen of their number had perished during the winter. Ten had been taken by the bloody flux and a fever, two had become lost while gathering wood, and it was thought they had been killed by marauding natives, another had been badly burned when a cauldron of potage had tipped over and the clumsy sod had died of gangrene from the burns. The last fellow was taken with a wracking cough.

The line companies of the Fifty-Sixth, under Blanchard, were to proceed directly to the town of Half Moon where they would bolster the doughty New England forces under command of General William Shirley, the former royal governor of Massachusetts.

St. Crispin was ordered by Old Barley to remain in New York and make final disposition for additional foodstuffs and ammunition to be sent up by baggage train to Half Moon. At Crispin's disposal would be a detail of men from Captain Frantom's company, who would provide escort when the train of carts and wagons had been assembled. Before leaving New York, however, he was to purchase for the colonel an additional mount as well as seeing to the transport of Blanchard's small pack of foxhounds. Beverly had spent considerable time (and no small amount of coin) picking out eight good dogs of provincial breeding that he presumed would make worthy coursers. Now that the campaign season was beginning, he thought it best to bring them along for diversion. After all, there would be few fetes and balls to attend once they had left the city behind, and he would need some source of diversion. Crispin, of course, was just the man to be handling hounds and horses, but Barley was unaware of Crispin's newfound talents in these areas and had merely set him at the task as a test of his ability to organize a sizeable and important, if boring, mission.

Crispin, however, was only too glad to be left behind, and the extra week in the city was one which he would not squander. After having spent weeks upon the trail and months out of touch with civilized society, he was in no hurry to rush head long into the wilderness and join the battle. Naturally, Crispin's action those two years earlier in Hart, along with his latest adventures, had set a rather dangerous precedent within the regiment and several of the captains and nearly all of the lieutenants felt obligated to live up to the standard so admirably set by the courageous Lieutenant Mull.

His fellow officers were clamoring to engage the enemy, and unless he was greatly mistaken, several of them would likely commit desperately foolhardy acts and wind up getting themselves slain in the melee of combat, thereby opening up the possibilities to promotion for those who remained unscathed. The opportunity to have one's head pulverized by a cannon ball or belly pierced by a bayonet was nearly certain if one stayed in the army long enough or sought valor too assiduously. To Crispin's way of thinking, Valhalla's halls were filled with brave sheepheads and his presence at Odin's table would not be missed. The fortunate soldier was the one who lived to tramp another march and draw another ration.

※

The few candles that were lighted flickered feebly off the damp stone walls of the Yellow Wasp, and Noddy Cope stood lurking in a shadowy corner, sullenly leaning against the wall, sipping at his ale. There were no patrons in the tavern this early and except for the Beast of Water Street and his deadly henchman. The only others present were the waifish young bootblack and the greasy barman.

Magoggle handed the bootblack a hapenny and then gently caressed the lad's dirty nine-year-old cheek. "Someday, my lad, you shall come to work for Old Nick, and you will have so many hapennies that all your friends will count ye a rich man. Look over there at Mr. Cope in his fancy coat. I bet you'd like to have nice clothes and a sword and sweets wouldn't ye? That would be grand, wouldn't it?"

The boy nodded and slipped the coin with the likeness of George the First into his pocket. Magoggle held out his tumbler and let the boy take a gulp of the warm spicy wine. The lad wiped his dirty mouth on the back of his sleeve, at the same time removing the snot from the end of his nose.

"You come back the day after tomorrow, and I'll have another little job for ye, an' perhaps yer own dram of the Jamaican. Yer a quiet lad, and ye do good work." The fat man looked at the flame reflected in his polished boots. "I like loyal little boys who know how to be silent. Now run along, and tell the other lads Old Nick treats ye right."

As the boy ducked out the door like some furtive yet grateful animal freed from a trap, he brushed by a pair of spindly legs clad in peach-colored sateen. He recoiled as though he'd just touched something rotten and backed into the street, tugging his forelock in deference. Trepan lifted his arm as though to backhand the boy, but by then, the lad had bounced into the cobbled street and was out of range.

"My dear Trepan, please don't harm the lad. It takes time fer me to tame them up enough to feed them from my hand. They're timid little things at that age but very trainable, and if ye don't get 'im young, they're often spoilt and useless later. Take my associate Mr. Cope for example. His mother fed him too much and sang hymns while he supped at her breast. Now where did that lead, I ask you? He spends too much time thinking about vittles and humming to himself, and his higher thoughts never did develop quite right. Still, he does as he's told, don't you, Cope?"

Noddy Cope dipped his chin toward Magoggle and went back to sipping his ale. Trepan sat down across the table from the fat man and waited until the barman had brought him his own tumbler of rum, and then the dirty publican receded back into the quavering shadows behind the caged bar.

"She's been washin' his things," stated Trepan flatly. "An' I think she's been givin' him extra service, if ye know what I mean. I don't like it much. Says she's workin' on him takin' her along with him when they march."

"She hasn't graced your bed again, has she? That's a plain shame, my friend. I'll see if I can't entice her to be a bit kinder. In the meantime, as soon as she has the lieutenant convinced to take her with him then you must high yourself to Albany, and keep your eye upon them until she learns where the treasure is hidden. Remember our deal my keen blade. You mustn't harm the young man. We divide the lucre, but the lad is mine. I'll give you the woman."

Magoggle reached into his pocket and took a gold coin between his thumb and forefinger and rolled it across the table toward Trepan, but halfway there, it just stopped, still standing on its edge. Trepan reached a dirty hand out for the coin. The fat man leaned forward, and the candle flickered just beneath his chin, and he seemed not to notice the heat as he grasped Trepan tightly by the wrist. The assassin could feel his bones grating together, and the pain was quite sharp, but he was a brazen one, and with his free hand, he withdrew the dagger from the cane and whipped it up underneath Magoggle's nose.

"You already gave me the woman," hissed Trepan. The dagger hovered under the Beast's nose. "Let go my wrist, or it'll cost ye yer life fatty!" Trepan had grown recklessly bold. Peg's lack of fealty to him, coupled with Magoggle's arrogance had left him surly and daring and, for once in his life, pathetically injudicious.

"Surely, my friend. No offense intended." The fat man released the smaller man's wrist and slowly leaned back away from the dagger's threatening point, a false grin barely bending his thick, full lips.

Trepan had not even given a thought to putting his dagger back in its secret lair when he felt a sharp prick in his ear, and a trickle of blood welled up and ran down his neck. His blade clattered onto the table as he realized that a sword had been placed in his ear and that any movement would likely cause it to be thrust straight into the sanctum sanctorum of his plots, designs, and secret most desires.

Magoggle sat with his fingers laced together across his great belly, and a now truly satisfied smile spread across his chubby face.

"You must never think ye can harm me. I don't know what to do now. You are a devil's man fer sure, but you must never try such a thing again, or I'm sorry you'll find it warmer than ye like by my fire."

The fat villain took a long pause and audibly breathed through his nose before he went on.

"Friend Trepan, do you know who yer in league with to find the treasure? O. Nicholas Magoggle. I've run things my way for longer than you can imagine, and I won't tolerate insubordination, not from anyone, most especially a junior partner. Keep the coin, and remember that what I give I can take away any time it pleases me. What I give with the right hand, I can take away again with the left. If I say I wish to let you keep the woman, she is yours only until such time as I decide to remove her from yer keeping. Do you understand now? The price of yer rudeness is the loss of yer share in the treasure. If you perform yer end of the bargain as promised, I'll think upon a reward. If you deny me or fail me in any way now, I promise you won't like the company where I send you."

Noddy Cope allowed the ensuing silence to continue for a long breath more. Blackness seemed to spread before the assassin's eyes, and it stretched on into an eternity in which wars were fought and babies were born without mouths to cry, and the stars winked out one by one as the firmament was wrapped in two almost infinitely black leathery shadows, and then, Noddy whipped back his sword and with his empty hand, punched Trepan squarely in the head with all of his considerable strength, snapping the assassin's head around and knocking over the chair and the cutthroat. Cope stepped over the prostrate form and swept up the sword and cane and without looking, threw them backwards toward the door where they landed with a clatter and bang. Sheathing his own sword, he grabbed Trepan by his lank, black hair with the one hand, scooped up the fallen man's tricorn with the other, and dragged him to the door. By the time they had reached the portal, Trepan was scuttling and scrambling to get his feet under himself. Noddy jammed the hat down upon Trepan's head and then planting his foot on the pickpurse's hinder regions, gave him a mighty boot out into the street.

Trepan, now propelled out into the center of the bitter, perpetually darksome lane, caught his balance just as he teetered on the brink of a large puddle. The cobbles had been gouged out of an area roughly the size of a wagon bed that was ankle deep with brownish water, in which floated the last semblance of something that might once have been a song bird. His arms had slowly stopped windmilling, and he thought he had regained his balance and had escaped adding insult to injury when his long thin dagger and cane struck him flatly in the back, catching him unaware, and once again more off balance than on, he stepped down into the muck and water. As his shoe filled with liquid, he stooped down to retrieve his weapon, and he thought in his rage of the glory he would feel when Noddy Cope was swinging from the end of a rope or was pinned through his heart like a great scarab beetle he had once seen in a portmanteau he had stolen. (The owner of the portmanteau and the beetle, an Egyptian diplomat, who was bringing the insect to the English King as a rare gift to add to the royal collection of useless oddities bestowed upon the disinterested monarch.) His nostrils flared, and Trepan slammed the cobra dagger back into the cane and then he walked stiffly down the street, his pride utterly whipped, until at last he was sure Cope could no longer see him, and then, he resumed his old foxy posture and slid into the early morning shadows, a thousand plots racing at breakneck speed through his scheming mind.

JUST DESSERTS

St. Crispin Mull had just finished feeding the last of the hounds and was settling down for the night in his white wedge-shaped tent. He didn't entrust the care of the hounds to anyone else and the black gelding he had bought for Old Barley, he had also attended to personally. The horse fidgeted at its picket, pawing the ground and reaching around trying to bite at Crispin's chestnut stallion, who was really quite calm for an uncut horse.

Earlier in the trip up from New York, the black had rolled his eyes back and lashed out with his rear hooves, neatly doubling over one of the privates who was bringing him a bucket of water. The fellow had basely beaten the horse over the head with the heavy bucket, and that was when Crispin decided it would be best if he cared for the animal himself, not even trusting the wagoner's or the lad who drove the cow and sheep.

Barley insisted on fresh cream, and so Crispin had purchased a small cow off a Dutch farmer, paying twice the going rate to the stubborn fellow. The sheep also would grace the colonel's table as roasted mutton, but at this juncture, they happily bleated and trotted along in front of the lad's long switch.

They were only a few days from joining the regiment, and Crispin wanted most to reach his commander without incident so that he could discharge his responsibility and rejoin the other young officers at cards and drink, which he sorely missed after having just regained them. On the plus side of the ledger, however, his bed was well warmed each night by the likes of none other than scar-faced Peg. She prepared his simple meals, kept his uniform well brushed and his small clothes spotlessly clean, and each night, she dallied with him until he seemed well satisfied, or so she judged by the sonorous sounds issuing from his mouth.

Then one night, rising without waking him, she slipped her feet into her brogans and wrapped a thick short cloak about her shoulders and, under the unblinking moon, sneaked off into the woods without even a candle lantern to light her way. She had scouted her route in the daylight while gathering wood for a cook fire, and after several minutes of quietly brushing branches out of her way, she at last stopped next to a large moss covered boulder that sat by itself in a small silvery green clearing amidst the black boles of ancient trees.

"Hsst! Don't move another step," the voice was deep and masculine but not in the least bit friendly or nice. "Put one hand up on the boulder, an' hike up yer skirts."

Peg obediently did as she was told. Out of the deep shadow of an ancient lichen covered oak stepped Noddy Cope with a leer across his face and a pistol in his one hand, pointed casually at her head and a slim cutlass in the other. His face did not seem anywhere near as dull as it usually did when he was in the presence of Magoggle.

"Ye can cover yer flanks now. I tell ye, yer a fool fer givin' it to Trepan or Magoggle," he said, nodding his head toward her bottom. "I'd have stroked yer soft spots gentle and covered 'em in pearls." He could see she hid no weapon. He nearly salivated, and there was a faint reek of rum about him, but he seemed steady enough on his feet.

Peg turned around and pulled her cloak close and blushing, looked for a moment at the ground between her brogans. His voice had been full of honey, and clearly, he meant what he said. Noddy tucked the pistol into his belt and leaned upon the sword like a walking stick. The silence was awkward, and he smiled a bit sheepishly, but the leer of the wolf lingered behind his eyes. Peg feared him in some ways more than the thief or Magoggle because he seemed to her a man of action like the Corsican, and somehow, this excited her.

"Do ye know where it is yet?"

"No, he hasn't confided in me, but I think he will before the week's out if I can pour enough rum in him," said Peg.

"What of Trepan? Is he lurkin' about? I shoulda kilt that one whilst I had the chance." Cope sheathed his sword but stayed in the shadow.

"He found me today near the picket line, but he didn't say a word. He just winked and barely nodded as I went by with Mull's slop jar."

Peg moved slightly, hoping she could lead Cope into a puddle of moonbeam where she could see him the better, both to admire so that she could watch his every move. While he had asked to look under her chemise, he unwisely hadn't checked beneath the cloak she wore. Formerly pretty Peg had cut away the underarm of her chemise so that she could reach in and draw out a wicked sharp kitchen knife she had secretly strapped beneath her arm by means of a thin canvass belt buckled across her bosoms.

She had fooled three very dangerous men into letting her help to steal a vast fortune from another, she thought, less dangerous man, and she knew she needed to take precautions. All in all, the situation had the ingredients of a fine disaster if she wasn't particularly careful. Naturally, her greatest fear was that one of them might discover her plot, and she would be murdered out of hand. Trepan and Magoggle were the ones to fear. Cope of course knew of her arrangements with the other two. While they, on the other hand, were blind to her scheming with Cope. Poor Crispin was oblivious to all. Trepan, already angry and jealous of Peg, thought he had his own plan to cheat everyone. Likely, the only thing that kept him from acting upon his passion and greed was a mortal fear of the bloated boss in New York.

One of her chilling plots, not yet fully cooked, was to lure Trepan and Cope to the same place and let them kill one another once she had cozened the handsome lieutenant. This still left Magoggle alive, however, and it was him she feared most of all. Magoggle's death would have to be engineered before Trepan and Cope were dealt with. If Magoggle were to survive, he would hunt her to the ends of the earth to gain his revenge; and while she was sure she could lead him a merry race for a time, it was certain that he would catch her in the end. She was unsure how far his reach extended, but she sensed that it went far beyond New York, perhaps even beyond the ends of the earth.

As she thought of the fat villain, a chill ran down her spine, and her thoughts went unbidden in a direction and to a place she dared not go before where the whimpers of unfaithful wives, and liars mingled with the titters and guffaws of murderers. She knew in her heart, if not her shriveling soul, that she would someday be escorted to that darkling pit. She recalled for a moment the afternoon when she had danced for him, like some lithesome marionette, and she shut her eyes tight and tried to focus on the glint of moonlight shining off Cope's sword.

Her deal with Cope was a simple one if he had the courage. Once the location of the treasure was known, she would split even with him if he killed Trepan and Mull and helped her gain a week's time before Magoggle came for her.

"I've to get back to New York, or Magoggle'll start to miss me. I told 'im I was goin' to my uncle's in Schenectady fer a wedding. I'll find ye agin in Half Moon." Noddy turned and was disappearing into the blackness of the trees. Somewhere in the infinite darkness a horse jangled its bit.

"You have to kill him," she whispered. A desperate but thorough plan had struck her like lightening.

Noddy stopped and turned back toward her slowly, and he was barely visible in the deep gloom.

"Kill Magoggle! Are ye addled? Ye can't kill 'im." Cope addressed her like someone who was insane.

"Kill him or we'll never get a shilling. As long as he's alive, we're in mortal danger. You kill him, and then, we'll both slice Trepan, and then you can have what you want." She lifted the hem of her chemise until it almost revealed her cursed treasure.

If she could convince Cope to remove the other three, then she would only have to poison his wine someday when he thought himself rich and safe. A similar plan to that she had tried to carry off with the aid of the Corsican—only this time, she would do the deed herself as she had with Goody. By her hand, Noddy Cope would vomit his spleen and then cease to breathe but only after the other three were stilled and the coin was well secured. No doubt, she would need to entertain him between her blankets and let him sup on many rich meals before his guard would be down sufficiently. *Not as handsome as the lieutenant*, she thought, *but he was not as stringy as Trepan either*. Wealth and the getting of it had its price.

"Garn! But yer a saucy one and bold. Half the treasure and you?" He crossed his arms and rested his chin on his chest, deep in thought.

"Aye! That's the offer if yer man enough!" She smiled and dropped the hem of her chemise. She could barely see his form but she knew he was watching her closely.

O. Nicholas Magoggle was no fool, and he trusted no one, not even his faithful henchmen. Noddy Cope was his, bought and sold, these twenty-five years. Magoggle had set his hooks deep in Cope, yet he knew that no *man* could truly be trusted. That was his specialty. Make them the very best at what they did for him and then never ever trust them again.

Cope returned from "Schenectady," but one had to say there was something different is his manner. He seemed both fearful and bold at the same time. While Magoggle had always told others what a simpleton Cope was, he himself new better.

The lad had been in his employ since he was a stripling. Cope's mother, a local hoyden, had been glad to collect the boy's wages until such time as she conveniently died of a fever, and the already fleshy criminal had cut the boy's wages in half and gave the youth the remainder in shiny coins each month. That was more than twice what he ever saw from his mother. A kind word here and there, combined with the coin, purchased loyalty, but the carefully chosen insults had left the young man unsure of himself, which was exactly as the bloated villain had planned.

For his part, Noddy knew he must not divulge his plan to a soul and that he must act swiftly, or he would lose his nerve. The chance to be free from insult and the control of Magoggle, along with acquiring vast riches, was a final temptation. The woman was right they would never be safe as long as the fat wolf drew a breath. Killing the likes of Magoggle would be nearly impossible, but to own the woman and the treasure she promised, along with his freedom, was worth the gamble. He pictured Peg reclining sensuously on a pile of coin without even a fig to cover her nakedness, and in that vision he found his courage.

The Yellow Wasp looked its usual self, which is to say unsavory and unwelcoming and bereft of warmth and companionship. It was a grog shop of the meanest kind, and on this day like all others, its darkened windows stared out like black eyes, and its central door stood open like a waiting maw. Noddy went in and kept to his usual habits, ordering a noggin of rum and a piece of salt fish for breakfast, and when it was delivered silently and sullenly by the barman, he went around the corner and toward the back. There Magoggle sat, enthroned, dribbling eggs down his chin and sipping at his warm spiced wine. It was at that moment that the great liar knew something was different about his man. Cope walked forward with large steps, a tumbler in one hand, a salt herring dangling from his lips, and his other hand resting lightly on his sword, but the look in his eyes was as though he wanted to beat a hasty retreat.

The Beast of Water Street knew that raising his great bulk from behind the table would only expose more of him to harm, so the fat one stayed ensconced in his chair. Something in Cope's manner made the fine hairs on Magoggle's thick neck prickle.

O. Nicholas reached into his pocket and pulled out his favorite weapon and, with a flip of his hand, threw it onto the table.

Cope was a stride away, and his hand had actually begun to withdraw the sword from its scabbard when the clank and thump reached his ears, and he saw a smile spread across Magoggle's face. Noddy stopped in his tracks.

"Well, lad, don't ye think it's time we talked about a bonus? Ye've stood by me lo these many years, and yer as like a son to me as any man could be. When ye entered into pact with me these twenty years ago, I was sure I had gained more than a convert. I must say, I thought I'd gained a trusted disciple." He pulled open the fist sized sack of coins and began counting out gold and silver. Some of the coins were ancient drachmas and others bore likenesses of kings centuries in the tomb.

Cope chewed the last of the fish and swallowed with an audible gulp while watching the stack of coin piling up in front of his mentor.

"I don't want to lose ye lad. I know ye fancy the girl I gave to Trepan, and I've decided to give her to ye instead. I can no longer trust the fellow, and I wish ye would handle it fer me."

The sword leapt into Cope's hand and sliced through the air with a hiss, coming down on the table with a cleaver-like thud. A stricken look came into Magoggle's eyes and his lips quivered as he pulled back his wrist, his chubby hand lay twitching on the table while blood fountained from the stump of his arm. The cuff of Magoggle's coat with its silver buttons was still attached to the now lonely hand that longed for its retreating arm.

"Twenty-five. I was let out to ye twenty-five years ago. After my kind mother took to the drink an' barkin' like a dog. God forgive her." Cope swept the coin into the pouch and tucked it calmly into his coat pocket. He looked over his shoulder to see the gape mouthed barman peeking from behind the corner.

Cope turned his attention back to Magoggle. "Ye taught me much boss, and I'll remember it all of my days. The most important lesson, you said, was never turn yer back on an enemy. You always said fools and cowards rest in a cold dark place where there's no teat, nor rum, nor fire to warm yer shanks."

The sword flashed out again, and the lone candle flickered and was extinguished by the gale wind of the passing blade. Unheard by the ear of any was the sound of maniacal laughter in the dark regions never pricked by heaven's light.

※

On his last night leading the plodding baggage train, Crispin had graciously asked Peg to sit with him while he ate the simple boiled beef dinner she had prepared him. He did not go so far as to invite her to sup with him. Rather than lower herself to eat with the enlisted men each night, she had dished a small share of the lieutenant's victuals into a trencher and set it aside to be consumed privately when she was done looking after Crispin's needs. Tonight was no different. Crispin was unaware of this arrangement but would have thought it well and proper and would have approved of her preparations. Certainly, there was a time when she could have sat at a gentleman's elbow during dinner, but that time was passed, yet still she was a small notch above a sergeant's wife no doubt.

Some few of the more senior sergeants had taken buxom, roistering wives from among the colonial drabs and one in their regiment had even brought his legal English (She was actually Irish.) wife with him. On this march, however, Peg was the only woman in the camp, and the men all knew she was sharing the lieutenant's company. It would be a breach of campaign etiquette for her to share familiarity with the men. The men themselves would not have trusted her in any case as they would have feared her tattling to the lieutenant about their idle talk and opinions, and not least, it would place the lieutenant in the queer place of requiring him to question her about the doings of the men.

All in all, it was considered healthier for women who chose to sleep with officers to keep their distance from the ranks and stay to themselves. The position had its rewards in better food and better bedding if not in warm and jovial company. Peg was a solitary creature by anyone's reckoning, and her years as a colonel's plaything and as Harding's wife had given her a sense of superiority to these honest soldiers and their coarse but sturdy mates. Everyone pretended not to notice that she was the same wanton who had once graced the colonel's bed.

"I think I shall turn in early," St. Crispin told her. He stood up and went into his tent and lit his small lantern with a stick he had taken from the fire.

His simple statement was a veiled command for Peg to meet him in the tent in a few minutes. This, of course, meant that she should either conjoin with him on an empty belly, or that she should bolt her food and wash the few dishes in the morning. She decided that she must eat, so while she nibbled on a boiled turnip, she quickly scoured the bowls with a wad of grass and set them aside until morning when she could heat the wash water after she made his dawn tea and while she brushed his coat. Through the tent, she could see the shadow of him disrobing, and this too gave her pause. There were few pleasures on the road or, for that matter, anywhere for a woman of her present station, but the delights of the flesh were a welcome diversion from the drudgery of camp life. The chance to sleep on a bed with clean bedclothes was for her now as an evening of dance and fine food had been in her more luxurious past.

She shoveled another mouthful in and then, wiping her hands on her apron, rose and headed for the glowing tent and the promise of pleasure.

✧

Their tumble ended and lying spent, Crispin thought of asking her what plans she had after they reached the regiment, but he thought it kinder not to remind her of her low and tenuous situation. She was well aware their agreement would reach an end in days, if not hours.

"What will you do after we've beaten the papists and the savages?" asked Peg as though reading his thoughts. "I mean, surely you can't live forever on a lieutenant's pay."

"I won't be a lieutenant forever. I suppose you wouldn't laugh if I told you I plan on being nothing less than a major by war's end? If I should be lucky enough to marry well, then I'll retire to Virginia."

"Quite a bit different, our fortunes now," she stated flatly, but not without a touch of irony. "I once was the girl all men desired and had more than most could expect, and here I am now, cooking for a subaltern. Not that I'm not appreciative, mind you. Why would you retire to Virginia instead of going home?"

"Let me see… I have little waiting for me in Scotland, and I have much waiting for me in Virginia. Besides, the weather is somewhat more pleasant. Just stay clear of the forests is my advice." Crispin gave her bosom a pinch and then prepared to roll over and sleep.

Peg knew she was close to the location of the coin and decided she had best press on as she mightn't have many more opportunities. She stroked his hair and encouraged his attention in more sensuous ways.

"You mean you have some provincial filly waiting for you in Virginia. Am I no longer pretty enough to hold your attention for more than a romp?"

"Some things are worth more than love," he said as he rolled back over to face her. "I will not wait for fortune to find me as I have already found it in Virginia. Well actually, the Carolinas to be specific, but it waits for me in Virginia. If I had it in hand, I would reward you for your service." He gave her another little nip and smiled.

"You think I can be bought like a common whore?" She feigned anger but then flashed a smile. Peg knew she was close now, and she stalked him like a huntress.

"Heaven forbid, your ladyship," jested Crispin. "I meant more the other things you have done for me,"—he paused—"and for this." He pulled her close, ready for another go.

"Mr. Randybuck, you haven't more than a shilling or two to your name, yet you brag like a banker! Have you bought land for a plantation, or do you have a buried treasure?" She said it as though she were jesting, hoping it would call him out.

"Ahh, land—no!" said Crispin chuckling. "What waits for me jingles a merrier tune than deeds or tobacco leaves."

They spent an hour locked in amorous union, and then, Crispin fell back exhausted and rested with his head on her shoulder, and Peg whispered to him as he drifted off into the folds of Morpheus's robe, but before he passed into unconsciousness, he unwittingly revealed that which Peg wanted most to know.

"I shall show you someday," he mumbled sleepily. "It's buried under the smith's forge in Williamsburg."

✯

"You'll not go by yerself! How am I to trust that you'd return? We may share a bed, but I'll tell ye no more till Trepan is out of the way. You say Magoggle will bother us no more, but what proof do I have of that?" Peg pulled her stockings up over her knees and buckled the garters.

While she stood bent over with her one foot on a stump and tying her brogan, Noddy was lying back buttoning his breeches up and considering her words.

"If I lay fer Trepan an' gut him like a pig, will ye tell me where it is then?" He took a long swig from his bottle canteen, which lay, on the matted grass next to his hurriedly discarded sword.

"Aye, after you kill the lieutenant as well. Then we have a chance, if ye've done fer Magoggle like ye said," stated Peg adjusting her bosoms within their armor like stays. She held her hand out to Cope to help him up from the grass. As he rose up from the grass he slid his sword from its scabbard and laid it in one fluid motion alongside Peg's neck. He kissed her lightly on the lips.

"Just remember, my sweet morsel, you might know where the coin is, but you'll not get near it without me.

Peg slipped her arm around his waist and laid the other on his chest ignoring the deadly sword entirely.

"You need not worry. I only want to be certain we see eye to eye." She pulled open the top of his shirt and pressed her lips against his skin as she lightly pushed the blade of the sword away from her neck. The razor's edge cut her palm, but she didn't notice as they twined together again like Daphne and Eros. Soon, she would own him, and he was becoming a slave to her pleasures, and it was her experience that the quickest way to a man's purse was the path through his breeches.

Formerly pretty Peg was plying her wares with great regularity back and forth between Messer's Mull and Cope. Trepan also had his eye on her (but not his hands) whenever possible, which was often since Crispin and his baggage train had arrived at last in Half Moon. The assassin seethed with hatred for Cope but was unaware that the henchman was in town or that anything untoward had befallen Magoggle. He had cornered the colonel's former mistress as she emptied the lieutenants cracked porcelain slop jar.

The latrine trench which was visited by all in camp with the reluctance of a bayonet charge and from which most retreated in haste was one of the few places sufficiently distant from the camp where he could speak privately and quietly with the fickle bawd. A number of the men from the ranks had spotted him loitering about the fulsome ditch for several days in a row, and he had now acquired to himself the nickname of Brown Lurker. The privates jested whenever they saw him near, calling out "Oy! It's the Brown

Lurker! The shit-colored ghost of the piss trench! Run!" and they would all scatter and bump into each other falling down in fits of hilarity. Invariably, someone would call out, pinching his nose between thumb and forefinger, "Oh, vile ghost get thee clean!"

Trepan sneered at their jests and, snarling quietly, promised himself that as soon as the woman told him the location of the gold he would sneak up in the night and kill every one of the arrogant soldiers where they lay. He imagined the sight in his mind as the company was ordered to fall in, and it was discovered that half of them were lying dead in their tents with sightless eyes staring up at the blank canvas. It had not occurred to him that he now sought to murder more people than he had ever dared to trust.

Anger and greed ate at his bowel, and his belly burned every day. Food was a momentary balm until his stomach began to churn, so he often skipped meals altogether. His face grew more gaunt than normal, and indeed, he began to look like an animated corpse or an opaque dung-colored spirit. The peach-colored sateen breeches pulled from the dead actor had become stained and dirty and were now a spotted beige.

Trepan, of course, remained as inconspicuous as possible whenever Crispin was about. He took himself into the woods not far from the regiment where he kept a miserable dirty camp. He had built a small shelter (flimsy and makeshift at best) out of limbs and boughs from a nearby pine tree, and there, with a pair of stolen blankets, he stayed with his thoughts turning round and round in his dark and angry mind until he became hungry enough to see what he could steal for his supper. He had learned to make a smoky fire with little blaze that kept off the bugs and didn't attract much attention to its feeble light.

The woman had promised him that if he met her near the latrines the next night, she would have learned the location of the treasure, and together, they would retrieve it. Of course, he had never told her that as soon as he knew the spot, he would kill the lieutenant while he slept and that once he was sure of the coin, she would be next in his bloody harvest. One couldn't trust a woman. It was a lesson he had learned from Granny Scopes and had momentarily forgotten. Dear old Granny, he hated her memory only slightly more than Peg. While Granny had gone out gurgling, the woman would beg for mercy, and he thought, *I'll let her think I'm relenting just before I pinch her wick.*

The days since his arrival at Half Moon had passed pleasantly for Crispin. He drilled with the regiment and passed the evenings in the company of his fellow officers and occasionally met Peg for a dalliance and in general relaxed after the travails of the highway. The summer weather was warm and in the deep silence of his tent, which he shared with another officer. Late at night, he dreamt of recouping his gold and of the life he would lead when the war was over. The provincial army, though rustic, seemed well enough drilled, and he fervently hoped that when it came to battle the Fifty-Sixth would be held in abeyance against the faltering of the colonial troops or left to drive home a final victorious charge. In either case, he hoped he would be far enough from cannon balls and musketry.

Peg visited Crispin less and made herself busy with chores as the night of the meeting with Trepan approached. Her eyes lost focus as she also thought of what she would do after she dipped her hands in the chest and let the cool shower of gold guineas, Maria Theresa's and Spanish reals cascade through her fingers. Her plot was about to bear fruit. If Noddy Cope was to be believed, then Magoggle was also no longer a looming menace, and now she knew the hiding place of the lucre. All that remained was to kill Trepan tonight and then do away with the lieutenant. Crispin had been good sport, and without him, her fortunes would be gloomy indeed, but nothing must be left to chance. As the sun began to set, she took down the soldier's laundry she had left to hang, and she put the great basket up on her shoulder and smiled to herself as she strode back down the company street.

Trepan waited in the darkness underneath a small lonely tree perhaps twenty or so yards from the trench and, without thinking, picked at a pimple on his upper lip. His belly growled, and a pang shot through his midsection as he expelled a smidge of odor from his hinder parts.

Peg sauntered towards the trench, holding her skirts up out of the wet grass, which was heavy with the evening's dew. It was hours past midnight, and after pausing at the edge of the ditch, Peg looked back toward the camp, making sure she was unobserved, and then she coughed low and soft. This was the signal that she and the nasty "ghost of the piss trench" had agreed upon.

Trepan moved slowly away from the tree just as the thick blanket of clouds broke and revealed the pale watchful moon above. He looked left, and the coast was clear, but as he turned to the right, he spied a figure coming at him at a swift walk, and he heard the subtle grating noise of a sword clearing the metal throat of a scabbard. Facing the sound of danger, he popped the long thin dagger from his cane and dropped into a wide crouch and thrust his swordish dagger in front of him ready to meet his attacker. Noddy Cope stopped two paces away with his sword held low as though inviting a charge.

"I'm going to kill you, little man," said Cope. "I should've killed you back in New York, but it'll be much better here. In the morning, they'll find the Brown Lurker floatin' in filth with all the other turds."

"Magoggle sent ye, didn't he? I knowed he was faithless. The divil he is, but he'll not get his due from me."

"You're as dumb as those turds! Magoggle has nothin' to do with this. Yer a greedy little fox ,Trepan, an' we can't enjoy the coin if we're always lookin out fer you!" Cope nodded at Peg, standing silent in the moonlight.

Without looking her way, Trepan addressed Peg. "I knowed ye was no good when ye up an left me that morning. Yer a cheap whore with a heart of stone."

Though he had never shown a moment's tenderness or mercy as has been noted earlier, it was plain as day that he was both heartbroken and truly believed she was more callous than he. Somehow even as he plotted her demise, the assassin had hoped in his sinful heart that he would convince her to go away with him and claim the treasure. Faced with the obvious betrayal of his would've been partner, he grew desperate like a cornered and tortured creature. He knew that his dagger was no challenge for Cope's sword, and on top of it, the other man was longer in leg and arm and younger by almost a score of years.

Without speaking a word, he dashed to his right and, in a single little bound, cleared the ditch and knocked Peg to the ground and then, rising above her, drove his dagger down in a last act of defiance, but not before Cope's sword, he had now leaped the trench as well, slid tightly into his chest.

"Damn ye ta hades!" Trepan let out a growl, and then there was a splash as Cope kicked him off his blade and into the slop, and Cope, dropping his sword altogether, shoved the little man's head down under the watery, stenchsome muck. Cope's nostrils were filled with smell of stale urine and night earth, and he nearly gagged and silently thought he would have to throw away his coat because the sleeve would be so permeated with the reek.

Meanwhile in the tent of a fellow officer, a mere two hundred yards from where fell deeds were being committed, Crispin blithely dealt the cards in a late night game of whist.

⚜

In the wee hours proceeding dawn, Crispin arose from his bed with a pressing need to visit the latrine. He had eaten much and drunk to the king's health too many times while they gamed. He lit the tin candle lantern, and then, wearing only his nightshirt, he slipped on his riding boots and began the short walk across the camp to the necessity ditch as he did not have a slop jar or even a bucket in his tent at present. The moon had set, but the clouds had hurried on, and the twinkling stars lit the firmament now, and setting the lantern at the ground next to his foot, Crispin hiked up his shirt and turned around into a squat and proceeded to relieve himself of the previous evenings repast. Uttering a grunt of satisfaction, he was about to clean his nether parts when he heard a choking groan in the darkness beneath his buttocks, which were still suspended over the trench. Whipping around, he thrust the lamp out over the muck and squinted into the filth. A great pile of excrement heaved as though trying to separate itself from the rest of the manure.

"God's holy trewsers! What in the name of hell is that?" He said in a loud and very shocked voice, forgetting to cover his lowland Scots accent. Not a soul in the camp stirred. The nearest guard who was some distance away merely thought he had heard someone talking in their sleep.

One end of the moving pile turned, and a single green eye surrounded by white popped open and settled square on Crispin. The eye bored through him, the only bit of white in a watery, brindle-brown soup of feces. Crispin staggered back a step and held his linen sleeve in front of his nose and mouth. A long moment of near complete silence ensued, punctuated only by the drip-drip of filth as it rolled off Trepan's chin.

A new stirring in the ditch had loosed a rank emanation that assaulted the nose. A sucking noise of release could be heard, and Mull once again peered down into the muck. Trepan had now freed one shoulder and struggled to push himself up into a sitting position. He hadn't died from the sword thrust nor the attempted drowning. As you have seen from the night that Crispin himself administered a drubbing to the assassin, Trepan was a difficult creature to eliminate as are most forms of vermin. His chest wound was invisible in the darkness covered as it was with excrement, which acted as a corrupt and filthy bandage.

His voice was no more than a raspy whisper. "Fate has put me here, Leftenant. Now likely you don't remember me, but we met in the teeth of a vixshus storm in Charleston, an' you near kilt me. Here I am covered in yer shit now with a hole in me chest from Noddy Copes sword an' but a minute to live." Crispin opened his mouth to speak, and Trepan with his back against the side of the ditch flapped a hand and motioned him to silence.

"That lovely bit of filly you mount has taken up with Cope, an' together, they're gonna steal yer treasure." He paused, gathering the strength to go on. "If I was you, I'd be gone after them and make 'em pay." He choked again, and a small bit of foamy blood collected at the corner of his mouth. "I myself was gonna kill ye, but as ye can see, that is most unlikely now, and I only ask that before ye shoot her down, tell her I'll be waitin' for her at the fiery iron gates."

Crispin closed his mouth and paused before he spoke. "Who the bloody hell is Cope? And how did you track me?"

"I sir am a first-rate knife or was, an' as fer trackin ye, it was no great feat. Cope is a despincable and dangersome fellow that the bitch took up with in New York. He is a fair hand with a blade, so just shoot 'im down. Take nothing less than a brace of pistols an a musket with ye." There was a rattle in his throat. "I've only one request after I cock up my toes. Would ye see to it that I'm washed off before they bury me? I doesn't like the notion of goin' to hell covered in shit." Trepan took a shallow breath and coughed.

"Yes, I'll see to it that they rinse you off. Do you want any rites said?"

"Nay says I. There is naught fer me but the flames I'm sartin." He slumped over with a splat and hissed a final word. "Go…"

Crispin turned on his heel and raced back to his tent to dress and arm himself. This was a private matter, and he did not wish to turn out the guard or rouse the entire camp.

ALONG COMES CRISPIN

Peg had tied her blanket roll upon her back, and sitting behind Noddy Cope on his horse, the two had quietly slipped out of camp and headed for Albany where they would catch a ship or a bateaux headed down Hudson's flood for New York. Crispin's inconvenient absence from his tent and the lateness of the hour had precluded the couple slitting the lieutenant's throat whilst he slept. They had argued briefly and hotly, but the plan, if that you could call it, was for Cope to creep into Crispin's tent and slash his jugular or for Peg to poison his drink.

Foolishly, they had not considered that he might be away or in the company of others. They dared not wait around until Trepan's corpse was found, and upon hurried reconsideration (hashed out in a moment of angry whispering), they decided that it was unlikely that Mull would couple Trepan's death and Peg's disappearance with a plot to steal the lucre. After all, he had no fore knowledge of Cope or Magoggle, and it was possible he might not even see or recognize Trepan's carcass.

Ever aware of her own vulnerability, Peg's natural and murderous overreaction was to poison, cut, or throttle her opposition — not always by her own hand. Fortunately, for the sake of those she thought to prey upon, they never saw themselves reflected in the dying ruby light she cast. Even Goody Harding had been blind to the rushing specter of death. Perhaps, the two decided, they had been in too great a hurry to tie up loose ends. Crispin's great good luck had intervened once again.

The heavy dew had left the road damp, and little did they look to see that their path was easily marked in the dampened dust that trailed beneath the horse's feet like a rope. Cope, having relieved Magoggle of his purse, had purchased for himself a new suit of handsome clothes, a pistol, and sundry traveling items but felt that he should also buy Peg a dress or two. Coupled with passage for them both to South Carolina, he feared he would be pinched for funds. The darkness had begun to retreat before the illumination of the rising eastern light, and neither of them had eaten a crust since the night before, so after putting several miles behind them, Noddy reined in at a wayside tavern, The Prince Rupert, for a pot of ale and a spot to eat before trotting the last few miles southward toward Albany. The sun shone warmly above the tall white pines beside the tavern before they had eaten their fill and mounted to ride on.

Noddy alternated his horse's gait between a trot and a hand gallop to cover the most ground as quickly as possible without pushing the animal past its limits. They passed no one in the minutes immediately following, but soon afterward, they saw a rider looming on the horizon. Riding on in silence, they said nothing, and Noddy slowed his animal to a walk as they came to a small stream that cut the road. The approaching rider had dismounted and was leading his horse. Coming abreast with the rider on his left, Cope noticed that the fellow carried a knife at his belt and a shiny blunderbuss slung upon his back. The man who was wearing a long brown oilskin greatcoat seemed hale and hearty and of middling age. At the front of his saddle, he carried two large thick leather pouches with buckles and, at the rear, a tightly rolled gray blanket. Whistling while he walked, the man waved at them and bid them good day, doffing his brown tricornered hat and fanning his face with it as he stopped to let his horse drink from the brook. Noddy knew a post rider when he saw one, and this one had not yet delivered his parcels and letters and was no doubt carrying something of value.

Opportunity was presenting itself again, and Noddy Cope was ready to shake hands with the devil (And, indeed, perhaps he already had.) if he thought he could make a profit and get himself closer to his goal in Charlestowne.

Crispin's horse was all in a lather as he came galloping around the bend and saw up ahead two horses and two figures standing in the road. He drew his horse pistol from his belt and gave the spurs to his mount, surging forward in a final burst of speed. His hat flew from his head as he bore down on the scene. The couple in the road was still a good distance off and one of them, a woman, almost certainly—Peg, he thought—ducked into the trees beside the lane while the other threw himself into the saddle of one of the waiting horses and then, kicking the animal hard, charged straight at him. There was no doubt in his mind that this was Cope, the man who had killed the diminutive and filthy villain in the ditch and who thought to make off with his, Crispin's, treasure. As the wildly pounding mounts closed to within mere yards of each other, Noddy took a quick aim with his new pistol and fired a shot at Crispin's chest. Then the horses were passing each other, going in opposite directions at terrific speed. By the time that Cope had reined in his mount and wheeled about for a second go, this time with the sword, Crispin had tumbled backward from the saddle and lay face downward, motionless in the byway with blood pouring from his head, his horse careening madly down the road, foam flying from its bit.

Peg darted from the bushes and grabbed the plunging animal before it could shy away and give warning to some industrious Dutch farmer heading for the mill or a barefoot and freckled cowherd driving his beasts to the field. A single gunshot and an empty saddle could only be highway robbery and, in no way, resembled the sounds and sights of war. Noddy trotted his mount passed Crispin and then, stopping, looked down and derisively spat on the lieutenant's waistcoat. Crispin had dared not wear his uniform and instead wore his only change of civilian clothes and had not even taken the time to don a coat. Lying there in the grass and ruts at the center of the road, he appeared to be nothing more than the unfortunate traveler, a victim of common highway bandits.

Having tied the skittish horse off to a sapling, Peg rifled through the post rider's pouches. Noddy now dismounted and gave Crispin's still form a nudge with his boot and then bent down to retrieve the unfired pistol from the damp earth. Peg let out a jubilant cry and held up the money belt that she had found hidden beneath the post rider's outer clothes, which explained why he was wearing the long coat on such a warm day. Noddy splashed across the creek and snatched the belt from her hand.

"Lord! There's a bit in here, or I'm not my pap's boy," he said, weighing it in his hand. Noddy did not trust his new partner. "I'll hold it. Now we gotta get rid of the lieutenant here and be quick about it. Take the rest of the letters and such and put 'em back in the pouches. Never did know my pap—whoever the bastard was. God rot his soul." The last part was more to himself than to Peg.

Peg snatched Crispin's pistol from Noddy's belt and pointed it at his belly. "Half a that is mine, my love!" She pulled back the cock and glared at Cope.

"Course it is, ya dimwitted tart! Right now, we need ta clean up the road and git ta Albany." He pushed the pistol aside and started picking up the letters she had scattered in the dirt, and he jammed fistfuls of them roughly back into the bags.

Peg quickly decided it best if Noddy understood that she was not some dull wench to be trifled with and that he had best treat her with more respect than Trepan, Isaiah, or Beverly had. She also feared that if Cope grew to bold, he might decide to rid himself of her. Copes dismissal and the flippant way in which he regarded her threat was maddening. She turned to the unconscious post rider and, pointing the pistol at his pallid face, called out to Cope.

"See here, don't ever think you can frighten the likes of me, Noddy Cope. I remind you. You'll get nothing without my help unless you know how to conjure back the lieutenant's ghost, and by the way, I don't think you had a father! Your mother lay with the devil to beget you, no doubt!"

She squeezed hard on the trigger, and the great pistol thundered and jerked upward in her formerly delicate hand. The post rider didn't even flinch, but a wisp of smoke rose from the smoldering hole in his head. She had not been prepared for the power of the gun, but she recovered from her surprise. She threw the empty gun at Noddy's feet and, without apparent hesitation, stooped and began picking up the last of the letters. Copes mouth fell open, and he paused for a moment, impressed by the murderous offhand manner of the drab. He had not thought her capable of such brutally direct violence. Peg too was surprised by her actions but not for long as she knew she must do whatever was necessary to safeguard her right to her portion of the lucre.

Getting back to the business at hand, as though they had merely fallen out over the price of nutmeg or whether the oxen needed shoeing, Cope took the blunderbuss from the back of the post rider and placed one of the now empty pistols next to the post rider's corpse, the other he stuck into Crispin's belt. The blunderbuss he decided he would keep for himself. Then with Peg's help, he threw bloody Crispin across the saddle, his gore drenched head dangling limply off one side. Peg, in turn, mounted the post rider's horse and lead Copes mount by the reins whilst Cope himself coaxed Crispin's horse complete with body down the road and up into the forest beside the track before he slapped the horse sharply on the rump after, of course, he had knocked unlucky Crisp off into the leaves and detritus. Taking a hand full of wax sealed letters, he scattered them hither and thither as he walked back to the road leaving a trail easy to follow. The letter pouches also he had left on Crispin's saddle.

How'd he find us I'd like ta know, he thought. *A fair bit of luck it was both a them comin' along like that at the same time. That bitch'll warrant watching though. She's a heartless bit of cunny.*

Returning to the road, Cope and the red-handed virago cantered on toward Albany a hundred pounds richer or at least, by Peg's reckoning, fifty pounds each. The silent post rider lay uncomplaining with his booted heels cooling in the stream, his arms outstretched in heavenly supplication, and with one eye socket smashed and filled with purple blood where the bullet had bored its foul hole. The other eye bulged outward from the force of the blast, seeing something far beyond the puffy sheep's wool clouds.

It would take several days riding over rough roads before the post rider's widow and children would learn of his fate at the hands of murderers and robbers. After a long and bumpy journey on the back of a wagon, the bones of Eliphalet Simms were gently returned to the dust. A rather ordinary and unremarkable headstone was stood up over his relics, and it tells the visitor naught of how he lived his life and little of how he died, except to caution the passersby that they will someday join him. The only distinctive marks upon the solemn monument are a Lorelei that flutters forebodingly at the top. Winged death seemed always to hover closely at Crispin's shoulder wherever he went, and it coursed more tightly with those who crossed his path.

To the governor—the Honorable Sir Charles Hardy

Sir,

It has come to my attention that you are not acquainted with the facts of this month concerning the terror to our highways. I will attempt to relate to you the events surrounding those dark deeds and the role of Sergeant Macaffee in bringing a dangerous rogue to heel.

It seems that on the morning of July 11, 1756, the post rider was coming from Boston Towne over the Post Road with his satchel running full but had been diverted toward the Prince Rupert Tavern on the Blockhouse Road. Most of the parcels were of the normal type, letters from kith and kin along with an odd assortment of seeds, books, the *Gentleman's Magazine* from St. John's Gate

London and, regrettably, the magnificent sum of over one hundred pounds sterling which the rider carried secretly in a leathern money belt about his waist. The post rider, one Eliphalet Simms, had been contracted by Mr. James Fitzhammond of Lincoln Township, Massachusetts, to quietly carry the coin to his brother Thomas Fitzhammond in Schenectady for the purchase of trade goods to be bought in Albany and used in a fur-buying venture in the west when the current hostilities end. Simms was still several miles short of his scheduled stop in Albany when treachery overtook him.

According to the deposition of Sergeant Macaffee of the Militia (a potter by trade), it seems that Simms had dismounted and was leading his horse to water when a then unknown assailant struck him upon the head and then shot him squarely in the face with a horse pistol. Sergeant Macaffee was on duty in the blockhouse when a local herd boy brought word that there was a body lying in a small creek that cut the road approximately three miles east from the blockhouse. Sergeant Macaffee took his two boys and a neighbor who was also at the blockhouse making repairs, and with their muskets went to investigate. Macaffee has some experience as a tracker having served on scouts against the Abenaki and the Huron at the onset of the present hostilities with the French. Macaffee confided in me that his first thought was that perhaps a drunken savage had bloodied his hands. There were he said at least two well-known Mohocks who reportedly when in their cups are given to barbarity and acts of violence. Upon arriving at the scene, Macaffee noted that the corpse had been pulled from the stream and lay as the herd boy had found it and that there were a welter of tracks belonging to at least five different individuals, easily noted by the distinct difference in boot types and the fifth set belonging to the cowherd who was unshod. The corpse still had a hip flask and all of his scelp, so the sergeant dismissed the notion of Indians. Tracing his way back up the road, Macaffee found the spot where Simms dismounted and began to walk, leading the horse. Simms went no more than one hundred yards before he paused at the rivulet. Apparently, Simms stooped to get a drink when the assassin, who must have lain in wait, struck him a blow to the head and then, rolling him over, finished his butchery with a blast to the face. Taking the money belt and the post satchel and stealing the horse, the bandit or bandits then rode down the highway until he or they reached a deer path a half mile further along and then exited into the forest. All this Macaffee was able to determine from the tracks and the corpse. The sergeant searched further but lost the trail in the brush and gathering darkness.

A storm cut short the day, so the expedition taking the corpse up on a litter made of sapling poles and regimental coats returned through the heat and rain to the blockhouse. That evening, Sergeant Macaffee sent word to me by one of his boys with the news of what had transpired. I dispatched two men that I deputed for the purpose of assisting Macaffee and also to assure that everything possible was being done to apprehend the murderous banditi. My next order was to call up another twenty-five men to man the blockhouse and patrol the highway until such time as it could be proven that the road was safe. Macaffee strongly complained that his business would fail and that he was no sheriff and that he was only a sergeant of militia. To this, I responded by applying to the colonel of his regiment for his promotion to lieutenant and gave him my utmost praise and approbation of the public faith in his ability as a tracker. Mr. Fitshammond of Schenectady, the supposed recipient of the stolen coin upon hearing of these events, has just posted a twenty-pound reward to the man or men who brought the cutthroat(s) to justice. We have since these measures were taken brought in a fellow who, it seems, is the highwayman. I further hesitate to explain to you that the rogue is no less than an officer in one of our own Crown regiments. Were he militia, I could go forward with his trial without a care. I cannot release him as no one wishes to take custody, and I know not how to go forward with a trial as I do not wish to do damage to his regiment nor bring embarrassment upon the Crown representatives. I pray that my plans so far meet with your approval and stand ready to receive correction or instruction from your esteemed and gracious office.

Hon. Pieter Van Zach
Albany County
July 1756

Here they were thought the doughty governor caught up in the midst of a war, which was threatening the very existence of the northern portion of his colony, and he had to be bothered with an idiot officer. No doubt the fellow had gambling debts or some other nefarious needs that could not be honorably met. Charles Hardy, the royally appointed governor of New York, dipped his quill in the Staffordshire china ink pot and began to scratch a note of praise to the stodgy Van Zach. The fat old Dutch fool had actually done something right for a change. The last time he had asked for the man's help, Van Zach had cozened the wrong member of the colonial legislature and set off a storm of protest. He sanded the note and set it aside to dry while he dashed off a note to Lord Loudon.

To General John Campbell
Commander of His Majesty's forces
New York

July 15, 1756

My Lord Loudon,
    One of your brave officers has recently been arrested by the constabulary for highway robbery. I am vaguely

acquainted with the facts. I have no doubt that there is an adequate explanation for the bloody events though it may be less than what we would pray for. This matter has been kept quiet for the moment in order that you and the Crown might be spared no small embarrassment. You will have my utmost assistance in this delicate matter. I would suggest that you begin with a discreet martial inquiry and that this matter be kept from the civil courts and public view and reckoning. Robbery is itself a most ignoble and dastardly crime, but the murder of a post rider casts a much darker shadow over the whole affair. Please feel free to contact my secretary if you have any needs. As you know, I shall have to distance myself from this troubling situation in order to attend to the many needs of the defense of the colony in these perilous times. It would be unseemly for the Crown's representative of this colony to be associated in a partisan manner with a crime as shocking as this. The leading citizenry must not see me as shielding a rogue from justice. The matter of the officer is, I think, best handled by soldiers. In other matters, I am pleading with some of the leading patroons of Albany to help supply the victualing needs of the militia upon whom you must needs rely. I will provide you with every assistance in destroying our popish enemy.

> I have the honor to be
> your most obedient
> and humble servant.
>
> Chas Hardy

The governor signed the letter in a neat hand with a small flourish and then sat back in his winged armchair, which was richly upholstered in a floral pattern of red and white. He steepled his fingertips and crossed his thick white silk stockinged legs. Hardy thought himself rather clever for putting the onus on the general. After all, this rogue officer was no affair of his, and if Lord Loudon

(John Campbell) couldn't keep his lads in check, then he should be the one to make the explanation. It was expected that the men of the ranks might slip the bridle, but officers in the king's service were expected to hold to a higher standard. Breeding and the price of commissions were supposed to weed out the garden and keep brambles from growing amongst the roses though the duke of Cumberland's reforms had opened the army's commissioning process to professionals and commoners. Hardy couldn't think of the last time an officer bearing a commission and wearing red had been executed for such common crimes.

It didn't hurt to remind the general who it was that exercised great power over the militia and who could make his life either pleasant or more difficult. If the general's troops needed vittles, then let him remember where those vittles came from and who influenced the granting of contracts. If Loudon wished to return to England in glory, then he needed the assistance of every governor, not least of whom was Charles Hardy. In exchange for Hardy's assistance and continued good office, he hoped his lordship would keep his regulars under control and the governorship and the colony from being sullied by peripheral association with foul deeds. Charles Hardy only wanted to see his nation prevail in this damnable war and was not in the mood for base ruffianism.

✵

The door to the cell opened silently on its well-greased, forge-blackened iron hinges, and Crispin looked up from the floor where his gaze had been riveted on a tamed wharf rat named Judge Vries who wore a little string collar strung with blue Indian beads. The judge searched each of the cells daily, looking for pitiful handouts from the prisoners. All other rats were smashed with the flat of a shovel or lured into a bucket of water to drown. Crispin occupied the only stool in the tiny chamber but he rose to offer it to his guest.

"Hmm. Seems you've a bit of trouble, Mull," said Barley Blanchard. "I never would have expected this foolhardy blackguarding of you." Blanchard shut the door and walked the two paces across the floor that separated them. "You're in a bad place, young fellow. Your shot is spent, and your sword is broken I'm afraid. Surrendering yourself to the general's mercy and a quick and gentlemanly death would seem the only honorable way out. I have come to ascertain the truth if I can and report to Lord Loudon on how I think we should best proceed with your disposition."

Crispin stood resignedly and listened, allowing a moment of silence to pass before he responded. "I don't know what to say, sir. I have no recollection of the events leading up to my capture other than that I recall some sort of a fight with a ruffian."

Crispin, of course, remembered all about his treasure and his conversation with Trepan at the reeksome latrine ditch. The truth be told, he was a bit fuzzy about the events of the morning that followed and how it was that he came to be found lying in the woods with the dead post rider's horse. "I have to mention, sir, that at no time have I spoken to anyone about any of the duties I performed for you before we departed England." That should give the old toper something to ruminate on. "And by my oath, I know nothing of this one hundred pounds that it seems I am accused of pilfering from the post rider. I am as perplexed as yourself and the sheriff."

Crispin well knew that he was in a very bad place, and three days of suffering in a damp cell with poor rations and only the occasional visit of a rat had made him more determined than ever that he should regain his freedom and claim his treasure. His luck had swung to and fro so many times that he was sure it would again. From captive to freeman and back to captive yet again and again. The maddening part of it was that if the dying assassin was right, then Peg was in league with someone else named Noddy or Neddy or Nobby or some such and they not only were after the hoard but were also the very same who had placed his head in the noose to say nothing of giving him a nasty gash on the head from a nearly lethal musket or pistol ball. He knew he had grappled but couldn't remember the particulars of the bloody action that had caused the wound or what the final outcome had been. He hoped the other fellow had received his comeuppance as well. Crisp would have been embarrassed and disappointed to know that Noddy had come off without so much as a scratch.

Now it was Old Barley's turn to take a moment and muster his thoughts. This Mull fellow was no fool and reminding him of the affair with Peg Fairchild was opening with trumps. Mull had shown himself a bright lad and one of action in the past. Clearly, Blanchard would have to see Crispin executed quickly or brought off safely and deeply indebted to his commander. The young man obviously meant to tell all if Beverly didn't save his fat from the fire.

"Discretion and patience are the finest virtues, Mr. Mull." Discretion was something Barley himself had learned the hard way. "I am sorry you don't have a memory of the events. I shall do all that I can to save you from the gallows. I can make no promises, of course. Can you tell me anything that might weigh well with Lord Loudon? Perhaps how you came to be on that stretch of road so far from camp or why you were with the post rider's horse or what might have happened to the hundred sterling?"

Crispin knew that there was no good story that he could concoct that would cover the circumstances resulting in his imprisonment, and he had already spent several days wracking his brain for an alibi. If he brought Barley in on the truth, then he might use both the truth about Peggy and Blanchard's greed to leverage the colonel's aid. Giving up half of the treasure was no small thing, but it was better to have half of something than none at all, and if he didn't get out of this mess quickly, then it was certain that Peg would get to the treasure before him. Was he to hang dishonored while others enjoyed his wealth. Perhaps living well as a junior officer was as much as he could dare hope for? For the moment, leaving this damp cell and his rodent warder would be enough. He held the confidence of one of Barley's secrets, and perhaps it was time to share his secret with another. There may be no honor amongst thieves, but he and Blanchard were no thieves, they were officers of the Fifty-Sixth Regiment.

"How many fine hounds and fancy saddles can you buy with four thousands, sir?" queried Crispin with a humble look, his shoulders slumped in what he hoped was a subordinate fashion. He knew it was time to be honest with one man. It made no sense to try and cheat, not now when he could almost feel the scratchy hempen cravat tightening about his throat. His spirit rebelled at the notion that the hewn timbers of eternity's gate loomed just beyond the barred window in the cobbled courtyard outside the gaol.

Blanchard's eyebrows beetled, and he looked the lieutenant straight in the eye, clearly wondering what Crispin was getting on about. Had the young fellow lost his senses, or was he shrewder than Barley gave him credit for? There was certainly no trouble in listening. After all, if he didn't like what Mull had to say, the lad could always be gagged and hanged.

Noddy and Peg had spent two sultry nights in New York, waiting for a vessel and hiding from any friends and associates of the Beast of Water Street who might be thinking of bloody revenge. The truth was Magoggle had never had a friend, and there being no one who was his peer and no one who desired his company of their own free will. Most silently reveled and cheered for Cope, still the Beast had his faithful and fearful adherents and they were not to be trusted.

The cellar of the inn was cool and damp, and Noddy had spent the days skulking about the wharves, waiting for a vessel while Peg had hid in the darkness amongst the barrels of cider and crates of turnips. She sat quietly with no one to speak with and with nothing to do but imagine herself richer than any woman she had ever known except, of course, Goody Harding.

At last, Noddy had found a pretty sloop, the *Blenheim* heading for Virginia with a planter family just returned from England. The trip would take only a handful of days, but the thieves would have to sleep on the deck with the captain and his crew beneath a stretched canvass tarpaulin as the Virginians had paid handsomely for the only cabin which was usually occupied by the captain and his first mate. Peg now dressed the role of a pleasant, steady New England goodwife moving with her husband to the tidewater where they would work as midwife and rifle smith. Their goods they explained would be following on another vessel, which explained to any who wondered why all that they carried were two small portmanteaus of stiff black leather with shiny brass buckles and a stubby blunderbuss.

Peg, at last, was now going to have her turn after serving the needs of others for so long. The thought never crossed her selfish mind that she had always seen to her own desires before the needs of others. Even her tiny daughter had been no more than chattel to be used like a bribe or traded like a note. The sun was hot and high in the sky shining like a gold coin dangling down temptingly from the heavens as the little ship slid away quietly to the south. Shore birds turned overhead and the Jersey shore lay like a dark thread off the starboard rail.

☆

Barley dug in the damp Virginia soil with the ferocity and ambition of a mad badger, and the dirt fairly flew between his knees as he scooped away the last of the earth. Crispin held the lantern aloft and. at last, came a hollow thump as Colonel Blanchard knocked lightly on the lid of the chest. Crispin set down the light and climbed into the hole behind the forge, and both he and his commander heaved mightily, and the box flew from their hands, falling to the ground with a very unsatisfactory bump as of something empty. The cracked lid swung open, and not even a lonely hapenny rolled out. The trunk was as empty as the Rub Al Khali, the great empty desert of Araby. The two men looked at each other blankly for long seconds before they leaped out of the hole and Crispin tipped up the box, shaking it vigorously as though it might magically cause a shower of gold to pour forth. Alas, the magic of the Djinn was not hidden in the banked coals of the smithery that night, and Crispin, at last, threw the casket across the room without a care for the noise he made.

A mangy dog up the road hearing the crash that rent the still night air set up a barking and Crisp was jarred from his confusion of anger and disappointment. His thoughts turned red as he imagined his hands clamping around the fine alabaster neck of Peg. Crispin thought that he would track her down, and someday, both she and her lover would pay in blood. For the moment, all that was left for him was the honest and manly occupation of a lieutenant of foot plying his trade on the battlefield.

Here ends the first tome in the tale of St. Crispin Mull of the Fifty-Sixth Regiment. Rumors of additional notes regarding the regiment and a ragtag officer have surfaced in Canada. As I mentioned at the beginning of this tale I hope one day to track down the fate of St. Crispin Mull, the lost fortune and the Cheviot Guards.

AUTHOR'S NOTES

It was common in the eighteenth century for aspiring officers to purchase their commission in a regiment. The price of the commission depended upon the rank and the regiment. The rank of colonel in a Royal Cavalry Regiment, for instance, was far more expensive than that of an ensign in a high-numbered infantry regiment

Regiments were often stationed around the countryside and only the most senior and important were placed in forts, castles, or near royal residences. It was not uncommon for regiments to be housed in what we would think were rather unusual circumstances.

Recruiters were well known for luring their target into taking the "king's shilling" thereby duping the lad into enlisting under dubious circumstances. Still, this was a slight step above the impressment practices of the Royal Navy. Taking the shilling was seen as accepting payment and by extension entering into a contract with the army.

Many of the Jacobites of the 1745 Highland Rebellion sought refuge in either the American colonies or in France. A great number of those migrated to North Carolina and Canada where they formed a nexus for loyalist forces in the American Revolution.

The various wars between Britain and France extended back hundreds of years and would not be resolved until the most recent French tyrant, Napoleon, was deposed. It is both ironic and worth mentioning that the French and English people share a common heritage through the martial successes of William the Conqueror in 1066 but have never called each other cousin.

The French Fortress known as Duquesne was located at the present site of Pittsburgh in Pennsylvania at the confluence of the Allegheny and the Monongahela rivers.

The Golden Age of Piracy was, at the time of the story, more than thirty years past, but pirates have always found employment. Remember that any story about St. Crispin Mull is subject to doubt, and there can be no question that the tales surrounding Red Mike DeVaca have swelled in the telling; however, the reader can rest assured there must be some kernel of truth or there would have been no treasure!

Mr. Galton was one of the five most prevalent manufacturers of musket locks for the British Government at the time of the Seven Years' War, yet it cannot be substantiated that a dwarf named Eben Octavius Drake ever worked for him.

Broken and rebellious Scots fled the highlands and islands for America and the West Indies in the 1740s following the example of their retreating leaders in the aftermath of the Jacobite defeat at Culloden. Many of the leadership escaped to France, the ancient ally and place of refuge for Scots in times of trouble. Men of ordinary means like Giant Hector Griffin chose a life of freedom in the colonies rather than see their highland traditions trampled and outlawed. It is estimated that as many as one in four American colonists was of Scots or Irish descent at the time of the Glorious Revolution.

In the days of our grandfathers, it was common for travelers in crowded taverns and inns to share a bed, sometimes three or more to a bed regardless of the social status of the sleepers. The preponderance of way houses today of course precludes this inconvenience, and it seems impossible to imagine these rude conditions.

Sir William Johnson the British Supervisor of Indian Affairs of the Northern Colonies was both a friend of the natives and one of the only ennobled colonists of his time. Best known by the Iroquois as Warraghiyagey (adopted brother of the Mohawk nation) and by the English establishment as the Baron of the Mohawk, Sir William was a staunch defender of the red man's rights and ironically of paternal English land and treaty privileges in North America.

King Philip also known as Metacom lead his noble woodland children in a war of self-preservation in 1675. Pilgrim sons made war on the children of the forest who had forborn the encroachment and insults of settlers for two generations. In the end, the redman lost as is ever the story where white men encounter natives, whether on the forests or the plains.

Fort Niagara built by the French in the last quarter of the 17th century is situated on the southern shore of Lake Ontario where the effluence of the mighty falls empties into the Great Lake. The English lead by Sir William Johnson would capture the Fort from the French in 1759, and finally, at the end of that century, it would be ceded by right of treaty to the United States.

Mer Du Nort is the French appellation sometimes used for the Atlantic ocean on maps of antiquity.

Baron Von Drais Walking Machine, of course, had not been invented in those far-off days, but the author hopes that it gives you a vision of Bedlam Eaton's final contortions. The Von Drais machine is a passing fad and only suited to the paved paths of parks and the chateau gardens of the idle wealthy. It is hard to imagine that it could ever challenge the practical strength and grace of equine transport. Perhaps if it were fitted with a steam engine, it might serve in some manner like the new trains.

Each regiment was composed of eight "hat" companies and two flank companies. The grenadiers who were the heavy shock troops in a bayonet charge were the most valuable of the flank companies and were made up of the largest and handsomest of soldiers

Subaltern is the archaic term for a commissioned officer below the rank of captain.